Siobha...

Siobhan Curham is thirty-three years old and lives in North West London. After a successful career in the film industry (she was promoted to assistant manager of her local video shop after just two months) she turned her attentions to writing. *The Scene Stealers* is Siobhan's third novel, she also writes a weekly column for the *Express and Star* newspaper and is currently working on her first screenplay.

Siobhan Curham

The Scene Stealers

CORONET BOOKS
Hodder & Stoughton

First published in Great Britain in 2004 by Hodder and Stoughton
A division of Hodder Headline

A Coronet paperback

1 3 5 7 9 10 8 6 4 2

A CIP catalogue record for this title
is available from the British Library

ISBN 0 340 73509 0

Typeset by Palimpsest Book Production Limited,
Polmont, Stirlingshire

Printed and bound in Great Britain by
Mackays of Chatham Ltd, Chatham, Kent

Hodder and Stoughton
A division of Hodder Headline
338 Euston Road
London NW1 3BH

For Jack

ACKNOWLEDGEMENTS

A huge thank-you once again to all the usual suspects; Judy Chilcote, agent extraordinaire and true friend. The Batman and Robin of the editing world, Sara Hulse and Wayne Brookes, thank you so much for your enthusiasm, support and expertise (not to mention the giggles – next time the baked potatoes are on me Wayne!) Lucy Dixon and everyone else at Hodder.

Thank-you as always to the Curham Clan, Mikey, Anne, Bea, Luke and Alice. And to my fantastic friends; Tina T – my partner in crime for the past three decades. Ginny and Jim – for keeping my local sales figures up. Jeanette and Steve – for everything (apart from the Medieval fort, Steve!). The one and only de-detoxified Sam Delaney – my second favourite Detroit boy after Eminem. Paul Molyneaux – the finest contact juggler in all of Amsterdam, if not the world. Lorraine Farrell – for the excellent removal service! Amit Kothari, Pinner's answer to Jack Kerouac and responsible for some of the finest poems on the web (www.amitkoth.com).

Thank you to Steve Porter at Harrow Arts and all the people who actually came along to the various readings I've given over the past year (even when Big Brother was on the telly!).

And of course a massive thank-you to Jack, for providing me with a meaning to all of this.

'At the least, I know that I have lived,
I have lived
And there has been a day
That was perfect.'

From 'Clear as the Taste of Day',
by Amit Kothari.

Chapter One

Sadie Jones hated birthdays. In much the same way she hated Christmas, New Year, Anniversaries, Valentine's Day and any other calendar date that came all neatly gift-wrapped and prefixed with the word Happy. It wasn't as if she was some wizened old crone, muttering 'bah humbug' as she recycled used wrapping paper and staged demos outside Clinton Cards. It was just that she hated the pressure these days brought. The pressure to celebrate and take stock; the invisible question mark following the word Happy, forcing you to face up to reality, rather than hide behind your customary façade.

The fact was, as Sadie awoke on the eve of her twenty-second birthday, she was far from Happy – a fact she could easily disguise on any other day, losing herself in daydreams of better times to come. For Sadie had always been an optimist – ever since she'd first heard the immortal words, 'your school days are the best days of your life', and had laughed so hard she'd been given a detention. Unable to accept that state-sponsored mind control and constant insecurity were the best life had to offer, she spent the majority of her childhood years fantasising about the perfect world that awaited her as an adult. A promised land of fulfilling work, fabulous clothes, and above all, freedom. Surely, if she visualised it hard enough, it was bound to come true?

Aided by the vivid imagination unique to an only child – and a vast array of Sindy paraphernalia – she would picture an average day in her adult life going something like this: Upon awakening she would stretch out her gazelle-like limbs and roll over to greet Action Man (or whoever her swarthy, crop-haired hero turned out to be). Completely undeterred by his darting eyes or worrying lack of genitals, she would luxuriate for a moment in his passionate embrace before casting off her satin sheets and leaping from her white four-poster for a quick rummage through her wardrobe. Finally plumping for the leather catsuit and legwarmer ensemble (unless of course she had an early morning ballet class, in which case she would pirouette her way into white tights and pink netting) she would cast an admiring glance in the gilt edged mirror of her spindly dressing table before kissing Action Man good-bye and hotfooting it to the film studios in her canary-yellow jeep.

So what a bitter disappointment it was for Sadie to awaken on the eve of her twenty-second birthday and realise that her childhood role-plays had been more a case of wishful thinking than some uncanny premonition of destiny. Rolling over to discover a lukewarm hollow in the bed next to her, she sighed. Yet again, GL had slunk out before her to use up all the hot water in one of his marathon shower sessions. From the living room below she could hear the thumping intro to 'Eye of the Tiger' – GL's weekly pre-sales meeting psych-up had begun. Thud – thud, thud, thud, boomed the bass line and Sadie slunk beneath the duvet and groaned. She could just picture him shadow-boxing his way around the settee, floating like a Burton's-clad butterfly, stinging like a sovereign-plated bee.

'Come to daddy!' GL roared, followed swiftly by the sound of breaking glass and a stream of expletives. Upstairs Sadie froze. He'd broken the mirror again – now he'd be in a foul mood before the week had even begun. Taking a deep breath she clambered out of bed and stumbled through to the bathroom. As she pushed open the door, a cloying haze of steam and Insignia fumes rushed out to greet her. Choking and spluttering, Sadie fished the damp towel from the floor and filled the basin with the tepid water that remained. After a quick wash she rummaged through the ranks of aftershave, moisturisers, hair gels and mousses amassed on the windowsill like some great invading force from Man at Boots, to find her own solitary can of deodorant and applied a quick squirt. Shivering in the wet towel, she hurried back to the bedroom to get ready for work.

As Sadie pulled her 'uniform' from her designated corner of GL's vast pine wardrobe, she thought wistfully of the fur-trimmed coats and funky disco attire that had lined her Sindy closet. It really came to something when you found yourself pining for dolly fashion of the late eighties. Why oh why couldn't she be pulling on a pair of black leather hipsters rather than these god-awful, ragged-bottomed cut-offs? Why couldn't she be shimmying her way into a spangly boob-tube instead of struggling into a red and black striped top emblazoned with a skull and cross-bones motif? As she fastened the huge gold buckle on her belt Sadie experienced a sudden panic attack. Where the hell was her cutlass? Catching a glimpse of gold plastic poking from beneath the bed she pulled it out and slotted it into the scabbard resting on her hip. Out on the landing she could hear GL barking his new voicemail greeting into his mobile. 'Hi there, you've reached the voicemail of GL Jenkins, Senior Account Manager, on Monday sixth January. Sorry I can't take your call right now, but hey, you know what to do. Nice and clear after the beep.'

Sadie sighed as she stared at her reflection in GL's Famous Old Grouse mirror. The young woman staring back at her from beneath the bottle of whisky bore no resemblance whatsoever to Sindy. Okay, so she had the lustrous chestnut locks, but a fat lot of good they were scraped beneath a scarlet bandana. And why the hell did she have to stop growing when she was about twelve? With her puny five-foot frame she looked more like Holly Hobbie than the lithe-limbed Sindy. Sadie grimaced as she inserted one huge gold hoop (circa 1983) into her left ear. It was extremely ironic that after all of those years spent dreaming of working in the film industry she should end up like this. Never in her worst nightmares had she pictured working in the film *rental* industry, being made to dress up in a hideous pirate's costume to toil for a pittance in her local video store. She rummaged about in her underwear drawer for her mascara and half-heartedly began applying a coat.

'Is it really worth it, babes?'

Sadie looked up to see GL smirking in the doorway, his gelled hair and veneered teeth glistening so brightly he looked as if he'd spent the night on the lawn and had woken up coated in dew.

'What do you mean?'

'The slap – is it really worth it? You work in a video shop in Ruislip Manor for Christ's sake, it's hardly Harrods. Besides, once you've got your eye-patch on the punters aren't even gonna see your efforts, are they?' GL snorted loudly. 'By the way, I've had a bit of an accident in the living room – the bloody mirror's broken. Clear it up for us, would you? I'm running a bit late.' He looked at his imitation Rolex and frowned.

'But so am I,' Sadie replied, putting her mascara back in the drawer and stuffing her eye-patch into her pocket. 'You know I have to get in early on Mondays to do the figures and the banking.'

GL scowled at her and scratched the side of his head, carefully avoiding the expertly sculpted peaks of hair that covered his crown like a miniature mountain range. 'Okay, let's just think about this shall we? It's Monday morning and

I'm running late for a sales meeting – a sales meeting to discuss the hundreds of Ks worth of business I'm going to be bringing in this week – and you're worrying about getting to your shop to bank some petty cash.'

'It's the whole weekend's takings,' Sadie mumbled, already mentally conceding defeat. In a discussion with GL there was no other outcome. Any attempt at debate was completely futile.

'Oh, I see,' GL replied condescendingly. 'And what are we talking here, Jim Lad? Exactly how many pieces of eight have you made in the shop this weekend?'

'Oh I don't know – about five hundred pounds.' Sadie could feel her cheeks begin to burn in anticipation of the ridicule to follow.

'Five hundred quid!' GL sneered. 'Hold the front fucking page! Babes, I'll have made five hundred pounds before I even get to the office this morning. You're looking at the man who just won Cromwell Communications an account with a projected annual revenue of one point five mil. Just get the mirror sorted, all right.'

And with that, Sadie's hero, her Action Man, turned on his elevated heel and was gone.

'Are you talking to me?' Terry checked himself out in the rearview mirror and pulled his finest Robert De Niro scowl. Admittedly, he was a bit older and rougher round the edges than De Niro in *Taxi Driver*, but they definitely shared the same brooding eyes and swarthy skin, of that there was no denying. Terry lit up a Superkings and took a swig from his can of Tennants Extra – the perfect breakfast for someone who had been up all night cruising the mean streets of Ruislip Manor.

'Car twenty-seven, what is your location please? I've got a school run come up for Lady Bankes Junior, over.'

Terry looked at his radio and frowned. He bloody hated school drops – horrible little brats sitting in the back like a line of garden gnomes, all gaudy backpacks and gormless faces, choking and spluttering at the slightest trace of cigarette smoke. He wound down his window and flicked his cigarette on to the rain-slicked street. Great start to the week this was turning out to be.

'Car twenty-seven, what is your location, over?' Mandy, the controller, squawked over the airwaves, her voice shriller than ever. God, what the hell was her problem? Probably rag week, Terry thought to himself with a grimace. Just as he was about to pick up the handset to respond, he heard a voice bellow above the roar of the rush hour traffic.

'Yo, taxi!'

Terry leant out of his window to see some spiky-haired flash git gesturing at him from across the road. 'Are you talking to me?' he asked, with what he hoped was suitable menace.

'Well, this *is* a taxi isn't it?' retorted the flash git, gesturing at the Manor Minicabs sign on the roof of the car as he darted across the road.

'Yeah.'

'Well then, take me to the Great West Road in Brentford and make it snappy. I'm late for a very important meeting.'

'Car twenty-seven, where the bleeding hell are you? Over.'

Terry grabbed his handset and yelled, 'I'm at the top of the Manor and I've just got a fare to Brentford – roger.' That's exactly what Mandy needed, Terry thought to himself as he turned the ignition – a damn good rogering. Not that he would be volunteering his services – in Terry's book there was nothing worse than a bird with tattoos, especially tattoos of fang-baring Bulldog mastiffs.

'All right, babes. How ya doing?'

Terry looked in his rearview mirror and scowled but just as

he was about to try another, *Are you talking to me?*, he realised that his passenger was in fact talking into a wafer-thin mobile phone whilst applying some kind of gel to the rain-sodden spikes on his head. Terry stared at the man's reflection and tried to recall where he had seen him before. He certainly wasn't one of Liam's mates with his flash suit and gold-plate jewellery, not to mention his ridiculous mockney drawl.

'Yeah, I've missed you too, babes. Don't worry, I'll make it up to you tonight – I'm getting a stonker just thinking about it!'

Terry pulled out on to a roundabout, right into the path of a Help the Aged minibus – in all his thirty years of driving he'd always had a bit of a mental block about this giving way to the right lark. Still, there was no harm done. He'd managed to brake in time. Just. 'All right, all right, keep your hair on,' Terry muttered to the old codger behind the wheel of the minibus, who for some reason seemed to be going into one. Sighing, Terry wound down his window and leant out. 'Steady on mate – no harm done. You want to take it easier at your time of life. You'll be no help to the bleeding aged giving yourself a heart attack at the wheel now will you? Bloody coffin-dodgers – shouldn't be allowed on the road.' Terry felt a tap on his shoulder and turned to see his passenger gesturing furiously at the splatters of gel adorning his puce face and pin-stripe suit. It looked as if a bird had shat all over him.

'I'll be sending you the dry-cleaning bill,' he hissed. 'You wanna learn to drive, mate. Call yourself a cabbie? You're a bloody menace!'

Terry leant back in his seat and sighed. What the hell was up with everyone this morning?

Lana watched as the minicab hurtled off around the round-about and her perfectly painted pout snaked its way into a

smirk. That coffin-dodger crack was really quite amusing –
she'd have to try and remember it. Although remembering
things these days seemed to be becoming increasingly difficult. She wouldn't have minded so much if she was one
of those doddery old dears in the back of that minibus,
shaking their heads and tutting like a bunch of blue-rinsed
budgerigars, but she was only forty-five and a young forty-five
at that. She was still a head-turner, not a coffin-dodger. As if to
reassure herself on this point, Lana made an extra effort as she
sashayed over the zebra crossing. Picturing her heroine Lana
Turner in her debut movie, *They Won't Forget*, Lana tilted
her chin out, pulled her shoulders back and swung her hips
from side to side like a velvet-clad pendulum. By the time she
got to the other side she had completely forgotten what it was
she was meant to be remembering. She hadn't forgotten what
had brought her out to the rain-soaked Ruislip Manor Parade
at such an ungodly hour however. The longing in the back
of her throat and the tension twisting knots inside her head
acted as a constant, inescapable reminder. As Lana pushed
open the door to the Asian mini-mart she resolved to stop
off at the video shop on the way home. The girl was always
in early on a Monday, poring over her paperwork with her
patch-free eye, and Lana was in just the mood for a bit of
Bogart with her breakfast.

Chapter Two

Upon arriving at Pirate Videos, Sadie's opening-up routine went something like this: Unlock door. Leg it to back of shop to reset the alarm. Lock door. Boot-up computer system. Put *Grease* on the video player. Turn on bank of television screens lining the wall next to counter. Refill and switch on kettle. Take petty cash from safe and place in till. Remove turd from outside toilet.

Ever since Sadie had become manageress of the Ruislip Manor branch she had been plagued by the phantom crapper. She had come to view it as yet another 'perk' of an outside toilet – along with the mildew on the toilet paper and the kamikaze spiders that would dive-bomb your lap without warning. Sadie had absolutely no idea who was responsible, but every morning for the past year she had got into work to find a huge faeces clogging up the pan. And today was no exception. As Sadie picked her way down the litter-strewn back steps she glanced apprehensively to her left, where the ramshackle outhouse leant against the wall of the shop like a urine-sodden tramp. Prodding the door open with the toe of her boot, she was greated by the unmistakeable stench of excrement – cutting right through the pungent aroma of rotting vegetation from the greengrocers next door. Sadie's stomach performed its customary lurch as she pulled the chain and watched the turd swirl off down the u-bend like some grotesque log flume ride. For a fleeting moment it crossed her mind that she didn't actually have to tolerate this crap –

not just literally, but from life in general. Surely she didn't have to put up with GL's barked orders or her crummy wages and antisocial working hours? Surely she could refuse, rebel, go on strike? Sadie took the bottle of bleach from the top of the cistern and applied a liberal squirt to the stained porcelain. On balance, she concluded, it seemed far easier to just go with the flow. The truth was, at the tender age of twenty-one years, three hundred and sixty-four days, Sadie was quite exhausted with life already. Besides, there were always ways to escape from the 'turds' fate might throw at you. She might not have her Sindy world anymore, but she had discovered something equally rewarding; a parallel universe in the world of film, in which she could cast herself with the persona or lifestyle of her choosing. Whether it be Sharon Stone as a crotch-flashing vixen or Olivia Newton-John as a mouse turned minx, over the years Sadie had developed a way of dissolving into the celluloid world like some form of osmosis via the screen. Hence why she tolerated the paltry wages and antisocial hours at Pirate Video Rental – what better place to indulge her escapism? As Sadie made her way up the wrought iron stairs into the back of the shop she could hear the opening credits of *Grease* fading out and suddenly life didn't feel quite so bad. After scrubbing her hands in the corner of the cupboard that Vince, the shop's owner, laughingly referred to as a kitchen, she made herself a steaming mug of coffee and returned to the counter.

On the television screen beside her, Sandy was arriving for her first day at Rydell High and talking about how she wished she were back at her old school. As always, this scene elicited a sigh from Sadie. How many times had she experienced that same longing as yet again she faced another first day at another strange school? By the time she was thirteen years old she had attended no less than six different schools, thanks to her father's job with the RAF. It was *Grease* that had sparked her love of films in the first place. In the character of Sandy, Sadie finally found somebody she could relate to. How many times had she had to encounter a scowling, gum-chewing Rizzo who would make her life hell for the first few weeks at each new school – sneering at her across the playground, making her move to another table in the canteen? How many times had she trudged home utterly dejected, her ears still ringing with the taunts, her wrists still stinging from the Chinese burns? But Sadie wasn't stupid. She might not have been brave enough to stand up to the bullies, but she soon developed a way to minimise their abuse. By erecting a barrier of blandness about herself they would quickly lose interest and swoop off in search of more satisfying prey; someone with ginger hair or a penchant for Star Trek for instance. Sadie kept her hair in a neat bob, wrote *I luv Take That* on her pencil case and never put her hand up in class to volunteer an answer. After the heartbreak of being parted from her first ever best friend at the tender age of five she also learnt not to form any attachments and would tag along with some equally inoffensive girl, usually called Susan or Jane, with whom she would discuss homework assignments and pretend to share in their love of horses. As a young teenager, the only time Sadie attended a sleep-over, smoked an illicit cigarette or talked about 'making out' was when she was pretending to be Sandy in *Grease*.

As the opening chords of 'Summer Loving' filled the shop, Sadie reluctantly opened a folder marked *Weekly Rental Figures*. Her eyes were drawn to the box in the bottom right-hand corner of the page – *Total Income for Week ending Sunday 5th January = £412.50*. Sadie could almost hear GL snorting in derision and he would have been right – it was pretty pathetic, but it wasn't her fault. What did Vince expect if he only ordered in one copy of the latest blockbusters? There'd almost been a riot when he hadn't bothered getting any copies of the

latest *Harry Potter*. God knows if it hadn't been for the endless
supply of tea and biscuits Sadie provided her customers, not to
mention the free counselling service, that box would probably
be displaying a big fat zero right now. GL might mock, but
she worked damn hard keeping that shop afloat, organising
kids' competitions, devising ever more original promotional
schemes – as the recent 'free pound of sprouts with every
Christmas movie hired' promotion so aptly demonstrated
– and sacrificing many a fingernail creating lavish poster
displays around the store. Anyway, it was the week after
New Year – they were still showing all the decent movies
on TV. Business was bound to be on the quiet side.

Sadie watched as Sandy and Danny gave their infamous
sigh, signalling the end of 'Summer Loving'. It still gave her
goosebumps, even after all these years, but before she could
get too dewy-eyed she was interrupted by a rap on the door.
Although it was almost half past nine, the leaden clouds filling
the sky still cast a shroud of darkness over Ruislip Manor.
Sadie could just make out a figure in black, pressed against
the glass door, beckoning at her furiously. It was only when
she was halfway across the shop floor that she realised it was
member 1540 – the actress (Sadie knew the membership
numbers of her most regular customers by heart – a fact
that she tried not to take too much pride in). She wasn't
absolutely certain that 1540 was an actress, but judging from
her flamboyant attire and vampish make-up she wouldn't
have been at all surprised; besides her name simply oozed
Hollywood. Lana something. Sadie frowned as she searched
for the front door key on her chain. Loveday – that was it.
Lana Loveday – if she wasn't an actress she certainly ought
to be, with a name like that. (Speculating on the private lives
of her customers was another occupational hazard.)

'Oh darling, thank you so much. I know it's terribly naughty
of me to arrive at such an ungodly hour, but I really didn't

want to have to come out again in such ghastly weather and I'm just craving *Casablanca*!' Lana swooped into the shop, bringing with her a shower of raindrops and a vapour trail of Obsession.

Sadie smiled as she locked the door behind her. Definite actress – she even had the mid-Atlantic drawl. 'Don't worry, go right ahead,' she replied, gesturing to the Golden Oldies wall – the most well-stocked section of the shop. 'I was just doing my paperwork.' As Sadie returned to her post, she glanced up at the shelves of videos lining the wall behind the counter. Row upon row of films clad in their uniform Pirate Rentals cases, with only the catalogue number at the base of their spine to identify them. As with her members, Sadie knew all of her favourites by heart. 602 for *Grease*, 1124 for *Pretty Woman*. Yet again she was reminded of the benefits of her job – where else could she get paid to have such a vast library of films at her fingertips and be free to watch them all day long?

Back on the screen, Sandy was asking what had happened to the Danny Zuko she had met at the beach, while John Travolta completely blanked her to put on a show of bravado for the rest of the T-Birds. Yet again, Sadie sighed. How was it that this film always seemed so relevant to her own life? How many times had she asked herself recently what had happened to the GL Jenkins she met and fell in love with at university? How many times had she felt as baffled as Sandy by his increasingly cocky demeanour and erratic mood swings? She only hoped that an 'electrifyingly' happy ending lay in store for them too.

Ever since GL had been promoted to Senior Account Manager he had crossed the fine boundary separating confidence from arrogance. There had been times recently when he seemed to have become a caricature of his former self, with all of his finest features becoming grotesquely contorted. His previously biting humour had edged into cruelty and the strength of will that Sadie had always found so attractive was beginning to feel quite oppressive. It was this development that troubled her the most. After a lifetime of turmoil and transition she had finally found security in GL's strength. She was quite in awe of the effortless way in which he charged through life and more than happy to coast along in his wake, like a bird adrift on a jet stream. But now, rather than carrying her, his power seemed to be turning against her, in the form of sarcastic put-downs and endless demands.

Sadie frowned. No, she was sure it was nothing more sinister than the pressures of his job. She would probably start acting erratically if Vince demanded she attend SAS survival courses in the name of 'team building' and reciting mission statements like, *Show me the lolly, Dolly!* before beginning a day's work. Getting dressed up as a pirate was quite literally child's play in comparison. Feeling a twinge of compassion for GL's plight Sadie picked up the phone to call him.

Lana held the covers of *Casablanca* and *Rear Window* in her hands and weighed up the choice. On her way to the shop she had been intent on some bad-assed Bogart, but when she spotted *Rear Window* she was instantly reminded of Jimmy Stewart and that chocolatey smooth voice and now she simply couldn't decide. The tension in her head was starting to reach critical point and the thought of the unopened bottle of Smirnoff in her bag was practically causing her to drool. To make matters worse, the shop-girl was now talking on the phone – to her boyfriend, judging by the simpering tone of her voice. Lana sighed as she moved a little closer to the counter; she never could resist the chance to sneak a peek into somebody else's life. It wasn't that she was nosey – more sadomasochistic, she reassured herself, as she winced at the girl's pathetic pleadings.

'But I don't understand. How can they expect you to do this at such short notice? It's my birthday tomorrow.'

Lana peered over the New Releases stand that formed a partition down the middle of the shop. The girl was hunched over the counter, her bandana slightly askew and her eye-patch pushed up on to her forehead. 'But please,' she implored, 'can't you ask someone else to go in your place?'

God, what was the matter with her, Lana despaired. Had the girl never heard of the concept *treat 'em mean, keep 'em keen*? On the wall of screens next to the counter *Grease* was playing – yet again – and Rizzo was having a ball making fun of Sandy and her prissy ways. Lana couldn't help thinking it was rather apt. There was something about Olivia Newton John with her dopey doe-eyes and ironed fringe that made Lana want to scream with frustration, and listening to the girl was like getting it in stereo – toe-curling subservience in surround sound. Lana needed a drink and fast. Slamming Jimmy Stewart next to Will Smith in the New Releases she marched over to the counter and flung down the cover to *Casablanca*.

The girl continued twittering away into the phone. 'I suppose so. Yes, of course I understand. Yes – I know, I'm sorry, it's just that I was so disappointed, with it being my birthday and everything. I know you will. Okay. I'll see you on Wednesday then.'

Oh purrlease! Lana sighed so heavily that it came out more like a groan and she tapped her diamante-encrusted nails on the counter impatiently. Her nerve-endings were constricting, her temples were throbbing, her entire body was crying out for an alcohol injection.

After an absolutely pitiful farewell, the girl finally put down the receiver and replaced her eye-patch. 'Sorry about that,' she muttered, taking the film cover from the counter and walking over to the back shelves.

'Don't worry about it,' Lana snapped, rifling through her handbag for her cigarettes. Hopefully a quick nicotine fix would see her through the walk home. She hadn't yet stooped to swigging on park benches, not direct from the bottle at least.

The girl stretched up to the top shelf for the video and put the cover in its place. 'My boyfriend's just told me that he's got to go on a training course in Newport Pagnell for the next two days and he's going to miss my birthday,' she explained.

Lana coughed. The old training course in Newport Pagnell excuse, eh? The rat was obviously as unimaginative as his girlfriend was sappy. 'Oh dear, how tragic,' she mumbled, handing the girl a five pound note.

'I know. I'm trying really hard not to be selfish because I knew when he got this promotion it would involve more travel and after all it's even worse for him – I mean, Newport Pagnell in January, what a drag. I just wish he didn't have to miss my birthday, that's all.'

Lana watched in disbelief as the girl stared mournfully into the middle distance with her uncovered eye, the five-pound note frozen in her grasp. Just get my damned change and then go get a life, Lana wanted to scream. It took every last reserve of willpower to muster a more civil response. 'Never mind, sweetie, I'm sure he'll make it up to you when he gets back.'

The girl gave her a feeble smile. 'That's exactly what he said.'

Hmm, I'll bet he did, Lana thought with a smirk. 'Anyway, I'd better get on – don't want to keep you from your paperwork.'

The girl's face flushed and she hastily handed over the video and the change. 'Oh yes of course, sorry. Well, have a good day.'

Lana flung the items into her bag and pulled up the hood on her black velvet cape. 'Yes, honey, you too,' but as she turned on her kitten heel and strode through the shop she heard the unmistakable sound of sobbing. Just keep walking, she told herself, there's nothing you can do or say that'll make the poor sap feel any better – in fact you're guaranteed to make things worse. But just as she reached the door there it came again, a pathetic little whimper, reminiscent of puppy dogs, newly born lambs and other such heart-rending bullshit. Lana rolled her eyes to the heavens and groaned. It was like mental torture – what the hell should she do? She stared out on to the street. The rain was falling in sheets now, sweeping through the Parade like a tidal wave. It was the kind of weather that probably gave John Frieda an orgasm, but this lady had no intention of de-frizzing her hair twice in one morning. No, she couldn't leave the poor girl on her own, she would stay and offer her a shoulder to cry on. Not literally of course – there was no way she was getting tearstains on her vintage lambswool sweater. What was needed here was what the Brits referred to as good old tea and sympathy and as long as the girl could provide the tea, Lana was sure she could summon up a smidgen of sympathy.

Chapter Three

As Sadie switched on the kettle, a stream of embarrassment coursed through her body, erupting like lava onto her cheeks. What the hell was the matter with her this morning? Why had she burst into tears like that? And in front of The Actress of all people. Lana seemed so glamorous, so strong; what on earth must she be thinking of her? As Sadie chipped away at the pot of solidified sugar she could almost hear her father's voice barking, *Stop your crying! Tears are a sign of weakness and weakness is an invitation for attack.* The first time Sadie had heard those words was at the tender age of three, following a particularly nasty fall from her tricycle. She remembered being hoisted on to the dizzying heights of the kitchen table, her mother dabbing at her grazed knee with TCP and gazing up at her imploringly – but it was no good, the combination of the shock from her fall and the searing pain from the antiseptic caused her to scream out in anguish. Her father's bellow had whistled about her face like a slap, instantly silencing her hysteria, and although Sadie hadn't understood what his words meant, their tone and the fear they seemed to instil in her mother provided a lesson that would remain etched upon her psyche forever – crying was wrong and to be avoided at all costs.

Squeezing all life from the teabags before despatching them to the bin, Sadie drew a deep breath and returned to the front of the shop. 'I'm so sorry about that,' she said, placing the drinks upon the counter. 'I don't know what's got into me this morning. You must think I'm a right idiot.'

'No – not at all,' Lana purred, exhaling a thin talon of smoke from her blood red lips. 'We all have bad days, honey. I don't suppose you have any tissues out back, do you? I think I may have a cold coming on.'

'Yeah, sure,' Sadie replied with a relieved smile. 'I'm afraid it'll have to be loo roll and it may be a little damp – outside toilet,' she added apologetically.

'No problem.'

As soon as Lana heard Sadie disappear off down the back steps she sprung into action, pouring half her tea into the rubber plant beside the counter and hastily topping it up from the bottle of vodka in her bag. She'd already had a couple of swigs while Sadie had been making the tea and the familiar tentacles of warmth were beginning to creep their way through her veins. Lana pulled down her hood and patted the carefully-set auburn curls framing her face. Perhaps this wasn't going to be quite so excruciating after all – with its intricate poster displays and borders of twinkling fairy lights the shop had a certain cosy charm, and the girl seemed to have regained control of her senses – yes, Lana could certainly think of worse places in which to breakfast.

'Here you go,' Sadie said, returning to the counter with a sheaf of toilet paper. 'I'm not surprised you've got a cold with the weather the way it is. It's absolutely pouring out there. Don't you just hate this time of year? It's so depressing, isn't it?'

Lana sighed. What was it with the British and their compulsion to talk about the weather? In the twenty years she'd resided in London she still couldn't quite come to terms with it. It wouldn't be so bad if they referred to it in neutral terms, merely reporting meteorological fact, but there always had to be a negative twist. Even on the most beautiful day they would revel in telling you that it wasn't going to last, that a cold front from Siberia was expected at any moment or that the heat was playing havoc with their hydrangeas. And the absolute cherry on the cake was when they would finish their diatribe with the immortal words *Still, mustn't grumble*!

'Mind you, we shouldn't complain – at least it isn't snowing,' Sadie continued, removing her sodden scarlet bandana and hanging it on the shelf in front of the electric heater to dry.

Lana watched as the girl shook out her chestnut curls. Combined with her heart-shaped face she had quite a cute, cherub-like quality about her. It was a shame she had to hide it all behind that ludicrous pirate's get-up. 'Thank you, honey,' said Lana, picking up the damp tissue with a grimace and placing it straight into her bag. 'Now I don't suppose you could do me one more favour?'

'Sure,' Sadie responded, still eager to make up for her embarrassing display of earlier.

'You couldn't put something else on the VCR, could you? It's just that every time I come into this shop you're playing *Grease*. How about something a little more – contemporary?'

Sadie blushed. 'Oh, yes, of course. Well, why don't you choose something.'

Lana furrowed her brow – now, what did the poor girl need? 'I know,' she declared. '*Thelma and Louise*. Do you want me to find the cover?'

'No, it's okay,' Sadie headed straight to the bottom shelf for tape number 1308. The Brad Pitt scene had been one of her favourite fantasies. It was such a shame things had never worked out between him and Thelma.

'So,' Lana said, tapping another cigarette from her mother-of-pearl embossed case. 'It's your birthday tomorrow?'

Sadie's face clouded over. 'Yes, I think I'll just forget about it this year though.'

'Don't be so silly,' Lana responded, before taking a large

gulp of tea. 'Birthdays are an achievement – they demand celebration. How old are you going to be, sweetie?'

'Twenty-two.'

Lana sighed. 'Twenty-two; why, you've got your whole life ahead of you. Wait until you're my age, then you'll have a real reason to weep and wail.'

In a bid to hide her embarrassment, Sadie bent down to fast-forward through the trailers. 'So— how old are you?' she ventured from beneath the counter. 'If you don't mind me asking.'

Lana laughed. 'Let's just say, I'm as old as my bones and about thirty years older than my breasts.' She brought her bejewelled hands together in prayer position, 'Thank the sweet Lord above for bestowing us with silicone – not to mention botox. I'm forty-five, honey, but let me tell you I don't feel a day under seventy – especially first thing on a Monday morning.'

Sadie emerged from beneath the counter, giggling.

'That's more like it,' Lana continued. 'You're far too young to be taking life so seriously. So your boyfriend's been called away on a course – why don't you go out with your girlfriends instead?'

Sadie attempted a smile. What girlfriends? She could just imagine Lana – the original American sweetheart with her immaculately coiffed hair and porcelain skin – growing up at the heart of a network of female friends, their lives joined together like patches on a quilt, a constant stream of slumber parties, followed by baby showers, followed by cake bakes. Just like in the movie *Steel Magnolias*, they had probably spent hours huddled on porch swings trading confidences as readily as cigarettes, all washed down with gallons of iced tea. Sadie sighed wistfully. The sad truth was that she had no 'girlfriends'. When she met GL in her first week at university he had rapidly become her closest and only true friend. The

rest of their group had come from his Business Studies course
and even now when they socialised it was with friends from
his work; other sales people whom Sadie had no real desire to
get to know any better. The only friends she had to speak of
were her customers, but these were more casual acquaintances
limited to over the counter gossips during working hours.

Sadie swapped her patch over to her left eye, 'No, I think
I'll just work instead. I could do with the extra money after
Christmas and besides I wasn't all that happy having to ask
one of my part-timers to do a twelve hour shift.'

The twang of country music filled the shop as Thelma
and Louise embarked upon their road trip, and Lana stared
at Sadie. 'What's your name, hon?' she asked, offering her
a cigarette.

Sadie shook her head. GL had decided they should both
give up for the New Year. 'No thanks, I've given up – New
Year's Resolution. My name's Sadie.'

'Sadie,' Lana repeated, removing her velvet cape to reveal a
skin-tight lambswool sweater in claret, teamed with a tailored
black pencil skirt. The huge ruby adorning her wedding
finger flickered like a flame as she extended her hand in
greeting. 'Delighted to make your acquaintance. I'm Lana.
Well, Sadie — has it ever occurred to you quite how dumb
New Year's resolutions are?'

Sadie sat back in her chair and frowned. 'What do you mean?'

'Well, it's the first of January. You've just enjoyed one of
the best weeks of the year – hopefully. You've exchanged
gifts with your nearest and dearest, munched chocolates in
front of the weepiest movies, feasted on the richest foods,
partaken of the finest wines,' Lana took a swig from her tea,
'and then you've seen out the old year drunk on a cocktail of
nostalgia and hope, gazing dewy-eyed at your beloved as the
clock strikes twelve.'

Sadie coughed as she recalled the previous week's New

Year's Eve party at GL's uncle's house. As Big Ben had struck twelve, GL's dad had struck his brother in the face with the remote control, yelling, 'You can stick your Dale Winton up your arse!' before storming back home to watch Jools Holland. To make matters even worse GL himself had disappeared off the face of the earth, only to resurface at ten minutes *past* midnight. Still, she understood the sentiment behind what Lana was saying.

'And then,' Lana continued, 'With Auld Lang Syne still ringing in your ears what do you do? You sit down and write out a list of resolutions guaranteed to make you feel as miserable as sin for the next twelve months.'

Sadie smiled. She had to admit the smell of Lana's cigarette was triggering a quite desperate craving in her.

Lana ground down the butt of her cigarette before pushing the ashtray across the counter. 'Yes, you set yourself impossible targets designed to starve and deprive yourself into depression – targets you know you'll never keep – so you end up spending the remainder of the year feeling a total failure as well as fat and hideously unhealthy.'

Sadie nodded as she thought of the list of resolutions GL had pinned to the fridge on New Year's Day.

- Give up smoking
- Join a gym
- Take another self-assertiveness course
- Do a bungee jump to impress boss
- Become a black belt in jujitsu
- Attend a gladiatorial re-enactment weekend
- Take driving test again – and pass
- Buy a Beemer (with alloy wheels and a mock-croc interior)
- Make first million

Lana was right – it was hardly achievable or inspirational stuff.

Lana drained the last of her tea. 'Wouldn't it make a lot more sense if we all just resolved to be happy?' she said, raising her arms with a flourish. 'I don't suppose there's any chance of another cup of tea before I go?' she enquired, turning on her most dazzling smile.

'Yes, of course,' Sadie took the mugs out to the kitchen for a refill. There was something quite hypnotic about Lana, with her flamboyant body language and husky drawl. It was probably what Hollywood directors and gossip columnists referred to as 'star quality'. She could quite happily make tea for her all day in exchange for basking in her reflected rays. 'I hope you don't mind me asking,' Sadie called from the kitchen. 'But are you an actress, by any chance?' There was a pause followed by a cough before Lana finally replied.

'Er, yes – I suppose you could say that I am a member of the acting community, sweetie. Although I don't really like to make a big deal about it. At the end of the day a job is a job.'

Sadie smiled as she poured the boiling water into the mugs and watched the teabags bob to the surface. She knew it. She wasn't often wrong in the assessment of her customers – apart from member 307 whom she could have sworn was a city banker with his penchant for pin-striped suits and lairy braces. She was absolutely stunned when he came into the shop one day in full lollypop-man regalia. And then there was the young man who owned the flat upstairs, Liam, whose hulking frame looked as if it ought to have been manning the door of a nightclub rather than hunched over a workbench carving fireplaces for a living.

'So what kind of acting do you do?' Sadie asked, returning to the counter with fresh cups of tea. She could just see Lana treading the boards of some West End stage – Mrs Robinson perhaps, or Lady Macbeth?

Lana emerged from behind the New Releases stand, pulling

the zip shut on her bag. 'Oh whatever I – or should I say, my agent – can get, honey. Commercials, voice-overs, stage roles.'

Sadie sighed wistfully. Oh, to be able to say you had an agent – it was like something out of *Heat* magazine. 'I can just see you on the stage,' she enthused. 'To be honest, the first time I saw you I thought you were an actress. I have this sort of game that I play,' she confided, 'where I try to work out my customers' occupations. I don't often get it wrong,' she added proudly.

'No, you're obviously a very shrewd judge of character,' Lana replied with a wry smile. 'I must confess I'm guilty of the same pastime. I do so love to people watch – it helps me with character portrayal you know; gives me an insight into what makes people tick.'

Sadie nodded enthusiastically. 'Oh yes, I suppose it would.'

Lana took a sip from her tea before continuing. 'I just can't help it – within seconds of meeting a person I find that I am analysing their body language, searching for clues to their true identity, reading between the lines of their dialogue for what they are really saying about themselves. I used to think it was a gift to be so perceptive, but in many ways it's become a curse.'

'How do you mean?'

'Well, after a time you become so good at reading people that life holds very little mystery anymore. It's like being given a pair of x-ray glasses; everyone becomes so transparent there are no longer any pleasant surprises.'

'Or nasty shocks,' Sadie added with a grin.

'Hmm, that's true, I guess.' Lana took a cigarette from her case and lit it. Inhaling deeply, she fixed Sadie with a penetrating stare. 'Would you like to know what I've figured out about you?'

Sadie felt her face begin to flush and she reached

instinctively for her tea. 'Okay,' she replied hesitantly from behind the mug.

Lana turned sideways to exhale a jet of smoke before returning her gaze to Sadie. Heavily framed in kohl, her huge eyes were like a pair of black-rimmed saucers. Or a pair of x-ray specs. Sadie squirmed.

'You're twenty-two years old, with the best years of your life ahead of you, and yet you seem deeply unhappy about something. You hide away behind that counter, behind that costume, watching that goddamn movie, *Grease* as though your life depended upon it, while all the time life is simply passing you by.' Lana gestured to the street outside where a gaggle of shopping-laden housewives were doing battle with the elements. 'I've seen the way you listen to your customers, laughing at their dumb jokes, pretending to be interested in their dreary little lives. You seem so anxious to please, but I get the feeling that you're never really pleasing yourself. Your boyfriend tells you he is going to miss your birthday and you burst into floods of tears which would suggest to me that a) you are deeply insecure or b) you have good reason to doubt him.'

Lana looked at Sadie's crestfallen face and bit her lip. Why did she always do this? Why couldn't she just keep her big mouth shut for once? 'Hell, what do I know? I've only just met you,' she declared in her best attempt at breezy, but it was no good; she could see Sadie's right eye filling up with tears. Oh Lord, why hadn't she just gone home and left the poor girl in peace? She could have been half way through *Casablanca* by now, not to mention the bottle of Smirnoff. 'Hey, please don't cry. Take this,' Lana fumbled in her bag for the toilet paper Sadie had given her earlier.

Sadie grabbed the tissue and dabbed angrily at her eye. What the hell was the matter with her this morning? She hadn't cried for years and yet now it seemed she was unable to stop. 'Could I have a cigarette?' she muttered, removing her eye-patch and casting it on to the counter.

'Sure,' Lana replied, eager to make amends, especially if it meant resolution-busting into the bargain. 'I'm sorry, I guess I had no right to say those things – I'm just an interfering old goose – see, I told you it was a curse.' Lana took a cigarette from her case and passed it to Sadie. 'Here, let me light that for you.'

Sadie inhaled deeply and sat back into her chair. Although she had only given up smoking for a week, the rush of nicotine made her feel quite light-headed. 'No, you were right – well partly. Things aren't too good between my boyfriend and me at the moment, but that's no reason for me to act like a baby. You must think I'm such a wimp.'

'No, not at all,' Lana lied, secretly congratulating herself on her accurate appraisal and wondering who the boyfriend was screwing.

'The truth is, I think he may be going off me – he seems so distant all of a sudden and everything I do or say seems to irritate the hell out of him, no matter how hard I try.'

'Maybe that's the problem,' Lana said.

'What do you mean?'

'Well, perhaps you're trying a bit too hard. Maybe you need to act a little less – needy?' Lana held her breath, but to her immense relief Sadie didn't burst into tears.

'Do you think so?'

'Yeah. Look, he lets you down over your birthday and you immediately start crying and decide to work all day instead. What kind of message is that going to send him?'

Sadie shrugged her shoulders.

'Well to me it's saying: hey buddy, you can let me down on my special day and I'll just take it, which only makes it all the easier for him to do it to you again. If, however, he gets back from his training course to find you full of tales of the fun birthday you had without him, well all of a sudden he's not Mr Indispensable. All of a sudden he realises that he'll have to start making more of an effort too.'

Sadie took a drag on her cigarette and forced a smile. She knew what Lana was saying made sense but there was no way she was going to own up to having no back-up supply of birthday celebrators.

Lana gazed at Sadie thoughtfully. Don't do it, she cautioned herself, it isn't your fault if the poor girl has no friends, just wish her a happy birthday and leave before it's too late. But before she knew it her mouth was opening and the words were spilling out. 'So, what do you say I take you out for a slap-up lunch tomorrow and we make it a birthday to remember. It's the least I can do given that you've made me gallons of delicious tea and all I've done is make you cry.'

Sadie's eyes widened. 'Oh – are you sure? I mean don't you have any work on or anything?'

Lana shook her head. 'I have a couple of radio commercials booked today, but tomorrow I'm as free as a bird.'

Sadie gave a cautious smile. 'Well, I suppose I could get my part-timer to do the day shift. If you're sure.'

'Of course I'm sure,' Lana replied, privately cursing herself. What the hell was happening to her? This could be a slippery slope. If she wasn't careful she'd be sponsoring a starving African next. 'Lunch it is then. I'll see if my agent can get us in somewhere nice. It's a bit short notice, but hopefully most of the regulars at the Ivy will still be skimming the slopes in Aspen.' At the sight of Sadie's beaming face Lana felt an unfamiliar twinge in the pit of her stomach – it was really quite nauseating. 'Anyway, I must fly, I'm supposed to be at the studio for midday.' Lana hurriedly put on her cape and picked up her bag. 'Here, take a couple for later,' she said, depositing two cigarettes on the counter in front of Sadie, 'What do you say we meet outside this place tomorrow at eleven o'clock?'

Sadie nodded enthusiastically, 'Great. Thank you. Are you sure you don't mind?'

'Of course I'm sure. Oh but do me a favour, honey – get rid of the pirate's costume. That Captain Pugwash look is so last season.'

Sadie giggled. 'Don't worry, I will.' As she watched Lana shimmy her way out of the shop she almost had to pinch herself. What a day it had been, from such a disastrous start to a lunch date at the Ivy with an actress. Who would have believed it? She couldn't wait to tell GL.

By the time Lana got home she was feeling seriously pissed off. Her video store encounter had left her feeling quite drained and work was the last thing she felt like doing. Opening the door to her nondescript semi, she shook out her umbrella and stepped into the hall.

'Hi honey, I'm home,' she called, her voice echoing throughout the empty house. 'Goddamn – it's darker than a Burt Reynolds' chest wig in here,' Lana muttered to herself as she flung her cape over the banisters and turned on the stained glass lamp. Catching a glimpse of herself in the Art Deco mirror on the wall, she grimaced. 'Gee, you're starting to make Morticia Addams look healthy,' she said to her reflection. Her reflection stared back, unblinking, and even in the dull glow of the hall lamp Lana could make out the telltale tinge of yellow in her eyes; the same tinge she had masked with foundation upon her face.

'I need a drink,' Lana announced, turning away from the mirror and delving into her bag for the bottle of vodka. Kicking off her shoes and clutching the bottle, video and cigarettes to her chest, she padded across the parquet flooring into the living room where she headed straight for the drinks cabinet in the corner. Half-filling a crystal tumbler with vodka she then made her way to the gargantuan television unit housed in one of the alcoves beside the fireplace. Lana inserted *Casablanca* into the video recorder and pressed Play. God, she really did not want to work today. Sighing, she flung herself onto the chaise longue opposite the television and picked up a huge marble lighter from the coffee table in front of her.

Pale light flickered throughout the room as the film began to play. Lana glanced at the heavy burgundy drapes still drawn across the bay window. There seemed little point in opening them on a day like today. Besides, now she had sat down she had no intention of moving until lunchtime at least. If only she didn't have to work. Lana lit her cigarette, adjusted the volume on the remote control and reached out for the telephone on the coffee table. Although it looked like a prop from a 1920s' movie with its circular dial and ebony effect, it had in fact been purchased from Argos for the bargain price of nineteen ninety-nine. Lana picked up the receiver and pressed a series of digits. She listened attentively for a moment before putting the phone back down. Within seconds it began to ring.

'Lord above!' Lana groaned, raising her eyes in despair before answering the call. 'Hello,' she purred into the mouthpiece. 'Yes, you have the right number. Why sure, I can do dominatrix. Whatever turns you on, honey. Whatever turns you on.'

Chapter Four

January 6th. Another day of ferrying filth from one stinking hellhole to another. You get to see all sorts in my line of work, would make your stomach turn the things that have gone on in the back of my cab.

Terry paused for a moment and chewed thoughtfully on the end of his pencil. This diary lark was beginning to do his head in. Robert De Niro made it seem so easy in *Taxi Driver*. How come everything he wrote about life on the mean streets of New York seemed so profound, while his own efforts – Terry glanced down at the spidery scrawl working its way across his battered notebook – well, writing never had been one of his strongest points. Perhaps if he made a bit more effort recreating the atmosphere of the film it might help stimulate the flow? Terry cast his eyes about his bedroom. With its nineteen-seventies furniture and white-washed walls, it certainly looked the part, and the frameless mirror hanging next to the window could have been pinched from the very set itself. Terry gave his reflection an admiring glance – the army jacket, faded jeans and brown cowboy boots were almost exact replicas of De Niro's. There was only one thing missing. Terry turned to the portable radio on the windowsill and searched for Jazz FM. When he finally managed to locate it they were playing 'What a Wonderful World' by Louis Armstrong, which was a little too feel-good for his liking, but at least he now had a soundtrack. He picked up his pencil and resumed writing.

*I get them all in the back of my cab. That fare to West
Hounslow earlier – they didn't fool me with their father and
daughter routine – I knew it was just some two-bit ho and
her pimp. All that talk of parents' evenings didn't fool me for
a second. Some day soon the rain's gonna come and wash the
scum off these Ruislip Manor streets.*

Terry looked out of the window. It was pitch dark but
he could hear the rain lashing against the wrought-iron fire
escape outside. 'Bloody country,' he muttered to himself.
'Never stops bleeding raining. I ought to get meself back to
the Costa del Sol.'

He cast his diary down on the bed in despair and looked
about the room for inspiration. 'Are you talking to me?' he
snarled at his reflection in the mirror before jumping to his
feet and reaching for the imaginary pistol on his belt. God,
he was bored. Grabbing the half-eaten tin of meatballs from
the table in front of him he marched over to the door and
flung it open. 'I'm just nipping downstairs to get a video,
Liam,' he called across the hall. 'Won't be long.'

Liam placed his razor on the edge of the bathroom sink and
groaned. Why was it every time he decided to get a video
out Terry always beat him to it? Now he would be subjected
to two hours of car chases and mindless violence or have
to spend the evening alone in his bedroom. Still, at least it
might mean that Terry was finally over his Robert De Niro
fixation. If he had to sit through *Taxi Driver* one more time he
wouldn't be held responsible for his actions. Liam wiped the
steam from the mirror and stared at his half-shaven face. With
his unruly mop of curls and his shaving foam beard he looked
like a cross between Father Christmas and Jon Bon Jovi (back
when he was still 'Living on a Prayer'). Even Liam realised
this was not a good look, especially if he was going downstairs.
He'd been meaning to get his hair cut for the past six months

now, but as with all of life's practical but essentially dull tasks, Liam never seemed to get round to doing it. It wasn't that he was some dozy old bum who couldn't give a toss – it was just that he could always think of far more interesting alternatives to the routine of everyday living. Like that time he had set off to the post office to pay his television licence but had ended up bumping into his old mate Jez. Jez, it turned out, was fresh off the Easyjet from Amsterdam, with a bag of magic mushrooms burning a hole in the lining of his rucksack. One thing led to another and before Liam could say TV detector van he was lying on his back in the park watching a flock of airborne elephants looping the loop through Technicolor clouds, whilst a marching band of pitbull terriers performed a mind-blowing rendition of 'Riders on the Storm'.

Liam pulled his hair back into a ponytail and with a few deft strokes of the razor scraped the remaining foam from his jaw. He'd go down to the video shop anyway – at least then he could stop Terry from picking anything too dire. It was his flat and his video player after all. Besides which, he'd been looking forward to seeing Sadie all day.

Sadie sat behind the counter and stifled a yawn. In the eight hours since Lana had left there had only been about four customers in the shop, one of whom (member 1127 aka Mr Top-Shelf) was currently hovering around the Drama section, pretending to study the cover of *Hamlet* whilst really plucking up the courage to lunge for one of the soft porn titles housed above.

'Greetings, pop-pickers!'

Sadie almost jumped out of her skin as Terry burst through the door brandishing a tin, his army jacket flapping about him in the breeze. His eyes lit up as they came to rest upon Mr Top-Shelf.

'Go on mate, don't be shy. Do you need a hand getting

it down or something? Here, Treacle, where's that step ladder?'

Sadie shook her head and frowned at Terry, but secretly she was quite relieved. With his greasy hair and pasty little hands, Mr Top-Shelf gave her the creeps; it was quite amusing to watch him squirm for once.

Terry draped a sinewy arm around Mr Top-Shelf's shoulders. 'I tell you what, mate – if it's porn you're after, you want to come to me. I can get you some quality action, d'you know what I mean? I'm talking hard-core, see what they've had for breakfast kind of stuff. None of your tasteful *Electric Blue* rubbish. Got a mate in Amsterdam, see.'

Pulling his raincoat tight around him, Mr Top-Shelf scuttled to the door and fled into the night.

'What did I say?' Terry asked, grinning broadly as he made his way to the counter. 'I was only trying to help the geezer.'

Sadie took one look at him and burst out laughing. 'Yeah right, just like that time you recommended *Silence of the Lambs* to that little old lady who was babysitting her grandkids. What the hell is *that*?' Sadie pointed to the open tin of meatballs Terry had placed upon the counter.

'That, my dear, is tea. Get the kettle on, Treacle, I'm bleeding parched.'

Sadie got up from her chair and smiled. Terry might be as annoying as hell, but with his twinkling eyes and impish sense of humour he had the unfailing ability to charm his way out of trouble.

'I tell you what, I've had a right mare of a day. You wouldn't believe the donuts I've had in the back of me cab.'

'Oh yes? Tell me more,' Sadie replied, taking a Christmas selection box of biscuits from the cupboard. With the kind of tea he was having it looked as if Terry could do with some dessert.

'This one bird – right dumpy old trollop – she wanted to go to the swimming pool? So I just points out that maybe if she walked the couple of hundred yards to the pool rather than order a cab, she might not have such a problem with her tonnage. D'you know what I mean?'

Sadie grimaced as she returned with a tray of tea and biscuits. 'And what did she say?'

'Well she went bleeding mental, didn't she. Wanted to know my name and number. Said she was going to report me, blah, blah, blah. So I says, "I suppose a tip's out of the question then?" and she says, "I'll give you a tip. You go home and wash your mouth out with soap, you horrible little man." And then she gets out of the cab without even paying her fare. Flabby old bint!'

Sadie took a custard cream from the tray and laughed. 'Serves you right. God, Terry, don't you know anything about customer relations?'

'With the likes of her? No thanks. She'd have to lose at least four stone before I'd even think about having relations. So, how was your day?'

'Well, it started pretty crap, what with the weather and everything.'

They both took a moment to gaze outside, where raindrops glistened like strings of glass beads against the pane.

Terry sighed as he turned back to the counter. 'I know, it's a shocker isn't it? I wouldn't mind if we got a decent summer, but we don't even have that anymore. It just seems to be rain, rain, rain all bleeding year round. Still could be worse, we could be roasting our nads off in some Third World country like Ethiopia or Sudanisia.' Terry speared one of the meatballs with his fork and popped it into his mouth.

Sadie put her biscuit back down. The sight of Terry chomping away, a trickle of gravy worming its way down his chin, was making her stomach churn.

'Yeah, right. Anyway something quite nice happened this morning. One of the customers asked me out for lunch.'

'I thought you had a fella?' Terry wiped his chin with the back of his hand. 'I tell you what, this is a blinding bit of meat. Do you fancy one?' He waved a meatball in Sadie's face, splattering the counter with gravy.

Sadie shrunk back into her seat. 'No thanks, I've already eaten. Yes, I have got a boyfriend, but don't worry, it was a female customer.'

Terry's eyes lit up. 'Oh yeah? And she asked you out for lunch, did she?'

'You can hold your pervy thoughts right there, Terry Leggett,' Sadie retorted. 'She found out it was my birthday tomorrow so she offered to take me out. Besides she's old enough to be my mother – about your age actually,' Sadie added with a grin. 'And you'll never guess what – she's an actress.' Sadie had been dying to tell somebody her news all day, but so far GL hadn't returned any of her messages.

'Fit, is she?' Terry enquired through a mouthful of meat-ball.

'If you mean, is she attractive, then yes she is, and she's American; but a bit out of your league, I'm afraid.'

Terry pulled himself upright and adjusted the collar on his army jacket, the streaks of gravy on his face blending perfectly with his olive skin. 'Says who?' he demanded. 'They don't call me Terry "De Niro" Leggett for nothing, you know.'

'They don't call you Terry "De Niro" Leggett at all.'

Sadie and Terry looked up to see Liam standing in the doorway, his towering physique practically filling the frame. 'Don't believe a word he says,' he remarked with a lop-sided grin, but although he was obviously addressing Sadie he seemed unable to make eye contact with her, staring at the New Releases stand instead.

Sadie felt her face begin to flush. 'Would you like a cup

of tea?' she asked, desperate for the chance to escape to the back and cool down.

'No, I'm all right, thanks,' Liam replied, picking up the cover of a James Bond movie and pretending to read the blurb.

'Are you sure?' Sadie pleaded. Even the backs of her eyes were prickling with heat.

'Go on mate, have a brew. She's got her festive biscuits out specially.' Having finally finished his meatballs, Terry was now studying the biscuits. He grabbed a pink wafer and stuffed it into his mouth whole. 'Here you go, Treacle – take this out the back, would you,' he said, handing Sadie the gravy-streaked tin and spraying the counter with wafer dust as he spoke.

'All right then, if it's no trouble,' Liam muttered, hurriedly replacing the video cover. What the hell was he doing picking up a James Bond? He couldn't stand the flash twat. Cars and guns did absolutely nothing for him, never had done. Even when he was a kid his solitary Action Man had ended up as a doorstop, staring up forlornly, his legs wedged beneath the door, his uniform in tatters, as Liam whittled countless figurines out of sticks with his penknife.

Sadie stumbled through to the kitchen and opened the back door. She gasped as the cold air rushed in to greet her, stinging her burning face. Although over the years she had managed to perfect a veneer of indifference between herself and the rest of the world, her cheeks constantly let her down. Like two beacons signalling her innermost thoughts and fears, they would flare up without a word of warning and often without any sense of logic. Like now, for instance. As Sadie poked her head out of the door and let the icy rain trickle down her face she felt quite bewildered. Ever since she'd met Liam he had always made her blush and she couldn't for the life of her work out why. It wasn't as if she fancied him. If anything he scared her. He was just so huge. His arms were the size of tree trunks and his hands were like great shovels, all scuffed and worn. Sometimes she couldn't help jumping when he'd plonk them down on the counter to deposit a video. His shoulders were the size of boulders and even his jaw looked as if it had been chiselled out of granite. He had lovely hair though; wild and tousled like a rock star's. She wondered what it would be like to run her hands through Liam's hair – it looked so soft and inviting, unlike GL's prickly spikes. Sadie slammed the back door shut and went to make the tea. Why hadn't GL phoned her? She'd been leaving messages all day. A wave of panic engulfed her. What if he'd had an accident? What if the train to Newport Pagnell had been derailed due to the wrong kind of rain on the line?

Sadie returned to the shop, smiling weakly to mask her concern. 'Here's your tea,' she called out to Liam who seemed engrossed in the cover of *Terminator*.

'Thanks.' Liam replaced the cover and made his way over to the counter.

'So – it's your birthday tomorrow, eh?' Terry asked, demolishing a custard cream. 'Your old man taking you anywhere nice?'

Liam looked up just in time to see Sadie shake her head.

'No, he's away on a course. So after my lunch date with the actress, I'm afraid I'll be stuck in this place.'

Liam couldn't help grinning as he picked up his mug of tea.

'What – they've got you working on your bleeding birthday?' Terry said, outraged.

'I don't mind. I could do with the money after Christmas and anyway I *am* going out for lunch.'

Terry frowned. 'Yeah, but still, working on your birthday – that's shitty, man. Tell you what, how about we have a bit of a knees up in here? I'll get a few cans and we can put a bit of music on. I can bring me Quo video down if you like.'

Sadie and Liam groaned and exchanged a shy smile.

'What?' Terry demanded.' 'It's better than that *Grease* shit you've usually got on. What's happened to that, by the way? Don't tell me you finally wore it out?'

Sadie smiled. 'No, I just fancied a change so I put *Thelma and Louise* on instead.'

Liam looked up at the bank of screens where Geena Davis was busy robbing a grocery store. 'Good film,' he muttered approvingly. His mum had played *Thelma and Louise* repeatedly the day she finally booted his step-dad out. As he watched it now, he remembered her throwing her head back and roaring with laughter, the years of stress and tension dropping away from her like an old skin.

'Couple of dykes,' Terry sniffed dismissively. 'So, is it sorted then? Are you pair up for a celebratory drink tomorrow or what?'

Sadie and Liam both nodded.

'Excellent. Well, I'll get meself down the offy, then and I'll see you in here about seven, all right?' Terry downed the rest of his tea, zipped up his coat and stuffed a handful of biscuits into each of his pockets.

'I thought you were getting a video?' Liam asked.

'Changed me mind, son. Think I might do a couple of hours graft instead. Catch the chucking out shift – I've got to get the cash for your extortionate rent somehow.' Terry leant over the counter and planted a kiss on top of Sadie's head. 'Good night, Treacle. I'll see you tomorrow.'

As Liam watched Terry bound from the shop, he couldn't believe his luck. Not only would he be able to watch the video of his choice, but he was also finally alone with Sadie. The problem was knowing what to say to her. It was ridiculous really; he never had this problem with anybody else. Okay, so he wasn't the loudest bloke in the world and next to Terry he was a bloody wallflower, but he was more than capable of engaging in conversation. Some mornings it would take him the best part of an hour to get from his flat at the top of the parade to his workshop down by the station due to his daily chinwags with the postman, the newsagent and Stelios in the caff. And if he got collared by Maurice Grimstead, the funeral director, he was looking at a good hour and a half – especially since that mix-up with the bodies last month. But when it came to the manageress of the video store, Liam found himself completely and utterly tongue-tied. It didn't help that she always seemed so nervous around him. The way she seemed to cower in his presence made him feel even more cumbersome than ever. Being six feet four certainly had its advantages when it came to having a good view at gigs or breaking up fights, but when it came to women, it was a nightmare. The only girls he seemed to attract were mouthy Amazonian types who seemed obsessed with sunbeds and nail extensions. Not really his cup of tea at all. Liam didn't want Lilly Savage minus the penis, he wanted somebody quirky and sweet, someone he could talk to about anything. He stared at the television screen for inspiration. Thelma and Louise had just been pulled over by a cop.

'Oh, this bit is brilliant,' he said.

Sadie smiled as she watched Susan Sarandon climb into the patrol car. 'Yes, it's great isn't it, especially when they lock the policeman in the trunk.' It had been strange watching *Thelma and Louise* again. She hadn't really got that much out of it before, apart from the Brad Pitt scene of course, but this time it seemed so much more emotive. Rather than feeling let down, Sadie had found herself almost cheering as the women hurtled into the Grand Canyon at the end. She'd even spent half the afternoon dreaming that Lana would turn up the following day in a 1966 T-Bird convertible to whisk her away on a road trip of their own, but of course the prospect of going bumper to bumper on the M25 was slightly less appealing than tearing along an open stretch of interstate.

'So, how old are you going to be tomorrow?' Liam enquired, in what he hoped was a suitably nonchalant manner.

'Twenty-two.'

Twenty-two. Liam tried his best to disguise a relieved sigh. He found it hard enough working out women's ages at the best of times, but with Sadie being so small it made it even worse. He had half expected her to chirp out 'seventeen,' before retrieving a copy of *Smash Hits* from beneath the counter. It would have been just his luck. Liam smiled. No, there was nothing wrong with twenty-two – nothing wrong with a five-year age gap.

'So, how does it feel then?'

Sadie stared at him blankly. 'How does what feel?'

'Being twenty-two – almost.' Oh, Christ. Liam groaned inwardly. Ten out of ten for the most unoriginal, irrelevant question ever asked.

'Oh, er . . .' Sadie's face flushed, but before she could reply the telephone began to ring. Sadie grabbed the receiver. 'Good Evening, Pirate Video. GL? Oh, at last. Where have you been? I've been leaving messages all day. I was starting to get really worried.'

Liam placed his mug on the counter. It was obviously the boyfriend. He'd only seen him once before, strutting around the shop as if he owned the place, criticising the out of date posters and laughing at the new releases on display, or rather the lack of them. Liam had been gobsmacked. He hadn't really pictured Sadie going for somebody so flash. With his poncey designer clothes and gold plate jewellery he was everything Liam hated in a bloke. It was this hope that Liam clung to when he thought about Sadie. Surely she couldn't be happy with the cocky little git?

'You were getting me a present? Oh, what is it? Okay then, I'll wait till Wednesday,' Sadie giggled coquettishly. 'Ooh GL, you'll never guess what happened to me today. Hold on, I'll just serve this customer.' But when Sadie looked up from the telephone, Liam was already half way out of the door.

Chapter Five

On Friday 30th May 1998 Sadie's mother was found dead in her car, a length of garden hose neatly taped to the exhaust and a carefully typed suicide note propped upon the dash. In death as in life everything had been 'just so'. Ten days later, Sadie had sat her first A level and never had she been more motivated for an exam. Her mother had found her escape route, now she must take hers. Sadie passed with two As and a B.

It wasn't until she returned home from sitting her final exam that the enormity of what had happened sunk in. As she let herself into the empty house and flung down her bag, it finally hit her that her mother had gone. But it wasn't her mother's laughter or conversation that were sorely missing – no, as Sadie examined the dust and grime and stacks of unopened junk mail accumulating in the hall, she realized it was her mother's cleaning skills that were glaringly absent. The truth was, as the years had passed and an icy gloom had descended upon her parents' marriage, her mother had immersed herself in housework, cleaning morning, noon and night. And the more she cleaned, the less she seemed to exist, scrubbing away at the already gleaming surfaces as if she were trying to remove every last trace of the reflection peering back at her. Every drop of energy she would have once spent doing things with Sadie was redirected into scrubbing floors and skirting boards, dusting lampshades and bookshelves and vacuuming every available inch of floor space. As far as

Sadie was concerned her mother had assumed a ghostly presence years before she actually died – drifting aimlessly around the house in her housecoat and slippers, offering only the occasional murmured communication between chores.

The exam-weary Sadie had looked about the hall in shock. Surfaces that had previously sparkled now lay thick with dust, flecks of mud peppered the thick oatmeal carpet and rather than smelling of beeswax and baking, the stale air hung heavy with the stench of eggs. Sadie picked up a note from the hall table. It was a message from her father, neatly printed in capitals, her billet for the day.

SADIE, HAVE HAD ACCIDENT WITH BOILED EGGS. PLEASE RECTIFY ASAP.

Sadie made her way into the kitchen to find a blackened saucepan soaking in the sink and a thick, yellow foam splattered about the room. The closer she looked, the more yellow foam there seemed to be; dotted over the counters, cooker and draining board and hanging in great clumps from the ceiling directly above the hob. Her head pounding from lack of sleep and the sheer concentration from the previous two weeks work, she began rubbing half-heartedly at a speck of congealed egg with a cloth, but it had set solid and refused to shift. Tears began coursing down her face as she flung the cloth into the sink. It felt as if her whole world was crashing down around her ears and she didn't know who to turn to or how to cope.

As Sadie looked about the kitchen in despair her sorrow began to transform into rage. Surely a housewife as proficient as her mother would possess an implement designed for ridding kitchen surfaces of exploded boiled egg? She seemed to have just about everything else in her neatly arranged cupboards and drawers, all beautifully lined in waxed gingham paper. One by one, Sadie opened the units and began flinging the utensils to the floor – a contraption for cutting crinkled chips, a yoghurt maker, three different kinds of tin-opener, a plastic 'cork' for half-drunk bottles of wine, great extended families of Tupperware boxes, a wire cheese cutter, egg cups, egg timers, egg cosies, little metal cases for poaching eggs in, but not one single exploded-boiled-egg-scraper.

'Don't cry, don't cry, don't cry,' Sadie hissed through gritted teeth as she flung useless utensil after useless utensil to the floor in disgust. But a welter of painful thoughts was bombarding her now. Why had her mother found it so impossible to face up to reality? Why had she chosen to throw herself into a frenzy of housework rather than face up to her sham of a marriage? Why had she chosen to take the coward's way out and left Sadie on her own? What was the use of all these gadgets anyway? All they did was keep everything perfect on the surface. Scratch beneath the veneer and the stain of misery was there for all to see.

As Sadie backed into a corner of the kitchen she realised that the devastation she had wrought was a far truer representation of her family life than the portrait of the highly decorated Air Force officer and family staring blankly from the wall. Her parents' marriage had been a cold, loveless union based upon bullying and fear, and all it had produced were a disappointment of a daughter and a suicide case.

Sadie wiped the tears from her face and grabbed a scouring pad from the pot by the sink. She wasn't like her mother though; she was strong, she didn't cry, she didn't feel pain. Sadie set upon the egg with a fury. She had got this far without snapping – successfully blocking out her parents' arguments, the trauma of endless new schools, the overwhelming lone-liness – she wasn't about to break now when the promised land of adulthood was just an exam pass away. As she set about removing every last trace of egg from the kitchen she felt another suit of armour clink around her heart. *No pain, no pain, no pain,* she told herself proudly, rubbing furiously with the scouring pad until both it and her fingers were in tatters. Sadie was initially shocked when she saw the blood oozing from her raw skin. But then her mouth curled into a smile. It was all the proof she needed – she was genuinely immune to pain.

On the first day of the new term Sadie's father gave her a lift to Norwich station. 'You've been a credit to this family,' he said gruffly, as he hoisted her suitcase on to the train. 'Conducting yourself the way you have, since your mother's – accident. A lesser female would have cracked, but not you.' And with that he gave her a firm handshake and turned to leave. For years she had longed for such a show of approval, but not any more. Sadie watched, emotionless, as her father strode off down the platform, shrinking until he was a dot upon the horizon, just like all the other dots scurrying about the station concourse like an army of worker ants.

When she finally arrived at the halls of residence of her London university, she plonked herself down on the rock-hard bed, cast her eyes over the barren walls and smiled. And smiled. At last she was free. At last her life could begin. After a shopping spree for a loaf of Mighty White, a jar of Coffee Mate and a selection of suitably 'studenty' posters, she nervously joined her fellow freshers in the Union Bar. It was here, over a pint of watered-down cider from a plastic glass, that she first met GL.

'Perhaps you can help us?' he'd called to her as she'd picked her way across the sea of denim-clad legs sprawled across the floor of the bar. The moment Sadie saw him she automatically glanced over her shoulder, so certain was she that the twinkling eyes and boyish grin couldn't have been directed at her. She'd encountered plenty of boys like GL at school, all cheeky quips and chewing gum, but they'd never bothered to acknowledge her existence. So when GL reached over and tugged on her sleeve, her heart had leapt. 'Me and my mates are thinking of starting a 'Bring Helen Daniels Back to *Neighbours*' Campaign and I was wondering if we could enlist your support,' he enquired gesturing at her to take the vacant floor space beside him. By the end of the night Sadie had felt giddy with excitement – she couldn't have wished for her new life to get off to a better start, especially when GL asked her if she'd like to go paint-balling with him the following day. She felt shocked and flattered. And more than a little apprehensive. Scrambling about in the bushes playing war was the sort of activity her father would call fun. But Sadie gritted her teeth and entered into the spirit of things, and despite her being massacred by a round of red emulsion pellets after just ten minutes, GL wasn't put off. If anything, her feeble display seemed to make him like her even more. 'You should have seen her,' he regaled them all in the Union bar afterwards, 'She looked like she'd done twelve rounds with a bottle of ketchup! Never mind, I sorted them out for you, didn't I, babes? Killed five of the fuckers in one go!' (GL's cockney accent stood out like a sheet of Perspex amongst the cut-glass vowels of his fellow students. Sadie was astounded when she learnt that his hometown of Chipping Sodbury was about one hundred miles due north of the Bow Bells.) To her immense relief, the next time they went out it was to the cinema. Admittedly it was to see *Spiceworld – the Movie* but it was a proper date, complete with popcorn, back row seats and everything.

Over the ensuing weeks Sadie invested everything she had in GL. She scarcely attended her lectures and snubbed invitations to drinks with the other girls on her corridor. All she wanted to do was be with him. Not only did it help block out the more painful thoughts still stalking her subconscious, but she finally had the chance to experience teenage landmarks first hand rather than through a screen. In GL she had finally met her very own Danny Zuko. After they made love for the first time Sadie lay on her back spluttering smoke up to the ceiling (GL had also introduced her to the delights of nicotine) and waited for the tidal wave of transformation to wash over her. She was finally a woman; after years spent living vicariously she had broken into the real world at last. But nothing happened. Although externally she had acquired a boyfriend, a social calendar, a life, inside she remained as numb as before. As GL rolled out of bed to dispose of his condom and reapply his aftershave she lay there in the darkness wondering, *surely this can't be it?* It was like waiting years for your favourite actor's new movie only to discover that it's a complete turkey.

Within a month Sadie had joined the Film Society, rented a TV and video and was seeking her thrills second hand once more.

Chapter Six

'Now, I do hope I haven't caught you fiddling with your wood!'

Liam put his hand over the receiver and groaned. There was only one thing worse than a middle-aged woman on heat and that was a middle-aged woman on heat who required a fireplace. He pulled his safety goggles down so that they hung around his neck and wiped his forehead with the back of his hand.

'No, you're alright Mrs Braithwaite, I was just giving my skew chisel a bit of a rub.' There, that ought to get her going.

'Oooh, sounds saucy!' Mrs Braithwaite cackled down the line. 'Well you know where I am if you need any help in that department – God knows I've done enough rubbing in my time,' she lowered her voice to a conspiratorial whisper. 'I'm especially good at polishing knobs, you know.'

Liam looked around the workshop in despair. Unfinished fireplaces were propped against every available inch of wall space, his business partner, Jim, was attending a Masonic convention in Kingston upon Thames and Tony the apprentice was off sick with alcopop poisoning. He really did not have time for this.

'Is there anything I can help you with, Mrs Braithwaite, or was this just a social call?'

'No, no. I was just ringing to see how my surround was

coming along. Have you remembered to add the extra cherub?'

Liam grimaced – Mrs Braithwaite's increasingly ornate fireplace was giving him even more of a headache. 'Don't worry Mrs B, it's all under control.' He glanced over to the far corner of the shop where an oak frame positively heaving with carved cherubs and crucifixes was awaiting a varnish. It looked more like a gravestone than a fireplace. That was probably the worst part of his job; having to obey the every whim of people with far more money than taste. Sometimes he wanted to scream with frustration as he desecrated yet another prime piece of oak or mahogany or pine with inane scallops and ludicrous swirls.

'I'm sure it is, lover, I'm sure it is.' Mrs Braithwaite purred. 'I tell you what, I'm popping down to the Manor a bit later for some flea powder. I'll call by then and have a quick peek.'

'Great, you do that.'

Liam put down the receiver and sighed. He had just about had it with women. Why did they have to make life so damned complicated? He and Terry had come up with a theory one night (after a particularly good smoke) that the reason women were so difficult was due to the two female hormones – *protest*erone and *beast*rogen. Liam stared bleakly across the shop and out on to the street where an unforgiving wind was whipping cigarette butts, chip papers and other discarded debris into miniature cyclones. From the moment he had woken, he had been experiencing his traditional January wanderlust. Every year it was the same; when the remnants of Christmas were all bagged up and awaiting the binmen and British summer was still light years away, Liam would experience the overwhelming urge to sling some shorts and a *Rough Guide* into a rucksack and head back out to Asia for a couple of months. He had thought this year was going to be different, with Sadie working below his flat. For the first time in ages he felt he had a reason to stay in Ruislip for the winter, but not after last night. From the way she was cooing down the phone to her bloke, she was obviously loved up and besides which, Liam had hardly floored her with his devastating conversational skills. No, he was far better off getting away for a while. Soak up a few rays, smoke a few spliffs. What did he want a relationship for anyway? He knew they were bad news. If his mother's catalogue of disasters hadn't been enough, the experiences of his mates should have convinced him by now. Any twinges of envy Liam may have felt as he made yet another best man's speech were soon replaced by an almost smug satisfaction when he saw his married friends transformed one by one into hen-pecked, despondent has-beens – glancing anxiously at their watches at the approach of last orders and sacrificing the football for trips to Sainsburys!

You're better off out of it, mate, Liam told himself before returning to his lathe, and for a brief second he was almost convinced.

Sadie shivered and drew her coat around her as she approached Ruislip Manor station. The wind gushing through the concourse brought with it a flurry of used tickets. It was absolutely freezing and for a brief second she longed for her pirate's outfit; at least the trousers kept the cold out, unlike the thigh-skimming dress she was currently wearing. As she drew level with Flaming Fires she felt her pulse begin to quicken – should she look in, and if so how? Opting for a surreptitious glance rather than blatant gawp Sadie lowered her head and peered discreetly through the fringe of curls that had conveniently tumbled forward. Was he there? Looking past the display of fires and surrounds neatly arranged in the window she could just make out a figure in the back, bent over some kind of machine, arms flexed around either side. Not even the icy breeze could prevent Sadie's face from beginning to flare. Why had Liam left so hurriedly last night – without even choosing a video? Of course she had her suspicions – she had probably bored him to death. As soon as Terry had left the shop it had felt like that excruciating moment in a nightclub when they turn off the music and turn up the lights – suddenly your every flaw is laid bare and you realise that you aren't Jennifer Beals from *Flashdance* after all. But why did she find it so difficult to talk to Liam? He had been trying really hard to make conversation as well. He must think she was a complete loser.

As Sadie trudged on, her worries only seemed to magnify. Was her outfit okay? Did they allow Top Shop clothes in The Ivy? Would Brian, her part-timer, be all right on his own all day in the shop? What if he set fire to the bin again? What would she talk about with Lana? Would Lana even show up? So preoccupied was Sadie with her litany of fears that she didn't even think to give her fellow shopkeepers a passing wave as she made her way up the Parade. Not even Raj the chemist, who was busy constructing a window display of bluebell scented talc, got an acknowledgement. By the time she reached Pirate Videos, Sadie was in a state of inner turmoil. This was hardly eased when she pushed open the door and was greeted by an ear-splitting screech of electric guitar. Sadie looked up at the bank of television screens just in time to see the unmistakeable cartoon image of a woman's vagina opening up to devour a penis. Brian was watching *The Wall* yet again.

'Brian!' Sadie exclaimed, 'You know you're not allowed to play that Pink Floyd tape in the shop – only films classified PG or U.'

Brian looked up sullenly from behind a pair of reflector shades.

'Oh cut me some slack, man – it's not as if anyone else is gonna see it, this place is deader than a morgue.'

Sadie turned to the Kids Section.

'How about a Scooby Doo movie?' she offered weakly. After all, with his sandy hair and sallow skin, Brian shared more than a passing resemblance to Shaggy.

Brian groaned. 'Oh come on, Sadie, you know I have to watch the Floyd when I'm working on my lyrics – they're my muse, man.'

Brian spent most of his employment at Pirate Videos hunched over the counter, composing lyrics in a battered notepad. Sadie had only ever seen one of his efforts on a crumpled ball of paper she found tossed behind the bin. Entitled 'Hellcat' it was a particularly vicious diatribe dedicated to a girl who had obviously spurned his advances. The first letter of each line had been highlighted in red to read ROT IN HELL BITCH. Sadie gave a nervous cough.

'Oh okay, then. Vince isn't back from Sardinia until next week so I don't suppose it matters, but you can at least turn the volume down a bit.'

'Where are you off to, anyway?' Brian could not have appeard less interested as he leant over to adjust the volume the merest fraction of a decibel. Sadie wondered if his eyes were even open behind those ridiculous shades. She had given up asking where his eye-patch was long ago, and to say his pirate's outfit had been heavily customised was something of an understatement. Sadie was pretty certain no pirate had ever sailed the seven seas clad in a 'Dark Side of the Moon' T-shirt before.

'Oh, just out to lunch with a friend – it's my birthday.' She didn't even bother telling him where she was going – after GL's lukewarm response the night before there was no way Brian would be impressed.

'One of your customers is taking you to the Ivy?' GL had

snorted. 'You're having a laugh aren't you? You'd be lucky if you got one of that lot to take you down the Wimpy Bar.' He'd been equally dismissive of Lana's profession. 'An actress, eh? And she lives in Ruislip Manor? More like she's a member of the local amateur dramatics society. Well, she's certainly *played* you for a fool. Ha! I dunno, babes, sometimes you can be so gullible.'

Sadie looked at her watch – it was almost five past eleven. Lana wasn't coming. GL was right – as always. How could she have possibly believed that Lana would want to take her to the Ivy, that anyone would want to take her to the Ivy? She may as well join Brian behind the counter and compose a duet about humiliation and ridicule. The first letters of each line could spell out WHAT A PAIR OF TWATS.

'Many happy returns, Sweetie. I hope you haven't been waiting too long, I'm afraid I overslept. I've got a role in *The Bill* coming up and I was up half the night learning my lines.'

Sadie turned to see Lana in the doorway, resplendent in an aubergine trouser suit and with what looked worryingly like a dead fox draped around her shoulders. Her hair was set in deep auburn waves about her heavily made up face and large emerald cubes glinted in each of her earlobes. In one hand, a cigarette smouldered away on the end of an ebony holder and in the other she held a diamante-encrusted clutch bag.

'Bloody hell!' Sadie heard Brian mutter, in what was either dismay or disbelief, but for once wasn't disinterest.

'Hi,' Sadie said shyly. 'You look fantastic.'

'Why thank you, honey. And so do you, so do you. It's so nice to see both of your eyes.' Lana sashayed over to Sadie and kissed the air on either side of her face. Mwah, mwah. 'Now, I'm afraid my agent couldn't get us in at the Ivy – it was very short notice, after all.'

Sadie's heart sank – surely they couldn't be going to the

Wimpy after all? A vision of Lana tucking into a burger, her fox stole draped forlornly over a red Formica table, sprung into her mind and she suppressed the sudden urge to giggle.

'But never fear,' Lana continued. 'We have a table for two booked at Le Caprice instead.'

Le Caprice. God, Le Caprice was always in *Heat* magazine. Sadie was sure it was where Tara Palmer-Tomkinson had thrown a fishcake at a paparazzi photographer. And where Kate Moss had once been spotted drinking a white wine spritzer whilst heavily pregnant. A huge smile swept across her face.

'Oh, fantastic. Thank you so much.'

'Don't mention it, honey. Now we really ought to get a move on as our reservation is for twelve.'

'Sure.' Sadie turned to Brian. 'Okay, I'll see you later, Brian. Any problems give me a call on my mobile.'

'Will do,' Brian muttered, picking up his pen, and as Lana and Sadie hurried from the shop he turned to a clean page in his notebook and wrote in capitals across the top; VIXEN YOU NEED FIXIN'.

Chapter Seven

As Sadie followed Lana up the steps and out of Green Park station the pale sunlight coursing down upon her face felt strangely symbolic. With every step she climbed, it was as though she were emerging from a gloom she hadn't even been aware of until now. For so long her life had been a matter of routine and even worse, a routine designed to fit in with somebody else's routine. Every day yo-yoing between work and home with only the occasional drink or takeaway to spice it up. Every day spent going through the motions, trailing in GL's wake. But now GL was miles away, in Newport Pagnell of all places – and she, Sadie Jones, was in the heart of London, right beneath – Sadie turned and craned her neck to take in the huge granite building looming over her. God, she was right beneath The Ritz itself and about to have lunch with her new actress friend. An actress friend who had a role in *The Bill* no less. Sadie gulped. The butterflies in her stomach seemed to be fluttering in time with the chatter in the air, as streams of people ebbed and flowed past her into the mouth of the station.

'Do we have far to walk?' Sadie enquired. Although the heels on her new boots were barely an inch high, her body felt completely out of tilt. She was also concerned about the effect the wind might be having upon her hair. At least her pirate's bandana kept her corkscrew curls under some sort of control. Any more icy blasts and she would end up looking like Macy Gray. All the way up to London on the tube she had tortured herself with visions of being turned away at the door of Le Caprice for being too scruffy, or ordered round to the tradesmen's entrance after being mistaken for a kitchen hand.

'Hell, no! Do you think I'd be walking more than thirty yards in these?' Lana pulled up one flared trouser leg to reveal a pair of savagely-pointed boots with a seven-inch spike heel.

As they rounded the corner of the Ritz, Sadie wasn't the only one feeling nervous. Glancing anxiously at her watch, Lana prayed that the receptionist at Le Caprice had swallowed the bullshit she'd given her yesterday about being a top literary agent. She looked over at Sadie who had her eyes firmly fixed upon the ground. Well, with her unkempt hair and dearth of make up she certainly had the look of a Booker-listed novelist who'd been locked away in a garret for the past two years!

Lana led Sadie down a narrow slip road behind the Ritz.

'Oh,' Sadie uttered in surprise. She had assumed the restaurant would be on the main road. But upon reflection it made far more sense for it to be tucked away like this. Discreet. Unpretentious. A-list. Never had she felt more out of her depth. Why, oh why couldn't they have gone to the Wimpy bar? As they approached the end of the road she spotted a electric blue neon sign bearing the words *Le Caprice* above a large revolving door. Of all the possible types of door this had to be the worst. *Don't get stuck, don't get stuck*, Sadie chanted in her head like a mantra as she followed Lana inside. Seemingly unable to raise her gaze above waist-level she studied the row of legs in front of her, some facing each other, others facing a panelled wall and she realised that they had to be in some kind of bar area. Every now and then the shiny black pole of a bar stool sprouted up between the trouser clad legs, displaying the daintiest feet, in the most delicate footwear, nestling upon golden rests.

Sadie sighed and prayed that she'd remembered to remove the Dolcis price tag from the soles of her boots.

'Can I help you?' the owner of a pair of kitten-heeled sandals enquired, as they clicked their way over the polished floor towards them.

'Yes, honey. I have a reservation for twelve o'clock in the name of Loveday – Ms Lana Loveday.' Lana's syrupy drawl was suddenly thicker than ever.

'Oh yes, Ms Loveday. Would you like to order a drink from the bar? Your table will be ready in just a minute.'

'Why, sure.'

'Can I take your coat, madam?'

Sadie momentarily plucked up the courage to raise her gaze, to see what had to be the most glamorous cloakroom attendant in the entire world, the white of her teeth and blouse glistening like fresh snow against her honey-coloured skin. Sadie struggled out of her coat and passed it to the woman. Please, please don't let the label of my dress be on display, she prayed, wringing her hands.

'And you, Ms Loveday – can I take your – fox?'

'Why, thank you,' Lana purred, plonking the flattened fox on to the woman's outstretched arm before striding towards the bar. She was home free. 'What are you having, Sadie honey?' It had been a stroke of genius plumping for the literary angle – what better cover for a marathon piss-up.

'Could I have a mineral water, please?'

Lana spluttered as she attempted to light a cigarette. 'Say *what*?'

'A mineral water?' Sadie's face began to smart under Lana's glare. She didn't really like drinking during the day, especially if she had to go back to work. She wasn't the most hardened of drinkers at the best of times, let alone at midday when alcohol seemed to be at triple strength.

Lana couldn't believe it. A supposed writing sensation, the

next Zadie Smith, ordering a miserable mineral water. They would be rumbled for sure.

'Don't be so silly,' she muttered through gritted teeth, 'It's your birthday, for Christ's sake. We'll have a bottle of Moet and Chandon, please,' she hollered to the barman, before swivelling her hips on to one of the leather-covered stools.

Clambering up on to the stool beside her, Sadie experienced a mixture of shame and anger. Why was everything so effortless for people like GL and Lana? Where did they get the confidence to assume control of every situation, leaving people like her kowtowing to their every demand? But as soon as she raised her champagne flute to her lips and felt that first fizz on her tongue her anger dissipated. Perhaps Lana was right. After all, it was her birthday. Surely one little glass wouldn't do any harm?

By the time they were seated at their table they were halfway through their second glass and everything – including Sadie – was looking up.

'I can't believe I'm actually here,' Sadie whispered, her saucer-wide eyes taking in the black and white prints on the walls, the weaving army of waiters and most importantly the other diners. Was that a wigless Joan Collins over there by the rubber plant? 'Thank you so much for bringing me.'

'You're welcome, honey, you're welcome,' Lana said, her face beaming as she topped up their glasses. 'Now, have you decided what you'd like to eat yet?'

Sadie hurriedly picked up her menu. In all the excitement she had completely forgotten about the food. She felt a stab of dismay as the first 'delicacies' her eyes happened to fall upon were the chilled beetroot soup and herb-roasted lambs kidneys. But a frantic search uncovered a couple of traditional offerings amongst the sea of foie gras and scallops.

'I think I'll go for the Caesar salad to start, followed by the deep-fried haddock and chips please.'

Lana stared sternly over her menu like an irate school-mistress peering over the register. 'Gee honey, why didn't we just go to the chip shop instead?'

Sadie ducked back behind her menu. Oh God, why couldn't she find anything she liked? She wasn't that fussy an eater. There was nothing else for it – she would have to bluff.

'Oh hang on,' she chirped, 'I didn't see the sea bass. I love sea bass. I'll have that instead,' and she put the menu back down praying that the accompanying Jerusalem artichoke mash wasn't quite as unappetising as it sounded.

Lana stifled a grin. 'Actually I was just going to recommend the salmon fishcake – the sorrel sauce is really quite divine – *and* you can have it with fries, or allumettes as they call them here.'

Sadie smiled gratefully, the fries were bound to be out of this world at Le Caprice and the fishcake couldn't be all that bad – after all if it was good enough for Tara Palmer-Tomkinson . . .

The fishcake, when it arrived on its bed of dark green spinach, was absolutely fantastic. Sadie closed her eyes and sighed as the fluffy fish and potato mixture melted like candy floss upon her tongue. Lana had been right about the sauce too; she had never tasted anything quite like it before, but it complimented the salmon perfectly. And as for the allumettes – well. Wimpy, eat your heart out.

'This is delicious,' Sadie murmured, taking a swig from her glass. The lunch was turning into a feast for all her senses, not just her taste buds. The clink of cutlery and the tinkle of the grand piano combined to form a symphony for her ears; the polished marble tabletops and leather seat covers were like satin beneath her touch, the cocktail of expensive scent mingled with rich spices was intoxicating, and as for her fellow diners, never had she seen such beautiful people. They were as vibrant and varnished as a set of Russian dolls. Sadie watched as Lana topped up their glasses once again. With her angular jaw and cat-like eyes she really was quite stunning – it was a shame she had to wear so much make-up though. Mind you it was probably force of habit in her line of work.

'So tell me about your part in *The Bill*. Are you playing a goodie or a baddie? Ooh, excuse me – I seem to have got the hiccups.' Sadie brought her napkin up to her mouth and tried desperately not to giggle.

Lana smiled – finally the girl was beginning to relax. Another bottle of bubbly and she'd be well away.

'Oh a baddie, naturellement. You can't see me in a pair of Dr Martens swinging a truncheon can you?' Lana thought of some of her more submissive clients' requests and gave a wry smile. 'No, they want me to play the madam of a brothel in Sun Hill – far more my style.'

As Sadie giggled she couldn't help a hiccup escaping.

'Wow, that's so cool. You must be really excited.'

'Well, when you've been in this profession as long as I have, honey, one job becomes very much like the last. But yes, I suppose it beats waiting tables for a living.'

'Or working in a video shop.'

'Oh, I don't know – at least you get to watch fi—'

'Well, well, who have we here?'

Sadie looked up to see a small middle-aged man, immaculately dressed in black polo neck and slacks, gazing down upon her, his tanned face beaming. A waiter stood beside him, back rigid, notepad at the ready, like a footman awaiting instruction.

'So you must be Sadie Jones?' The man held out his hand in greeting. 'I am Chris – one of the managers at Caprice,' he explained, 'And I would just like to welcome you and check that everything is okay with your meal.'

Sadie glanced over at Lana, who suddenly seemed extremely preoccupied with the contents of her handbag.

'Thank you,' she stammered, shaking his hand. 'Yes, everything's wonderful – the illuminates are delicious.'

The manager looked down at her plate. 'The allumettes? Ah yes, they are a favourite of mine also.'

Sadie flushed. Oh God, why had she said illuminates? He must think she was a complete imbecile, but what was he doing talking to her anyway? Why wasn't he over congratulating Joan Collins on her bravery in facing the public sans hair? And how did he know her name? Oh no, Lana must have told him it was her birthday – no wonder she was looking so shifty. Sadie's heart sank as she remembered her twenty-first birthday the year before. GL had arranged for them to go out for a meal at the local Beefeater with a group of his friends from clay pigeon shooting. Everything had been going all right until her Knickerbocker Glory arrived laden with sparklers and she had been surrounded by surly-looking waitresses droning Happy Birthday. Surely they weren't going to pull a similar stunt here in Le Caprice? Although she had been revelling in watching all the other diners and speculating upon their identities she would die if the tables were turned and they all fixed their gaze upon her.

'And you must be Ms Loveday?' To Sadie's immense relief, the manager turned his attention to Lana. Lana looked up from her bag and smiled nervously.

'Yes, honey, pleased to meet you.'

'Well, give my regards to Marcus, won't you – he must be so proud of your new find.'

As he gestured towards Sadie she gave Lana a bewildered stare. What on earth was he going on about? At least the shock seemed to have cured her hiccups.

'Why yes, he is,' Lana purred, reaching for her glass. 'We all are,' and she smiled at Sadie the way a mother would at her newborn child.

'Okay, well, all the best with the book,' the manager said, returning his gaze to Sadie. 'Tell me, what is it about?'

Sadie gazed up at him blankly.

'What b—'

'Now, now,' Lana interrupted. 'I'm afraid we can't give anything away at this stage. I've just negotiated exclusive serialisation rights with the *Daily Mail*,' she added in hushed tones.

'Ah, I see,' the manager whispered back. 'Well listen, don't you dare leave without having dessert, ladies – I recommend the iced berries with white chocolate sauce,' and once again he took Sadie's hand and shook it vigorously. 'Good luck, my dear, good luck, I will be watching this year's Booker Prize with baited breath.'

As he turned on his heel and strode back towards the bar Sadie looked at Lana in confusion.

'What on earth was that all about?' she whispered. 'What did he mean, all the best with the book?'

Lana took two cigarettes from her case and passed one to Sadie.

'Er, well—' For once she seemed lost for words.

'And what was all that about serialisation rights and the *Daily Mail*? Serialisation rights to what?'

Lana lit both of their cigarettes and stared out of the window.

'Your book,' she muttered, her mouth sloping into a sheepish grin.

'But I don't understand,' Sadie replied. 'What book?'

'Shhh – keep your voice down,' Lana hissed and she leant across the table towards Sadie. 'It's like this. I haven't been totally honest with you, honey, and for that I truly apologise. But you seemed so down yesterday and I wanted you to enjoy yourself on your birthday. The trouble is I'm just too damned big-hearted.' Lana sighed theatrically, exhaling a plume of smoke. She glanced at Sadie hopefully only to see that her doe-eyes seemed even more bewildered than before. 'Have you any idea how difficult it is to get a table in a place like this?' she whispered.

Sadie shook her head. 'But I thought you said your agent was sorting it out for you?'

Lana laughed and took a swig from her glass. 'There is no agent, honey. I had to pretend to be *your* agent.'

'My agent? But I'm not the actress, *you* are.'

'No, neither of us are *the actress* – but you, my dear, are the writer.' Lana leant back in her chair and grinned.

Sadie frowned as she tried to put all the pieces of the puzzle together. It didn't help that the champagne seemed to be having the same effect as treacle upon her brain, completely clogging up her powers of deduction. 'So you booked a table pretending to be my agent and you said that I was a writer,' she said slowly.

'That's right honey, but not just any old writer.'

Sadie looked up, 'Oh my God. Who do they think I am?'

'Well, I had to make sure it would work, so I told them you were the next big thing – that Zadie Smith and JK Rowling were going to be quaking in their boots. Oh, and I think I may have mentioned the Booker Prize somewhere along the line.'

'The Booker Prize?' Sadie shrieked, before hurriedly lowering her voice. 'Oh my God.'

Lana hardly dared look up – she just knew the girl would be in floods of tears – and how the hell was she going to explain that one? Writer's block – that was it. Trouble with the second novel, she would whisper knowingly to the manager as she chased out after her. But when she finally summoned the courage to glance across the table Sadie was not leaping to her feet, tears streaming down her face – far from it She was reaching for the bottle of bubbly and topping up their glasses, grinning from ear to ear.

'I don't believe it – this is brilliant. They actually think I'm some kind of budding author.'

Lana smiled. 'A literary sensation no less.'

Sadie chuckled. 'I can't believe you had the nerve. So have you ever been here before at all?'

'Once or twice, a long time ago – in my previous job.'

'Oh – so you *used* to be an actress?'

Lana smirked. 'No, honey, I used to be a call girl. Waiter, could we get some dessert?'

Chapter Eight

'Now – let me get one thing straight,' Lana declared, as their desserts were set down before them on sugar-dusted plates. 'I was never from the Divine Brown school of prostitution – I can't think of anything tackier than displaying your wares on a street corner like a honey-glazed ham in a butcher's window – but you can probably tell that just from looking at me.'

Sadie glanced across the table and watched as Lana inserted a spoonful of berries into her mouth, expertly removing the molten white chocolate from her lips with a deft flick of her tongue. In the ten minutes since Lana's shock revelation she hadn't known what to think. She'd never met a real life prostitute before, let alone been taken out to lunch by one – Terry would be having kittens if he'd known. Sadie supposed she should have been feeling outraged at being lied to (and about) and appalled at her lunch date's professional background, but bizarrely all she really felt was excitement. She had the sudden realisation that in Lana's company almost anything was possible and rather than feeling alarmed at the prospect, she felt exhilarated.

'So, what kind of, you know, were you?' Sadie asked.

'Oh my sweet Lord, try this dessert, it's absolutely luscious.' Lana said, gesturing at Sadie's untouched plate.

Sadie looked down at the crimson berries protruding like drops of blood against the swirls of white chocolate sauce. As she closed her lips around the first spoonful it was as if a sparkler had ignited in her mouth. Tart explosions of juice erupted on her tongue, only to be soothed away by the creamiest chocolate. 'I was an escort,' Lana confided. 'But I'm talking top-drawer, twenty four carat escort. I only ever had a handful of regular clients – Saudi princes, ageing business tycoons, that kind of thing – absolutely no Tory MPs,' she added firmly.

'But why? I mean how?' Sadie stammered. 'How did you get into it in the first place?'

Lana sighed. 'Well that's a long story, honey. Let's just say that contrary to popular belief, the streets here in London are not exactly paved with gold and when I arrived here back in the eighties I was in urgent need of some reserves.'

'Yes, but surely there were other jobs. What made you choose that one?'

Lana looked up sharply – the last thing she needed was a lecture from Little Miss Panty Starch – but Sadie's wide-eyed gaze seemed far more one of fascination than disapproval. Lana leant back in her chair and sighed. 'Well, when I first arrived I did manage to get some modelling work, but the trouble was you never knew how long you'd have to wait between jobs and I got sick of hauling my ass around endless castings only to be told by some middle-aged, pot-bellied lech that I could do with losing a few pounds. I was brought up in the Deep South,' she explained. 'My parents' generation spent half their lives living off squirrel pie and grits, there is no way on God's earth you are going to make me stick my fist down my throat to puke up perfectly decent food.'

Sadie nodded in agreement as she savoured another mouthful of her dessert. God, she pitied the poor supermodels who had to dine in places like this regularly. It seemed an absolute travesty to indulge in such delights only to hurl them back up again minutes later in the marble-topped toilets downstairs.

'So anyway, one day at a Pretty Polly shoot, one of the

other girls told me about the escort work she'd been doing
on the side and when I heard the kind of money she was
being paid – it was like the answer to all of my prayers.'

'But didn't you feel awkward at first? Wasn't it embarrassing?'

Lana smirked as she remembered her first ever client. *Take
off your dress*, the doddery old fool had ordered the minute
she'd walked in the door. She had soon set him straight.
That's really no way to talk to a lady, she'd barked back,
marching over to the mini-bar to pour herself a stiff scotch.
*Now why don't you be a good boy and take off your pants
– let me see what I've got left to work with*. To her surprise
he'd absolutely loved her show of bravado – she'd nearly
spilt her scotch all over the shag pile when she turned to
see his beaming dentures and shrivelled little penis on full
display. Lana looked at Sadie staring at her expectantly and
she altered her smirk to a bashful smile.

'Oh, honey – it was excruciating, but when your back's
against the wall, when you have nowhere else to turn, when
the chips are down, it's staggering the hurdles one manages
to overcome. It's all about the triumph of human spirit in
the face of adversity, I guess.'

Sadie nodded sympathetically. 'I know exactly what you
mean,' she said, 'Sometimes in life you just have to go
on to automatic pilot and do whatever it takes to get you
through.'

Lana stared at her in surprise. Sadie's voice had taken on
a harder edge and her doe-eyes were focused on something
in the middle distance – some skeleton from her own past
perhaps, or perhaps she was simply referring to how she
got through the ordeal of working in a video store dressed
as a pirate.

'So you don't do it any more then?' Sadie asked, returning
her gaze to Lana.

Lana shook her head and scraped her spoon around her plate, determined not to squander a single drop of chocolate sauce. 'No – I gave it all up a couple of years ago. I'd made my money, bought my house – unlike a lot of the other girls I didn't have a drug habit to finance,' Lana poured the last of the champagne into her glass. 'So now I just do a bit of freelance work from home to keep me in life's little luxuries.'

'What, you mean you have clients coming to your house?' Sadie asked.

'Oh, good lord, no,' Lana shuddered at the thought as she passed Sadie a cigarette. 'They phone me instead.'

'I don't understand.'

'I have a sex line,' Lana explained. 'They call me, I talk dirty for a bit, they come, I get two bucks a minute.' God, what was up with her today? Why was she giving the girl so much information? It was as if the champagne had oiled her jaw and now she couldn't stop it from yakking. How was she going to be able to go back into the video store after this? She'd probably be barred – and then she'd have to join *Blockbusters* and that was a bus journey away *and* they didn't let you smoke in the shop – dictatorial assholes. But once again Sadie surprised her – for instead of looking horrified, she looked downright excited.

'So what kind of things do they say to you? What do they ask you to do?' Sadie asked, leaning across the table in anticipation.

Lana grinned. She was starting to feel quite pleasantly pissed.

'Oh, honey – you would not believe how dull they are.'

Sadie looked deflated.

'Really?'

'Yes. Most of them simply have no imagination. I tell you, if I hear the words *tell me what you're wearing* one more time!'

Sadie giggled.

'So, what sort of things do you say to them, then? Do you have a set script?'

'Honey, I have a cupboard full of *set scripts* – I wasn't totally lying when I told you I was a member of the acting community. I must have a script for every possible perversion going. Submission, domination, flagellation, flatulation – you name it, I can talk it.'

'Flatulation?' Sadie asked, puzzled.

'Why, yes. Haven't you heard of that one? I call my script for it The Wind in the Weirdos.'

'What, you mean they get turned on by – farting?'

Lana nodded. 'And belching. I have one regular who phones me up just to hear me belch.'

Sadie shook her head in disbelief. 'And that makes him orgasm?'

'You'd better believe it. Still, I must say, I have perfected the most sensual burp going.'

Sadie giggled. 'How can a burp be sensual?'

'Okay, you asked for it.' Lana raised her glass to her lips and downed the contents in one. She then closed her eyes and began to moan, gently rocking backwards and forwards on her chair. 'Oh yes,' she sighed, 'Here it comes. Oh baby. Oh my God. It's going to be a huge one. Oh my, oh my . . .' Tilting her head back and opening her immaculately painted lips Lana proceeded to emit the longest, lustiest belch Sadie had ever heard.

Lana opened her eyes to realise that a deathly hush had fallen over Le Caprice – even the gossip columnists at the bar had stopped talking. Everyone was staring at her in horror. Everyone, that is, apart from Sadie who was doubled up in mirth and banging the table with the palm of her hand.

'That – is – so – gross,' she gasped between guffaws.

'That's nothing – you want to hear one of my farts. Fanny

the Fart Fantastic, I call myself.' Lana paused to hear the collective intake of breath from her outraged fellow diners. 'What's up?' she roared. 'You guys want to hear me fart or what?'

Sadie clapped her hand to her mouth and looked around in shock – all eyes were fixed upon them and she could see the manager making his way towards their table, doling out apologies as he went. It was just like the faked orgasm scene in *When Harry Met Sally* – in an extremely warped kind of way. As the manager drew level with them there was really only one thing she could say.

'Er, I'll have whatever she's having,' she stammered, before collapsing on to the table in fits of laughter.

Chapter Nine

Life's a bitch and then you marry one!

Or get one rubbing herself against you while she's pretending to examine her new fireplace, Liam mused, as he read the graffiti plastering the wall of the stairwell. He grimaced at the recollection of Mrs Braithwaite creeping up behind him while he was applying the final coat of varnish to her vile surround. 'Who's a clever boy then,' she'd whispered and the sound of her sixty-a-day rasp right in his ear had caused him to drop his brush in fright.

'Jesus!' he'd exclaimed, before retrieving his brush from the floor. 'You shouldn't do things like that – you could have given me a heart attack.'

'Oooh, I'm sure it would take more than little old me to frighten a big strong man like you,' she'd countered, licking her fuchsia lips with a resounding slurp. As he'd backed away from her, wielding his brush in a pathetic attempt at self-defence, he'd sent the tin of varnish flying, covering the floor in a syrupy pool. It had taken the best part of two hours to get the place straight again – forty-five minutes of which had been spent trying to convince Mrs Braithwaite that, no, the varnish had not made him all 'sticky' and no, he did not need her help to 'strip it off'.

Reaching the top of the stairs, Liam turned on to the balcony overlooking the Parade. He had never felt so relieved to get home. All he wanted to do was put some Stones on the stereo, take an ice-cold beer from the fridge and have a long soak in the bath. He marched past the row of tatty front doors and ill-fitting windows until he reached his own flat, a welcome beacon at the end of the row with its double-glazing and freshly painted walls. Two garden gnomes clad in England kits stood guard on either side of the solid oak door – another benefit of being built like Lennox Lewis was that he seemed immune to the local sneak thieves. As soon as he opened the door, Liam's heart sank. A cacophony of brass instruments rushed out to assault his eardrums – Terry had that bloody Jazz FM on again and from the sounds of it they were having some kind of new-wave, alternative night. Not only that, but the flat was filled with the most revolting smell. Liam couldn't quite put his finger on what it was, but it was exactly how he imagined the smell of rotting corpses when he watched news correspondents reporting from war-torn countries comment on the stench of death. But this wasn't a war-torn country – this was his flat, his home. Liam didn't hold any truck with all that Englishman's home being his castle bollocks – he'd rather watch *An Evening With Anthea Turner* than hang a flock of china ducks on his wall, but still. This was too much. After the day he'd had this was really taking the piss.

'Tel!' he called out, but there was no reply. Probably couldn't hear him over the din. Liam glanced through the door on his right, but the living room was empty. Actually, that wasn't strictly true. The living room was quite full. Full of crap. Liam cast his eyes around it in despair. Copies of the *Racing Post* littered the coffee table, spilling down on to the rug below, completely obscuring the intricate carvings he had spent months toiling on. That table had been one of his finest pieces of work; now it wouldn't have looked out of place in a bookies. Liam strode through the swathes of paper to the hi-fi system in the corner and turned off the radio. The sudden silence was almost as deafening as the jazz. All around his feet lay discarded CD covers and inserts, emanating out from the stereo like ripples on a pond, reaching as far as the monster settee under the window and even on top of the huge flat screen TV on the opposite side of the room.

'For fuck's sake,' Liam muttered, picking up an abandoned remote control in a vain attempt to bring some sort of order to the chaos. The remote felt unusually light in his hand and he turned it over to see that the back cover had been removed and the batteries pillaged, leaving just an empty shell. Liam looked around in despair. The only part of the room that was free from clutter were the walls, painted a burnished orange and adorned by a huge black and white print of Jim Morrison. And – Liam rubbed his eyes in disbelief as he noticed a new addition by the door – a calendar of Page Three Stunnas.

'Terry!'

As Liam marched down the passageway to the far end of the flat the gut-wrenching smell became stronger and stronger, obviously emanating from the kitchen. Liam took a deep breath and flung open the door. Once again there was no sign of Terry, but his recent presence was very much in evidence. A cigarette was smouldering away in an ashtray on the counter, leaving behind a perfectly formed finger of ash and on the stove a pan was bubbling, showering the surrounding counter with brown specks.

'Bloody hell,' Liam sighed as he turned off the hob and extinguished the butt. What was he thinking of having such a liability for a lodger? How much longer would it be before he returned home from work to find the place razed to the ground, with Terry sitting grinning sheepishly on the mound of ashes that was once his flat? That was the trouble with Terry – he could be the most infuriating little shit going, but then he would give you one of his grins or make one of his ridiculous jokes and before you knew it everything was back to normal. Well, not this time. This time he had gone too far. Liam was not going to stand for him sodding off out somewhere and leaving the stereo blasting, a fag burning and – Liam glanced apprehensively into the saucepan – what looked and smelt like a pot of diarrhoea simmering on the stove.

Liam placed a lid on the saucepan and flung open the kitchen window. He needed a beer more than ever before, but when he opened the fridge it was completely bare (apart from the tub of Flora and half-eaten chicken chow mein from last Saturday). This really was the last straw. Liam sat down at the kitchen table, held his head in his hands and moaned. When he'd arrived at the Manor Arms that Friday night all those years ago and seen the name of the live entertainer plastered on the blackboard outside, he should have known that it spelt trouble. *Wayne Kerr – singer / comedian – he'll shock you, he'll rock you,* proclaimed the brightly coloured chalk. And like a fool Liam had sauntered in and taken his usual place at the bar, completely oblivious to the curse that was about to blight his life for the next two years.

When Terry had raced up on to the podium at the rear of the pub and bellowed out, *Greetings pop-pickers!* to a scream of feedback from his mike, Liam had actually laughed. 'Looks like we've got a right one here,' he'd chortled to his mates, staring in disbelief at Terry's gold satin Superman outfit, with its unfortunate hole in the crotch. And Liam didn't stop laughing for the next hour as Terry alternated between telling dire jokes about muff-diving and absolutely massacring all-time rock classics such as 'Layla' and 'Bohemian Rhapsody'.

Until the riot kicked off, he had found Terry absolutely hilarious – it was by far the worst Friday night's entertainment he had ever seen down at the Manor, and that took some doing. But then it all went sour. It was calling the landlord's girlfriend a frigid dyke that did it. Admittedly she was a bit on the severe side, but you could hardly blame the poor girl for not wanting to put her hand down Terry's pants to retrieve

his 'banana'. And when he accused her of looking like Ann
Widdecombe with a charisma by-pass, all hell broke loose. In
one leap, the landlord was over the bar and launching himself
upon Terry, shouting, 'That's my bird you're dissing, mate.'
To which Terry had expressed his sincerest apologies and
commented on how admirable it was for the Manor Arms
to have employed a blind member of staff and didn't it make
your heart glow, this care in the community lark. As Terry
disappeared beneath a flurry of punches Liam had put down
his pint with a sigh and waded over to the rescue. However,
his attempts at keeping the peace ended with him being rather
unceremoniously barred, along with 'Wayne Kerr' who was
told that he would never work in the pub entertainment
industry again. United by their sense of injustice, the two
men had trudged off to the chippy, Terry still clad in his gold
Superman suit, which caused a few raised eyebrows behind
the counter. Completely unwittingly Liam had invited him
back to his flat for a couple of cans. If only he had known
then that a couple of cans would end up becoming a couple
of years.

For the next few hours Terry had regaled Liam with his
life story – his childhood on the fairgrounds, his lengthy
career as a petty crook, culminating in a five year stretch
at Her Majesty's pleasure and his subsequent determination
to go straight. He ended up crashing the night and he never
left. Liam need a lodger and Terry needed a new abode –
since leaving the nick he'd been kipping on the back seat
of his friend Del's motor which wasn't exactly ideal – after
all, it was only a Mini Clubman. Liam had felt sorry for the
bloke – he was obviously a lonely old sod, with no family
to speak of and very few mates – and more than that,
he genuinely liked him. Life was certainly never dull with
Terry around. Over the past two years he had watched with
amusement as Terry had struggled to stay on the straight and

narrow, pursuing a string of wildly unrealistic and hopelessly unsuitable careers.

Liam smiled to himself as he remembered the day Terry had decided to become an Avon lady, getting Sadie to apply on his behalf. At the thought of Sadie, Liam leapt to his feet and looked at his watch. It was almost half past seven and he still hadn't had a bath or wrapped her present. Or bought any wrapping paper to wrap her present with. Just at that moment he heard the front door slam and the sound of footsteps stomping down the hall.

'All right, son,' Terry greeted him with a cheery grin. 'Just been down the offy to get some beers in for tonight – you were right out of them. And don't you worry about grub – I've got one of me concoctions on the go. Oh,' Terry paused as he noticed the saucepan on the counter, 'Cheers mate. Ready, was it? Well, don't be shy. Tuck in. I bet you're Hank Marvin, aren't ya?'

Liam grimaced. He was indeed starving but there was no way on this earth he was going to eat one of Terry's 'concoctions'.

'Actually, Tel, I'm all right as it goes. I think I'll just grab one of those beers and dive in the bath before we head downstairs.' And with a sigh of defeat Liam made his way to the door.

'Right you are, mate. There should be enough hot water left – I don't think I used it all.'

Chapter Ten

'So I says to this bird, what do you mean Sly Stallone is an over-rated hasbeen? Rocky Balboa would piss all over Mike Tyson. Are you still there, babes? You've gone a bit quiet.'

Sadie brought the phone back to her ear and stifled a yawn. Like a fickle friend, the champagne of earlier had begun to turn against her, leaving her hot, dehydrated and with the beginnings of a thumping headache. GL's rambling phone call was not exactly helping matters.

'Sorry – I'm not feeling too good that's all. I'll be glad when it's closing time and I can go home.'

'Blimey, you're not still moping because I had to go away for your birthday, are you? Look, I told you I'll make it up to you tomorrow. I tell you what, as soon as I get back I'll take you up the St Georges Centre and get you something nice – a new frock or something.'

'But I thought you already had my present,' Sadie responded, her heart beginning to sink.

'Well, yeah. That was it. I was going to take you shopping, but now you've ruined the surprise.' GL's cockney whine was as shrill as a parrot's squawk in Sadie's ear.

'Oh. I see.'

All last night she had lain in bed, like an over-excited kid on Christmas Eve, wondering what GL's surprise gift might have been, and hoping fervently that it was the newly released *Grease* DVD. She wanted to kick herself for being so stupid.

'Don't worry, a shopping trip will be great,' she lied. 'I haven't been to Harrow for ages. Anyway – I'd better go now, I've got a customer.'

Sadie put down the phone and stared forlornly around the empty shop. When she'd taken over from Brian at five o'clock she had felt euphoric – she'd even turned a blind eye to the huge bong she had found on the kitchen draining board and the distinctive aroma of cannabis lingering by the back door. 'Don't forget your drugs, man,' she had called after Brian with a giggle, causing him to peer over his sunglasses at her in shock.

From the moment she and Lana had been ejected from the restaurant to the moment they rolled off the tube at Ruislip Manor, they hadn't stopped laughing. 'The public expulsion of bodily gases *really* isn't part of the etiquette here at Le Caprice,' Lana had said as their train pulled out of Green Park, mimicking the manager perfectly and sending Sadie careering into a bemused commuter as she clutched her side in mirth. To dine at Le Caprice was hip, but to get thrown out – that was positively rock and roll. But nearly three hours on her own in a deserted shop had ensured the early onset of a hangover and Sadie was feeling an all too familiar gloom start to descend. Terry and Liam hadn't even bothered to show up. Yet again her philosophy on life had been proven – the minute you open yourself up to happiness and hope, in behind them slip pain and disappointment, like a pair of gatecrashers intent upon wrecking the party. When would she ever learn? Just as Sadie turned to search the back shelves for *Misery*, she heard the shop door burst open and a horribly out of tune chorus.

'Happy birthday to you, happy birthday to you, happy birthday, dear Treacle, happy birthday to you!'

Sadie turned to see Terry standing in the middle of the shop holding a Battenburg cake with a solitary candle flickering away on top. Standing behind him, grinning awkwardly, was Liam, laden with *Thresher* bags.

'Happy birthday,' Liam grunted, seemingly to the ashtray beside the New Releases.

'Thanks,' Sadie replied, unable to prevent her mouth morphing into an inane grin. 'I didn't think you were coming.'

'Yeah, sorry about that,' Terry said as he made his way over to the counter, 'It was young Liam here. He was tarting himself up in that bathroom for bleeding hours.'

'I was waiting for the water to heat up,' Liam retorted through gritted teeth.

Sadie glanced over at Liam. For once his hair wasn't tied back in a ponytail and it hung, still damp, in curls around his chiselled jaw. Combined with his brightly checked lumberjack shirt and faded jeans he looked as if he'd just walked off the set of an INXS video. For some bizarre reason Sadie's hands began to tremble.

'Here you go then, my darling – don't forget to make a wish,' Terry said as he plonked the birthday Battenburg on the counter before her. 'Bleedin' 'ell – what's all this? Don't tell me you're getting into the Floyd in your old age.' Terry gestured at the bank of screens where a dishevelled Bob Geldof appeared to be having some kind of nervous breakdown.

Sadie blew out her candle and smiled.

'No, Brian had it on when I got here – I just couldn't be bothered to change it,' she explained.

'Oh – Brian,' Terry replied knowingly. 'Right fruit and nutcase, ain't he? Indulged in a bit too much of the old puff the magic dragon if you ask me.'

'Do you want a beer?' Liam enquired, taking a bottle from the bag and promptly dropping it on to the counter with a clatter. For once Sadie wasn't in that awful pirate's costume. She was actually wearing a dress, and a short dress at that.

Liam averted his gaze and quickly picked up the bottle. 'Sorry,' he muttered, 'it slipped out of my hands.'

'As the actress said to the bishop,' Terry chortled.

'I'd love one,' Sadie replied, much to Liam's surprise. He hadn't really had her down as a beer drinker; this was a definite bonus.

'So have you had a good day then?' Terry asked, before cracking open three bottles of beer with his teeth.

Sadie smiled. 'Let's just say it was interesting. Anyone for a slice of Battenburg?'

Two slices of cake and a bottle of beer later and Sadie's birthday cheer had come flooding back. Terry had even persuaded her to put on The Shadows' Greatest Hits and was busy imitating their uniquely naff dance routine (complete with air guitar) in the middle of the shop.

'Here – I got you this.' Liam muttered, passing Sadie a small package, wrapped in what looked suspiciously like newspaper. 'I kept the receipt, so I can take it back if you've already got it. Happy birthday.'

Sadie took the parcel nervously. With the amount of alcohol she had consumed there was no way she could possibly prevent herself from blushing. 'Thanks,' she stammered. 'I like the paper.'

Liam grinned. 'Yeah, apparently the newsprint look is all the rage in the gift-wrap industry at the moment. It's amazing how they've managed to make it look so much like a copy of the *Racing Post*. The print even comes off on your fingers and everything.'

Sadie laughed as she struggled with the reams of Sellotape binding the package. 'God, I think I'm going to need a hacksaw to get through this lot.' In desperation she picked up the knife she'd been using to cut the Battenburg, but this only served to make the parcel stickier.

'Here, let me,' Liam offered, producing a Swiss army knife

from his pocket and flicking it open. 'If this doesn't work, I'll nip upstairs for my blow-torch.' Thankfully he managed to slice his way through the tape and handed the now even tattier looking present back to Sadie. 'Sorry about that,' he said with a sheepish grin. 'Gift wrapping never was my strongest point.'

'Don't worry,' Sadie reassured him. 'It's the thought that counts.' When she opened the package to see a limited edition DVD of *Grease* nestling amongst the shredded newspaper she was completely dumbstruck. 'How did you know? I – I don't know what to say,' she whispered, her eyes scanning the back cover – it even contained previously unseen footage of the Greased Lightning scene! 'Thank you. Thank you so much.' And before she could stop herself she'd leapt to her feet, standing on the bar of her chair for additional height, and kissed Liam lightly on the cheek.

Liam coughed and looked down at the floor. 'Oh, that's all right. You always seem to be playing the video so I thought it was a pretty safe bet. I thought someone else might have got it for you though.'

Sadie shook her head. 'No – I was hoping that they would, but they didn't. This is fantastic. Thank you so much.'

He shoots – he scores! Liam felt like charging down the shop punching the air. That cocky little shit of a boyfriend might strut about the place as if he knew everything, but he didn't know what his girlfriend really wanted for her birthday. He wasn't even *here* for her birthday, but Liam was *and* he'd managed to get a birthday kiss.

'Do you want another beer?' he asked, making direct eye contact with Sadie for the very first time.

'Did I hear somebody say beer?'

Sadie looked up to see Lana propped in the doorway, her previously pristine hair looking as if it had been charged with static and her cosmetic mask sliding down her face. She looked like a walking, talking, morning after the night before. Or in this case, night after the morning before.

Terry stood transfixed in front of the bank of screens, fag dangling from mouth, air guitar still held aloft, as Lana stumbled past him, her bedraggled fox stole trailing along the floor behind her like some tragic victim of the Beaufort Hunt.

'Well hello, young man,' she purred to Liam, her drawl as thick as porridge. 'I don't suppose there's a beer in that bag with my name on it?'

'Well now, that all depends on what your name is,' Terry said, recovering his faculties with remarkable speed and bounding over to the counter.

Lana peered down her nose at him as though she were surveying an open sewer. Then, glancing longingly at the bag of beers, she extended a somewhat unsteady hand. 'Lana Loveday,' she announced, 'Delighted to make your acquaintance.'

'Lana Loveday, eh?' Terry replied, taking her hand and shaking it vigorously, 'I'm Terry – Terry Legget. Me mates call me Tel.'

'Well, Terry, how about it? How about we all have a birthday toast?' and she gazed up at Liam imploringly.

Sadie couldn't help smiling when she saw the expression on Liam's face. He looked absolutely terrified.

'Er –, Liam, Terry, this is my friend Lana, the one I went to lunch with today.'

'Oh – the actress,' Terry exclaimed, opening a bottle and passing it to Lana. 'Do you know what, I think I might have seen a couple of your movies, Miss *Loveday*.'

'Somehow I very much doubt it,' Lana retorted, taking a hasty swig. 'What the hell is this trash?' she asked, gesturing towards the screens where The Shadows were still busy strutting their drainpipe-clad legs and strumming their guitars. 'I don't know – I thought *Grease* was bad enough, but this—'

Sadie smiled apologetically at Liam and Terry. It was blatantly obvious that Lana was drunk; hopefully they wouldn't take her remarks too personally.

'Now, just you hold on a sec,' Terry snapped. 'I'll have you know Hank Marvin is an all-time guitar great. The only geezer who comes close to him is Rick Parfitt from Status Quo – that riff in 'Margarita Time' was pure genius.'

Sadie and Liam exchanged bemused glances before dissolving into laughter.

'Yeah, that's right, mate,' Liam retorted. 'Eric Clapton eat your heart out.'

'Are you telling me that the Quo aren't legends?' Terry demanded.

'Legends in their own living room, sweetie,' Lana sneered. 'And obviously your bedroom, but I really don't think you can compare them with the like of Clapton. Cigarette, anyone?'

Brushing her pearl embossed cigarette case aside, Terry marched towards the door. 'I'll show you,' he shouted over his shoulder. 'If my Quo video hasn't got this party rocking in five minutes I'll eat my – my flak jacket.'

To Sadie's shock (at least when she had sobered up some fifteen hours later) Terry was absolutely right. Within five minutes of Status Quo being on, the four of them were careering around the shop, thumbs in imaginary belt hooks, flinging their shoulders this way and that.

'Oh my God!' Sadie eventually gasped, stumbling sideways into Liam as 'Caroline' came crashing to an end. 'I need another drink.'

Liam looked down at her flushed face and grinned. He'd never seen Sadie so animated, or so inebriated come to that, and it was rekindling all of his previous feelings – and then some. She finally seemed relaxed in his company, especially when 'Down Down' had come on and they'd ended up having a limbo-dancing contest through the aisle in the New

Releases. Liam followed Sadie to the counter and handed her a beer.

'Shall we stop for a fag break?' Terry asked Lana as 'In the Army' began resonating around the shop.

Lana smirked. 'If you asked that question where I come from, you'd probably be strung up from the nearest tree. Okay – lead the way, kind sir.'

Terry led Lana to the counter, the fox wrap draped around his neck providing an interesting contrast with his camouflage jacket. 'This is a blinding song,' he sighed. 'All about the folly of war, it is – the lyrics are well deep.'

'Not nearly as deep as 'Down, down, deeper and down',' Liam commented, causing Sadie to erupt into peals of laughter.

Never in her wildest dreams had she imagined her birthday ending up like this. She couldn't remember the last time she had had so much fun. Sadie cleared her throat and prepared to speak.

'I would jusht like to shay,' she slurred. What the hell had happened to her mouth? It felt as if her tongue had doubled in size and was flopping out over her lips like a dead halibut. Taking a deep breath, she tried again. 'I would just like to say, thank you all for making this one of the best birthdays ever.' She turned to Liam and smiled, 'Thank you so much for the DVD and Terry thank you for the cake and the beer—'

'And the Quo,' Terry interrupted.

'Of course, how could I forget the Quo,' Sadie laughed as she turned to Lana. 'And Lana, thank you for such an interesting lunch. I won't forget that burp for as long as I live.'

Terry and Liam stared at her, puzzled.

'What burp?' Liam asked.

Sadie and Lana exchanged knowing smirks.

'Lana has a unique gift,' Sadie explained. 'She can bring grown men to orgasm with one of her belches, can't you Lana?'

Lana nodded modestly. 'One of my many hidden talents,' she replied, attempting to nudge Liam and ricocheting into the counter.

'Sounds right up your street, Tel,' Liam joked, swiftly side-stepping Lana's stumble.

'Go on then,' Terry encouraged. 'Give us a belch.'

Lana looked at Sadie and Sadie nodded, passing her a bottle of beer.

'Okay, here goes,' she declared, before downing half the bottle and inhaling deeply. Then, clutching the counter for support, Lana began swaying backwards and forwards, moaning and sighing, 'Ooooh yes, oh baby, here it comes, yes, yes, yes . . .' before emitting a roaring belch that must have lasted at least ten seconds.

'Bloody hell!' Terry exclaimed, his eyes beaming with admiration. 'That was a belter. Respect is due,' and he shook Lana's hand vigorously.

'That was nothing,' Sadie cried. 'She did one at least twice as long as that right in the middle of Le Caprice – it's a really swanky restaurant, full of celebs,' she explained to Terry. 'Joan Collins was there and everything. The whole restaurant went silent – it was just like that scene in *When Harry Met Sally* where Meg Ryan fakes an orgasm.'

'That's a brilliant scene,' Liam said, nodding enthusiastically.

'Absolutely blinding, 'Terry agreed. 'There's no way that Ryan bird was faking it though. She must have had a dildo under the table or something.'

'I like the bit where one of the other diners turns to the waiter and says *I'll have whatever she's having*,' Liam continued.

'Yeah me too.' Sadie agreed. 'That's exactly what I said to the manager when he came over to throw us out.'

'You got thrown out?' Liam asked incredulously. With her demure appearance and diminutive stature he couldn't imagine Sadie being thrown out of anywhere, least of all some swanky five star restaurant.

'Yeah, it was brilliant. I thought I was going to wet myself I was laughing so much, especially when Lana told Joan Collins that if she really wanted to be sexy at seventy she ought to start belching more.'

When they eventually stopped sniggering, the four fell silent and sipped on their beer.

Finally Liam spoke.

'So if you could recreate any movie scene and cast yourself in the lead role, which would it be?' he asked, addressing no-one in particular.

'That's easy,' shouted Terry, pulling himself upright. 'I am Spartacus!' he bellowed, causing the others to jump out of their skin.

'No – I'm being serious,' Liam protested. 'If you could do what this pair did today and re-enact any scene from cinematic history what would it be? Obviously you would have to choose something practical. You'd probably get sectioned if you dressed up in a toga and marched down the Manor shouting, "I am Spartacus!"'

Terry scratched his head. 'Oh, I've got yer. In that case I'd be Travis Perkins when he goes on that killing spree in *Taxi Driver*.'

Liam sighed and returned to his drink.

'I'd probably choose something from *Grease*,' Sadie offered, picturing herself serenading GL with 'Summer Loving'. Suddenly feeling nauseous, she rummaged beneath the counter for a piece of chewing gum.

'Now there's a surprise,' Lana slurred. 'What is it with

you and that movie? You need to broaden your horizons, young lady.'

'All right then, what would you choose?' Sadie retorted, gripping hold of the counter. Like a ship on an extremely choppy crossing, the shop was starting to tilt before her very eyes and she felt dangerously close to capsizing out of her chair.

'I don't know, something with a bit of balls, something that I'd never dare to do in real life. It was quite liberating, you know, doing that belch in the restaurant – sticking two fingers up at the establishment and their goddamn etiquette. In fact I would highly recommend it. Although a shooting spree might be taking things a little too far,' she added, glancing sideways at Terry.

'All right then, Liam,' said Terry, helping himself to one of Lana's cigarettes. 'You're the one who asked the question. Which scene would you choose?'

Liam frowned.

'I don't know, but I wouldn't mind giving it a go. It would be a laugh, wouldn't it? Just think about how many times you've watched a film and wished it was you on that screen? What's to stop us from having a go?'

Terry thought wistfully about the scene in *Taxi Driver* where Robert De Niro takes Cybil Shepherd on a date to a porn cinema. 'Yeah, but aren't you forgetting one small fact?'

Liam stared at him blankly.

Terry raised his eyebrows in despair. 'What about the supporting cast, you donut?'

Liam scratched his head. 'Well, it depends on which scene you choose. Obviously it can't be something involving a cast of thousands, but if you got a couple of mates in on it, it might be possible.'

'We could all help each other,' Sadie suggested, glancing

around for the waste paper bin. With every ring of smoke that Terry puffed into her face she could feel her throat constrict and her stomach contract.

'What, like some sort of film fanatics anonymous?' Lana said with a smirk.

'It worked in the restaurant today, didn't it?' Sadie stumbled to her feet. Maybe if she just got a breath of fresh air . . .

'Mmm, I suppose so,' Lana conceded. 'Are you all right, honey? You're looking a little peaky.'

'Yes I think so. I just need some—'

When Sadie came to, she was propped up on the back step of the shop with Liam staring down at her, all four of his eyes wide with concern.

'Are you okay?' he asked, both of his mouths talking in perfect stereo.

Sadie nodded and her head seemed to shatter into a million pieces, shimmering like stardust in front of her eyes.

'I think so. Wass happened to your face? Why have you got two mouths?'

'Is she all right?' From somewhere in the distance she could hear Terry's voice, muffled as if he had been gagged with cotton wool. At the thought of Terry's mouth overflowing with cotton balls she keeled over sideways with laughter.

'Yeah – bit of the old double vision going on, but I think she'll live,' she heard Liam reply as he grappled to prop her back upright. Putting out a hand to steady herself she gasped at the icy coldness of the stone step beneath her. What was she doing out here? Why wasn't she in the shop?

'Oh God, I've got to lock up the ship, I mean shop. What time is it? How am I going to get home?' Sadie tried in vain to scramble to her feet but her legs felt about as supportive as a pair of springs.

Liam placed a huge hand on each of her shoulders. 'Don't

you worry about the shop. Terry's taking care of it – he's broken into enough of them in the past; I'm sure he'll be able to lock one of them up. And don't even think about going home – you can crash upstairs for the night. There's no way I'm leaving you on your own in that state.'

And before Sadie could even begin to formulate an argument, Liam had whisked her up into his arms and begun carrying her up the fire escape to the back door of his flat.

Chapter Eleven

One of Liam's earliest recollections was of waking in the middle of the night to find himself home alone. He was only six years old and had been having a terrible nightmare about his mother being eaten by a tiger. Just as the ferocious beast had dunked his mum head first into a dollop of ketchup and opened its cavernous jaws Liam had wrenched himself from sleep and shot out of bed. His Superman pyjamas were dripping with sweat but for some reason he couldn't stop shivering. Padding across the cold linoleum into the hallway and discovering the flat steeped in darkness, he raced into his mother's room and flung himself upon her bed, only to find that it was completely empty. The tiger had got her after all. Liam struggled beneath her neatly tucked blankets – the bed hadn't even been slept in – and sat there hugging his knees, trying to work out what to do. He hadn't minded when his dad had disappeared; he'd been quite relieved, in fact. Everything had become so much more relaxed; his mum had started singing along to the radio and wearing skirts and funny shiny things on her legs. But now she had gone too – and he didn't have a clue what to do. Liam pondered the possibilities. He could always stow away on a ship like that little boy called Tim in his favourite picture book, earning his passage scrubbing decks and helping peel potatoes in the galley. But Liam had no idea how to get to the sea, other than the fact that it involved having a lift in the back of his Uncle Dave's van, like the previous summer when he and his mum had gone to stay in that caravan.

At the thought of the caravan, six-year old Liam had begun to sob. He remembered snuggling up against his mum in the little fold-down bed, listening to the rain ricocheting off the metal roof, twisting strands of her hair around his fingers and feeling warmer and safer than he'd ever done in his life. Now, no matter how far he wriggled beneath her blankets, he felt chilled to the bone.

When he'd finally heard the jangle of keys in the lock and seen his mother's silhouette in the doorway he had frozen with fear. Her ghost had come to get him. Apparently it had taken her an hour to calm him down and convince him that no, a tiger had not gobbled her up and no, she was not a spooky ghost, but that she had had to take on a part-time job in a pub in order to pay for yet another new school uniform for her ever-growing son. Despite her teary promises that she would never leave him again Liam had insisted upon sleeping in the living room from then on, forcing his eyes to remain open for as long as possible, watching his mother like a hawk as she let down the hems on his trousers and converted his shirts from long to short sleeves. Some nights it would be hours before he finally succumbed to the hypnotic flicker of the black and white portable dancing across her face and was lulled into sleep by the murmur of endless soap operas and sitcoms.

Liam leant back in his armchair and watched the images blinking away silently on his widescreen TV. It was the graveyard shift in the schedules and a moustachioed Magnum PI was busy solving a murder whilst fending off the advances of a bevy of Hawaiian beauties. He knew he really ought to go to bed but he didn't want to leave Sadie alone in her drunken state. He smiled as he glanced over to the sofa where Sadie lay curled on her side, coils of her dark hair spilling on to her milky white face. Noticing that her blanket had begun to slide on to the floor, Liam tiptoed over and pulled it back up to her shoulders. It felt strange being so close to Sadie without her even realising. Part of him felt as if he were trespassing, but he couldn't help lingering, crouching beside her to watch her heart-shaped mouth tremble as it gently exhaled little puffs of air. She looked just like one of those cherubs he had spent most of last week carving on Mrs Braithwaite's surround. Before he could stop himself, Liam reached out a finger and gently stroked her face as if tracing the grain in a piece of wood. Suddenly Sadie opened her eyes, causing Liam to topple over backwards into the coffee table in shock.

'What's going on?' she mumbled, rubbing her eyes with the backs of her hands.

Liam could feel his face begin to smart with embarrassment. This was just typical. Now she was going to think he was some sort of sordid sex pest who brought intoxicated women back to his flat to have a wank over – or worse. In his haste to clamber to his feet, Liam slipped on a copy of *The Racing Post* and shot head first on to the sofa. On to Sadie. He could hear Sadie yelping from beneath him as she struggled for air.

'Oh my God. What are you doing?' she gasped, her tiny fists pummelling at his chest.

'I'm sorry,' he cried, rolling off her on to the floor and hitting his head on the corner of the coffee table with a resounding crack. 'Ow! Jesus! Oh God – my head.'

Sadie attempted to haul herself upright and quickly glanced beneath the blanket. To her immense relief she still appeared to be fully clothed.

'What were you doing?' she repeated. 'What am I doing? Where the hell am I?'

Liam sat up, gingerly rubbing the side of his head. 'You're

in my living room. You were really drunk. Don't you remember passing out in the shop? I didn't want to leave you on your own, that's all.'

Sadie frowned. It was as if someone was busy drilling holes inside her head and she could scarcely hear herself think.

'But what about Lana?' she asked. 'Where did she go?'

'Terry gave her a lift home – you were both pretty shit-faced.'

Liam glanced at Sadie to see that she was staring at him – her eyes wide with horror. Oh God, he could just see the headline in the *Ruislip Gazette* – 'Local Carpenter Gets Life for Attempted Rape'. Mrs Braithwaite would probably be the key prosecution witness.

'Oh my God,' Sadie cried. 'Your head, it's pouring with blood.'

'Really?' Liam couldn't help sighing with relief – at this point anything was preferable to being banged up for fifteen years alongside a load of nonces.

'Here, let me take a look at it.'

Liam edged forwards nervously, aware that any slight lurch or stumble would mean criminal charges for sure. Sadie perched on the edge of the sofa and gently brushed Liam's curls to one side to reveal a nasty gash on his temple.

'Oooh,' she winced. 'It looks pretty bad.' A strange tingling sensation began rushing up her fingers. Liam's hair was just as she had imagined it.

As Liam cautiously got to his feet a large drop of blood fell upon Sadie's dress.

'Oh shit – sorry. I've got blood on your dress. I'll go and get a cloth.'

'Don't worry about that,' Sadie replied. 'Just go and see to that cut. Would it be okay if I made us a coffee? I've got a terrible headache.'

Liam nodded and smiled. 'You're not the only one.'

When Liam returned to the living room, his wound patched together with some cotton wool and a jagged strip of elastoplast, Sadie was curled up in the corner of the sofa, sipping from a steaming mug.

'How's the head?' she asked, gesturing to another mug, balancing precariously on the paper mountain that had once been a coffee table.

Liam grimaced as he brought his hand up to his dressing. Right now he knew that the sympathy vote was all that could save him and he was determined to play it for all it was worth (hence the streak of dried blood he had failed to remove from his cheek).

'Pretty bad,' he half muttered, half groaned. 'How about yours?'

'Getting better,' Sadie replied with a weak smile. 'The caffeine seems to be doing the trick.'

'Good, good. Listen, about earlier. I don't want you getting the wrong idea or anything. Your blanket had slipped off and I'd just come over to pull it back up and then you woke up and scared the hell out of me and I slipped and I landed on top of you – but it was an accident. I mean, I don't want you thinking I'm some kind of sex pest or anything.' Liam slumped down into his armchair in despair. What was that saying about digging yourself out of a hole?

Sadie smiled. 'It's okay. I was just a little bit disorientated, that's all.'

'Yeah, but I know what it must have looked like. I wasn't trying to force myself on you or anything. I'd never do anything like that. I'm not that kind of bloke. I really respect women – and their rights.' Oh God. Liam felt like legging it from the room and crawling under his bed in shame. He'd just remembered how that saying ended – you have to know when to stop digging.

Sadie looked at him and laughed. 'Honestly, it's okay. I know you're not like that.'

'Really?' Liam looked over at her hopefully.

'Yes, really.'

Liam sighed with relief.

'Liam?'

'Yes?'

'I like the calendar.'

His heart plummeting, Liam followed Sadie's gaze over to Terry's new calendar, where Miss January had one hand down the front of her sequinned G-string, her bee-stung pout almost as full as her pendulous breasts.

Chapter Twelve

'Can I ask you a question, Ms Loveday – do you have a death wish or did you simply not understand the warning I gave you at your last appointment?'

Lana stared blankly across the desk at the jumped-up little juvenile posing as a doctor. 'The way I'm feeling this morning, doc, I have to say that death is looking like a pretty favourable option,' she quipped, but the miserable shit refused to grant her the faintest trace of a smile, glaring at her sternly over the gold rim of his glasses instead.

'When we spoke last time I thought I had made it abundantly clear that you should be avoiding alcohol at all costs. I can tell just by looking at you that you have chosen to ignore these instructions.' The doctor sighed and drew his chair closer to the desk. 'You have suspected liver disease, Ms Loveday – not some common-or-garden cold.'

As Lana stared at him through bleary eyes, she had to concede that he could have a point. Suspected liver disease or not, yesterday's bender had not been the smartest of moves, not with the benefit of hindsight and a megawatt hangover. She wondered how Sadie was feeling.

'Now as you know, we've had the results of your liver function tests back and they would indeed confirm the possibility of cirrhosis.' The doctor seemed to take particular delight in this last word – rolling each syllable off the tip of his tongue like marbles off a chute – CIRRH – O – SIS!

Lana scowled. He was starting to seriously piss her off,

with his exasperated sighs and accusing stares. She could tell just by looking at his mean little mouth and piggy eyes he was one of those doctors who thought the world owed him a living. And all because he'd spent seven years at med school and swallowed a Latin dictionary.

'So, what does it all mean, doc?' she asked with a sigh.

'It means that I will need to refer you to the hospital for an ultrasound scan and a series of x-rays in order to ascertain the extent of the damage to your liver.'

'Sod my liver, doc, what about the damage to my head? I swear to God it feels like a marching band are holding a jamboree in there! You wouldn't be a sweetie and write out a little old prescription for about ten dozen paracetamol, would you?' Lana leant across the desk and attempted her finest Princess Di gaze from beneath her false eyelashes.

The doctor visibly recoiled, rolling his chair backwards, his face creased with disgust. 'I'm afraid that these are the only things I'll be giving you today,' he replied in clipped, polished tones, handing her some leaflets.

'*Cirrhosis – the Causes and Effects,*' '*Alcohol and Cirrhosis,*' '*Alcoholics Anonymous*'. As Lana cast her eyes over the leaflet headings she felt a surge of white-hot rage welling in her stomach, forcing its way into her chest and throat, until it finally spewed from her mouth.

'Who the hell do you think you are, kid?' she snarled, heaving herself to her feet. 'What the hell do you know about anything, anyway? Look at you sat there all high and mighty behind your big desk, barely out of diapers and talking to me as though *I'm* the child!'

'Well, maybe if you started acting a little more responsibly, I would be able to treat you accordingly,' the doctor retorted. 'Your actions so far have hardly been constructive, have they?'

'How dare you!' Lana yelled. 'You don't know the first thing about me, or what I've been through. How dare you speak to me as if I'm something you scraped off the bottom of your shoe. Alcoholics Anonymous?' she spat, scrunching the leaflet into a ball. 'You're lucky I don't take twelve steps right around this desk and shove this leaflet into that smug mouth of yours.'

The doctor raised his hands slightly, as though in semi-surrender. 'Now come on, Ms Loveday, I really think you ought to calm down. Anger and frustration are quite common-place upon learning of a potentially serious illness, but I can assure you it is far more beneficial to deal with things in a more rational and ordered manner.' He turned to consult the monitor on his desk. 'Now, let's get you fixed up with this ultrasound.'

'Oh, go to hell,' Lana hissed, flinging the leaflets at him and heading towards the door.

'Ms Loveday, you really aren't doing yourself any favours adopting this kind of attitude. Please sit back down.'

Lana flung open the door and glanced out at the waiting room packed with old codgers gazing morosely into space and other sickly-looking types pretending to enjoy their copies of *Knitting Monthly* or *The People's Friend*. She'd show that cocky little shit who was the smart one.

'Do you think I came down in the last shower, doctor?' she yelled, causing several people to drop their periodicals in fright. Pretending to fumble with her bra strap, Lana stumbled into the middle of the waiting room to assume centre stage. 'I came to see you because I have an earache – since when has that warranted a breast examination?' Fired up by the collective, rather raspy intake of breath all around her, she continued, 'And don't expect me to believe that was a thermometer you had in your pocket either! It's out-rageous!' she cried to her captive audience. 'He ought to be struck off. You'll be hearing from my attorney, sonny Jim' she bellowed over her shoulder before marching indignantly towards the door.

Chapter Thirteen

For somebody who had only got about two hours sleep and on a sofa at that, Sadie was feeling remarkably chipper. Not even the scene of devastation awaiting her in the shop could put a damper on her mood. She merely rewound the Status Quo video, pressed play and skipped about the place singing along to 'The Wanderer', flinging empty beer bottles, cigarette packets and the remnants of the birthday Battenburg into a bin-liner as she went.

She and Liam had ended up talking for most of the night. As usual Sadie had managed to sidestep the spotlight, firing a stream of questions at Liam, which was hardly an arduous task, as the more she got to know the more inquisitive she became. Although she hated to admit it, her powers of perception seemed to have let her down quite badly with Lana and Liam. But in both cases she had ended up feeling pleased rather than disappointed. As Liam had always seemed so intimidating, she had taken it for granted he would be a typical bloke's bloke; someone with a Millwall season ticket and a shelf full of Bruce Willis videos. It had been a delight to discover that he preferred films of a more cerebral nature, *Twelve Angry Men* being his all-time favourite. But perhaps his most surprising – and attractive – quality had been his lust for adventure. Sadie had sat in awe as he rattled off the list of countries he had been to; not just the usual backpacker trail but places like Cambodia, Vietnam, even Uzbekistan – 'I lost a bet,' he explained ruefully.

'I have this phobia about wasting time,' he had gone on to confide, over yet another coffee and a packet of Hobnobs. 'My worst nightmare would be to end up chewing on my gums in some twilight rest-home, with nothing to look forward to and bugger all to look back on. Besides, you've got to have something to bore the grandkids with, haven't you?'

Sadie couldn't see any grandchildren of Liam's being bored by his vivid accounts of fishing on the banks of the Danube or feasting on cream of beetroot soup at the Samarkand Bazaar.

They must have finally dozed off at about five o'clock only to be rudely awoken two hours later by Terry crashing into the room, a stream of expletives spewing from his mouth.

'Who the hell do they think they are? That's what I want to know. A bloke's entitled to his privacy, ain't he?' Terry seethed as he plonked himself down on the end of the sofa, right on top of Sadie's feet. 'Sorry, Treacle. Here Liam, you awake over there? Any chance of making the brews? I'm in a state of shock, mate.'

Liam hauled himself upright in his armchair and groaned. 'Bloody hell, Tel, I'd only just got to sleep.'

Ignoring his protestations, Terry fumbled down the side of the settee for his cigarette papers and baccy. 'I'm doing you a favour, son – you'd have needed to get up for work in a couple of hours and if I hadn't come home you might have overslept. Tell me something – am I having some kind of nightmare or are we living in a fascist state, like Saudi A-bleedin'-rabia or something?'

'What's happened?' Sadie enquired sluggishly. Her tongue felt as if it had been coated in wallpaper paste.

'What's happened? I'll tell you what's happened. I've lost my job, that's what's happened. But you know what, like I says to that bitch of a controller, Mandy, I'll have them for invasion of privacy, you see if I don't.' Terry lit his roll-up, his gnarled brown hands quivering with rage.

'I don't understand,' Sadie responded, stifling a yawn. 'How did they invade your privacy and why have you lost your job?'

'Well, it was after I dropped your mate off last night – *the actress* – all over me like a rash she was, but I says to her, no, no, my love, I wouldn't like to take advantage of your currently pissed state. You come back to me when you're sober, my darling and then we'll talk 'ow's your father – I never did like me birds plastered,' he confided to Sadie, 'not since this one piece called Brigit passed out on me after a few too many Pernod and blacks – it was like shagging a corpse. Anyway, after I drops the lovely Lana off, I decide to clock on down the cab office, so I goes in and while I was waiting for a job to come up I thought I'd record a few thoughts in me diary. At about four o'clock I got a job taking this pregnant bird up to Great Portland Street – about to drop she was, but I think I calmed her down when I told her how few women snuff it in childbirth nowadays compared to Victorian times. By the time I got back to the office Mandy was standing behind the desk looking like she was chewing on a wasp.

'"What's up," I says to her, "you auditioning for hostess on the *Weakest Link*, or something?" But then I realised she'd got my diary in her hand and before I knew what was what, she was screaming on about me being a sick individual and a liability to the firm and how there was no way I was working for Manor Cars a second longer, or I'd end up costing them their license.'

Sadie glanced over at Liam to see his face obscured by a cushion and his huge shoulders trembling like rocks about to come loose in a landslide.

'What exactly had you written in the diary?' she asked, trying desperately to contain her own mirth.

'Well, that's just it,' Terry replied indignantly. 'All I'd been doing was keeping a record of all the filth and perversion that's rife on our streets these days and saying how it needed someone to come along and wash it all away in a river of blood. But the way she was carrying on you'd have thought *I* was one of the sickos! I don't think she was too impressed with what I'd written about her either,' he added, 'but it's true – she does need a good shafting. There's no way I was going to be the one to do it though – she's a right ropey old mare.'

When he failed to elicit any response from Liam or Sadie other than a prolonged fit of coughing, Terry got to his feet. 'Don't worry about the tea, son,' he said sorrowfully, 'I think I'll just hit the sack instead. I need a bit of time on me Jack Jones to get me case for unfair dismissal sorted.'

'Oh my God,' Sadie spluttered as soon as Terry left the room. 'Sometimes I seriously worry about that man.'

'At least you don't have to live with him,' Liam muttered. 'Thank God I've got a lock on my bedroom door. You know what this means, don't you?' He grinned at Sadie. 'He'll be back on the job market again. I hope you've got your career adviser's hat at the ready. What was that promotion he tried to run during his one day stint as an Avon Lady?'

Sadie groaned at the recollection. 'Free in-house massage with every purchase – offer not available to the over-sixties or mingers.'

Deciding that there was little point in trying to get any more sleep, Liam and Sadie had dragged themselves across the road to the greasy spoon for one of Stelios's legendary bacon butties. Cocooned in the cosy world of red Formica and hissing urns, the condensation on the windows obscuring the unforgiving weather outside, Liam regaled her with tales of his life with Terry. Sadie had laughed so hard she had given herself a stitch. And when they finally spilled out on to the pavement, flushed from the steamy heat and laughter, she had felt a pang of disappointment almost as raw as the icy wind whistling up the Parade. Now she had finally managed to master the art of conversation with Liam she didn't want to stop. Nor, it would seem, did he.

'Here you go,' he had said fishing into his jeans pocket and pulling out a slightly battered-looking business card. 'Give us a ring if you get bored later, I'll be on my own all day.'

Ashtrays emptied, shelves tidied, air-freshener sprayed, Sadie took up her post behind the shop counter and examined the business card in the palm of her hand. *Flaming Fires*, it read, with the dot over each i replaced by a tiny flame. *Liam Costello ~ Carpenter and Joiner* it said beneath, along with his work and mobile numbers.

Liam Costello. Sadie rolled his name around her head as if she were tasting a new wine. It had a nice ring to it. Much nicer than GL Jenkins, or Gary Lee Jenkins in its full glory. Liam Costello. Sadie Costello. Sadie's cheeks burned. What on earth was the matter with her? She was already in a relationship and besides there was no way someone as worldly as Liam would be interested in a dullard like her. When it came down to it, she had done absolutely nothing of any possible interest in her twenty-two years on this planet. The best she had to offer were accounts of her daydreams and childhood role-plays. Somehow she couldn't see Liam being riveted by tales of her Sindy-assisted escapades. *Did I ever tell you about the time my Sindy ran away from ballet school to elope with Action Man?* No, it just didn't compete with the travelogue of a wandering spirit.

Meanwhile, at the other end of the Manor Parade, Liam was busy carving yet another cherub for Mrs Braithwaite's elaborate surround. For once she hadn't actually requested this addition, but Liam was feeling in a generous mood and what was the harm in the occasional freebie – it was good for customer relations. Not that he had any desire to improve his relations with this particular customer. The truth was, he couldn't stop thinking about Sadie and, after a lengthy hibernation, it was as if he had been fired back into life. He wanted to preserve this feeling, for experience had taught him that moments like this were few and far between and if you didn't find some way of capturing them right there and then, the moment would be lost forever. All morning Liam worked away, recalling from memory the contour of her cheeks, the coils of her hair, whittling the wood as if it were as pliable as dough. At one o'clock the growling from his stomach finally forced him to down tools. He wondered if Sadie was hungry too.

Sadie was seriously starting to wonder if she was still drunk. Perhaps the alcohol in the beer from last night was on some kind of time release mechanism, like the vitamin C capsules GL liked to take during the winter to avoid any unsightly colds. After all, it was Terry who had supplied the beer so anything could be possible. But on the other hand, it was probably more to do with the fact that she had consumed her usual alcohol quota for a year in the space of one day. She would probably be drunk until Thursday and hungover until June. Either way she was determined to enjoy her current sense of euphoria for as long as it lasted. As she looked around the shop she finally understood what Terry meant when he talked about beer-goggles. Never had the place seemed more attractive. Oh, the things she could do with this store – if only it belonged to her. Sadie's mind brimmed full of ideas for eye-catching poster displays and profit-boosting promotions. She could run a competition for the local kids – get them to draw their favourite film character, advertise it in the toy shop down the road, then by getting the children in, hopefully the accompanying parents would splash out on a video too – a golden oldie obviously.

With the unique selling point of being the only video store in the area with barely any new releases, let alone DVDs, Sadie was forced to rely upon her boundless imagination to drum up trade. But today rather than feel frustrated by such limitations she rose to the challenge. Today, anything seemed possible. There hadn't even been a turd awaiting her in the toilet. Life was finally looking up. Sadie picked up Liam's business card and flicked it over in her hand, her stomach turning in tandem. 'Give me a ring if you get bored,' he had said, but had he meant it? He wouldn't have given her the card if he hadn't meant it, would he? Or maybe he was just being entrepreneurial? Maybe he gave his card to all new acquaintances in case they ever required a new fireplace. What she needed was a reason to ring him, a cover to avoid any embarrassment. She felt the beginnings of hunger rumbling like a distant storm in the pit of her stomach. Perfect. She would ring Liam and see if he fancied anything from the sandwich bar. With Vince still away she would be able to shut up the shop and pop down the road without any fear of being caught.

Sadie picked up the receiver and took a deep breath, but just as she was about to dial the number she heard the door open. It was such a rare sound that combined with her already nervous state it caused her to drop the phone to the floor with a clatter. The sight that greeted her when she looked up hardly soothed her nerves. The minutes she saw the man in the black balaclava she thought, *stick-up*. Her second thought, *panic button*, was swiftly replaced with a third, *tight bastard*, as she remembered Vince's decision to have the alarm disconnected in a bid to cut overheads. Sadie glanced sideways at the safe in the adjacent wall and grimaced at the thought of the grand sum of thirteen pounds and fifty two pence that sat inside, two pathetic little bags of loose change, more suited to the interior of a kid's piggy bank than a safety deposit box. The robber was hardly going to be impressed. What if he decided to help himself to something else as a form of compensation? Stay calm, Sadie told herself, strike up a rapport with your attacker and you have more chance of staying alive. That's what they always advised on programmes like *Crimewatch*, before telling you not to have nightmares.

'What do you want?' Sadie asked, far too brusquely for one meant to be building bridges. Sod it, if she moved fast enough she could probably make it to the back door.

'Have you got any copies of *Philadelphia*?' came the muffled reply.

Sadie nodded, numbly. Of course they had copies of *Philadelphia*, it was about twelve years old, wasn't it? She felt herself begin to relax but then brought herself up with a start. Perhaps this was just a ruse to distract her attention so that while she was rummaging around the shelves the robber would let himself behind the counter and launch his assault. Or even worse, perhaps it was some warped burglar with a penchant for Tom Hanks. Maybe he had just hit *Blockbusters* and had ten copies of *Forrest Gump* in his bag. Sadie looked at the sports bag on the floor by the robber's feet. There was something strangely familiar about the plethora of extreme go-karting stickers covering the canvas. Come to think of it, there was something quite familiar about the robber himself, with his stocky build but distinct lack of height.

'GL, is that you?'

'All right, babes? Have you missed me?'

Sadie's sense of relief at not being about to lose her entire Tom Hanks back catalogue was tempered slightly by a feeling of confusion. What was GL doing back so early and—

'Why are you wearing that balaclava?' she asked.

GL peered out uneasily from the eye slit. 'I was just a bit

cold, that's all,' he retorted. 'So have you got *Philadelphia* or not?'

Sadie hurriedly looked up the film's catalogue number on her computer and took it down from the back shelf. 'There you go,' she said placing it on the counter. 'Well you're back nice and early – do you fancy going on that shopping spree when I finish here at two?'

GL trudged over to the counter and placed the video in his bag. 'To be honest babes, I'm completely knackered. I was up half the night working on a proposal I've got to give in the morning. All I want to do is crash out and watch a movie. I tell you what though, why don't you go and treat yourself.' GL took his wallet from his back pocket and pulled out a sheaf of twenty-pound notes.

Sadie stared at the money glumly. There was a time when she had been overwhelmed by GL's sudden bursts of generosity. They were so incongruous to his usual penny-pinching ways that she always felt honoured when suddenly, out of the blue, he would peel a couple of hundred pounds from his wad and tell her to 'go wild.'

'Thanks,' she muttered.

'Well, that's charming, that is,' GL replied, hoisting his bag over his shoulder. 'Have you any idea how hard I've been grafting for that money while you've been sat on your arse watching videos all day?'

Sadie shrunk back into her seat. There was something about the tone of his voice, a familiar steely edge that rendered her frozen with fear.

'I'm sorry – I wasn't thinking.'

'No, you weren't. That's your problem, babes, you never do.' GL leant across the counter, practically spitting the words through the slit in the balaclava. 'The world doesn't revolve around you, you know. I've got a lot on my plate right now and any decent girlfriend would show a bit more understanding.'

Sadie nodded meekly. 'I know, I'm sorry.'

GL sighed and shook his head. 'Are you though? I don't know, babes, sometimes I wonder if maybe we shouldn't just call it a day.'

Sadie felt a surge of panic course through her body and she had to sit on her hands to prevent them from shaking. She would have nothing without GL, she would be nothing without GL. In all their time together he had never talked about ending it. 'No. Please. I *am* sorry. I was being totally selfish. You go home and unwind and I'll see you at teatime. Is there anything you want me to get you from the shops?'

GL stood staring at the floor for what seemed like an eternity before finally replying. 'No, you're all right, but how about coming round here and giving your old man a hug before he goes.'

As Liam marched down the parade, cheerily saluting his fellow tradesmen along the way, he rehearsed his opening gambit to Sadie in his head. *All right, do you fancy a roll?* Liam winced. Talk about straight from the Sid James school of double entendres, and after his behaviour of last night he couldn't afford to cause the merest whiff of sex pest. *I was feeling a little peckish and I wondered if you fancied a nibble.* Jesus Christ, what was the matter with him? He'd only left her a couple of hours ago but already he could feel his old Sadie-related speech impediment coming back to haunt him. He would just stick with a simple hello and take it from there.

But when Liam reached the shop, he saw something so stomach-churning it killed his appetite stone dead. Sadie was standing in front of the counter, her arms flung around a man's neck and her head buried into his shoulder. Although the bloke was wearing some kind of woolly hat he could tell from his height or lack of and the slogan on the back of his sweatshirt that it had to be the boyfriend. '*The nutter in front is from Corporate Sales – Newport Pagnell 2002,*' the top read. *And the arsehole inside is one lucky bastard,* Liam thought glumly, before turning swiftly and striding back down the street.

Chapter Fourteen

'You really are the most maggoty excuse for a man I have ever come across,' Lana hissed into the receiver, her dark eyes glinting with rage. 'No wonder you have to phone me – I bet you can't even get it up when you're actually with a woman, can you? Or maybe you just can't get a woman, period. What should I call you – Mister Limp Dick or Mister No Dick?'

There was a muffled gasp from the other end followed by a click, cutting the phone line dead. Lana glanced at the clock on the mantelpiece. Less than two minutes – a new personal best for *Mister Treat-Me-Like-Scum-and-See-How-I-Cum*. Perhaps he could sense that her contempt for him was real this time rather than just the bored recital of a worn-out script. This morning Lana felt nothing but hatred for everything and everyone. She hated all men, from the perverts who called her phone-line to that dreadful little cab-driving friend of Sadie's who had practically tried to rape her the night before. She hated doctors, especially doctors young enough to be her son who insisted upon lecturing her as though they were her father. She hated her liver for letting her down and spying on her, like some CCTV camera for the medical world installed inside her very own body. She hated life, but even more she hated death for plaguing her like some deranged stalker, determined not to let her forget.

The only thing Lana loved in this world was booze. It was

the sole thing she could rely upon; her best friend, elixir and painkiller all blended and bottled into one. Before a drop had ever passed her lips she had succumbed to its charms. As a young girl she would watch spellbound as her screen heroines helped themselves to snowy white cigarettes from silver boxes and fixed themselves martinis from polished mini-bars. There had been something so seductive about the clink of bottle upon glass, the silky flow of the liquor as it cascaded down, the way the women would tease the olive around the brim before devouring it with their perfectly painted mouths. The whole ritual associated with drinking seemed so sophisticated, so sensual. Of course you never got to see Lana Turner or Joan Crawford with a severe attack of jaundice, crouched over a toilet, vomiting blood. This part of the ritual was strangely omitted from the films, discarded cuts destined for the editor's floor.

Lana logged off her phone and got to her feet. She suddenly felt stir-crazy, stuck there in her dingy living room, humouring perverts and torturing herself with stupid thoughts. She would go pay Sadie a visit, see if there was any scandal from last night – after all, when it had come to their escorts home Sadie had most definitely drawn the long straw.

As Sadie sat slumped behind her counter, she felt as shrivelled and deflated as a burst balloon. *Maybe we should call it a day.* GL's words kept echoing around her head, causing her to flinch in horror. She had no idea he was so unhappy with her. Yes, he had been becoming increasingly irritable, but she had put that down to his job, not her. What if he decided to dump her? What would she do? Where would she go? She had no money and the thought of returning to her father cap in hand was unbearable. Her entire childhood had been spent dreaming of the day she would be free from his reign of terror. Although life with GL hadn't exactly been a picnic recently, she could never go back to East Anglia. As far as she was concerned both her parents were dead. GL was right, she had been incredibly selfish. While he'd been away working hard she had been out getting drunk and spending the night with another man. Okay, so nothing untoward had happened, but she had found herself entertaining the kind of thoughts a loyal, loving partner would never have. What had she been thinking of? She and Liam had absolutely nothing in common. GL was her steady boyfriend, her only boyfriend. He was the one who had saved her who had given her a brand new life and how did she repay him? Sadie felt thoroughly ashamed of herself and thoroughly sick of the Status Quo video banging away at her eardrums like a pneumatic drill. As Sadie replaced it with *The Wall*, ready for Brian's shift, she felt as if her beer goggles had been wrenched from her face and stamped upon leaving her with no alternative but to face up to reality. As she looked forlornly at the trades description defying 'New Releases', the dearth of DVDs and the tatty poster display peeling away from the wall she felt a pang of dismay. She didn't own this shop and the way business was going it was highly doubtful she would even have a job there for very much longer. Just as she may not have a relationship for much longer. She had never seen GL so dejected. Normally he came back from sales courses all high fives and snappy slogans. He would usually want to go extreme skateboarding to unwind, not chill out with a movie. The kind of movies GL watched were not the sort to 'chill out' to anyway, unless you found high-speed car chases or graphic war scenes particularly relaxing. And GL most definitely did not. He watched films the way that other people snorted coke – for an instant high. She would never forget the time they had taken out *Saving Private Ryan* and he had actually whooped throughout the opening Normandy landings scene – the bloodier the effects, the louder his bays. Sadie shuddered at the recollection. No,

GL was more a Tommy Lee Jones than a Tom Hanks man. And *Philadelphia* of all films, it was just so – sensitive.

'Well, hello, my fellow Caprice outcast. You're still alive then?'

Sadie looked up to see Lana in the doorway, a bottle green silk scarf swathing her head and a huge pair of shades hanging over her face like two black shutters.

'Appearances can be deceptive,' she replied with a watery smile.

'Don't tell me,' Lana said holding up her hand in a stop gesture. 'Your head feels like lead, your mouth is drier than sandpaper and your body feels as if it's gone ten rounds with Mike Tyson?'

Sadie laughed. 'That's amazing! You ought to be a doctor.'

Lana snorted as she reached the counter and plonked down her vintage Chanel handbag. 'Please don't talk to me about doctors, hon. I do however, know just what the doctor would order in a case like yours.'

'You do?'

'Uh-huh,' Lana nodded sagely and peered over her shades. 'Yes, it would appear that you require an urgent prescription of smores.'

'Smores?'

'Yes. As in, please momma, may I have s'more? Now, what time do you get through in this godforsaken place?'

Sadie glanced at her watch. 'In exactly ten minutes.'

'Great – I'll go get the ingredients and meet you back here. Then we'll go round to mine for a smore overdose.'

Upon seeing Sadie's bewildered expression, Lana leant over and gave her a reassuring pat on the shoulder. 'Trust me, my dear, on a day like today they are manna from heaven,' and with a swirl of her cape she was gone.

Sadie smiled with relief. After recent developments she

really hadn't fancied trudging around Harrow town centre spending GL's hard-earned cash on herself. The thought of getting to see Lana's house made for a far more intriguing prospect.

Chapter Fifteen

'So, do you live alone then?' Sadie asked, running to keep up with Lana's stride as they wound their way through the labyrinth of back streets emanating from the Manor Parade.

'I most certainly do.'

Prior to yesterday's revelations, Sadie had pictured Lana living with a distinguished old actor of the Laurence Olivier mould or a houseful of cats *à la* Brigitte Bardot, but now her imagination was running riot. Her head was awash with images of red lights in front windows and pimps clad in a camel hair coats manning the door. God, why had she ever let Terry talk her into watching *Taxi Driver?*

'Here we are – home sweet home,' Lana declared, as she barged her way through a wooden gate hanging precariously from a solitary hinge, like a child's tooth just one tug away from the fairy. Sadie felt quite disappointed to discover the house was almost identical to the row of others tapering off into the distance, with their uniform double-glazing and their handkerchief sized front lawns. The only thing to differentiate Lana's house from all the rest was the ornate scroll that had been taped to the glass panel in the front door.

THINK BEFORE YOU KNOCK

Milkmen: I am perfectly capable of fetching my own milk, thank you very much and have no desire to purchase one of your appalling sounding 'Dairy Diaries'.

Assorted Bible Bashers: I worship Satan and am way past redemption.

Double Glazing Salesmen: Perhaps you would like to invest in some glazing for your eyes as any fool can see I have a perfectly fine set of windows and doors.

Betterware: I have no need for plastic containers or any other gimmicky gadgetry for my kitchen – I do not do cooking! Leave your hideous catalogues at their own peril.

Trick or Treaters: I put razor blades inside apples.

Save the Children and other do-gooders: Charity begins (and ends) at this home.

Binmen: Here's a festive tip – try removing the garbage rather than just rearranging it over my lawn.

Sadie couldn't help gasping as she worked her way through the litany of abuse and then giggling as she looked down to see the WELCOME mat upon the floor.

'Let me assure you that my doormat is an entirely post modern ironic purchase – some of us Yanks have grasped the concept of irony you know,' Lana added wryly. 'Not that *you* aren't welcome, honey, it's just that I am quite a private person and one thing I can't abide is the uninvited visitor. Now come on, let's get a fire going before we catch our death of cold.'

Sadie followed Lana through the hallway into the living room, her eyes squinting in the gloom. To her relief, the house was far closer to her initial imaginings – displaying elegance of the Hollywood rather than whorehouse variety, albeit rather faded. The layer of dust on the velvet curtains, the threadbare patches on the chaise longue, the peeling varnish on the drinks cabinet and coffee table, the faded portraits of faded stars hanging slightly skew-whiff in their cobweb fringed frames, all gave the room a rather unsettling air of Miss Haversham. Sadie shivered.

'Don't worry, sweetie, once I get this thing going it'll be hotter in here than the front of Brad Pitt's jockey shorts,' Lana declared, grabbing a huge marble lighter from the coffee table and kneeling in front of the fireplace.

Sadie watched as Lana carefully arranged some crumpled balls of newspaper amongst the blocks of wood in the hearth.

'This was the only reason I bought this house – the thought of a proper open fire,' Lana explained as she ignited the paper balls one by one. 'I figured if I was going to freeze my ass off for eight months of the year in this Godforsaken country then I may as well have a roaring fire to come home to. There.' Lana sat back on her haunches and took a cigarette from a silver box on the coffee table. 'Help yourself to a smoke, hon.'

Sadie shook her head. 'I think I'm going to have another go at giving up,' she said, staring at the coals as they began to glow red. 'So, is it very hot in the part of the States that you come from?'

Lana stood up and removed her cape, revealing a charcoal woollen sweater dress draped over her curves. Sadie noticed that the wool had started to bobble slightly. As with her house, Lana's sartorial elegance had a certain faded quality about it.

'Is it hot in South Carolina?' Lana replied. 'Is the Pope a geriatric? Put it this way. We don't have much call for fires, unless of course we're camping. Which reminds me.'

Lana cleared a space on the coffee table and tipped her carrier bag onto it. A bag of marshmallows, a huge slab of Dairy Milk, a packet of Jacobs crackers and a quarter bottle of vodka all spilled out.

'Hair of the dog,' Lana explained hastily, following Sadie's gaze to the vodka. 'Take a seat, hon and we'll get some smores on the go.'

Sadie perched on the end of the chaise longue, praying that these famous smores did not include vodka. The last thing she wanted was another drink; to return home to GL half cut would be catastrophic.

'Okay, first we have to assemble the crackers and chocolate,' Lana explained, ripping open the packet of Jacobs. 'Back home we use Graham crackers, but these ought to do the trick.'

Sadie frowned as she watched Lana lay out a line of cream crackers and then cover each one with squares of Dairy Milk. She was far more accustomed to having cheese with her crackers than chocolate. Mind you, Americans were famous for combining peanut butter and jam. At least Lana hadn't bought a jar of Sunpat on her shopping spree.

'Okay,' said Lana. 'Now we need to toast the marshmallows. Have you ever been camping before?'

Sadie nodded. 'Yes, once with my parents for my seventh birthday. I was heavily into the *Famous Five* at the time,' she explained.

Lana opened the bag of marshmallows and smiled. 'What a wonderful present.'

Sadie nodded. Actually, it had been awful. Her dad had run the entire operation as if he were their drill sergeant; getting her and her mum up at the crack of dawn to stockpile firewood and lecturing them incessantly about the nutritional value of the common earthworm and the most effective way to skin a rabbit. Then, when the handle of his billycan had snapped, causing soup to spill all over his trousers, he'd lapsed into an irretrievable sulk. Nothing her mum could do or say would appease him and they'd ended up returning home two days early.

'Yeah, it was great.' Sadie replied with a sigh.

'Well, hopefully this will bring back plenty of fond memories.' Lana said, grinning broadly, I'll go get the forks.'

Sadie made her way around the coffee table and knelt in front of the fire. As she watched the flames licking greedily at the wood, she thought of the tent her mum had erected out of blankets and a clothes-horse as soon as they'd got home and her father had returned to the base. Sadie smiled as she recalled the vast amounts of jelly babies they'd pretended to roast over a 'fire' constructed from Twiglets and red crepe paper flames.

'So, do your parents live locally?' Lana asked upon returning, handing Sadie a fork.

Sadie shook her head. 'No. My dad is an officer in the Air Force and he's currently based in East Anglia and my mum – my mum's dead.'

Lana looked up with a start. 'Oh, gee, I'm sorry, hon.'

'Don't worry, it was a long time ago.'

'How old were you?'

'Eighteen. Go on then, pass the marshmallows.'

Lana stared hard at Sadie as she passed her the bag, but try as she might she couldn't detect the slightest flicker of emotion upon her face. 'Okay – the desired effect is to get them golden brown all over – think George Hamilton's hide,' she added with a smirk.

Sadie took a marshmallow from the packet and stuck it on to the end of her fork. 'No problem,' she declared, waving her fork in the fire. Within seconds a flame had shot up from the marshmallow itself. 'Oh my God,' Sadie cried. 'My marshmallow's on fire!'

Lana smirked. 'Hmm. I can see your camping skills need a little bit of honing. The object is to gently toast them, my dear, not incinerate the poor bastards.' Inflating her heavily rouged cheeks like a pair of bellows, she puckered up her lips and extinguished the flame.

As Sadie scraped the blackened remains from her fork, she watched Lana hold her own marshmallow a few inches from the fire and slowly but surely the snowy white surface turned gold.

'Here we go,' said Lana, 'One perfectly toasted mallow. Now you just pop it on top of one of the crackers like so,' she deftly planted the marshmallow in the centre of a chocolate topped cracker, 'And then sandwich it with another.' Lana pressed another chocolate-topped cracker on top of the marshmallow and held it tightly. 'The heat from the marshmallow melts the chocolate, see.' Lana handed the bizarre sandwich to Sadie. Sadie could feel the heat seeping through the holes in the cracker and as the chocolate began to melt, the sweet smell of cocoa and vanilla began spiralling up her nostrils. As if triggering an aroma-sensitive alarm, her stomach began to rumble.

'Don't be shy, tuck in,' Lana urged as she began toasting another marshmallow.

'Oh my God,' Sadie murmured as she bit into the crackers and the whole sandwich caved into the chocolatey mixture inside. 'This is delicious.'

'What did I tell you?' Lana beamed. 'Luvverly jubberly, as that prick, Jamie Oliver, would say.'

Sadie giggled at Lana's Dick Van Dyke style cockney, and sent a shower of crumbs over the carpet. 'Whoops. Oh no.' Chocolate began dribbling down her chin and oozing on to her fingers and the more she tried to lick it away the messier she became.

Lana smiled as she watched Sadie grappling with her smore. She looked so childlike with her chocolate-stained face and dimpled cheeks. And yet she had lost her mother just four years previously. As Lana knew all too well, this had to be one of the worst blows fate can deal you – to lose the very person who gave you life, the person who nurtured you, protected you – how much pain lay behind Sadie's smiling façade? Lana slammed her fork on to the table.

'Fancy a drink,' she said, more as a statement than a query, before fetching two crystal tumblers from the drinks cabinet and unscrewing the lid from the bottle of vodka.

Sadie looked up in surprise. 'Oh, not for me, thanks,' she replied, licking her fingers.

Lana ignored her to pour two huge measures into the glasses. 'I insist,' she said. 'You have to have something to wash down the crackers, and besides, we could both do with a hair of the dog.'

Sadie grimaced. The mere thought of neat vodka on top of all the chocolate made her want to hurl. Lana must have a cast iron stomach. 'Do you have any mixers?' she enquired half-heartedly.

'Why sure, honey,' Lana replied with a beaming smile. 'How about a little tonic.' After a good deal of rummaging about in the recesses of the drinks cabinet she managed to locate the remnants of a bottle of tonic water and added a splash to Sadie's glass. Sadie could tell from the lack of accompanying fizz that it was as flat as tap water.

'So tell me,' Lana said, taking a swig from her own, straight vodka and returning to her toasting. 'Is there any gossip to report from last night? I have to say you certainly came out tops when it came to our escorts home – if indeed you were escorted home. It hasn't escaped my attention that you appear to be wearing the exact same outfit you had on yesterday.'

Sadie gulped and tugged on the hem of her dress. 'Nothing happened. After I passed out Liam didn't want to leave me on my own so he took me up to his place, that's all. I slept on the couch. Honestly.'

'Well how gall-ant,' Lana remarked with a smirk. 'But what a lost opportunity. How could you resist that physique? The man is an Adonis.'

Sadie frowned. 'I don't know what you mean. I've already got a boyfriend and we're very happy, thank you very much.'

'Ah yes – Mr Newport Pagnell. So tell me, when is he due to make a reappearance?'

'He's already back, if you must know,' Sadie took a sip from her drink and fought the urge to retch. Lana's questioning was beginning to seriously piss her off.

'Oh.' Lana removed her marshmallow from the fire and began constructing another smore on the coffee table.

'Yes, he called by the shop earlier with my birthday present.'

'Really?' Lana pressed the smore together, her bejewelled fingers glimmering in the firelight. 'So, what did he get you?'

'Well he gave me some money actually – I asked him to. You know what men are like, I'd rather chose something that I really want.' Sadie could feel her cheeks begin to burn but she wasn't sure if it was from the fire, the vodka or the shame of having to lie.

'I see,' said Lana, staring at Sadie while she bit into her smore.

Squirming under her gaze, Sadie took another marshmallow from the bag and skewered it with her fork. 'So, tell me more about you,' she said, holding the fork gingerly in front of the fire. 'What was it that made you come to Britain in the first place?' Sadie watched enviously as Lana licked her lips, somehow managing to devour her smore without the slightest trace of chocolate escaping her mouth.

'Well – one guess, honey. What is it that lies behind every heartache and life-changing decision in a girl's life?'

Sadie had seen more than enough weepy melodramas to know the answer to that one. 'A man?' she replied.

'Exactly.'

'So you came to Britain to be with a man?'

Lana put down her smore and shuddered theatrically. 'Good Lord, no. I came to Britain to *escape* from a man.'

Sadie watched as Lana took a cigarette from her box, her hands visibly shaking as she lit it.

'Sorry. I didn't mean to pry. It's none of my business.'

'No, no, it's okay. In a way I'm glad you asked. My therapist said I shouldn't bottle up what happened to me, but some things are so painful – even years after the event it's still a little raw to relive.'

'I know,' Sadie nodded. 'I know.'

'Of course you do,' Lana took another large swig from her glass before topping it up. 'His name was Frank. Frankster the Prankster everyone called him, on account of his jovial demeanour.' Lana snorted and arched her pencilled eyebrows ceiling-ward. 'He moved to our town when I had just turned sixteen. I'll never forget the first time I saw him.' Lana's gaze drifted towards the fire. 'I was mooching along Main Street on my way home from school – all alone because my best friend Hanna Beth had clarinet practice – when suddenly I spied the most glorious vision in frayed denim, leaning against the gas pump by the crossroads.' Lana sighed wistfully. 'I tell you, I don't think I'd ever witnessed a finer specimen of masculinity. His skin was the color of maple syrup and his eyes – why, they made cornflowers seem dreary. "What does a guy have to do to get a date in this place?" he called out after me as I walked past. Of course I pretended not to hear him, but then all of a sudden he was bounding alongside me, grinning the most dazzling grin, and I don't know if it was the heat or my hormones or the heat from my hormones, but the next thing I knew, we were sitting in a diner chatting over two chocolate malts as if we'd known each other for a thousand years.'

'Wow,' Sadie gazed dreamily into the flames, trying hard not to think about her own encounter with Liam in the caff that very morning.

'Yeah, wow,' Lana retorted bitterly. 'It's amazing isn't it, how your instincts can betray you. How they can trick you into feeling you're luxuriating in a heavenly dream when all the while you're about to embark upon the worst nightmare of your entire life.'

Sadie stared at Lana. 'What do you mean? What happened?'

'Well, let's just say Frankster the Wankster would have been a more appropriate alias,' Lana replied, drawing so heavily on her cigarette that she created almost an inch of ash.

'Why? What did he do?'

'Well, he was very clever – I'll give him that. He had everyone fooled with his Jack the lad routine and his boyish charm, and none more so than me. I gave up everything for that man, a scholarship to stage school, my dreams of a Hollywood career, it all went up in smoke the moment I set eyes upon him. Oh, if only I'd taken up the clarinet like Hanna Beth, then our paths might never have crossed.' Lana ground out her cigarette in a huge marble block of an ashtray. 'It was as if he became my entire purpose for living – and it damned near killed me.'

Sadie shivered and took another swig from her drink. It went down a lot easier this time. 'What did he do to you?'

Lana sighed. 'What didn't he do? As soon as he had that ring on my finger he changed. Why, on our very wedding night he up and disappeared. And although he swore he'd just been feeling restless and been out walking, when he got back the next morning I could smell the perfume on him and I knew he was lying. But I was so young and so in love, I just turned a blind eye to it all. The silent phone calls, the nights away from home, the traces of lipstick on his collar. And then when I finally started to ask questions, he got so mean. "Who do you think you are," he would yell, "my fucking mother?" And then he started turning the tables on me, quizzing *me* all the time about where I had been and who I had seen. It got so that I didn't bother going out any more; it was easier just to avoid other people. That's when he started inventing reasons to pick on me.'

Sadie felt a lump begin to form in her throat. Suddenly

everything seemed to make sense. No wonder Lana was so bitter about men, no wonder she had no qualms about making money from sex. She remembered a show *Geraldo* had done about the 'real Pretty Women' and every one of the prostitutes featured had come from an abusive background. 'What do you mean – he'd invent reasons?' she asked.

'Oh, if he came home from work and thought the telephone had been moved he'd accuse me of calling my lover. He became so damn anal about the house being immaculate. If anything was slightly out of place it would be an excuse to berate me – or worse. The cans being unsymmetrical in the cupboards, the towels not hanging neatly in the bathroom.'

'God, that's just like *Sleeping With the Enemy*.'

Lana frowned. 'Yes – well – it didn't take long before the beatings started and then one night . . .' Lana lowered her voice until it was barely audible. 'One night, he came back from a car auction in Charleston and he – he forced himself upon me.'

'Oh my God!' Sadie didn't know what to do. Although she couldn't see Lana's bowed face she was almost certain she was crying. 'Oh, don't cry. Please. I'm sorry, I never should have asked. Here, take this.' Sadie picked up the chocolate stained tissue she had been using to wipe her face and brought it over to Lana. Putting an arm around Lana's hunched shoulders, she gave them an awkward little squeeze.

Lana took the tissue and pressed it over her eyes. 'I'm sorry, hon. I'm really not the greatest company right now. Perhaps it would be best if you left. We can get together another day. You see, I only need to think of him and it sends me right back there.'

Sadie got to her feet. 'Yes of course, if that's what you want. Are you sure you're going to be all right, though? I feel really bad leaving you like this.'

'Oh, I'll be fine. I'll come see you in the shop tomorrow.'

Lana kept the tissue firmly clamped to her face as she listened to Sadie shuffle about the room.

'I'll see myself out then,' Sadie said.

'If you don't mind,' Lana replied, remaining motionless in front of the fire. There was no way she was going to get up or Sadie would see that she hadn't been crying.

'Well – if you need to have a chat or anything you know where I am.'

'Okay. Thank you hon. I'll come by real soon, I promise.'

Just go, Lana thought. Get out of my house and take your misguided sympathy and compassion with you. *Don't you understand,* she wanted to call out after Sadie as she heard the front door click shut and her footsteps fading off down the street, *I don't deserve your friendship; I don't deserve anyone's friendship . . . I've just sat here feeding you a pack of lies and watching you swallow them hook, line and sinker. Why would you want to be friends with someone like me?* Lana poured herself another drink and downed it in one. Why would anyone want to be friends with someone like her – she was nothing but a drunkard, a liar and a worst of all – a killer.

Chapter Sixteen

Everything about Lana was a fabrication. From her screen siren name to her silicone-enhanced breasts. The moment her plane touched down at Heathrow, almost twenty years previously, she had set about constructing a web of lies so tightly woven that at times even she found herself entangled between fact and fiction.

Her husband Guy had started it all off in that poky little interview room in Immigration Control. 'I always intended coming back to the UK when I was ready to start a family,' he'd informed them, in lie number one. 'It's a personal dream that my children should be Oxbridge educated too. And then of course there's the accent.'

They'd shared a little snigger at that one, Guy and the two Nazi-style interrogators, whilst Lana had forced her mouth into the dumb little smile of the dumb little wife, all the time her heart breaking for the children she now knew they'd never have. Then she'd heard the stamp of rubber upon her visa and knew that it was official – her fraudulence had been authorised and now there was no turning back. Not that she wanted to turn back. All Lana wanted to do was run and never stop. Even in the nightmares that plagued her she would be racing up a hill, eyes fixed on the ever-distant horizon, ignoring the outstretched arms and anguished cries reaching out to thwart her.

She and Guy had taken a cab to a small hotel in Earls Court, the type with plastic sheets and a Durex machine in the lobby. As they'd perched on the edge of the bed and Guy had written her out a cheque – essentially her severance pay – Lana had felt numb with disbelief. How had it all come to this? It hardly seemed a week ago that Guy had been carrying her over the threshold of the penthouse suite in the newly built Trump Tower and they had gorged on caviar and champagne in celebration of their union.

'Thank you,' she muttered as she studied the cheque.

Pay Mary Latimer, fifty thousand pounds only, her loving husband had written. So that's how much I'm worth, Lana thought, with morbid curiosity rather than anger – that's how much it costs to make me disappear.

'That should be enough to sort you out with somewhere to live. My solicitors will be in touch, once the dust has settled, about the divorce,' Mary Latimer's loving husband had declared as he headed for the door. But why should he have wanted to stick around? God knows, if Mary could have escaped from herself she'd have been out of there like a shot too. So she did the next best thing. From that day forward, Mary Latimer ceased to exist and Lana Loveday was born.

Calling herself Lana had been one of her most effortless lies. With its virginal, whiter than white connotations, the name Mary had in many ways felt more of a pretence. Like a poorly-fitting hat, it had always sat awkwardly upon her headstrong, tearaway character. Similarly her childhood in Springfield, Missouri (or Misery as she preferred to refer to it) was another clumsy mismatch. A small town in the heart of Middle America's bible belt was no place for an aspiring drama queen to be raised. Amid the sleepy diners and dreary malls there was precious little to fire her lust for romance and adventure, let alone sate her voracious appetite for life. Why oh why couldn't she have been born a Southern belle? The only thing Lana could do to prevent the ground swell of frustration swallowing her up from the inside out was to run. And run. Before school, after school, at weekends and holidays, sometimes in the middle of the night when she awoke drenched in sweat, she would pull on her sneakers and sweat pants and take to the road. She wouldn't relax until she had fled her own neighbourhood of stucco-coated bungalows, with their shabby porches and tatty front yards and made it to the top of the hill where the streets opened out. Then her breathing would slow and her pace would ease and she would practically glide along the maple-lined avenues, occasionally glancing sideways to admire the grandiose Colonial style houses, with their brightly painted front steps and rolling lawns and imagine she had managed to run all the way to the Deep South, where the women flung themselves down staircases and the men frankly didn't give a damn.

At least back then she was running *to* something. Back then it was freedom that was firing her up, not fear. And on the day of her high school graduation she grabbed the opportunity to break free with both beautifully manicured hands. Having outgrown her childhood obsession with the South (she never had acquired the taste for catfish) she had set her sights on New York – after all, what better place to claim your liberty? Winning a scholarship to study the performing arts at NYU, she bade her infuriatingly strait-laced parents farewell and boarded the Interstate Greyhound bus, never to return again. Not even six years later when everything went apocalyptic did she consider going back to Missouri. The truth was, her farm-hand father and her seamstress mother were about as alien to Lana as the name with which they had christened her and besides, she wouldn't have been able to bear the knowing look upon their faces. Far better to leave them with the fantasy that their daughter had quit her modelling career to begin a new life overseas with her British stockbroker husband.

Lana had lasted just one semester at NYU before her old feelings of boredom and frustration began to set in. Even

the social whirl of freshman parties failed to satisfy the
hunger within her. There really was no logical cause for
the hollow feeling that plagued her. It certainly wasn't a
lack of popularity. Like some bewitchingly exotic scent, her
understated elegance and total self-belief attracted a stream of
admirers both male and female. And her course was a world
away from the childish drivel that had infuriated her so at high
school. But still she wanted more. It had taken her a lifetime to
get to New York and now she had arrived she didn't want to
waste another second waiting on tables or dozing in lectures.
She wanted instant gratification, instant glamour and if she
couldn't become a Hollywood star overnight then she would
do the next best thing. Lana was signed up by the first model
agency she approached and quit school the following day.

Finally Lana had found a lifestyle to match her own frenetic
pace. As she bustled her way through departure lounges,
sashayed her way along catwalks and guzzled her way through
magnums of champagne, the void in her life appeared to
diminish. But the accompanying sense of relief was to prove
short-lived. Rather than being satisfied, her appetite had
merely been whetted. Whether it be a cover rather than
an inside spread in *Vogue* or a crate rather than a bottle
of champagne, she was haunted by a constant craving for
more. In this respect she and Guy were a match made in
heaven.

A high-flying Wall Street trader hailing from London,
England, Guy Latimer's hunger was solely confined to money.
For him greed wasn't just good – it was God. As soon as
Lana saw him, flicking pretzels over the balustrade at the
Metropolitan Charity Ball, she knew she had to have him.
With his raven hair, Wedgewood blue eyes and clipped
accent, he was like Clark Gable and Richard Burton all
rolled into one. 'What are you doing?' she had giggled,
as a ripple of consternation broke out on the dance floor

below. 'Waiting for you,' he had replied, pulling her out of sight. The attraction was instant and mutual and although Lana was certainly no stranger to spontaneous sex, this was different. *Guy* was different. As he led her into the restroom and locked the door behind them, the heat they generated was searing. Before his lips had even touched hers she could feel them scorching her skin, blazing a trail along her cleavage and up her neck before finally combusting into a kiss. Afterwards, when she stumbled out to rearrange herself in front of the wall of mirrors, she half expected to find her body erupting in blisters.

Over the weeks that followed Guy became her new source of craving. Intoxicated and bleary eyed from the heady mix of alcohol and an almost permanent state of arousal, she staggered between his bed and her assignments, her head awash with romantic notions of the power of love at first sight. And how Guy had fulfilled those notions, how he had fed her craving, with his twenty-four carat engagement ring and whirlwind wedding ceremony at Trump Tower!

Why hadn't she realised all those years ago as she'd lain there beneath him, her skin smouldering and her heart pounding, that she truly was playing with fire, and sooner or later she really would be burnt?

Chapter Seventeen

All the way home Sadie had oscillated between feelings of sympathy and gratitude. Sympathy for Lana's plight and gratitude for her own good fortune. Never again would she moan about GL's dedication to his job or his occasional mood swings. Okay, so he could be a bit bossy and domineering, but at least he didn't demand an itinerary of her movements – far from it, in fact. And okay, some of his remarks could be a little on the cutting side, but at least he wasn't abusive. He was just highly motivated, that's all.

However, when she walked into the living room and saw GL slumped in front of the television, with Bruce Springsteen wailing about Philadelphia in digital surround sound, he appeared far more morose than motivated. He hadn't even bothered to take his customary post-work shower, and was still clad in his suit, his loosened tie hanging like a noose around his neck. As Sadie took off her coat and sat down beside him on the sofa she noticed that his face was covered in dark red blotches, as if somebody had been pelting him with spoonfuls of damson jam.

'God, GL, what's happened to your face? Are you okay?'

'I dunno, babes,' GL replied morosely. But he knew only too well what lay behind his hideous disfigurement. Watching *Philadelphia* had confirmed his worst fears. At the tender age of just twenty-two and with his whole life ahead of him, he had contracted AIDS. If only he hadn't had that knee trembler with his nephew's German au pair on New Year's

Eve. Her thicket of a minge should have been enough of a warning, God knows what kind of infestations had been lurking amongst all that undergrowth. The worst thing was that he was normally so careful. In this day and age a bloke just didn't know what he could be dipping his wick into and GL never normally went out without a clap trap tucked inside his wallet. But he really hadn't expected to pull on New Year's Eve – not at his Uncle Mike's and certainly not with Sadie in tow. That's what had made it all the better at the time – the fear that at any moment someone could have caught them at it, up against the crates of dog food in the utility room. Well he'd been caught out all right, but unfortunately by the Grim Reaper rather than the missus.

'Perhaps it's chickenpox,' Sadie offered, scrutinising his blemished face. 'Can you remember if you've ever had it before?'

GL nodded glumly. 'And measles.' He'd already phoned his mum for a rundown of his childhood illnesses. There was no two ways about it. He had AIDS and he was going to die. GL shuddered as he thought of all of the lost opportunities ebbing away from him like a tide destined never to turn. Those orders he could have won, the spondulicks he could have earned, the birds he could have shagged, that bungee jump off the Clifton Suspension bridge. Still, things had changed since Tom Hanks' day. With the right medication AIDS no longer needed to be a death sentence. Look at Mark Fowler – he'd gone on for ages riddled with HIV, flogging his fruit and veg to the residents of Albert Square. GL grimaced; he didn't know which was the worst prospect and for the first time in years he genuinely felt scared.

'Come here and give us a cuddle,' he said forlornly, arms outstretched.

Sadie's heart soared as she nestled against GL's chest.

Perhaps her relationship wasn't doomed after all. GL's harsh words of earlier may just have been down to a mixture of tiredness and worry about his skin complaint. After all he did take extraordinary pride in his appearance – GL was the only man she knew who was aware of the cleansing properties of seaweed.

'Oh, you've started smoking again,' she commented, noticing the near empty cigarette packet on the arm of the sofa.

'Yeah – stress related,' GL replied, wearily. And to think he'd been worried about getting cancer. 'So how was the shopping spree?'

'It was okay.' Sadie buried her head deeper into GL's chest.

'What did you spend my hard-earned dosh on, then?'

'Oh, er – the new *Grease* DVD,' Sadie replied. Her mouth had become so dry she felt sure it would splinter into pieces if she attempted to swallow.

GL yawned. 'Well there's a surprise. So, have you missed me?'

'Yes, of course – I had good fun at Le Caprice though,' she added, remembering Lana's advice about making GL feel dispensable.

'Le Caprice? Blimey, is that still open? Ow, shit.'

At the sound of GL's groans, Sadie sat upright and watched with concern as he writhed with pain. 'Are you all right?' she asked.

'Yeah, just feeling a little tender, that's all,' GL replied. Ever since he'd woken that morning and seen the eruptions upon his face, every twinge in his body seemed to have taken on gargantuan proportions. Slight tension in his brow became evidence of a latent brain tumour and symptoms previously associated with heartburn now signalled imminent cardiac arrest.

'You really ought to go to the doctor,' Sadie suggested,

feeling her way through the sovereign rings to stroke the back of his hand.

'I was hoping I might get a bit of nursing at home,' GL murmured, gazing at Sadie dolefully.

Much as she felt sorry for him and relieved at his obvious warming towards her, Sadie couldn't help feeling a pang of dismay at GL's suggestion. She had long since given up the hope that sex was anything like it was portrayed in the movies – all writhing limbs and panting and moaning. For her, sex was practically an out of body experience – in the worst possible sense. Similar to some people's accounts of coming back from the dead, during sex with GL Sadie would often find herself floating above the bed, lost in world of daydreams while her body lay as motionless as a corpse below. Not that GL seemed to care. He seemed far too involved in his own enjoyment, not to mention the bizarre running commentary he liked to employ as he built his way up to climax. 'Your mission – should you choose to accept it – is to make this little lady cream!' he would announce at the start, before burrowing beneath the duvet to perform cunnilingus for twenty-seven seconds exactly. Sadie could be sure of the duration because she had timed it on several occasions. He would then resurface with the words, 'Double O Seven at your service, ma'am, with a license to thrill,' before thrusting himself inside her and humping away for a further two and a half minutes (five if he was having trouble reaching his weekly sales target).

GL obviously was having trouble reaching his target, Sadie concluded as she glanced miserably at the clock on the VCR. He had been pounding away at her now for almost ten minutes and with each thrust a searing bolt of pain coursed throughout her groin and the carpet fibres tore into her back like bracken. Perhaps she ought to do something to help chivvy him along. The problem was, she didn't really know what. GL had been her only sexual partner and right from the start he had seemed more than content with her passivity. Initially she had been relieved, as she was terrified of making some dreadful sexual faux pas, like blowing where she ought to suck or spitting where she ought to swallow. But over the years her relief had been replaced by feelings of boredom and disillusionment. Akin to unblocking the plugholes and taking out the rubbish, sex had become yet another chore she performed to keep GL happy. But perhaps it was time for a change. Perhaps that was what had been behind his recent consternation – he had secretly been longing for her to become more animated in bed.

She thought of Lana letting rip in the Le Caprice and felt a drop of confidence trickle its way inside her. If Lana was able to fake orgasms in front of a restaurant full of A-listers, and on the telephone to complete strangers, then surely she, Sadie, could conjure one up for her boyfriend. Sadie took a deep breath, closed her eyes and let out a little moan. Completely oblivious, GL kept pounding away, muttering, 'Come to daddy,' over and over like a mantra in her ear.

'Oh yes,' Sadie whispered. 'That's so good.' But rather than the words flowing from her lips like molten chocolate, they squeaked out in staccato beeps.

'What did you say?' GL asked, abruptly ceasing his humping and wiping the sweat from his blotchy brow.

Sadie's face flushed. 'Oh nothing, it doesn't matter. Carry on.'

'You did, I heard you. You said, "that's so" something.'

'Good,' Sadie muttered, mortified. 'I said, that's so good.'

'What's so good?'

'It is. You are.'

'Oh babes!'

Sadie felt GL quiver as he resumed his pounding. She gritted her teeth and braced herself for the onslaught.

'Tell me again. What am I?'

'You're so good,' Sadie stuttered, wishing that the carpet would just open up and swallow her whole.

'But am I the best? Am I the best fuck you ever had?'

Sadie shuddered. Rather than open up and swallow her whole, she felt as if the carpet had transported her magically to the set of one of those God-awful soft porn videos that Vince insisted upon stocking in the shop. Like *Debbie Does Dallas*, Sadie was doing Ruislip Manor.

'Yes, you're the best,' she whispered – and it wasn't a lie, it was just that GL also happened to be the only lover she had ever had.

GL let out a strangulated yelp, shouted, 'Ger-fucking-ronimo!' and collapsed on top of her. 'Thanks babes, I needed that,' he said, before rolling off and leaping to his feet, the used condom dangling like a latex teat from his limp penis. 'I'm just going to jump in the shower. Be an angel and make me a Lemsip.'

So that was what had been at the root of his bad mood of earlier. Sadie had been selfish and neglectful – spending the night with another man, being unresponsive in bed – and it had almost cost her her relationship, not to mention the roof over her head. Well, not any more. As Sadie staggered to her feet and fumbled behind the sofa for her knickers she resolved that from now on things were going to change. *She* was going to change. She was going to fake orgasms with the best of them and GL would never have cause to dump her ever again.

Chapter Eighteen

Terry had been dreaming about revenge. Literally. For the eight hours or so he had been asleep – and while the rest of the world went about its daily business his subconscious had been staging a montage of increasingly bloody acts, starring him as swarthy avenger – armed rather bizarrely with an industrial-size can of meatballs and accompanied by an unfeasibly buxom blonde sidekick. Not one of his enemies had escaped his wrath, from the cross-eyed control freak who had made his life hell in his first foster home, to Mandy at Manor Cars who met a particularly sticky end, drowning in a vat of gravy.

But as Terry started to come to, realising it had all been a dream and that his head was actually buried between a pair of pillows rather than breasts, his spirits began to sink. Nothing had changed. He was still Terry Leggett, loser extraordinaire, not a hero like Robert De Niro, or Hulk Hogan. He had no money, no family, no place of his own – and even worse, he had no job. Terry couldn't bear being out of work. It did his head in, all that sitting around watching crap TV. It gave a bloke too much time to think – and Terry was a doer, not a thinker. If he sat too long in one place his skin began to crawl like there were a million ants scrambling about all over him, eating away at him, until they finally burrowed inside his brain to torment him from within and not even the promise of a night of topless darts on *Men and Motors* could ease his woes.

Terry sat up and squinted at the illuminated display on his clock radio. He'd acquired it from his mate Rancid Ron down at Wembley market for a bargain two pounds fifty. The only problem was that the top part of the display didn't light up, which could prove pretty tricky when trying to ascertain the time, especially if you'd had a skinful the night before. From what Terry could make out it was either 1:05 or 7:05. He scratched his head and pondered. Judging by the pitch darkness enveloping his room, he deduced that the hour had to be seven. Too late to find himself a job so he'd settle instead for a video – he knew Sadie would give him a tab. Not like that jobs-worth little shit in the mini-mart. Terry smirked as he recalled a flashback from his dream in which he meatballed Taj to death before cramming his corpse on top of the out-of-date TV dinners stored in his chest freezer.

Terry leaned over to turn on the faded Arsenal lamp beside his bed, but the sight that greeted him made him want to bury his head right back under the duvet in despair. Dirty dishes, piled on (and probably stuck to) the window sill, overflowing ashtrays strategically placed so that there was never one more than an arms length away, mugs containing coffee-based cultures in various stages of cultivation and clothes strewn all over the floor. Terry picked up the pair of boxer shorts nearest the bed and gave the crotch a sniff.

'Jesus!' he exclaimed, flinging them back down in disgust. They smelt like an extremely potent packet of cheese and onion crisps. Wrapping the duvet around his wiry and completely naked frame, Terry clambered out of bed in search of more pants. There was little point looking in the MFI chest of drawers leaning precariously against the bed. For a start the handles had all fallen off and secondly he only had about three pairs of kecks to his name and he couldn't remember the last time he'd paid a visit to the launderette. He

gingerly rifled through the jumbled mass of t-shirts, jumpers
and trousers until he came upon another pair. Bright tartan,
they had never been his favourites, but they had been free
(abandoned in the tumble drier by a previous customer) and
at this point in time he was hardly in a position to be fussy.
Terry held the pants up to his nose and sniffed, a little more
cautiously this time.

'Bleedin' 'ell!' Recoiling in disgust, Terry hurled them into
the far corner of the room where they managed to attach
themselves to the cigar being brandished by his prized bust
of Winston Churchill (nine pounds ninety nine, courtesy of
Rancid Ron). This pair seemed to smell of smoky bacon.
What was going on here? Why did his pants smell like a
Walkers selection pack? Deciding to not even bother trying
to locate his remaining pair – he didn't think he could
stomach a whiff of prawn cocktail – Terry opened his door
and leant out. The flat was steeped in darkness. Gathering
the duvet about his shoulders, Terry tiptoed along the hall
and cautiously opened the door to Liam's bedroom. As he
turned on the cluster of spotlights Terry frowned. It didn't
make sense. How could a geezer living on his own keep the
place so tidy? Okay, so there was a stray sock on top of the
tower of LPs by the door and the huge oak-framed bed was
unmade, but other than that Terry could have been standing
in a bird's bedroom, what with the coordinated green colour
scheme and the carefully arranged wooden artefacts adorning
the ornately carved shelves.

Still, at least he knew that, as with a bird's room, there was
bound to be a well-stocked underwear drawer. Terry cast his
duvet on to the floor and padded over to the fitted cupboards
lining the far wall. One by one he pulled out the drawers until
he finally found what he was looking for – a veritable pants
fest. Plumping for a pair of Calvin Klein briefs – after all if
he was going to wear 'hot' pants he might as well do it in

style – Terry couldn't help giving them a cursory sniff. To his immense relief they smelt nothing like crisps and just like washing detergent. He let out a contented sigh.

'What do you think you're doing?'

Terry turned to see Liam standing in the doorway, his mouth agape and eyes aghast.

'Okay, babes, I'd better love you and leave you.' GL said with a sigh, as he adjusted Sadie's bandana.

Sadie smiled as she let him out from behind the counter. She couldn't remember spending a more pleasant day in his company. Not since the early days at university had things felt so relaxed between them.

When GL had woken up to find precious little improvement in his facial sores he had decided to call in sick. And although it seemed horrible to delight in someone else's misfortune, Sadie couldn't help wishing he were ill a little more often. He just seemed so cuddly and affectionate all of a sudden. Vulnerable, almost. She was seriously contemplating replacing his vast stocks of ginseng, Echinacea and other herbal elixirs with dummy pills such was the transformation in his character.

'I don't know what I'd do without you,' he'd whispered in her ear, causing Sadie to radiate happiness. At last the self-sufficient, self-motivated GL actually needed her for something. Like fast-forward footage of a blossoming flower, she could feel herself begin to unfurl with pride; a process that had been going on all day.

'You take the first shower,' he'd said. 'I suppose I ought to make an appointment with the quack.'

When he hadn't been able to get a doctor's appointment until the following day he'd actually offered to come to work with her – after ensuring that she would lend him her magic-concealer to camouflage his blemishes first. They'd spent the whole afternoon snuggled behind the counter, munching on toasted Mighty White, watching assorted weepies and reminiscing about Uni.

'Do you remember that first term, when we used to sleep all day and have breakfast in bed watching *Countdown*?' Sadie asked, as she waited for *Terms of Endearment* to rewind.

'Yeah, and I always massacred you on the conundrum,' GL replied with a chortle, before setting off to find the cover for *Love Story*.

Since watching *Philadelphia* the previous day some kind of emotional floodgate seemed to have opened inside GL, leaving him with an unquenchable thirst for Hollywood melodrama. Sadie had even caught sight of a beige-streaked tear rolling down his face at one point. But when she had asked if he was okay, GL had simply gathered her to him and rested his spiky head upon her shoulder.

'As long as I've got you, babes. As long as I've got you.'

Every time Sadie thought things couldn't get any better, GL would spring something else upon her.

'You've done all right in this place, you know,' he'd said at one point, gesturing at the shop. 'Considering the shite stock and the fact that you've had no training in creating displays. My very own Captain Pugwash.' And he'd pinged her eyepatch playfully.

But the icing on the cake, the fairy on the tree, had to be when he invited her to his work's Christmas do.

'The tight-wads have it every January to keep the costs down,' he'd explained, showing her an orange embossed invite to the Brentford Office Fancy Dress Party (theme – Hollywood Musical) at the Trusthouse Forte, Greenford. It had been arranged for the following Saturday. 'I suppose you'll be working, though,' he'd added wistfully.

'Well, I'm meant to be,' Sadie replied, her brain going into overdrive. GL had never invited her to a work's party before.

In fact, she'd been led to believe that partners were strictly off limits, not '*more than welcome*' as the invite indicated. Who would she go as? What would she say? How would she possibly fit in with all of those highflying sales types? Sadie took a deep breath and told herself not to be so stupid. After all, wasn't she out dining with Joan Collins only two days previously? Not only had she lunched at one of London's most salubrious restaurants, she had also been banned for life. For all Sadie knew she and Lana could be featured in next week's *Heat* magazine under the banner, *Boisterous Belch Ruins Joanie's Brunch*. A night at the Trusthouse Forte, Greenford should be a veritable breeze by comparison.

'I'll see if I can get Brian to cover my shift,' she had replied with a smile.

And she was still smiling as she booked out *The Champ* for GL. Things were definitely starting to look up. She had a new friend and her relationship was finally back on track – it seemed hard to believe she had been so dejected only a few days before. So dejected she had ended up seeking solace in ludicrous dreams of another man. Sadie shuddered.

'Will you be all right making your own way back tonight?' GL asked as he pulled up the hood on his sweatshirt and prepared to leave. 'It's just that I don't think I'll be up to coming out in the cold again today and I want to get an early night before I see the doc tomorrow.'

'Of course I'll be all right,' Sadie replied. She'd been all right every other night she'd locked up and walked home alone, hadn't she? Still, it was nice of GL to think to ask. 'You go home and take it easy. Are you sure you want to watch *The Champ* though? Wouldn't you prefer something a bit more light-hearted? How about *Police Academy*?'

'Nah, this'll be fine, babes,' GL replied with a bit of a grimace. 'I'm not really in the mood for slapstick. I'll see you later.'

No sooner had GL left the shop than Lana appeared, displaying a similarly tortured expression upon her face.

'Are you okay?' Sadie enquired, pleased to see her new friend and yet concerned at her less than radiant appearance.

'I've been better, honey, put it that way.' Lana replied with a frown as she approached the counter. Her hair seemed rigid and lifeless, like a home-made doll whose curls had been fashioned out of pipe cleaners, and there was a sallowness about her complexion not even her heavily rouged cheeks or the huge ruby choker, glinting at the base of her neck, could disguise.

'Oh God, I feel awful. I shouldn't have been so nosey yesterday, asking all those questions about your past. I'm sorry.' Sadie said, horrified at the thought that she may have triggered some kind of post-traumatic stress disorder in Lana.

'Oh don't be so silly, 'Lana retorted, grabbing on to the counter with a rather unsteady hand. 'My current malaise has nothing to do with what we discussed yesterday – although I must admit our conversation did leave me a little shaken. No, I think I must have been stricken by some kind of stomach bug – gastric influenza perhaps. I've been getting the most unbearable cramps and feeling quite light-headed all day. I only came out because I'd run out of painkillers.'

'Here,' Sadie said, pointing to the chair next to hers behind the counter. 'Why don't you come round and take a seat? I'll make us a cup of tea.'

'Oh, are you sure? I wouldn't want to get you into trouble.'

As Lana gazed at her in anticipation, Sadie couldn't help notice something odd about her eyes. The whites were displaying a definite yellowish tinge, as if nicotine stained. Sadie hastily raised the flap at the end of the counter and beckoned her to come through. 'It's fine, honestly – my boss doesn't get back until next week. You come and take the weight off your feet and I'll make us a cup of tea.'

'Did someone say tea? Here, Liam, how's that for timing?'

Sadie and Lana looked up to see Terry march into the shop, a dishevelled-looking Liam trailing in his wake.

'Well, well,' said Lana with a smirk. 'If it isn't my taxi driver from the other night. Tell me, have you figured out where your gear stick is yet?' And she fixed Terry with a piercing stare.

'Oh, I know where me gear stick is all right – it's you Yanks who needs the practice.' Terry stuffed his fists into the pockets of his jeans and swaggered over to the counter. Hopefully the stuck-up cow would see the designer label pants protruding over the top.

'So, what's with the underpants over the trousers look? Don't tell me you're trying to recreate a scene from *Superman*?' Lana sneered.

Sadie giggled. Terry had on the most gargantuan pair of pants, pulled up so high over the top of his jeans, and even worse, his jumper, that they practically encased his entire ribcage. 'If you are then don't ask me to be your Lois Lane.' she said with a smirk.

Liam, who until now had been lurking around the Kids' Section, began to trudge over. 'Is it a bird? Is it a plane? No, it's Superpan – t!' he exclaimed, at which everybody, including Liam, groaned. 'Sorry, it's been a long day,' he explained.

Sadie smiled as she watched Liam raise his hands in mock surrender. It obviously had been a long day; judging by his appearance he had come straight from work. His hair, tied back in a loose ponytail, was flecked with what looked like wood shavings and his face and hands were streaked brown. She felt a strange fluttering sensation in the pit of her stomach

– or perhaps it was lower down. Sadie sprung to her feet. 'I'll just get the kettle on,' she muttered, horrified at her body for such an act of betrayal, not to mention harlotry.

When she got back from the kitchen with a tray full of steaming mugs she found the others engrossed in a discussion about the scenes they wanted to recreate.

'Oh God, you're not still talking about that, are you?' Sadie groaned. 'I was hoping that conversation had all been part of some horrible dream – along with limbo dancing to Status Quo,' she added, casting a sideways grin at Liam.

Liam turned away, his face flushed. 'Where's your sense of adventure,' he muttered, scuffing his foot upon the floor.

'Yeah, come on girl, live a little,' Terry piped up, grabbing one of the teas. 'It'll be a right laugh. The whole film world is our lobster. I quite fancy doing one out of *Bonnie and Clyde*,' he confided, helping himself to one of Lana's cigarettes.

'You're kidding,' she retorted. 'Don't you think a bank job might be a little out of your league, honey? Perhaps you ought to just stick to lifting other people's smokes.' Lana grabbed her cigarette case from the counter and stuffed it into her bag.

Terry snorted and looked at Liam. 'A little out of my league, she says! Ought to stick to pinching cigs! That's like telling Evil Knievel he'd be better off riding a scooter. Do you have any idea who I am?' he asked, hands on Calvin Klein clad hips.

'I could hazard a guess,' Lana replied. Her eyes were beginning to spark back into life, Sadie noted with relief.

'I am – or rather I was, until Her Majesty requested the pleasure,' Terry paused for dramatic effect and a drag on his cig, '—The Basildon Bandit a.k.a, also known as, The Prime Sinister.'

Lana and Sadie stared at Terry blankly, whilst Liam cleared his throat.

'The Prime Sinister?' Lana enquired, her voice laden with sarcasm.

'Yep, that's right. Ringing any bells is it?'

'Hmm – only alarm bells,' Lana muttered to Sadie. 'So tell me, Prime Sinister, when was the last time you saw your shrink?'

Terry nudged Liam in the ribs and grinned knowingly. 'She don't believe me, Liam. Obviously you're not an avid viewer of *Crimewatch*, sweetheart, otherwise you'd know only too well what I was on about. For nearly two months I terrorised the building societies of Essex, armed only with me pump action water pistol and me John Major mask. If it hadn't been for that old biddy flooring me with her motorised shopping trolley, I'd probably still be at it today. So don't you go telling me *Bonnie and Clyde*'s out of my league. Anyway, for your information, it ain't a bank I've got me sights on.'

Observing Liam's pained expression, Sadie could barely contain the urge to laugh. 'Who have you got your sights set on, then? I can tell you now not to bother with this place – we've only got about two pounds sixty in the safe,' she said.

'Don't be silly, Treacle – I wouldn't dream of doing this place over, not even when that donut Brian's working. Golden rule of organised crime – never shit on your own doorstep. No, I want to get that twat in the mini-mart.'

'Now you're talking,' Lana said with a chortle. Every time she went in there, the price of vodka seemed to have gone up. Taj was currently asking two whole pounds more for a litre of Smirnoff than Tescos.

'So what exactly are you going to do?' Sadie asked, suddenly troubled by the prospect of Nick Ross unveiling her photo-fit to the nation. Could she already be classed as an accessory to the crime?

'I dunno yet,' Terry replied. 'I'm going to get the video out tonight and study it for inspiration. How about you others, have you had any ideas for your scenes?'

Lana shook her head and shrugged her shoulders. 'To be truthful I hadn't given it a lot of thought – other things on my mind,' and she glanced at Sadie, 'But I have to say you've certainly got me thinking. It would be a wonderful opportunity to have a little fun. I guess I'd better do a bit of viewing over the next few days too.'

'Well, I've got mine sorted,' Liam announced, heading to the drama section.

'Oh?' Sadie said, failing miserably to conceal her curiosity. 'What is it? What are you going to do?'

Liam returned and placed a copy of *Mutiny on the Bounty* upon the counter. 'There you go,' he declared, almost defiantly.

Terry began to guffaw and leant over the counter to tap Lana on the shoulder. 'And you think *I'm* radio rental,' he bellowed. 'So tell me, son, what exactly is it you're planning here? Thinking of staging an uprising on a P&O ferry are we? Mutiny on the Booze Cruise is it?'

Liam's face flushed as he met Sadie's bewildered stare. 'No – I'm not going to stage a mutiny, but I am going to re-enact Fletcher Christian's journey to Pitcairn Island.'

A shocked silence fell upon the group.

Terry was the first to break it. 'Are you sure?'

To Sadie's dismay, Liam nodded, his jaw clenched in determination.

Terry scratched his head. 'But Pitcairn Island, that's right down by Australia ain't it?'

'New Zealand,' Liam corrected. 'That's where I'm flying into and then I'll have to hitch a ride on a boat.'

Lana whistled. 'Boy, you sound like you've got it all mapped out.'

'I have. I went and booked the tickets yesterday. I'm leaving next month. Don't worry, Tel, I'll probably only be gone for a few weeks and of course I'll be needing a flat-sitter.'

Terry's expression lifted slightly at the prospect of uninhibited nights of porn and uninterrupted pillaging sprees, but then he remembered the previous year when Liam had buggered off to Asia for what seemed like an eternity. The truth was, despite his bird-like obsession for neatness, he had missed having Liam around. Terry attempted a feeble grin. 'No problem, son, I'll make sure the place stays ship-shape.'

'Sadie, honey, these boys are putting us to shame. Please tell me you've thought of a scene,' Lana beseeched as she removed a compact from her bag and gave her face a liberal coating of powder.

'Yes, I have,' Sadie replied. 'I've just got to nip to the loo, and then I'll give you the details.'

Sadie couldn't get out of the shop quick enough. Her head was reeling from Liam's news. Why did he have to pick a scene set on the other side of the world? Why couldn't he have chosen something from an Ealing Comedy or some obscure film set in Ruislip – there had to be one in existence. And why was she so bothered by it anyway? She perched on the icy cold porcelain and waited as slowly but surely the cold seeped into her body and shocked her back to her senses. Liam's life had nothing to do with her. She hardly even knew him – although after their marathon conversation of the other night/morning this didn't quite ring true. But the fact was she had a boyfriend, with whom she was more than happy, especially since his unexpected disfigurement. Hastily recalling her enjoyable day with GL, Sadie got to her feet and adjusted her scabbard. The notion she had been toying with all afternoon now seemed like the ideal solution. Not only would she have a scene to re-enact, but she would hopefully give her relationship a welcome boost into the bargain.

'I've decided to re-enact a scene from *Grease*,' she announced, upon her return to the shop.

'Now there's a surprise,' Lana said, arching one eyebrow. 'Don't tell me, you're going to have a sleepover and perform, 'Look at me, I'm Sandra Dee'.'

'No,' Sadie replied, tartly. 'I'm going to re-enact the final scene.'

'What, the one where Sandy turns *bad*?' Lana enquired, unable to disguise her obvious shock.

'The one where she wears that black leather number and you can see her knockers?' Terry asked with a grin. 'Nice one.'

'Yes. Although obviously I'm not actually going to re-enact it at a graduation day.'

'Where are you going to do it then?' Liam enquired casually – or so he hoped.

'Well, my boyfriend, GL is having an office party next Saturday and the theme is Hollywood musicals. He thinks I've got to work, but I thought I'd surprise him and arrive unannounced, all made up to look like Sandy from *Grease*. I'll probably need your help with the makeover part,' she said to Lana. 'I thought I'd get the deejay to play 'You're the One That I Want,' especially for us. What do you think?'

Once again a deathly silence fell upon the group and once again Terry was the first to break it. 'I think it's a blinding idea, Treacle, and if you need any help getting into your outfit you know where to come.'

'You come straight to me, that's where,' Lana said sternly. From the little she had garnered about Sadie's relationship with Mr Newport Pagnell she couldn't help but feel a terrible sense of foreboding about Sadie's idea, not to mention surprise. Quite frankly she couldn't see the timid little mite having the balls to vamp it up in the privacy of her own bedroom, let alone on a crowded dance-floor. Still, it would be fun to give her a makeover, and a bit of slap and a pair of six inch heels certainly never harmed a girl's confidence. 'By the time I've finished with you, hon, he'll be eating out of your hand. Now then, I'd better get a few films of my own out – it seems I've got a bit of catching up to do.'

As Sadie booked out the others' videos she felt a steely determination begin to grip hold of her. Just as GL appeared to be mirroring Danny Zuko's transformation from cockney wide-boy to sensitive soul so she intended to transform herself into the orgasm-faking, leather-clad babe of his dreams, and ensure that from now on she would always be the one that he wanted.

Chapter Nineteen

'Of course I still want you, babes.' GL propped his mobile phone between his ear and his shoulder and ripped open his prescription package. 'No, I'm not avoiding you. It's just that I've had this bleeding skin complaint, haven't I, and I've had to lay low for a couple of days.' GL fished the tube of ointment from the bag and unscrewed the lid. 'I've just got back from the doc's and he reckons it's some kind of allergic reaction. He's given me this anti-histamine cream to put on it.' Adjusting his position in front of the hall mirror, GL carefully began applying dabs of white ointment to the angry red blotches covering his face. 'You know what I think it was? I think it was that aftershave you got me for Christmas. Well, it makes sense doesn't it? The first time I wore it was when you gave it to me at the sales course and bingo, the very next morning me face goes into one.' GL examined his polka-dot skin and sighed. He hadn't looked this rough since he was stricken with acne at the onset of puberty and his mother had had to blitz his zits with toothpaste. 'No, don't worry babes, you weren't to know. I guess my skin just isn't used to that cheap stuff. It always has been pretty sensitive – a bit like me really. Ha!'

Although the carnage that had been wreaked upon his complexion was not really a laughing matter, GL was so relieved that he hadn't been diagnosed with AIDS he found it impossible to get in a strop. In fact, since leaving the doctor's surgery he hadn't stopped grinning. He had almost bought a copy of *The Big Issue* from the tramp outside the station – until he realised it cost one pound twenty. He might be happy, but he wasn't insane. 'Yeah, I'm missing you too, babes, especially after Tuesday night. I certainly got you going, didn't I, eh? Listen, how about we take up where we left off at the Brentford do next Saturday? – Nah, she's got to work. – Yeah, Hollywood musicals. – Fuck knows. I don't know why they couldn't have done Hollywood action heroes, we could have gone as Rocky and Adrienne, ha ha! All right then babes, better love you and leave you. Yeah, I'll catch up with you in the office. Laters.'

GL flipped his mobile shut and bounded into the living room. He was in just the mood for a bit of Sly Stallone. *Rocky 4* ought to do the trick – the bit where he gave that Russki a good hiding was one of the best moments in cinematic history. GL grimaced as he removed *The Champ* from the VCR. A brush with death obviously did funny things to a bloke. The sooner Sadie took all that mushy crap back to her shop the better. At the thought of Sadie, GL gave another grimace. What was he thinking of yesterday, opening up to her like that? Now she'd probably be all over him – like a rash. GL chortled to himself; God, he was on form today. Shame he wasn't back at work really, he'd probably cream his targets. Still – at least Sadie was out shopping, not running around after him like some eager-to-please puppy. Why the hell had he given her two hundred quid for her birthday anyway? That exercise bike he'd got her for Christmas should have been enough. The trouble with Sadie was if you gave her an inch she wanted a mile – sometimes her neediness made him want to puke. At barely five feet two, GL had learnt long ago that life was all about survival of the fittest, and yet there was something about Sadie and her dependence upon him that also gave him a bit of a sick thrill. She was like a motorway pile-up, stomach-turning and yet strangely tantalising all at the same time.

GL got to his feet and puffed out his over-pumped chest. '*I am the greatest!*' he declared in his finest Mohammed Ali before attempting to moonwalk over to his leather-bound *Rocky* collection.

Sadie pulled up the zip on the unfeasibly tight leather trousers and thanked God that the shop she was in had individual rather than communal changing rooms. She felt ridiculous. It wasn't that the trousers didn't fit. They did, perfectly, maybe a little too perfectly around the crotch area. It was just that they weren't *her*. But then they weren't supposed to be her, were they? They were supposed to be Sandy from *Grease*. *She* was supposed to be Sandy from *Grease*.

'Cooeey! Is anyone home?' A voice trilled from the other side of the curtain.

Sadie jumped. What the hell did they want?

'Can you do me a favour?' The voice enquired, so close to the crack in the curtain that Sadie could smell the cigarette fumes on the owner's breath. With a hefty sigh, she pulled back the curtain to reveal the most extraordinary sight. A huge, semi-naked woman stood before her, her breasts drooping over the cups of her greying bra like two lumps of suet and a leather thong slicing into her fleshy hips like a pastry cutter. Gathered in a ring around her ankles lay some kind of leopard skin garment.

'I don't suppose you could zip me up, could you, lover?'

'Oh. Yes, sure,' Sadie replied, stepping from her cubicle.

'Nice trousers,' the woman commented, hoisting her leopard skin number over her hips. 'Very classy.'

Sadie smiled. 'Thanks. Nice – er, dress?'

As the woman jostled the garment over her errant breasts it was hard to tell whether it was a dress or indeed a boob tube. It left absolutely nothing to the imagination, not even the rampant bikini line, Sadie noted with horror.

'Yeah – I'm looking for something for me wedding anniversary.' The woman paused from her grappling to grip Sadie's arm, 'It'll be twenty-five years this Sunday. To be honest I never thought we'd see twenty-five days, what with him screwing that bingo caller on our honeymoon, but somehow we've got to a quarter of a century, so I thought I ought to make a bit of an effort. Okay love, zip her up.'

Sadie pulled cautiously on the zip, trying hard not to nip the mounds of flesh that were making a desperate bid for freedom. 'There you go,' she said, as she finally managed to yank the zipper up to the top.

'Well – what do you think?' the woman enquired, giving a little twirl. 'Saucy or what?'

'Yes, it's lovely,' Sadie lied, but as she watched the woman pouting and purring at her reflection she couldn't help feeling a little reassured. If her fellow shopper could look in the mirror and see Liz Hurley rather than Les Dawson, then surely she, Sadie, could look in the mirror and see Sandy from *Grease*.

Chapter Twenty

Unfortunately, by the day of the party all Sadie saw when she looked in the mirror was a nervous little girl playing dressing-up. As she studied the slightly skew-whiff wig, the worryingly errant boob-tube and the sky-scraping stilettos she couldn't help feeling as if she'd just raided her mother's wardrobe. Not that her mother's wardrobe had ever contained anything remotely skin-tight, strapless or spike-heeled, but the point was, rather than making her feel grown-up, her outfit simply made her feel like a huge impostor. Or rather a tiny, weenie, impostor. Sadie kicked off her shoes and sighed. Why oh why couldn't she have been born with Lana's style and poise? Not to mention her stature.

With just ten hours to go until the party began, Sadie's dress rehearsal was making her more anxious than ever. It certainly hadn't helped that GL's new-found attentiveness seemed to have faded along with his blemishes and she had barely seen him all week. What with her twelve hour shifts (Vince was back from Sardinia and had demanded a complete stock check of the shop) and GL working late to catch up on the time he had had off sick, they had communicated more via post-it notes than verbally.

Gone golfing with the lads, this morning's message had informed her. *Going straight to bash after and kipping at Wilko's, so don't wait up*. Sadie could have kicked herself for not waking up before GL had left. Then she would have been able to tell him of her plan and they could have gone to the party together. She was beginning to dread the prospect of arriving unannounced. What if GL was looking forward to a night with the lads? What if nobody else had invited their partners? But GL had invited her; the *invitation* had invited her. He wouldn't have shown it to her if he hadn't wanted her to come. And besides the whole point of the exercise was to introduce the element of surprise and excitement into their relationship. As Sadie yanked off her wig and reached for her pirate's outfit, she only hoped it was surprise and excitement she would be bringing to the party, rather than shock and horror.

Shock was certainly the order of the day when, two hours later, halfway through Sadie's cataloguing of the Action Adventure Section (she had no idea Jackie Chan had made so many movies) Terry arrived clad in full biker regalia. He looked like a cross between Lemmy from Motorhead and Olive from *On the Buses*, with his scuffed leather jacket and outsized riding goggles.

'Here, Treacle, have you got any copies of *Easy Rider*?' he enquired, swaggering into the middle of the store where he paused to light a roll-up.

Sadie put down her notepad and pen and smiled. 'Yeah, sure. That's if Brian hasn't taken it out again. I'll just check. Got time for a cuppa?'

Terry frowned and studied his watch. 'All right, just a quick one, mind. I don't want to be late for me first day at work.'

'You've got a new job? That's brilliant. What is it?' Sadie asked, hurrying behind the counter to put the kettle on.

'I'd rather not divulge that particular piece of information at this moment in time. Not until me contract's been sorted.'

As Sadie rustled up the tea she pondered Terry's latest career move – it was very unlike him to be so coy, and what on earth was the biker's gear all about?

When she got back to the counter Terry was studying the cover of *Easy Rider*, his goggles pushed up on to the top of his head, and was humming 'Born to be Wild' under his breath.

'It's all right, Treacle, I found it. Here, I've been thinking of growing me hair into a mullet, what do you reckon?'

Sadie stifled a giggle. 'Hmm. Well, it would be interesting . . . and if velour jogging suits can make a comeback I don't see why the mullet can't. What's going on, Terry? Why this change of image all of a sudden? I didn't even know you had a bike.'

'I don't. At least not yet.' Terry tapped the side of his nose and gave Sadie a knowing nod. 'Don't worry, you'll know soon enough.'

'This isn't to do with what we were talking about the other night, is it? You're not getting involved in anything dodgy?' Once again, Sadie was plagued with the image of a sombre-faced Nick Ross addressing the nation.

And as with so many underworld crimes, the brutal robbery of the Ruislip Manor Mini-Mart was orchestrated by a matriarchal figure. Cracking under the pressure of intense police interrogation, the accused, one Terrence Leggett, confessed that he had been led astray by his local video store manageress, Sadie Jones – or Treacle, as he likes to call her.

Sadie pictured a photo-fit of herself, complete with menacing eye-patch, flickering on to the screen, whilst Nick Ross shook his head soberly and urged the viewers not to have nightmares.

Terry's chesty guffaw brought her crashing back to reality – or at least a reality of sorts. 'Nah – a job like that takes planning, timing, casing. I won't be doing my scene for a few weeks yet. Not like you and young Liam.'

'I thought Liam wasn't doing his until next month.'

'Well, that was supposed to be the plan, but now he's on

about bringing it forward. Do you know what, sometimes I worry about that lad, I really do.'

'What do you mean?' Sadie was baffled and she couldn't help wondering how Liam would feel if he knew Terry was worrying about him. Extremely worried, she presumed.

'Well, always roaming off about the place, never able to settle down. I call him the wanderer,' on cue Terry launched into a round of Status Quo.

'Yeah, but surely that isn't anything to worry about,' Sadie butted in at the earliest opportunity. 'At least he's out there living his life, experiencing the world, having adventures,' she mused, gazing wistfully towards the shop window.

Terry frowned. 'There's living your life and there's trying to escape it. Sometimes it's hard to tell the difference. You got any biscuits?'

'I don't understand. What would Liam be trying to escape from?' Sadie asked as she fetched the remains of her Christmas selection box from beneath the counter. 'It seems to me like he's got it all – his own business, his own flat.' A gorgeous body, a voice from somewhere inside her head couldn't help adding. The voice of her *Crimewatch* alter ego, no doubt.

'Well now, that's not really for me to say,' Terry replied, solemnly. 'He ain't happy though, you mark my words.'

As Sadie marked Terry's words she couldn't help feeling a little concerned. Not only for Liam, but for herself. Why was it that lately any sign of another's misfortune seemed to fill her with reassurance? Firstly GL's skin disorder and now this. Although she felt worried for Liam she couldn't help feeling more than a little comforted by the thought that maybe his life wasn't so perfect after all. But why?

'But why?' she asked Terry, trying desperately to edit any sense of urgency out of her voice.

Yet again, Terry remained uncharacteristically coy. 'It really ain't my place to say, Treacle.' He dunked a custard cream into his tea and crammed it into his mouth. 'Shumtimes, figs ain wah vay zeem.'

'What?'

Terry took a swig of tea. 'I said – sometimes things ain't what they seem. Sometimes the most popular bloke in the world can also be the loneliest. You ask that Robbie Williams geezer, or Wacko Jacko – they'll know what I'm on about. Anyway, it's time this cowboy hit the road.' Terry pulled his goggles back down and adjusted his leather jacket. 'Good luck tonight, Treacle – or should I say, Olivia Neutron Bomb. He's a lucky fella that boyfriend of yours, you knock him dead. And if you need any help getting into your clobber I'm only upstairs.'

Like a child let loose in a Pick 'n' Mix section, Lana grabbed two indigestion tablets and three aspirin from the mounds before her on the coffee table and stuffed them into her mouth. Taking a huge swig from her bottle of vodka, she slumped back on to the chaise longue and closed her eyes. She felt completely out of it. From the moment she had awoken she'd been suffering from the most unimaginable cramps in her stomach and pounding in her head and over the course of the day it had just got worse. Her entire body seemed to be seizing up on her, torturing her with wave upon wave of pain, completely immune to any form of medication. To make matters worse, Sadie was due to arrive at any moment for her 'Sandy' makeover. Lana had had enough of a struggle applying her own make-up, let alone somebody else's. Her hands were shaking so much she'd nearly blinded herself twice with her eyeliner and she'd completely shattered her compact when she'd dropped it on the floor. Lana couldn't help giving a wry smile at the prospect of the seven years bad luck that would now befall her. 'How the hell am I going to tell the difference?' she'd enquired into the broken mirror and then recoiled as she caught sight of her jaundiced skin and bleary eyes. With the crack from the mirror forming a jagged scar across her reflection, the ominous picture was complete. It was then that Lana had felt the first traces of fear creep into her body, tingling its way up her arms and legs and gathering at the ends of her spine before converging upon her chest, where it took hold like a vice. Consumed with panic, she finally allowed herself to acknowledge what was happening. *As ye sow, so shall reap ye,* she could just hear her parents hissing at her over the tops of their bibles, like some God-awful scene from *Carrie*. It was then that she had decided to get pissed, but even the vodka seemed to be letting her down, failing to numb the pain or the panic.

The doorbell's chimes shattered the silence like a hammer blow to glass and Lana brought her hand to her heart and gasped. 'Get a grip, girl,' she scolded herself as she shuffled into the hallway and fumbled with the lock.

'Sadie, honey, come on in,' she heard herself cry, but her voice sounded crackly and thin, as if it were coming down a long distance telephone wire.

Sadie gusted into the hall, practically pumping adrenalin. 'Hi. Oh God, Lana, I am *so* nervous. I don't know why I suggested doing this scene. I think GL is looking forward to a night with the lads and I've got this awful feeling that my turning up is going to be a complete disaster. And then there's the wig. I can't get it to stay on straight; it seems really loose. I don't know if you've got any tips. Have you ever worn a wig before? I thought that maybe in your previous line of work? And I'm really not sure about the trousers – they are *so* tight. Mind you, there was a woman in the shop and I swear she looked just like Les Dawson in drag – are you familiar with Les Dawson? Famous, overweight comedian from the seventies and eighties, dead now? Anyway, she was trying on this skin-tight leopard skin number that was at least two sizes too small, but she was so confident it made me realise that life's all about attitude rather than appearance, isn't it? So I've just got to have a bit more confidence in myself and I'll be fine. Have you got any vodka, by the way? Blimey, it's a bit dark in here, isn't it? Is everything okay?'

To Lana's relief Sadie finally shut up, and like a spent tornado collapsed in a heap into an armchair.

'I'm fine, honey, just fine. Now, let me fix you a drink. Did you bring the movie?'

Sadie fished her new *Grease* DVD from her bag and passed it to Lana. 'But what are all those pills for? You're not still sick, are you?'

Lana nodded as she inserted the DVD into the machine and pressed play. 'Just a touch of indigestion, that's all, nothing to worry about.'

Thankfully Sadie's arrival seemed to work where the vodka and painkillers had failed; within minutes Lana's own panic had subsided and even her stomach cramps had dispersed into a dull bloated sensation; the girl was nervous enough for the both of them.

'Take a chill pill, honey. You're going to do fine,' Lana soothed, upon attempting to manicure Sadie's trembling fingernails.

'Sure. Which ones are the chill pills?' Sadie asked, gesturing to the miniature pyramids of pharmaceuticals on the coffee table, at which point they both dissolved into fits of laughter.

'Don't you worry, by the time I've finished with you you'll make Olivia Newton John look like an old trout,' Lana purred, gesturing dismissively towards the television screen, before tentatively applying a coat of ultra translucent foundation to Sadie's already ultra translucent complexion. Her hands seemed far steadier now; either that or they were simply quivering in perfect harmony with Sadie. 'DM won't know what's hit him.'

'GL,' Sadie corrected.

'Sorry. GL. What does that stand for anyways?'

'Gary Lee. He insists on being called GL though,' Sadie explained. 'He even got it changed by deed poll. He thinks it sounds snappy and businesslike – I think he was inspired by J.R. Ewing.'

'Or J.R. Hartley,' Lana offered. 'Does he have a particular fondness for fly fishing?'

Sadie giggled and closed her eyes. While Lana powdered and painted away at her face, humming along to the *Grease* soundtrack as she worked, Sadie could feel the nervous tension begin to seep from her body like coffee through a filter. So this was what it was like to prepare for a girls' night out. How many hours had she spent dreaming of evenings like these? Picturing herself giggling with girlfriends, gossiping about men, exchanging beauty tips and singing along to music. How many times had she watched the sleepover scene in *Grease* and longed to be transported into that soft focus world of satin cushions, silky negligees and sneaky cigarettes? Sadie inhaled deeply and revelled in the scent of perfume, nail varnish and smoke flooding her nose; all proof that her dream had finally come true.

One hour, half a bottle of vodka and twenty Marlboro Lights later and Sadie had been transformed. Lana stretched out on the chaise longue and surveyed her rather timid-looking masterpiece.

'Well go on, don't be shy, give us a twirl,' she encouraged. It was ludicrous really, but as Lana examined Sadie's huge eyes, made all the more striking with the benefit of smudgy frames of kohl, her milky skin and plump rosebud of a mouth, she couldn't help feeling a surge of pride. It was how she imagined a mother might feel on the night of her daughter's first prom. Part of her wanted to sit Sadie down and warn her of the dangers of letting a young man touch her knee. Another part of her wanted to puke at such sentimental hogwash.

Sadie stumbled into the centre of the room. She wasn't sure if it was vertigo from the six-inch heels or drunkenness from the vodka that was causing her head to spin, but either way things were feeling pretty wobbly at her new elevation. 'How do I look?' she asked, not even daring to meet Lana's gaze, for fear that she might catch the trace of a smirk.

'You look amazing,' Lana sighed. 'Of course it's hardly surprising. I do seem to be blessed with magical powers when it comes to giving a makeover.'

Sadie nodded enthusiastically. It certainly felt as if Lana had cast a spell over her, transforming her from naïve little girl into sultry sex kitten with one wave of her mascara wand and sprinkling of glitter. And now Sadie's face looked the part the rest of her outfit seemed to fit too. Her blonde wig shimmered rather than clashed, her boob tube tantalised rather than titillated and her skin-tight trousers flattered rather than revealed. She had never felt so glam – or so giddy. Sadie plopped down on the end of the chaise longue, beside Lana's feet. 'Did you order the cab?' she asked, lighting herself a cigarette and wishing she had mastered the art of smoke rings to go with her new sultry image.

'I most certainly did,' Lana responded, picking up the remote control. 'But you have to watch the scene before you go – final dress rehearsal and all. Here we are.' Lana pressed play. 'Okay girl, let's go – I'll be Danny.' Lana hoisted herself to her feet and stared at Sadie, perfectly mimicking John Travolta's shocked expression filling the screen. 'Sandy – is that you?' she gasped, gesturing at Sadie to get up.

Sadie let the cigarette dangle from her cherry red lips and swaggered across the room to face Lana. As the opening chords to 'You're the One that I Want' struck up Lana grabbed a candle from the mantelpiece and began singing into it as if it were a microphone. Round and round the coffee table the two of them strutted, gasping for air as they giggled and yelled their way through the song. It wasn't long before Lana had clambered on to the coffee table to hold her microphone aloft and bellow out the chorus. Not wanting to be outdone, Sadie leapt on to the chaise longue, almost breaking her ankle in the process, shrieking ooh, ooh, ooh and attempting to shimmy her way to the end.

'Was that the doorbell?' Sadie asked, mid shimmy.

'No – it was just my falsetto,' Lana quipped, giving an impromptu pelvic thrust.

Sadie collapsed to her knees in fits of laughter. 'Your false what?'

'My false-etto. Oh my Lord, there's somebody looking in the window.' Lana threw herself on to the floor in alarm.

'What? Are you sure?' Sadie collapsed into a seated position and straightened her wig.

'Sure I'm sure. I can see his eyes glinting at me underneath the net curtains.' Lana hit stop on the DVD and the room fell silent. 'What do you want, you – you peeping Tom?'

'Meeeeeess – your taxeeeeeee, it is readeeeeeeeee!' A heavily accented voice called from outside.

'Shit – it's my cab,' Sadie cried. 'Okay, I'm just coming,' she yelled, adjusting her wig and fumbling beneath the coffee table for her handbag. 'Right, are you sure I look okay?' she asked, having one final glance in the mirror above the fireplace. Her cheeks seemed to have flushed a rather alarming shade of scarlet, making it hard to tell where they finished and her lips began.

As Lana hauled herself up from the floor she felt a sudden blow to her head, as though someone had just clouted her with a mallet. 'Jesus,' she gasped, but when she opened her eyes she saw that Sadie was on the other side of the coffee table armed with nothing more offensive than a tube of lip-gloss.

'Are you all right?' Sadie asked, her hand frozen mid-application.

'Yeah. Just a little dazed. Must have gotten up too quickly, I guess.' Lana reached out for the arm of the chaise longue to steady herself and as she did so she felt her entire insides lurch upwards.

Sadie rubbed her lips together to even the sheen and clipped her bag shut. 'Thank you so much for tonight,' she said, negotiating her way over to Lana. 'You don't know how much better I feel now. I can't wait to see the expression on GL's face when I walk in.' She hesitated briefly before giving Lana a hug. 'Come down to the shop tomorrow and I'll tell you all about it.'

It took every ounce of strength for Lana to twist her mouth into a rigid smile and when she nodded it was as if somebody had ignited a firework inside her head, causing a shower of sparks to errupt behind her eyes. Somehow managing to manoeuvre one foot in front of the other, she followed Sadie into the hall, but with every step she could feel a terrible sensation welling up inside her, like an impending storm over which she would soon have no control. A scorching heat exploded into her face and yet bizarrely, her body began to shiver. As she watched Sadie tripping and giggling her way down the garden path she wanted to call out, but her mouth seemed paralysed. Numbly raising her arm in response to Sadie's wave, Lana watched helplessly as the taillights of the taxi faded into the night, like the disappearing image from a television screen when you hit the off switch and everything goes black.

Chapter Twenty-One

As Sadie wiped a circle of condensation from the cab window and pressed her nose to the glass she felt a wave of sentiment wash over her, the like of which she had only previously experienced watching *Dead Poets' Society*. So what if her cab driver was fresh off the back of a lorry from Bosnia and didn't know his Hangar Lane Gyratory from his North Circular Road. Wasn't it wonderful that he had escaped from his oppressive homeland to be offered the chance of a bright new dawn in Ruislip Manor? And so what if his grasp of the Queen's English was pitifully pidgin and he failed to understand even the most basic of instructions – like 'TURN RIGHT!' and 'STOP!' and 'THIS IS A ONE WAY STREET!' He'd made it half way across Europe, for Christ's sake; eventually he was bound to venture upon the Trusthouse Forte, Greenford. Sadie smiled contentedly as she watched the stream of sodium light rush past her eyes. It was Saturday night and rather than being stuck behind the counter of a shop she was racing around the outskirts of London, part of the great social whirl coursing its way between the capital's bars, clubs and restaurants, like over-excited children scurrying through a maze. God, exactly how fast was her driver going?

By the time they hurtled to a halt outside the hotel, Sadie's rose-tinted view of the world had been somewhat obscured by a fog of motion sickness, blurring her vision and sticking at the back of her throat.

'Keep the change,' she muttered, flinging a twenty-pound note at the driver and capsizing from the car. Pulling herself upright, she gasped as the icy night air bit into her bare arms, shoulders and cleavage. Why on earth hadn't she brought her coat? Still, she was here now and she could always borrow GL's for the journey home. As Sadie glanced over to the brightly lit foyer of the hotel she felt a stab of fear. How would she know where to go? What if they had more than one function room? What if it wasn't clearly sign-posted? She'd ask the receptionist for directions, of course. But what if they had a guest list? Her name wouldn't be on it. Sadie pictured a haughty receptionist, all manicured claws and bared teeth, barking at her 'if your name's not down you're not coming in.' But GL's name would be down, she could just explain that she was his partner and had arrived late. But what if they didn't believe her and thought she was a gatecrasher with a particular fetish for telecommunications companies' post-Christmas parties? Oh God! Sadie fished in her bag for a cigarette and thought of Lana. What would she do in this situation? Stuffing her cigarettes back into her bag, Sadie took a deep breath, lifted her head up high and strode over to the doorway. She was going to the party, goddammit, and no son of a bitch was going to stop her.

'Good evening, my dear,' the Thora Hird look-alike behind the counter clucked, glancing up from her – Sadie peered nervously into the old woman's lap – needlepoint portrait of the Queen Mother. 'If you're here for the Fancy Dress party you need to go through those double doors on the left and follow the corridor round until the end. It's in the Terry Wogan Suite.'

Nodding her head in thanks, Sadie sashayed over to the double doors. Well – that had been a piece of cake; she'd shown that receptionist who was boss. The poor old dear had probably felt quite intimidated by her new found glamour and woman-of-the-world air. 'Ow!' Sadie yelped as she slammed into the door, the impact causing a chain reaction of pain bucking up the right hand side of her body, from her stiletto heel, to her ankle, to her knee, to her hip.

'It's pull, lovey, not push,' the receptionist called out, helpfully.

'Yeah, thanks.' Sadie yanked the door open and stumbled down the corridor. From somewhere in the distance she could hear the bass line from *Saturday Night Fever*, pounding in time with the blood that was now pumping into her face. Calm, calm, she told herself, praying for a Ladies toilet in which she could take refuge to miraculously appear. Seemingly in answer to her prayers a door up ahead of her shot open and two women clad in chorus line attire came staggering out. Their bottle-tanned skin was the colour of crème caramel and their hair had been set in bouffant helmets above their over-made-up faces.

'So, do you reckon you'll shag him tonight or not?' One enquired of the other as they careered down the corridor away from Sadie.

'Depends,' her friend replied, hoisting her bustier. 'Blimey, I wish I'd remembered my tit tape.'

'Depends on what?'

'On how many more rum and blacks he's going to buy me!'

Sadie watched as the two girls opened the doors to the Terry Wogan Suite and were immediately swallowed into the darkness within by a wave of sound. Raucous laughter mingled with the clink of glasses, all set to a disco beat. Sadie dived into the toilets. Thankfully they were completely deserted, apart from the fug of hairspray and cigarette smoke suspended in the over-heated air, like some laboratory reconstruction of global warming.

'Oh no!' she groaned, catching sight of her reflection in

the harshly lit mirror upon the wall. With her flushed cheeks and lop-sided wig she looked more like a lagered-up lagger at closing time than a disco diva on the verge of making her grand entrance. Splashing cold water upon her neck and wrists (an invaluable hint acquired from *Beauty Tips of the Rich and Famous* one particularly dull shift) Sadie waited patiently for her body temperature to return to the right side of radioactive.

One swift wig adjustment, two coats of lip gloss and three anxious puffs on a Marlboro Light later and Sadie was ready. As ready as one was ever likely to be when they were about to risk complete and utter humiliation. *It's all about attitude not appearance*, she reminded herself, straightening her shoulders, thrusting her bust and pursing her lips. 'I am Olivia Newton John,' she whispered, as she opened the toilet door. *All I have to do is enter the function room, march over to the deejay and make my request.* As Sadie approached the doors of the Terry Wogan Suite she pictured herself strutting on to the dance-floor as 'You're the One That I Want' struck up. The other revellers would utter a collective gasp of admiration as they stepped back from the spotlight, leaving just her and an awestruck GL on the dance-floor. She visualised all his friends gathering around, patting him on the back and offering words of encouragement, tinged, of course, with envy. '*Nice one, mate*,' they would say. '*Cor, I should be so lucky!*' Sadie frowned as GL's imaginary friends began morphing into Kylie Minogue. This was worse than going to the dentist for root canal treatment. She was beginning to go out of her mind with fear.

BANG! Her hand hit the door and she pushed it open. BANG! She walked straight into a wall of sound, heat and fumes. Sadie gasped for breath as her lungs were filled with a potent mixture of exhaled smoke, perspired alcohol and over-applied perfume. Caught off balance by the sudden darkness, Sadie reached out to steady herself on what she thought was the back of chair.

'Steady,' a voice bellowed out from somewhere above her. 'How many have you had, darling?'

Sadie squinted to see that the back of the chair was in fact an arm. Not the arm of a chair, but the arm of a man. A huge barrel of a man with a pair of over inflated lips curled into a lecherous grin.

'I tell you what, love, while you're down there.' His lips had obviously been inflated to match his ego.

Sadie stood rooted to the spot as the man turned to his weasel of a friend.

'Here, Smithy, did you hear that?' He shouted, nudging his friend in the ribs and pointing at Sadie with the smouldering stub of a cigar, 'I just said to her, all right love, while you're down there.'

Sadie stared on in horror as both men fell about laughing.

'It's all right love, you can get up off your knees now,' Rubber lips gasped, between guffaws. 'Oh fuck me, she is up already.'

'Can I get you a drink?' The weasely one enquired, thrusting his pointy little face right into Sadie's.

Sadie recoiled at the stench of stale lager upon his breath. 'No, thank you, I'm looking for someone.' Why oh why couldn't she have a repertoire of one-liners like Lana's at her disposal? How she would love to cut these two arse holes down to size with a razor-sharp wit.

'So I suppose a fuck's out of the question?' The weasel retorted, looking up to his fat-lipped friend as if for approval. Look at me, his desperate gaze seemed to imply, I can be just as much of a twat as you.

Sadie thought of Lana. How would *she* deal with this situation? Sadie inhaled deeply on her cigarette and blew a jet of smoke into the Weasel's eyes. 'You want a fuck? I'll give you a fuck,' an unfamiliar voice emerged from her mouth, tinged with a slight drawl. 'Why don't you both fuck off!'

Unfortunately, however, at exactly that moment the theme from the *Blues Brothers* came on and Sadie's cutting put-down was drowned out by a huge cheer and a stampeding mass of men in suits, shades and pork pie hats racing to the dance-floor. Spotting a darkened corner over to her right, Sadie skulked toward it to try and get her bearings. Her eyes now adjusted to the darkness, she began 'casing the joint' as Terry would have put it. At the thought of Terry, Sadie gave a wistful smile. Oh, to be in the shop now, hearing all about the Prime Sinister's latest exploits over a steaming mug of tea. Rather than stuck in the Terry Wogan Suite of a Trusthouse Forte, dodging perverts over – Sadie felt something brush against her leg and looked to the floor in horror – over what would appear to be a steamy mass of bodies. Oh God! Sadie was unable to tear her eyes from the tangled limbs thrashing about under the table next to her. What the hell was wrong with these people? Had she been directed to the wrong fancy dress party and ended up at a Spearmint Rhino post-Christmas bash instead? But no – surely they would hold their parties in the privacy of one of their own clubs. Sadie glanced around the Terry Wogan Suite anxiously, half afraid that rather than re-enacting *Grease*, she had unwittingly walked into the orgy scene from *Eyes Wide Shut*. Thankfully there didn't seem to be any other acts of fornication taking place amongst, on top of, or beneath the drinks-laden tables. The handful of people who had not converged upon the dance-floor to pogo around to 'Everybody Needs Somebody to Love' stood in huddled little gaggles, quaffing champagne direct from the bottle and puffing away on cigars. There seemed to be an awful lot of heads being thrown back and backs being slapped. Everything was loud, loud, loud.

From the speaker-blowing music, to the braying laughter, to the grunting and groaning beneath her. Sadie looked down at the flailing legs. The *five* flailing legs. Blinking, she recounted. One, two, three, four, five. Three clad in fishnets, the remaining pair bare apart from a pair of trousers rucked about the ankles. Oh this really was too much. Sadie paused briefly to consider what Lana might do in this situation, but concluding that she might very well join in, she decided to beat a hasty retreat to the Ladies to regroup.

'I think you'll find the Seven Series has much better leg room – or should I say leg-*over* room,' a middle-aged man clad in a *Lion King* outfit was reporting to a group of wide-eyed transvestites, as Sadie barged her way past towards the door.

With their sycophantic laughter still ringing in her ears, Sadie stumbled into the toilets and locked herself into the first cubicle she came to. Shutting the toilet lid, she collapsed down, removed her stilettos and sighed. What a complete nightmare. How on earth had she ever imagined she would have been able to pull this off? There was no way on this earth she was going to be able to recreate the scene from *Grease* in front of that lot. She would be heckled all the way into reception. Either that or gang-raped. No, the best thing to do would be to discreetly return and find GL. Her appearance would still hopefully provide him with a pleasant surprise. Massaging her aching feet, Sadie leant back against the cistern and closed her eyes. All she needed was a moment's peace and quiet to regain her composure.

'Oh, babes!'

Sadie's eyes flew open. It was GL. But how? Why? What was he doing in the Ladies toilets? He must have followed her in. But no – she hadn't heard the door go and besides, his voice was coming from the far end of the cubicles. Sadie's heart skipped a beat. Surely in her haste she hadn't fled into the Gents by mistake? But even if she had, why was he talking to her? And how did he know she was in here? Sadie held her breath – perhaps she had imagined it. After all, she had just been thinking about him.

'Oh yeah, that's right, go all the way down, babes.'

Sadie's eyes widened in horror as she heard a gasp followed by a splutter from the far end of the toilets.

'How – was – that?' A girl's voice enquired in breathless little bursts.

'That was blinding,' GL replied. 'Nah – better wash your mouth out if you want a kiss, you know the thought of tasting me own jism makes me go all funny.'

'Oh, all right,' the girl conceded with a sigh. 'You'd better get me another rum and black to wash it out with then.'

'Your wish is my command,' GL replied. Sadie flinched as she heard the sound of a zip being pulled up. 'But first of all, how's about a little bit of Columbia's finest?'

Sadie squirmed. What the hell was 'Columbia's finest'? Surely she wasn't going to have to sit there while some – some *tart* performed a bizarre South American sex act upon her boyfriend. A stabbing pain began emanating from her rib cage, causing her entire body to seize up. Pulling her knees up to her chest and burying her face upon them, she huddled into a ball. Other people, such as Lana, might march from the cubicle screaming threats of castration and worse, but Sadie had been rendered paralysed with pain and fear. From the far end of the cubicle she heard the rustling of some kind of wrapper – a packet of condoms perhaps?

'Easy does it,' GL muttered.

Sadie pictured him easing himself inside the little trollop, her words still echoing around her head. *You'd better get me another rum and black to wash it out with then.* Why did they sound so familiar? *Depends on how many more rum and blacks he's going to buy me!* It was one of the girls she'd seen leaving the toilet earlier, the one with the beige skin and bulging breasts. Sadie fought the overwhelming urge to retch. Surely this couldn't be happening. She heard a long hard sniff from the end of the toilets.

'Fucking hell!' GL exclaimed, before sniffing again. 'That is one blinding bit of charlie. Come on, put your tits away and let's get back to the dance floor.'

The entire row of cubicles reverberated as a far door was flung open and two pairs of footsteps made their way past Sadie. Two pairs of footsteps belonging to her cocaine-snorting boyfriend and his bit on the side. Sadie felt as if all sense of reality had fled from her life like a criminal's accomplice, leaving her helplessly stranded in some *News of the World* style parallel universe, right at the point where even the undercover reporters would have made their excuses and left. But she couldn't leave. She was frozen rigid, her heart rattling away like machine gun fire, her teeth chattering and her hands shaking uncontrollably. Her eyes faded in and out of focus as they filled with tears and it seemed as though the walls of the cubicle were about to fold in upon her, as if they were constructed from nothing more than paper. A suitable analogy for her whole life, really.

She heard the outside door slam shut, the tinkle of the girl's laughter echoing along the corridor, and then a sudden burst of noise as they returned to the party. Then all she could hear was the hum of the completely ineffective air-conditioner and a muffled voice inside her head. *You've got to get out of here*, the voice instructed, calmly, authoritatively. *Walk into reception and order a cab. If you can get yourself to Lana's house you will be all right. Get back to Lana's house and you will be all right.*

Chapter Twenty-Two

Where Sadie's first cabbie had not been able to speak much English, the driver on her return journey seemed completely mute – much to Sadie's relief, for she wouldn't have been capable of feigning even a passing interest in his unfulfilled aspirations as a Hollywood screenwriter or his unresolved hatred for 'that Ken Livingstone geezer'.

The last time Sadie had felt this numb was one scorching summer's day four years previously, when she had unexpectedly been summoned to her headmaster's office half way through History. As soon as she entered the room and saw her father staring blankly out of the window, her bog standard, *oh-my-God-I've-got-to-see-the-head* jitters had been replaced by an altogether more sinister sense of foreboding.

'Dad?' she'd enquired timidly.

'Your mother's dead,' he replied, without even bothering to turn around, his hands remaining neatly folded behind his poker-straight back, his voice as even as the hum of the portable fan on the headmaster's desk.

Sadie stared helplessly towards him, but it was as if somebody had suddenly cranked up the sunlight, turning the rays coursing through the window from gold to brilliant white, their intensity burning on the backs of her eyes. 'Dead?' she whispered, blinking furiously.

'Yes. She was found in her car at nine thirty-three this morning,' her father replied, his silhouette framed like a negative image against the dazzling backdrop.

And this bizarre attention to detail was the only thing to register with Sadie throughout the fog of numbness that followed. Her mother had been found at *nine thirty-three*. What had she been doing at nine thirty-three? Sadie had cast her mind back, but try as she might she could not recall exactly what her History teacher had been saying at precisely that moment. Precisely the moment her father had returned home and opened the garage door to be hit by a choking cloud of exhaust fumes.

Similarly, as Sadie sat slumped in the back of a cab, speeding her way back to Ruislip Manor, all she could think about was rum and black. What kind of person drank rum and black? What did the black stand for anyway? Sadie felt pretty sure it was blackcurrent, but she couldn't say for certain. One thing she could say for certain was that Lana would know. Hopefully she had a supply of rum and black in that drinks cabinet of hers and she would fix Sadie one for research purposes.

It was only when Sadie was halfway up Lana's garden path and spotted the front door ajar that her numbness began to subside, allowing reality to prick its way back into her consciousness like an acute attack of pins and needles.

'Lana?' Sadie prodded the door open cautiously. 'Oh, shit!' In the gentle glow of the hall lamp she could just make out a dark pool of what looked ominously like blood seeping over the parquet flooring and filtering off into scarlet rivulets across the oatmeal rug.

'Lana!' Sadie cried, stepping into the hall, into the blood and hitting the light switch with the palm of her hand. 'Oh no! Oh, Lana!' Sadie raised her hand to her mouth in shock. Through the living room door she could just make out one of Lana's stockinged feet, her kitten-heeled slipper dangling limply from her big toe. 'Oh God, Lana, what's happened?' Sadie tried to push the living room door open, but it was jammed. Peering through the gap she realised that Lana's body was the obstruction, stretched along the base of the door like a draught excluder. Gingerly Sadie forced the door open little by little until finally there was a space large enough for her to slip through. Lana was lying sprawled with her back to the door, her face obscured by a fan of auburn curls and one hand resting upon the telephone receiver. The telephone itself lay toppled on its side facing her.

Sadie fell to her knees and gently brushed Lana's hair from her face. Up this close her skin seemed leathery and sallow, her upturned cheek sunken and smeared with blood. Pushing Lana's pearl choker back down to the base of her neck, Sadie pressed her fingers to her throat and held her breath. Please, please, be alive, she silently implored, searching desperately for a pulse. After what felt like an eternity, Sadie finally managed to locate the faintest of beats. Without a moment's hesitation she set the telephone upright and grabbed the receiver, her finger trembling so much she must have hit the nine at least five times.

As Sadie cast her eyes about the Accident and Emergency unit she began to wonder if someone had spiked her cup of insipid, machine-brewed tea. Everywhere she looked she was greeted with a mind-bending clash of colour and sound; from the purple walls and olive chairs to the screams of babies and curses of drunks. It was all made even more unbearable by the strobe effect of the flickering strip lights overhead.

'I told you I can fight me own battles,' screeched a spindly, peroxide blonde from the other side of the room.

Sadie glanced across at the woman's companion, a great hulk of a man with a face the colour and texture of corned beef, nursing what looked suspiciously like a stab wound to his arm. At the sight of the blood oozing out from beneath his makeshift tourniquet, Sadie shuddered. When were the doctors going to bring her news about Lana? When Sadie had first seen the blood in the hallway, her initial assumption had been that Lana had fallen victim to a violent burglary. But once the ambulance crew arrived they soon put paid to her theory. 'She must have vomited the blood,' one of them informed her as they eased Lana on to a stretcher and checked inside her mouth for obstructions. 'Does she have any stomach problems that you're aware of?' Sadie had shaken her head, before remembering the piles of pills on the coffee table when she had arrived earlier that night. 'She had been feeling a bit under the weather – she thought it was gastric flu,' she offered. The ambulance man had looked at his colleague and raised his eyebrows. 'I think this is a little more serious than gastric flu,' he muttered ominously.

Sadie suddenly felt very afraid and very alone. What if Lana were about to die? What if she had already died and the doctors were on their way to tell her? She wasn't sure she could cope with a double whammy of abject horror in one night. Sadie studied her fellow A and E inmates. The bickering couple opposite, the anxious parents fussing over their screaming baby, the Chinese man with the gingham tea-towel draped over one hand, his concerned wife clinging on to the other, the teenager with the two black eyes, exchanging gangsta jargon with the rest of his posse; even the drunkard, pebble-dashed in vomit and bellowing Frank Sinatra, was accompanied by a mangy-looking Labrador. Sadie was the only one on her own. She fumbled in her handbag for her purse, her fingers trembling as they tried in vain to prise apart the wad of advantage, loyalty and store cards crammed inside. Finally she located a business card amongst all the plastic, but as she tugged it out her bag spilled onto the floor, sending her mobile clattering across the lino.

'No mobiles allowed, sweetheart,' the drunk seamlessly interrupted his raucous rendition of 'New York, New York' to inform her, pointing unsteadily to a sign on the wall that also told her she was not allowed to smoke cigarettes or consume alcohol. Bugger! Sadie could feel every nerve ending in her body being stretched to breaking point. Retrieving her bag and phone with one hand and clutching the battered business card with the other, she hobbled from the waiting room and down the short corridor towards the exit. The smell of disinfectant was so overpowering she could practically see the fumes evaporating from the polished floor. As Sadie burst through the door into the welcome darkness outside, she took a deep breath. The air was crisp and clear and smelt of distant bonfires. Sadie turned on her mobile and the illuminated display informed her that it was twenty minutes past twelve, which seemed ludicrously early given everything that had happened. It was as if she had been dropped slap bang in the middle of an episode of the *Twilight Zone* and all sense of time and reality had ceased to exist. But at least the relatively early hour meant that Liam should still be up.

Chapter Twenty-Three

By the time Liam arrived at the hospital, Sadie felt as if she had become fossilised to the wall of the A and E unit. Although she could still just about move her head, the rest of her body was frozen stiff.

'Bloody hell! What are you doing out here?' Liam asked, immediately removing his fleece and handing it to Sadie. 'You'll get hypothermia.'

'Oh well, at least I'm in the right place,' Sadie muttered through chattering teeth.

'Let's get you back inside,' Liam said, peeling her from the wall and steering her gently through the door.

As Sadie entered the foyer and pulled Liam's fleece over her head everything went dark. 'What's happened? Has someone turned out the lights?' she asked, fumbling about with her hands.

'It's your wig,' Liam explained. 'It's come down over your face.'

Sadie groaned as she reached for the wig and yanked it from her head. In all the pandemonium she had completely forgotten about her fancy dress get-up. There she was looking down her nose at the others in the waiting room when all the while she had probably been in a sorrier state than the lot of them. 'I totally forgot,' she cried. 'I totally forgot.'

'Hey – don't worry about it,' Liam soothed, taking the wig from her hands, and placing it over his head-sized fist. 'How about we get a cup of tea and you can tell me what happened. I take it you never made it to the party then?'

'Oh, I made it all right.' Sadie began rolling up the sleeves on Liam's jumper. They were about twice the length of her arms, causing her to feel like a gibbon – even worse, a gibbon in six-inch stilettos. 'Let's just say my scene didn't exactly go according to plan.' She bit hard on her lip to stop it from trembling and began making her way up the corridor.

'Oh, I see.'

Sadie looked over at Liam. His hair was dishevelled and she noticed that his lumberjack shirt had been buttoned up all skew-whiff. 'I didn't get you out of bed, did I?' she asked, leading him towards the vending machine.

'No. Well yes, but I wasn't asleep.'

'Oh – I'm sorry, I didn't know who else to call.' Sadie turned away in embarrassment. What kind of sad indictment was it upon her life that in a case of emergency the only person she could call upon was a customer? A customer with whom she had only had a proper conversation once before. Admittedly, it had been something of a marathon conversation, but even so. In a frenzied assault, the brutal facts of her life seemed to be raining down on her from all angles; her father was a cold-hearted control freak, her boyfriend a drug-taking cheat, her only friend may be about to die and her mother . . . Sadie slumped against the side of the drinks machine and held her head in her hands. This wasn't an episode of the *Twilight Zone* she was starring in – this was her real life and no matter which way she turned, she could no longer escape it.

'Sadie? Are you all right?'

Sadie could feel Liam alongside her now, his body as sturdy and unyielding as the drinks machine, one huge arm reaching around her shoulders, drawing her closer to him. Oh, to be able to collapse into those arms, to just let somebody else carry her burden for a while. She felt like a small child all over again, clambering on to her father's lap, desperate for him to envelop her in a hug rather than nudge her awkwardly back on to the floor.

'Miss Jones?'

Sadie peered around Liam's chest to see an anxious looking doctor clutching a clipboard. His pale blue eyes were ringed with shadows and his forehead creased into a frown.

'Yes,' Sadie replied, edging her way around Liam.

'Your step-mother is asking to see you.'

'My what? Oh – right. You mean Lana?' Sadie held her breath, praying they hadn't confused her with someone else.

The doctor nodded and glanced at his clipboard. 'I'm afraid you can only stay for a couple of minutes. She's lost an awful lot of blood and is still very weak, but she was quite insistent that she saw you before we take her up to the ICU.'

'ICU?'

'The Intensive Care Unit,' the doctor explained.

'Is – is she going to be okay?'

The doctor continued to frown. 'It's very difficult to say at this stage. We won't really know anymore until we've carried out her liver scan tomorrow.'

'Her liver scan?'

'Yes. Your stepmother has suspected cirrhosis of the liver. We think this is what may have caused the internal bleeding tonight.'

Sadie heard Liam emit a low, hollow whistle behind her.

'Cirrhosis? But isn't that fatal?'

'It is certainly very serious. I'm sorry, I assumed you knew that your mother had already been for some tests.'

'My stepmother,' Sadie automatically corrected, or should that have been incorrected? Sadie no longer seemed sure of anything much. 'No, she hadn't mentioned it at all.'

'Well, the next couple of days are going to be crucial, and as I say, until we get the results of the scan we really have no idea of the severity of the damage to your stepmother's liver. Now, if you'd like to follow me.' The doctor turned to Liam. 'I'm afraid you'll have to wait here, sir.'

Liam raised his wig-clad hand in a gesture of acknowledgement. 'No problem. I'll be right here, Sadie.'

Incapable of even turning to face him, Sadie nodded her head and followed the doctor like an obedient puppy out of the waiting room, along an aisle of curtained-off cubicles and around a corner until they reached a door at the far end of the corridor. A picture of a mobile phone with a line slashed through it hung in the middle of the door. Sadie knew she had switched off her phone straight after calling Liam, but she couldn't help fumbling in her bag just to make certain.

The doctor placed his hand on the door handle and then paused to turn to Sadie. 'Now as I said, the next forty-eight hours are critical, and it is imperative she gets as much rest as possible – so I can really only allow you to stay for a minute.'

'Yes, of course.' Sadie felt as if her brain might explode with the amount of information it was being asked to assimilate and the endless stream of questions that were being generated as a consequence. Why had Lana never mentioned her suspected liver disease? Why had she dismissed her symptoms as gastric flu? What was she doing drinking alcohol with suspected cirrhosis? What was she doing drinking *so much* alcohol with suspected cirrhosis? Shoving the uncomfortable conclusions she was drawing to the back of her mind, Sadie slipped past the doctor and into the room. Lana lay motionless on a metal-framed bed, her waxen face bathed in an eerie pool of green light from a monitor beside her. Every couple of seconds the monitor would bleep and a neon trail would run across the screen. A figure in the right hand corner appeared to be recording something. 87–88–90–87. Sadie watched the figures change with baited breath. She had seen enough episodes of *ER* to know that any sudden fluctuation in these numbers was likely to bring a swarm of green-gowned medics racing into the room, yelling things like *stand back!* and *we're losing her!*

Sadie tiptoed over to the bed and gazed down at Lana. Somebody had removed the blood from her face and the pearl choker from her neck. A tube had been taped to her cheek and up into her nose and another one had been hooked into her arm. She was barely recognisable.

'Sweet Lord above!' Lana exclaimed, opening her eyes with a start. 'You scared the shit out of me.'

Sadie took a step backwards and stifled a scream. The number on the monitor jumped to 91 then fell back to 87.

'Ditto,' Sadie replied, trying desperately to compose herself.

Lana sighed and closed her eyes.

'How are you feeling?' Sadie asked, immediately wanting to kick herself. How did she think Lana was feeling, having vomited about a gallon of blood and been diagnosed with suspected cirrhosis of the liver? She could just imagine the kind of withering reply she was going to get. But none came. Lana just lay there, breathing shallow little breaths, her false eyelashes flickering in time. Sadie glanced anxiously at the monitors but nothing seemed untoward. 'Lana? Are you okay?'

Lana reached out her hand and beckoned at Sadie to come closer.

'I – need – you – to – do – something – for – me,' she said in a faltering whisper.

Sadie shivered. She had seen this scene played out in count-less different ways in the numerous weepies she had recently viewed with GL. This was where the dying hero/heroine made their last, deathbed wish before departing for loftier planes. Sadie bit her lip and prepared to make a mental note of

Lana's funeral play-list or the desired location for her ashes to be scattered.

'Sure,' she replied, taking hold of Lana's hand. It looked so pitifully gnarled and bare without its usual dazzling array of rings. 'What is it?'

Lana opened her eyes and stared straight into Sadie's. 'You have to bring me my make-up bag and a mirror. The National *Hell* Service might have taken away my freedom, but they sure as hell aren't gonna deprive me of my Estée Lauder!' Lana paused to catch her breath before continuing. 'As Whitney Houston once said – before she met Bobby Brown, obviously – no matter what they take from me there's no way on this earth they're taking away my dignity!'

Chapter Twenty-Four

'Do you fancy coming back to my place for a coffee?' Liam looked out of the cab window and fought the urge to groan. Why did everything he said to Sadie always seem so laden with cheesy innuendo? *Because you're desperate to get her in the sack, you dirty old sod*, a voice not unlike Terry's retorted inside his head, instantly making his skin crawl with embarrassment.

Sadie breathed a sigh of relief. There was no way she could have faced going back to GL's house, and the prospect of returning to Lana's to clear up all the blood was hardly an appealing alternative. 'Yes, I'd love to,' she replied, a tad too eagerly perhaps, but she was way past caring. Her third cab driver of the night – Sadie wondered if she might qualify for some kind of 'Mini-cab Miles' discount by now – gave a contented chortle before losing himself once more in his dire compilation of Music Hall Greats.

'Well, it's looking pretty hopeful if Lana's already asking for her make-up,' Liam mused, fiddling with the leather friendship band around his wrist. It had been a gift from a Canadian girl he'd met on his last sojourn to Thailand. He didn't know why he kept it really, it just made him feel good knowing it was there; a talisman to protect him from the agonies of British life and remind him of that whole other world beyond the Ruislip Manor horizon. A world full of beach parties and magic mushroom tea and meaningful liaisons with Canadian blondes – what was her name again?

Sadie smiled. 'I know. I was really scared she was going to ask me to oversee her funeral arrangements.'

Liam shifted slightly in his seat to face Sadie. 'She's quite a character, isn't she? How long has she lived in Britain?'

'About twenty years, I think. She came over here to get away from her husband.' Sadie lowered her voice, 'He used to abuse her.'

Liam raised his eyebrows in surprise.

Sadie looked at him. 'What?'

'Oh nothing – it's just hard to imagine Lana as a victim,' Liam explained. With her cutting putdowns and withering stare she certainly scared the hell out of him.

'I guess she's had to toughen up over the years. It can't be easy having to start all over again in a strange country – and now with this happening she's probably terrified. I don't suppose you know anything about cirrhosis, do you?'

Liam shook his head. 'Not really. We'll have to wait and see what the doctors say once she's had her scan.' Liam didn't have the heart to tell Sadie that as far as he knew cirrhosis was incurable, with a liver transplant being the only hope of survival.

'Cirrhosis, you say?' the cabdriver piped up, mercifully turning Noel Coward down a notch or two.

Sadie caught his glance in the rear view mirror and nodded.

The cabdriver shook his head and whistled. It was the same kind of low-pitched whistle Sadie had heard Liam give in the hospital earlier. 'A rum old business that is,' he muttered gravely. 'Why? You know someone with it, do you?'

'Yes, a friend of mine,' Sadie replied. 'She was diagnosed with liver cirrhosis earlier tonight.'

'With *suspected* liver cirrhosis,' Liam corrected, praying for the cabbie to keep his mouth shut, which he realised was a little like praying for sunshine on a Bank Holiday. Once you made the mistake of asking for a cabbie's opinion on a subject it was like opening the gates to Bullshit Central.

The cabbie tutted and sighed and tutted once again. 'Cirrhosis,' he finally declared, his voice laden with doom. 'Usually means last orders at the last chance saloon I'm afraid. Bit of a drinker is she, your mate? Likes a sherbert or two, does she?'

'Well, I don't know. No more than most people,' Sadie replied defensively, although the cab driver did seem to be reaffirming her worst suspicions. Did Lana have a secret drink problem? After what she had been through at the hands of her ex-husband, not to mention her somewhat dubious career path, it wouldn't exactly have been unjustified.

'Let me tell you something, sweetheart, you don't get cirrhosis of the liver from the occasional martini and lemonade. Nah, it comes from years of alcohol abuse, something my dear Uncle Brendan, God rest his soul, would vouch for if he were still with us today. Two bottles of scotch a day for twenty-five years he got through before he keeled over and died in *MacFisheries* one Friday. They did a nice bit of cod, *MacFisheries*, still I don't suppose you remember, do you? A bit before your time it was. Before all the bleeding superstores took over and killed off the high street traders.'

Liam and Sadie exchanged glances of despair before staring out grimly into the night.

'Okay mate, you can drop us off here,' Liam yelled gratefully as soon as he spotted the twinkling frame of fairy lights in the Pirate Video Store window.

'Are you sure, son?'

'Yes – I live right above that video shop,' Liam explained, thrusting a twenty pound note at the driver.

'Oh blimey, you must be Terry Leggett's lodger,' the cab driver replied. 'Give him my regards, won't you? Manor Cars hasn't been the same since he left. Got himself a new job yet, has he?'

'What?' Liam replied, completely gob smacked. Terry's lodger? Jesus Christ, what the hell was the dodgy bastard telling people? Liam composed himself sufficiently to respond, albeit through gritted teeth. 'Yes, I think he's found something, but I'm not exactly sure what.'

'Say no more, son, say no more,' the cabbie replied, winking into his rear view mirror. 'Now, where did I put that change?'

'Don't worry about it,' Liam muttered, fumbling with the door handle. This cab journey was starting to bring him out in a cold sweat – and if he had to hear that shite singer imploring Mrs Worthington not to put her daughter on the stage one more time . . .

'I tell you what – one of these days I'm gonna swing for Terry,' Liam fumed, once he and Sadie had been deposited safely on the pavement outside the shop, the opening strains of 'My Old Man Said Follow the Van,' fading off down the deserted Parade. 'I can't believe he's been telling people that I'm *his* lodger.'

Sadie laughed. 'So he hasn't told you what his new job is then?'

'No,' Liam replied, ushering Sadie up the stairwell to the flats. 'All I know is that it involves riding a motorbike at all kinds of weird hours.' Liam glanced at his watch and prayed that whatever Terry's new occupation was, it would still be keeping him occupied at half past one on a Sunday morning.

'Perhaps he's some sort of courier,' Sadie said, trying hard to picture Terry hurtling around the West End, crashing red lights and leaving swathes of mown down Japanese tourists in his wake.

Liam chuckled as he fetched a huge bunch of keys from

his pocket. 'He's probably got himself involved with some kind of Albanian drugs baron without even realising it – the daft old sod probably thinks he's delivering consignments of self raising flour or something.'

Sadie's heart began to pound as she followed Liam into the flat. It had been a lot easier the last time she'd visited. Ironically, being carried up the fire exit in a drunken stupor had proved far less embarrassing. Still, she knew there was nowhere she would rather be after such a god-awful night. There was a calmness and strength about Liam, not only physically but in his whole demeanour, that left her feeling reassured and safe.

Liam opened the door to the living room, took one look inside and hastily backed out again. 'I think we'll go to my room,' he said. 'If you don't mind. It's just that Terry's in there and he's fallen asleep on the couch.' Much to Liam's relief Sadie nodded obligingly. Not only was Terry asleep, but he was asleep with one hand down the front of his pilfered boxer shorts and *Confessions of a Window Cleaner* panting and groaning away on the TV. 'Make yourself comfortable,' Liam said, opening the door to his bedroom and gesturing Sadie to go inside. 'I'll rustle us up some coffee – white no sugar, right?'

Sadie nodded and walked into the bedroom, her eyes widening with surprise. In her (admittedly limited) experience, a man's bedroom seemed to say little about its owner, apart from that he may have an aversion to picking up dirty underwear and a penchant for characterless chrome furniture. But not Liam's. His room was crammed full of clues to his identity, from the intricately carved gargoyles on the headboard of his bed to the variety of books lining the shelves. Sadie scanned the titles; leather bound encyclopaedias jostled for space amongst the rock biographies, carpentry manuals and – Sadie squinted to make sure she wasn't seeing things –

Collected Poems of Dylan Thomas. Loyd Grossman would have had a field day looking through this particular keyhole. Sadie edged her way further into the room. From the kitchen she could hear the reassuring clunk of cups and the first splutters of the kettle. Liam's bedroom had been painted a rich dark green, perfectly matching the gold-flecked throw upon the bed. She put her hand down to stroke the glistening fabric. With its elaborate brocade and tiny glinting mirrors it was obviously from Asia. Sadie could just picture Liam bartering for it in some far-flung bazaar – along with the ebony figure of Buddha squatting on the mantelpiece, she assumed. There was a hollow in the bed, where the throw had been flung back, and a dip in the pillow where Liam's head had obviously been resting when she had phoned from the hospital. Sadie sat down on the edge of the bed and traced the ridge in the pillow with the tips of her fingers. The bed seemed to glow in the warmth of the adjacent lamp and all of a sudden she felt intoxicated by tiredness. Like Goldilocks alone in the Three Bears' house, all she wanted to do was clamber into this daddy bear-sized bed and fall into a deep sleep. Then she caught sight of something on the bedside table that woke her up with a start – a bulging British Airways wallet propped against the *Lonely Planet Guide to New Zealand*. Sadie couldn't help picking up the wallet and taking a peek. A letter addressed to Mr Liam Costello detailing his flight information had been folded inside, on top of the wad of tickets and luggage labels. Sadie scanned the letter for the relevant information. *Departure date: Tuesday 18th February, Return date: open.*

Return date: open – what did that mean? Sadie felt a pang of despair as the awful truth dawned upon her. Liam was leaving in just two weeks time and he might never be coming back. What had she been thinking of, harbouring hopes of turning to him for support? He had his own life; his own happy life crammed full of action and adventure, no matter what Terry might have implied to the contrary. What did Terry know anyway? His whole existence seemed to be based upon an endless string of fantasies. How the hell would he know how Liam was feeling? All of a sudden Sadie felt completely foolish. What was she doing here? What was she thinking, leaving herself open to be hurt yet again? Hadn't she learnt anything from tonight's events? Hadn't she learnt anything from her *life's* events? The only person she could truly count upon was herself and from now on if anyone was going to be doing the leaving it was going to be her. Sadie jumped to her feet just as Liam returned to the room with a steaming mug of coffee in each hand and a packet of chocolate digestives tucked under his arm.

'I've started hiding my food in the hall cupboard,' he confessed. 'Living with Terry's like living with a squirrel with the munchies. Are you all right? You look as if you've seen a ghost.'

Sadie smiled weakly. 'I'm really sorry,' she said, edging her way over to the door. 'But I think I ought to be getting home.'

The packet of digestives slid out from under Liam's arm and crashed to the floor.

'But what about the coffee?' he asked, placing the cups on the bedside table, on top of the Lonely Planet book. He'd only been gone a couple of minutes – what could have happened to have caused such a change in Sadie? Liam's heart sank as he scanned the room for something Terry might have planted; his copy of *Animal Farm* perhaps, or even worse his scrapbook of Readers' Wives Cuttings, entitled '*Well Fit Wives*'.

Sadie paused as she reached the bedroom door. With her tousled hair and smudged make-up, not to mention the grunge effect of the outsized fleece and stiletto combo, she looked uncannily like Susannah Hoffs from *The Bangles*. A look that

Liam could get used to and certainly didn't want to say good night to just yet.

'I'm sorry, it's been a really long night and I'm feeling very tired all of a sudden. Besides, my boyfriend will be worrying about me.'

'Oh, right,' Liam replied, unable to disguise his disappointment. So she hadn't split up with him after all. When she'd seemed so bitter about the party he had secretly hoped she'd finally given the little twat the elbow. Liam wanted to kick himself for being so stupid. 'I'd better walk you home then.'

'No, no!' Sadie yelped, her stilettos buckling beneath her as she backed out of the door. She had to get out of there before she was engulfed by the flood of tears welling behind her eyes. 'I'll give you a call,' she cried over her shoulder as she yanked open the front door and stumbled out on to the balcony to be enveloped in a mesh of icy drizzle.

Chapter Twenty-Five

When Lana drifted back into consciousness the following morning, the first thing she thought of was death. It was hard not to, stuck in that godforsaken place, wired up to those godforsaken machines, whose sole purpose with every bleep seemed to be to remind her of her own mortality. It was ironic really – that it should be so easy to take another person's life, and yet being confronted with the prospect of your own demise was just about the hardest thing on earth to comprehend. All it took to extinguish another's existence was a simple chain of events, as random and as effortless as an accident. Although Lana knew full well nothing ever really happened by accident. Those fancy-Dan defence attorneys Guy had hired may have been able to pull the wool over the jury's eyes, but she knew the truth. Everything in this life happens for a reason. It's a scientific principle for Christ's sake – cause and effect. Cause: Lana, effect: death. It had happened before, some twenty years previously and now it was happening again, only this time it was her own death she was precipitating.

Of course, she had thought about ending it all back then – killing Mary Latimer off literally instead of just figuratively – but the truth was she had been too afraid. What did it feel like to die? That was the question that had plagued her over the years, particularly at night when it would send her half-crazed with its endless taunts. And the answers to the question only terrified her all the more, the fear creeping through her flesh and erupting through her skin in cold patches of sweat, like a dank November fog. It seemed so infinite, this event she had so carelessly inflicted upon another human being and yet never had the guts to bring upon herself. At least not immediately, anyway. No, being the chicken-shit coward she was, Lana had chosen the easy route, staggering towards death, blissfully anaesthetised against the pain.

Until now. Her insides were wracked with the most intense pain, the simple act of breathing causing her to wince in agony. God, she could murder a drink. Lana gave a hollow chuckle. Now there was an ironic statement if ever she heard one. If only she could be sure death was just one long deep sleep, then she would embrace it with open arms. But despite all her attempts to block out her parents' incessant Bible-bashing with daydreams and liquor and boys, they must have had some effect on her subconscious, for Lana couldn't shake the notion that what awaited her on the other side was an eternity of hellfire and damnation.

The staccato bleeps of the monitor continued to pierce the air, like Morse code informing the world she was still here – for the time being anyway. Lana thought of her liver, a shrivelled, scarred mass hanging on for dear life inside her body, another of her victims. Cause: Lana, Effect: cirrhosis. Any minute now it could give up the ghost completely and the bleeps would blend into one continuous note, the green lines on the screens flattening out in unison. And she would be gone. Lana tried to imagine a world without her in it. Governments would rise and fall, fashions would swing in and out and back in again, just as they had since that fateful date in April 1982, but now *she* would no longer be there to witness them. All at once she found herself pondering the most ridiculous scenarios. Knowing her luck, the week after she died some smart arse would finally invent female contraception that didn't come accompanied with weight gain, acne, heavier periods or the risk of cancer. Knowing her luck, they would also develop a pain-free Brazilian wax. Her head filled with the wonderful innovations that were bound to emerge after her demise. Calorie free chocolate, ladder resistant pantyhose, a man you could keep in your closet and only take out for sex and household maintenance.

When Sadie arrived about three hours later, which felt more like three years, Lana could barely contain her relief.

'Sadie, sweetie, you came,' she whispered, beaming from ear to ear. 'Do me a favour, honey, go nab yourself a doctor's coat and one of those damn clipboards and get me out of this place. We'll tell them you're my consultant and you're flying me to an exclusive clinic in LA for specialist treatment.' Lana paused for a moment to stare at Sadie. 'Jeez, what the hell's happened to you, hon? You look like shit.'

Sadie, still displaying her council estate meets heroin chic look of the night before, shuffled over to the bed. After leaving Liam's she had removed her stilettos and run barefoot all the way to Lana's house, where she had spent what felt like an eternity cleaning up the blood before collapsing on to the chaise longue for a few hours fitful sleep. To say she looked like shit was something of an understatement. She managed to summon up a watery smile. 'Funny, I was just about to ask you the very same question,' she said, plonking herself down on what was possibly the most uncomfortable chair ever constructed. Sadie winced as the plastic edges cut into her aching limbs.

Lana chortled and shrugged her shoulders. 'Okay, fair point. You did remember to bring my cosmetics, didn't you? If I don't get a pair of tweezers to my eyebrows in the next sixty seconds I'm going to end up looking like that Neanderthal from Oasis.'

Sadie nodded and plonked a carrier bag on to the bed.

It had felt really strange going through Lana's belongings
– just being alone in her house had unnerved her – but it
was what Lana had wanted. And needed by the looks of
things. Sadie tried hard not to stare at the washed-out figure
propped before her on the bed. It was as if Lana had aged
ten years in as many hours. She seemed shrunken somehow,
her shoulders drooping forwards, her skin hanging from her
cheekbones like parchment, all yellowing and crinkled. Her
usual exotic fragrance had been replaced by a strange bitter
smell, as if it had been stripped away by paint thinner.
Sadie hurriedly reached inside the bag. 'Here you go,' she
said, placing Lana's leather cosmetics case in front of her.
'I thought you might be wanting these as well,' she added,
producing a bottle of Chanel No.5 and a black satin negligee
she had found draped over Lana's pillow.

Lana's bedroom had been exactly as she had pictured it,
crammed with the most exquisite antiques: the four-poster
bed covered in heart-shaped satin cushions, the oak chest
at the foot of the bed, the slightly battered gramophone
in the corner, and the silver jewellery box on the dressing
table. The dressing table itself was the focal point of the
room, with its huge three-sided mirror, framed with tiny light
bulbs, in true Hollywood starlet fashion. Sadie had perched
upon the velvet-upholstered stool and gazed at the array of
lotions, potions and perfumes on display. A huge ivory tub
of face powder lay open in front of her, a great rabbit's tail
of a powder puff abandoned next to it. It was when Sadie
had held the powder puff up to her nose and breathed in the
floral scent that she had finally allowed herself to cry. Lana
couldn't die – she was too vibrant and glamorous. She was
too strong.

But she certainly didn't appear to be any of those things
now as her hands fumbled clumsily with the zip on her
make-up bag.

'Darn! I seem to be all fingers and thumbs. God knows what they're putting in those drips. Sadie, honey, you couldn't help me out here, could you? Just slap a bit of foundation on me and a bit of blush, I'll take care of the lips.'

'Sure.' Sadie took the foundation eagerly and squeezed some on to the palm of her hand. Anything to get the old Lana back.

'So tell me – what happened last night? Why did you come back to my place? Not that I'm complaining, you understand, but I take it something must have gone wrong with your scene.'

Sadie grimaced. 'Oh, you don't want to hear all about my disaster. It would only depress you.'

'Are you kidding?' Lana shrieked, her voice cracking from the effort. 'Look at the state of me, girl. Believe me, there's nothing you could do or say to make me feel any lousier at this point in time. To be brutally honest, hearing your tale of woe might even make me feel a little better.'

Sadie couldn't help chuckling at this. 'Oh well, if you put it that way.' She sighed and began smoothing the foundation into Lana's skin, instantly fading the yellow hue to ivory. 'Well, as you know, I got the taxi from your place and about two hours later I finally made it to the venue. The cab driver was from Bosnia and hadn't quite mastered The Knowledge yet,' she explained.

Lana chortled. 'Oh, don't. I had one the other week who seemed to think a pedestrian crossing was some kind of exercise in target practice.'

Sadie fetched a powder compact from the bag. 'Okay, close your eyes.' She gently began dusting Lana's forehead and nose with powder. 'When I eventually got there I have to admit I was starting to feel a little bit nervous,' she continued.

Lana smiled and nodded her head against the pillow. From

what she could recall, the poor girl had been having kittens before she'd even left the house.

'So I went to the toilet, to freshen up and have a quick smoke, you know, and I saw these girls on their way out. Really tarty types.'

There was something about the acid tone of Sadie's voice that made Lana open one eye a fraction and study her face. Her normally placid expression had been replaced with a steely glare.

'They were discussing whether one of them was going to shag some bloke later on – and do you know what she said?'

Lana shrugged her shoulders.

'She said, "It depends on how many rum and blacks he buys me." Can you believe it? I mean what kind of girl uses sex to get a few free drinks? It's like being a—'

Lana coughed.

'Oh – sorry – I didn't mean.' Sadie felt her face begin to smart. 'Anyway, I finally plucked up the courage to go into the function room. Oh, Lana – it was horrible. It was even called the Terry Wogan Suite.'

Lana snorted with laughter. 'Classy,' she drawled.

'Exactly. And believe me, it turned out to be extremely fitting. It was crammed with the most obnoxious people I've ever seen. They were all so loud and full of themselves and – well – horny!'

Lana opened both of her eyes. 'Horny?'

Sadie continued to blush. 'Yes – or maybe pervy would be a more accurate description. Seriously, some of them were even shagging under the table!'

Lana smirked as she recalled a Roman orgy one of her clients had once dragged her along to. Although naturally it had taken place in the rather more salubrious penthouse suite of a Park Lane hotel.

'I couldn't see GL anywhere and this horrible creep with huge lips had tried to hit on me, so I decided to go back to the toilets to rethink how I was going to play my scene.'

Lana smiled fondly as she pictured poor Sadie surrounded by a bunch of lairy arseholes on heat, hopelessly out of her depth despite her six-inch heels.

Sadie put the powder compact down on the bedside cabinet and stared out of the window forlornly. When she finally resumed speaking her voice was barely more than a whisper. 'I locked myself in the first cubicle I came to and was just about to light a cigarette when I heard GL's voice. For a moment I thought he was talking to me – I thought I was the only person he called babes,' she gave a bitter little laugh. 'Shows what a fool I am really, doesn't it?'

Lana looked up at Sadie, her eyes suddenly wide with concern. 'Sadie, honey? What happened?'

Sadie felt one of Lana's hands come to rest on top of her own. 'He was in there with somebody else, that's what happened – the girl I'd overheard earlier.'

'The rum and black girl?'

'The rum and black girl. Obviously he hadn't bought her enough of them, because she was only giving him a blow job.'

'Oh my God! Oh, sweetie!'

'And then – if that wasn't quite bad enough, I had to listen to him snorting cocaine. Cocaine! I thought the only drug GL took was ginseng. Oh Lana, what am I going to do? I feel like I've been such a fool, my whole life seems to have been built on a tissue of lies,' Sadie's voice began to quiver. 'And the worst thing is, I've been the biggest liar – kidding myself that everything was all right when I knew deep down that it wasn't.'

Lana stared at Sadie, for once completely lost for words. There was something so heartbreaking about the anguish

etched upon her face, tainting her usual doe-eyed innocence.
Lana felt an unfamiliar feeling stirring within her – she
couldn't quite put her finger upon it – some strange mixture
of outrage and concern.

'So what did you do? Did you confront him? Does he
know that you know?'

Sadie laughed bitterly. 'Of course not, I'm too gutless for
that. I just hid there like the spineless little doormat that I
am and waited for them to leave. Then I came straight back
to yours and that's when I found you.'

Lana felt terrible. What must it have been like for Sadie to
have come back and found her in such a horrendous state?
Although the events of the previous night were a little hazy,
Lana would never forget vomiting all that blood. She had
thought it was never going to stop and she was sure it
was her own blind panic that had eventually caused her
to pass out. What must it have done to poor Sadie, on
top of everything else she had just been through? And to
have then had to accompany her to the hospital and wait
patiently for her to come round, while all the time her own
world was crashing down around her ears. Lana felt a burning
sensation at the corners of her eyes. God, were they feeding
her neat progesterone through those drips or what? If she
wasn't careful she would start weeping next and that was the
very last thing Sadie needed. Taking as deep a breath as she
could muster she grasped hold of Sadie's hands.

'Don't talk about yourself that way,' she scolded. 'He's the
asshole, not you, and don't you ever forget that. Besides, it's
good that you didn't go rushing out there and chop his balls
off or brain that old trollop with a bottle of rum.'

'It is?'

'Why, sure. Have you never heard the saying, revenge is
a dish best served cold?'

Sadie nodded.

'Well believe me, never a truer word was spoken. Revenge is so much sweeter when you've had time to cool down and savour the after-effects. You need time to plan your strategy, stockpile your ammunition, co-ordinate your strike.'

Sadie couldn't help smiling – Lana was starting to sound frighteningly like her father.

'Don't you worry, my girl – with me as your Chief of Defence, revenge will be sweeter than a tray full of smores.'

Chapter Twenty-Six

As it transpired, Sadie did not have to wait very long at all to wreak her revenge. In fact, the necessary 'ammunition' presented itself within a matter of hours.

'What do you mean by ammunition?' she had asked Lana. 'A pair of scissors to slash his suits with? A pot of water to boil his *Rocky* videos in?'

'Good Lord, no!' Lana had exclaimed. 'That whole bunny boiler scene is so Eighties. You need something way more original than that. It's all about psychology. You have to figure out exactly where his weakest spot is before launching a precision attack. Think of it as the mental equivalent of kicking him in the balls – just as painful, but a hell of a lot slower to heal.' A devilish grin began spreading across Lana's face, re-igniting the spark in her eyes. 'Don't worry, hon, we'll think of something, and in the meantime I want you to go get your things and move them into my place. I'm afraid the spare room could probably use a bit of a clean, but it's yours for as long as you need it.'

'Oh no – I couldn't,' Sadie had stammered, but Lana wasn't having any of it; she fixed Sadie with a determined stare.

'Nonsense. You can't go back to that asshole and besides, you'll be doing me a favour. I need someone to keep an eye on the place while I'm stuck in this hell-hole, and when I finally get discharged I guess I'll be needing someone to keep an eye on *me*.'

Sensing there was little point in arguing, and feeling

overcome with relief, Sadie had bowed to Lana's instructions without further hesitation. Thankfully, when she got to GL's house she found it empty. *GONE EXTREME GO-KARTING!* the note attached to the hall mirror exclaimed, the boldly printed letters seeming to swagger across the page. As Sadie cast her eyes around the hall, she felt as if she had been away for months rather than just overnight. It was like that period of readjustment after returning from a holiday. Everything that had once felt so familiar now bore an unsettling new slant. For a start she realised that she had never viewed this house, with its wall-to-wall burgundy shag-pile and Dolby surround sound speakers, as home. In her mind it had always been GL's place – as indeed it was on the mortgage. She would never have chosen the theme from *The A-Team* for *her* doorbell, or hung one of those irritating singing trout upon *her* wall.

'Don't worry, be happy!' the plastic fish warbled as she walked past. Sadie stopped in her tracks. She had never realised quite how much she hated that fish until now. She grabbed one of GL's golf clubs from the bag at the foot of the stairs and brandished it at the fish.

'Don't worry—'

SMASH! She brought the club crashing into its scaly belly.

'Beeeeeeeeeeee – huuuuuuuuppyyyyyyy,' it groaned, one of its beady eyes popping out of its head on a spring.

Sadie gasped. What was she doing? Although GL was undoubtedly fond of his singing trout and regularly pissed himself at its idiotic warblings, it was hardly his most vulnerable point. Still, skewering it with an eight-iron had proved immensely pleasurable. Sadie decided to look upon it as the mental equivalent of a quick dig in the ribs before getting stuck into GL's figurative balls (whatever they might turn out to be). The beginnings of a smile twitched at the corners of her mouth as she mounted the stairs two at a time. She would have a quick wash and change of clothes before grabbing her things and heading to Lana's.

But upon entering the bathroom she experienced a similarly choking feeling of irritation to that in the hall. Why the hell did GL need so many damned cosmetic products? Fair enough, every man needed shampoo, aftershave and deodorant, but was it really necessary to purchase about ten different types of each? And what about the ridiculous names and descriptions? Sadie began grabbing bottle after bottle from the windowsill. *Java for Men. Arabian Nights. Nights in White Satin. Sensual Musk Pour L'homme. Sahara Spice. Anti-dandruff protection for the man on the go. Twenty-four hour protection for the athletic man.* Oh pur-lease! Sadie wanted to vomit. GL wasn't an athletic man – he was a pumped up little prick.

It felt as if somebody had turned the shower on full blast. A red mist descended upon Sadie. What kind of a man used facial moisturiser, for Christ's sake? The kind who was concerned about the 'environmental hazards of the modern day world,' the label informed her. What kind of a man needed to buy dental polish? A vain arsehole in search of the perfect, self-satisfied smile, that's who.

Sadie yanked open GL's tub of seaweed enriched, deep-cleansing clay and spat into it. He was so damned hygienic as well, with his fifty-seven different mouthwashes and his anti-bacterial soap, shampoo and shower-gel. It wasn't natural to be so paranoid about a few little bacteria. Everybody knew that exposure to germs was essential for building a healthy immune system. Sadie stirred her saliva into the pot of clay with the tip of her little finger. Oh dear . . . oh no – was that her nose she could feel beginning to run? This cold weather was playing havoc with her sinuses. Sadie pressed a finger over one nostril, the way she had seen footballers do on the television and blew hard through the other one. A jet of snot flew into the jar, its green hue blending perfectly with the aquamarine clay. But surely that wouldn't be enough. Poor GL's body must be crying out to be introduced to some bacteria. It was down to her, as a parting gift, to make the introductions. Sadie glanced about the bathroom until her eyes alighted upon GL's electric toothbrush standing in all its sterile glory inside its case beside the sink. Sadie took it out and knelt down on the floor in front of the toilet. Was Rum and Black in this position as she administered her blow job, she wondered, as she began scouring the inside rim of the toilet pan with the toothbrush – the part where even the most meticulous cleaners cannot reach. Sadie wondered if GL had got Rum and Black to rinse her big painted mouth out with disinfectant prior to the act? After all, this was the man who purchased his condoms by the caseload, who had to scrub his penis raw the second after he had come. There were no post-coital cuddles with GL – no, the moment he shouted Geronimo he had to hotfoot it to the bathroom to douse his beloved member in antibacterial penis delouser. Sadie was certain that if she looked hard enough she would find a bottle of the stuff stashed away somewhere. But surely his behaviour couldn't be normal? Although she had no other experiences of her own to draw upon, she had watched enough steamy sex scenes in movies to know that GL couldn't be representative of the male population. In *9½ Weeks*, Mickey Rourke didn't bound out of bed for a quick douche every time he made love to Kim Basinger. In fact, Sadie could not recall a single film in which this had occurred. She sat back on her haunches and smirked as the sad truth dawned upon her – it would appear that GL's weakest spot, both psychologically and physically, *were* in fact his balls. So it would be his balls she would go after.

Sadie gathered together the liquid soap dispenser and the four different brands of shower gel. One by one she unscrewed the lids of each and lined the open bottles on the shelf beside the sink. Then she bent down to have a look in the cupboard beside the toilet where cleaning paraphernalia was stored. GL wanted a sterile penis? She would be only too happy to give him one. Removing the Domestos from the cupboard, Sadie carefully poured a generous helping of bleach into each of the open bottles, her brow furrowed with concentration. As she stood there, like some deranged professor poring over a row of test tubes in an old *Frankenstein* movie, a strange transformation seemed to be coming over Sadie. For the first time in her life she felt a sense of control. For the first time ever she was in charge of events and instead of an anxious chorus raising their doubts and fears in her head, there was just one voice, calm and collected, repeating just one word, over and over again. *Bastard, bastard, bastard.*

Once she had replaced all the lids and returned all the bottles to their rightful places, Sadie made her way into GL's bedroom. What kind of a *bastard* has a poster of himself stuck on his wall, she thought, staring scornfully at the mock sepia print of GL dressed up as a bandit from the Wild West. *WANTED – DEAD OR ALIVE!* the caption beneath read. Sadie rummaged through the desk drawer for a marker pen. Crossing out the words *DEAD OR ALIVE*, she replaced them with *FOR BEING A WANKER.*

Next stop was the condom supply beneath the bed. Sadie lay on her stomach and lifted up the valance. In the darkness she could just make out two medium sized boxes. She pulled them out. Immediately recognising the smiley face motif on the condom container, Sadie wrenched off the lid. It was like gazing into the pensioners' favourites at a pick'n'mix counter with the assortment of brightly coloured foil wrappers on display. Every imaginable type of condom was there, from ribbed to gossamer, from featherlite to extra strong. Perhaps GL had worn a condom while that tart had been sucking him off. He had probably bought some rum and black flavoured ones especially. Sadie leapt to her feet and went to her designated corner of GL's wardrobe. Pulling her pirate's top from the shelf, she removed her name badge and returned to the box. Sitting cross-legged on the floor, she slowly and methodically made her way through the condoms, piercing a hole with the badge pin right through each of the foil packages, counting as she went. One, two, three . . .

Sixty-four, sixty-five, sixty-six. Sadie stabbed the pin through the final condom and looked at the multicoloured pile glistening on the floor beside her. Sixty-six condoms equals sixty-six shags, enough to have lasted her and GL over a year. But now she knew he would have worked his way through this lot in just a couple of months. As with his house she was suddenly seeing GL in a whole new light. Or maybe she was finally seeing things, full stop. After all, hadn't GL always been a bit of a ladies' man? Hadn't he always had a habit of disappearing off on 'lads' weekenders' and overnight courses? He'd certainly had ample opportunity to cheat on her over the years. But she had been so damn desperate for a boyfriend, for someone to play Danny to her Sandy, that she had turned a blind eye to all the incriminating evidence that now seemed to be gliding before her eyes as if on a conveyor belt. Sadie felt like a contestant on the *Generation Game* as she recalled the mood swings, the silent phone calls, the nights working late at the office. And of course the *pièce de resistance*, the equivalent of the game show's state of the art Teasmaid, GL's insistence on separate bank accounts. What a prize fool she'd been.

Sadie began slinging the punctured rubbers back into their box. In all the time she'd lived with GL, she had never laid eyes on one of his bank or credit card statements. They always seemed to be spirited off as soon as they arrived. She wondered what further damning evidence they would detail. Payments to swanky restaurants perhaps, or Interflora? Probably a standing order to Bacardi and Ribena – not to mention Durex. Sadie's eyes fell upon the other box. It was about the size of a shoebox, but metallic rather than cardboard, with a label built into the lid. '*Important Documents*' GL had informatively scribed upon it. Sadie removed the lid and looked inside. Her heart sank as she rifled her way through the wads of certificates inside. Advanced Sales Skills, Jujitsu White Belt, Under Nines Soccer Summer School, Half a Length with armbands for the Chipping Sodbury Tadpoles. God, he had even kept his cycling proficiency certificate. Sadie frowned as she studied the documents. Nearly all of them had his first name tippexed out and 'GL' written over them. Was he so obsessed with his image that he even felt the need to go back over his childhood records and readjust them? What was so wrong with the name Gary Lee anyway? Sadie reached absent-mindedly into the bottom of the box and brought out an old style passport. She flicked it open to the back cover, where a teenage GL smirked out at her. His face was slightly spotty and his hair slightly flatter, but there was no mistaking that cocky grin. Sadie's eyes skimmed the information. Place of birth: Bristol, Avon. Next of Kin: Mrs Petronella Jenkins. Sadie grimaced. She had never liked GL's mother, with her phoney American accent and obsession with fondue parties. And what a name. Petronella – it sounded like an air-freshener for dogs. It was almost as bad as – Sadie nearly dropped the passport in shock. She rubbed her eyes and squinted them back into focus. No, she had not been seeing things. It was written down there quite clearly in black and white, right next to 'name'. But how? What? Why would somebody choose to call their beloved only son such a truly monstrous name? Did such a name even exist? Sadie could only conclude that a lifetime's resentment at being christened Petronella could have led to such a choice. She felt a quiver of excitement shimmy up her spine. In ammunition terms this was a state of the art, heat-seeking weapon of mass destruction and as far as GL was concerned it had fallen into entirely the wrong hands.

Chapter Twenty-Seven

Liam pressed fast-forward on the remote control and waited until the tape counter reached two hours, nine minutes. He had watched *Mutiny on the Bounty* so many times he knew precisely where to locate his favourite scene – in all three versions. It was the Marlon Brando version he had spent most of Sunday night watching – but try as he might, it just didn't seem to be working its usual magic. Liam pressed play. Bang on cue the outline of Pitcairn Island filled the screen, but rather than experiencing the usual tingle of excitement at the prospect of retracing Fletcher Christian's footsteps, Liam felt about as flat as the glassy sea on which the Bounty was drifting. He gazed blankly at the screen as the ship's crew danced about the island like kids in a sweet shop, all tanned skin and sun-bleached hair as they grabbed armfuls of papaya and yams and breadfruit, and shouted excitedly about there being enough wild game to feed the entire English Navy. Not even the sight of the golden rays filtering through the fringes of palm leaves or the bevy of beautiful Tahitian women singing around the campfire could lift Liam's spirits. The only woman he could think about right now was Sadie.

Liam couldn't work Sadie out for the life of him. She was like one of those bloody Rubik's cubes that had baffled the entire nation throughout the eighties. Just when you thought you'd got it sussed, you'd turn it over to find a bloody great line of yellows running right through the reds. Similarly, every time he thought he was getting somewhere with Sadie, when she finally appeared to be relaxing, something would happen and she would retreat back into her shell – or even worse, back to her creep of a boyfriend. After Sadie's hurried exit the night before, Liam had followed her out on to the balcony and watched as she raced along the Parade. She had even taken her shoes off and run in bare feet, such was her haste to get away from him. But why? Liam had returned to his bedroom and hunted high and low for some kind of incriminating evidence that could have led to such a panicked exit. But all he could find was the Cliff Richard album lurking towards the back of his collection of LPs. If only Sadie had stayed around long enough he could have explained that yes, the pink tank-top Cliff was wearing was a crime against humanity, and yes, so was the music, but it had belonged to his mum, not him. Liam had borrowed it when he was about fifteen years old for the guitar riff on 'Devil Woman,' and never got round to giving it back, that was all. But try as he might to shift responsibility for his spectacularly disastrous luck with women on to Cliff Richard, Liam knew deep down he only had himself to blame. Try as he might, he had never quite managed to master the art of being a 'Charmer'. And if he was totally honest, he didn't really want to either. Blokes like Nigel Havers, with their slicked-back hair and even greasier patter made his skin crawl. Why did women fall for that bullshit? Why were they taken in by those corny lines lifted straight from the *How to Get a Guaranteed Shag Manual?* Why were they so impressed by bouquets of flowers, all picked, packaged and even delivered by somebody else? Why did they always seem to prefer men who were all style over substance? Men who obviously spent far more time looking in the mirror than looking at them? Men who were so busy spiking their hair and strutting around in flashy suits, they didn't even know what their own girlfriend wanted for her birthday.

Liam flung down the remote control in disgust.

'Easy, tiger.'

Liam looked up to see Terry enter the living room, and for once he felt relief rather than irritation.

'All right, Tel.'

'Should I keep this on, or what?' Terry enquired, gesturing to his crash helmet and staring pointedly at the remote control on the floor.

Liam smiled sheepishly. 'Nah, you're all right, mate. I was just feeling a bit sorry for myself, that's all.'

Terry removed his helmet and sat down on the settee next to Liam. He frowned as he bent forward to study a rip running up the front of his jeans. 'Bloody joy-riders,' he muttered under his breath.

Liam followed his gaze. 'Are you okay, Tel? What happened? Did you come off the bike?'

Terry nodded. 'Yeah, a bunch of kids pulled out right in front of me down by Budgens. I tell you what, they should bring back National Service, that'd soon wipe the smirks off their spotty little faces. If they want to go tear-arsing around the place put 'em in a tank and send them over to Baghdad. Then we'll see who's smiling.' Terry reached into the inside pocket of his leather jacket for his roll-ups. 'I dunno, all I want to do is go out there and earn an honest crust and all I get is hassle and abuse.'

Liam couldn't help laughing. 'The day you earn an honest crust is the day I start believing in the tooth fairy. Go on, Tel, what is it you've been up to this past week? I don't think I can take much more of this suspense.'

Terry's eyes darted around the room shiftily. 'Promise you won't say nothing – especially to that stuck up Yank bird.'

Liam nodded. It was the first time he'd seen Terry all weekend so he'd yet to tell him that Lana had rather more pressing matters on her mind than Terry's new occupation.

'You know you can trust me – did I ever tell anyone about those knock-off teapots?'

Terry groaned. 'Bleedin' 'ell. I was stitched up good and proper that time, wasn't I?'

Liam chuckled and retrieved his can of beer from its rather precarious position on top of Terry's pile of biking magazines on the coffee table. 'Oh, I don't know. There's something quite challenging about a handle-less teapot. It gives the whole brewing experience a new element of excitement.'

'There's nothing bleeding exciting about third degree burns, I can tell you,' Terry retorted, fishing into his pouch for a pinch of tobacco. Liam waited patiently as Terry placed the baccy in the middle of a cigarette paper and with one deft turn of the wrist and slither of the tongue constructed himself a smoke. 'I told you, son, straight up, it's no more dodgy business for me. Leastways, not until I recreate my scene from *Bonnie and Clyde*. I tell you what, that Taj geezer is going to rue the day he ever refused to give me credit. I only wanted a couple of cans of Tennants Super.'

'All right, all right, I believe you. Just tell me what it is you've been doing on that bike of yours. Where have you been keeping it, by the way? I still haven't seen it.'

Terry paused to take a puff on his cig. When he did finally respond, his voice was barely more than a mumble.

Liam frowned. 'What did you say?'

'I said, I've been delivering pizzas for Dominos. The bike stays at the shop.'

Liam burst out laughing, spraying beer all over the sofa. 'Oh cheers mate, I needed that,' he gasped, dabbing at the spilt beer with the sleeve of his jumper. 'So all this *Easy Rider* bollocks, all this swaggering around the flat in your leathers singing 'Born to Be Wild', like the Manor's answer to Meatloaf, was because you've got yourself a job delivering pizzas? Jesus!'

Terry scowled. 'I can't win, can I? I try to go straight and all I get is ridicule. I bet Buster Edwards never got this much grief after he turned his back on train robberies and he ended up flogging flowers, for Gawd's sake.'

Liam wiped the tears from his face with the back of his hand. 'I'm sorry, Tel, but you've got to admit, it is a bit comical. All this time I've been imagining you out there on some fuck-off Harley and you've been poodling about on a little blue and red scooter. Still—' Liam's whole body began to reverberate with laughter once more. 'At least you weren't bullshitting when you said you were earning an honest crust. Stuffed crust was it, or just plain?'

Terry began to grin. 'Don't. I'm getting sick of the sight of bleeding pizza. I've been having them for breakfast, lunch and dinner. Still, mustn't grumble, beggars can't be choosers, and all that. I just wish they had meatballs as a topping. I reckon they'd be on to a winner there. Give it a bit of a Bolognese flavour.'

Liam grimaced and shook his head. 'I can't believe you didn't tell me. I was discussing it with Sadie last night – we reckoned you were working as some kind of drug runner.'

Terry snorted. 'Yeah, right. Let me tell you, the only herb I've been supplying this week is bleeding oregano. So how is Treacle? I'll have to pop down there meself tomorrow. Tell her the good news before you do.'

Liam's face instantly fell.

'Blimey, what's up? You look like you've just caught your old mum shagging Ozzy Osbourne. Sadie's all right ain't she?'

Liam frowned. He didn't really want to have to recount the disastrous events of the night before to Terry and besides which, the image of his mother in a clinch with rock's Prince of Darkness was casting a rather unsavoury shadow across his mind. But for the first time ever he seemed to have Terry's undivided attention; for once he was not humming Status Quo or wrestling with a piece of ear wax or other orifice obstruction, but simply sitting there staring at him intently.

Liam took a swig from his beer and, staring glumly into his lap, he began to recount his sorry tale: the tearful, late night phonecall from Sadie, the unexpected visit to the hospital, Lana's suspected diagnosis (at which point Terry interjected with a low pitched whistle) and Sadie agreeing to come back to the flat for a coffee.

Terry's eyes lit up at this point and he swivelled sideways on the settee so that he was directly facing Liam. 'So she came back here did she? But I don't get it. When I saw her on Saturday she was all geared up for her big *Grease* scene at her geezer's work do. How come she ended up at the hospital with the septic tank?'

Liam shrugged. 'I dunno. I think something must have gone wrong. She was in a right state when I got there.'

Terry frowned.

'Anyway,' Liam continued, 'by the time we got back here she seemed okay again. Lana had regained consciousness and as I said, we were even having a joke about your new job.'

'So why the long face then?' Terry asked, rolling himself another cig, the butt of the previous one still smouldering away on his bottom lip.

'Well, I took her through to my bedroom—'

'Oh, yeah?' Terry laughed, little clouds of smoke puffing from his mouth with each chortle.

'Well, I could hardly bring her in here, could I? You were asleep on the couch with your hand down your kecks and *Confessions of a* bloody *Window Cleaner* on the box.' Liam searched through the carnage on the coffee table for something to smoke. Retrieving half a cigarette from one of the ashtrays he lit it up before continuing his tale. 'So I took her to my room and told her to make herself comfortable while I went to make the coffees.'

'Yeah,' Terry cried, his eyes glinting with excitement, 'and did she?'

'Did she what?'

'Did she make herself comfortable?'

'Oh, for Christ's sake. This isn't some Channel Five movie we're talking about here. I didn't get back to find her draped over the bed in a leopard skin thong, if that's what you're on about.'

Terry's face fell.

'Far from it, in fact. She looked as if she'd seen a ghost. Seriously, Tel, she couldn't get out of here quick enough. She didn't even stop for her coffee or a chocolate digestive.'

'What chocolate digestives?' Terry enquired accusingly. 'We haven't got any chocolate digestives – have we?'

Liam reached down the side of the settee for the remainder of the biscuits and slung them at Terry. 'I can't work her out, Tel. One minute we're laughing and joking together and the next she's out of here like – like—'

'Like a bat out of hell?' Terry offered, through a mouthful of digestive.

'Exactly.' Liam sighed and stared mournfully at the blizzard that was now engulfing the television screen. 'I don't know what I'm doing wrong, mate. The only women I seem to have any luck with these days are all old enough to be my mother.'

'There's nothing wrong with that – you just point them in my direction and I'll sort them out,' Terry replied. 'Correct me if I'm wrong, but have you got a bit of a soft spot developing for young Sadie?'

Liam groaned and prepared himself for the inevitable piss-take. 'No. I mean – well – of course I like her, but not like that. I just want to be mates, that's all. Anyway, she's already got a bloke.'

Terry snorted. 'Have you seen him? Flashy little twat. I tell you what, son, you'd easily have him in a fight – no contest.'

Liam groaned again. 'This isn't the Wild West, Tel. I'm not going to take some bloke outside over his girlfriend. There's not going to be any gunfight at the video store corral. Besides, she's made it quite clear who she prefers. She couldn't get back to him fast enough last night.'

Terry frowned. 'Don't be so quick to jump to conclusions,' he said and something about the unfamiliar gravity in his voice caused Liam to look up in surprise.

'What do you mean?'

'I mean, things ain't always what they might seem,' Terry mused. 'Do you know what, sometimes I worry about that girl, I really do.'

'Why?' Liam stared at Terry intently.

'Well, as I said, sometimes things ain't exactly what they seem.'

'Meaning?'

'Meaning just because she's going out with the bloke, don't mean she's happy with him.'

'But you don't know that for certain, do you? Do you?'

Terry shifted in his seat to avoid Liam's gaze. 'It ain't really my place to say, son. All I will say is don't be so quick to write things off all the time.'

Liam ran his fingers through his hair and frowned. 'I don't understand.'

'Oh, I think you do,' Terry uttered sagely, before peeling the remnants of his previous roll-up from his lip. 'When are you going to stop running away from everything, eh? Isn't it about time you stuck around and faced the music?'

Liam could hardly believe what he was hearing. 'Now, hang on a minute,' he began.

'Oh, I know what you're going to say. What right have I got to criticise you? Me, who's spent me whole life on the run from something or another. Fucking hell, son, ever since I was a kid I've been trying to escape from someone; first the social services and then the old Bill. I've never had somewhere to call home, somewhere to run to instead of from. But that's why I'm warning you now. Don't go making the same mistakes I did. If you want something – or someone – go after it, don't run away.'

'But I *do* go after things,' Liam protested. 'What about all the travelling I've done? Look at all the places I've seen while my mates have been stuck here in their shitty nine to five lives. If I set my mind on something I get off my arse and do it. How can you say I don't go after things? Jesus, I'm going to be on the other side of the world in two weeks time, retracing Fletcher Christian's footsteps.'

'Exactly,' Terry retorted.

'What do you mean, exactly?'

Terry paused to light his new roll-up. 'And what was Fletcher Christian doing when he landed on that island of his?'

'He was having an adventure, discovering uncharted territory, building a future for himself.'

'Bullshit.'

'All right, what *was* he doing, then?'

'He was on the run, just like you. He'd led a mutiny against a Naval Officer, a treasonable offence, and he needed somewhere to hide. And, according to the *Sunday Sport's* exclusive report last year, he ended up dying a sad old man suffering from knob rot.' Terry got to his feet, clutching the packet of chocolate digestives. 'Anyway, son, it's time I hit the sack, this pizza lark is doing me in. No hard feelings, eh? It's just that I worry about you sometimes, that's all.' And with that Terry shuffled from the room.

Liam sat in the darkness and contemplated this latest turn of events. It was like the final awful twist in a horror movie when the hero realises that his closest friend is in fact the psycho killer and he has nowhere left to turn. Not only was Liam a disaster when it came to women, but now even Terry was worrying about him. Liam looked around the room in despair before retrieving the remote control from the floor and pressing rewind. Well – he'd show the lot of them. What was that song his mum used to play every time she chucked all their wordly goods in the back of her mini and they left her latest arsehole bloke? 'When the Going Gets Tough, the Tough Get Going.' There was nothing weak about moving on. It was called being decisive. Wasn't it?

Chapter Twenty-Eight

'Good morning, Pirate Videos, Sadie speaking.'

'Good morning, babes. What the hell happened to you last night?'

Sadie held the telephone receiver away from her ear and drew a breath. A myriad of panicked thoughts jostled for attention in her head, like a gaggle of gossips debating the latest episode of a soap. *Why was GL phoning her? Why was he still calling her 'babes'? Why wasn't he angry? Why wasn't he suffering from third degree burns to the foreskin?*

Cautiously she brought the phone back to her ear. 'What do you mean?' she asked.

'Well, I ended up staying the night at Wilko's. We went for a few bevvies after go-karting and as he only lives round the corner from work I thought it would be easier to crash there instead of coming all the way home. I must have called at least a dozen times to let you know, but you never picked up, and your mobile was switched off too.'

Once again Sadie clasped the receiver in both hands while she listened to the flurry of answers that now flooded her mind. *So he hasn't even been home. He doesn't even know what I've done. He doesn't even know that I've left him. He hasn't even had a shower – at least not with his newly enhanced, anti-bacterial shower gel.* And then the final, sickening realisation: *He's been with that tart again.*

Sadie took a deep breath and attempted to regain her composure. 'Oh, I'm sorry, *babes*,' she replied, barely able to conceal her contempt. 'They asked me to work an extra shift in the shop yesterday and I was so tired when I got back home I went straight to sleep. I must have been out like a light to have missed the phone ringing so many times.'

'Hey, don't worry about it.' The relief in GL's voice was palpable. 'Tell you what, why don't you bring home a copy of *Speed 2* tonight and we'll get a bargain bucket from the KFC? I feel as if I haven't seen you for ages.'

'Yeah, great,' Sadie replied, not even bothering to feign enthusiasm at the prospect of a night spent watching GL slaver over Sandra Bullock and a tub of greasy chicken. And yet just a week ago such a proposition would have made her day. Could she really have been that desperate? 'Anyway, I'd better go now,' Sadie added. 'Vince is coming down for a staff meeting.'

'Ooh, bloody hell, high-powered stuff,' GL sniggered. 'I'd better get cracking too, I've got to give a presentation to the whole unit about that deal I set up last week. Even Bob Tanner, the Sales Director, is going to be there. Catch you later, babes.'

Sadie sat motionless for a few seconds, staring numbly into the shop while the dialling tone hummed in her ear. What she was feeling now went way beyond anger; it transcended the fitful rage she had experienced the previous day as she had sat puncturing condoms and scouring toilets with toothbrushes. No, this was something different altogether. It was a deep-rooted thirst for revenge and she knew exactly how she was going to quench it.

'All right then, peeps, let's get down to business, yeah?'

Sadie jumped as a voice bellowed out from behind her; an infusion of Mediterranean and cockney accents, under-scored by a forty-a-day rasp.

Vince was standing in the entrance to the kitchenette, legs astride, hairy hands on hips. He looked like a cross between

John Wayne and Englebert Humperdink. 'Now where the fuck has that hippy got to? I haven't got all day, you know. I'm a busy man. I've got to be in the Willesden Green store for eleven thirty, you know what I mean?'

Sadie nodded weakly. She could have told Vince it was asking far too much of Brian to make an appearance at such an early hour. He probably didn't rise from his coffin until gone midday.

'I dunno, I go out of my way to help you guys, give you a bit of my time and expertise and what thanks do I get?' Vince frowned and scratched his head, instantly flecking his coarse dark hair with a powdering of dandruff. He pulled up the sleeve on his undoubtedly elegant but completely wasted designer suit, revealing a gold Rolex nestling on a carpet of black fur. Sadie had never known a man as hairy as Vince. Even his eyebrows looked more like a pair of badgers. 'I give him five more minutes and then that's it – finito! You know what I mean?'

Once again, Sadie nodded. By the end of an encounter with Vince she always felt like one of those dogs people attach to the back shelf of their cars, her head bobbing aimlessly in agreement, as though on a spring.

Vince marched past her, trailed by his usual fog of Paco Rabanne fumes. 'I don't know, Sadie, sweetheart, that poster display's looking a little bit tatty,' he remarked, standing in the middle of the shop and frowning at the display surrounding the television screens. 'Isn't it time you replaced it with something a little more up to date? You know what I mean? How about that new Nicole Kidman movie? I'm sure I sent you a box full of posters. The one where she's leaning on that fence and you can see her left raspberry?'

Sadie nodded and sighed. 'Yes I know the one you mean, but we still haven't been sent any copies of the film. I didn't see the point of advertising it until we have it in stock.'

Vince raised his hands in disbelief. 'You aren't getting any, sweetheart, but that's not the point. At least if we've got the posters up we won't look like a laughing stock. You know what I mean?'

Sadie automatically went to nod, but then stopped herself. 'No, actually, I don't know what you mean. Surely we look more of a laughing stock advertising a film that we haven't got? And *why* aren't we getting it? It's up for about eight Oscars. What's going on, Vince. We haven't had a new release for about a month now.'

Vince stared uneasily at his mock-croc cowboy boots. 'What are you talking about? I sent you at least five new true life dramas last month, didn't I?'

'Yes I know, but there isn't exactly a huge market for Farrah Fawcett at the moment,' Sadie responded defiantly. She had never been quite this forceful with Vince before, she had always been too wary of what he might tell her, too afraid that he might confirm her worst suspicions and announce that the shop was about to be closed down. But after the events of Saturday night, nothing seemed to faze Sadie any more. It was as if her life was on a collision course with calamity and she was determined to see the ride through until the bitter end.

'What are you talking about? Birds love that kind of stuff!' Vince exclaimed, marching over to the new releases stand and grabbing a cover. 'All that *my husband got my grandmother pregnant* bullshit.' Vince paused for a second to pore over the blurb. 'Bloody hell – that's sick! Still, they've got a top-drawer cast. Didn't she used to be on *Knot's Landing*?'

Refusing to look at the cover, Sadie stared dejectedly at the floor. Vince may be incredibly stupid, but surely even he realised that with average weekly takings down to less than two hundred pounds the shop was hardly what you might term a goldmine.

As if he were reading her mind, Vince replaced the film

cover on the shelf and strode back over to the counter. 'Don't worry, sweetheart. Whatever happens you'll always have a job with Pirate Videos. There's always vacancies in our Brixton and Putney branches, you know what I mean?'

Sadie nodded. She knew what he meant all right. The Ruislip Manor branch was on its way out and if she wanted to remain in employment she would have to transfer to the gun-crime capital of England.

'But I tell you what,' Vince continued, grabbing his cigars from the counter. 'That opportunity will not be on offer to the hippy. And you can tell him that from me, yeah?'

Sadie nodded, although she had no intention of telling Brian any such thing. It would probably make his day to learn the shop was about to close; they probably wouldn't see him or the Pink Floyd videos for dust.

When Brian did finally materialise, a full hour after Vince's departure, the first thing Sadie did was grab her coat and bag and head for the door. 'I'm going to do the banking,' she explained, a laughable prospect as the weekend's takings had come to the grand sum of twenty-three pounds and fifty-seven pence.

Brian stared at her blankly – at least she assumed that's what was going on behind those reflector lenses. 'But I thought we were having a meeting,' he muttered.

'We were. We did. Two hours ago,' Sadie retorted.

Brian sighed and slung his canvas rucksack under the counter. 'I might as well have stayed in bed then,' he said, making his way to the back shelf, no doubt to find himself *The Wall*.

'Oh, I wouldn't bother putting Pink Floyd on, either, 'Sadie added as she reached the door. 'Vince wants us to play kids' videos all week. It's part of a new promotion. Can you start off with number 1257 please.'

Sadie chuckled to herself as she walked out on to the Parade. The thought of Brian having to sit through *Teletubbies, Series One* was hugely satisfying. She seemed to be developing quite a sadistic streak all of a sudden. Sadie the Sadist – yes, it certainly had a ring to it. But Brian's torment was nothing to what she had in store for GL.

Walking straight past the bank, Sadie headed up to the roundabout at the top of the Manor and made her way to Pierre's Internet C@fe on the corner. She had spent most of the previous night lying awake in Lana's spare room trying to devise the most effective deployment of the ammunition that had fallen into her lap so unexpectedly, like a gift from the Gods. After much deliberation she had concluded that in terms of reliability and maximum impact there could be no better conduit than the Information Superhighway. After purchasing her token, Sadie sat down at a PC and keyed in her ID number. As soon as she was online, she went straight to the AOL site and logged on to GL's personal e-mail account.

Name: GLJenkins, she punched into the keyboard.

Password: Goldfinger. *God, what a twat.*

Once she had entered his account she hastily retrieved his old passport from her bag and took a photocopy of the inside cover. Scanning the copy into his personal pictures file she then clicked on COMPOSE MAIL and began to type.

Dear Friends and Work Colleagues,
    Since I have known you I have always gone by
the moniker, 'GL' and many of you may have been
wondering why this is. As a fan of the programme Dallas
I realised at an early age that all the greats tend to be
known by their initials – from the legendary oil magnate,
JR Ewing to the literary giants JRR Tolkien and of course

JK Rowling, not to mention the international statesman, George W. Bush. I decided that by going by my initials I would create an aura of power and mystique about myself that would make me stand out in a crowd. And events certainly seem to have proved me right. Those of you who knew me at university will agree that I was one of a kind – a Svengali type figure for the other kids to look up to, even aspire to, as I clambered to the dizzy heights of red belt in jujitsu and was crowned Paint-balling Champion for two years running. However, this all paled into comparison with the success I have enjoyed since entering the heady world of commerce. Those of you who have experienced the white knuckle ride of working with me at Cromwell Communications (you know who you are you bunch of nutters!) will know all about the ball-busting deals I bring in week after week. Culminating in my greatest success to date, when I recently secured an account with a projected annual revenue of £1.5 mill. Even our very own Sales Director, Bob Tanner, doesn't know how I do it. He practically creamed when he saw my end of quarter results.

So what is the point of this mail? Basically I feel as if I have nothing left to prove. Oh don't worry Bob, I'm not about to throw the towel in – as Rocky Balboa once said, 'I ain't about to quit, Adrienne.' No, I just don't see the point in hiding behind a pair of initials anymore. I'm proud of who I am and I want to share that fact with the world. From now on I want you to address me by my full Christian name (please see attached copy of my passport) and leave the initials to other, more pretentious wankers. Yours, loud and proud,

Gaylord Jenkins.

Sadie sat back in her chair and smirked. She'd show that jumped up little arsehole. Without further ado, she attached the copy of Gaylord's passport to the mail, entered his bulging address book and clicked on SEND EVERYONE.

Chapter Twenty-Nine

'You stupid little bitch.'

Sadie looked up from *Fatal Attraction* to see GL standing in the shop doorway. At least she assumed it was GL; his body was the same, but his features seemed to have been contorted beyond recognition. The cocky grin had been twisted into a menacing scowl and his eyes had narrowed to the size of two dart-heads, aimed straight at her. Steam billowed from his mouth, casting a shroud around him, like dry ice against the cold night air.

Sadie felt an old familiar stab of fear, a feeling that dated way back to before she had ever met GL. If she closed her eyes now she knew she would see her mother kneeling on the kitchen floor, her whole body trembling as she tried to scrape up the remnants of her father's dinner from the floor. 'How many times have I told you I don't like pork, you stupid little bitch?' her father demanded, his voice as cold and controlled as GL's. 'I'm sorry,' her mother had stammered, nipping her finger on a sliver of china and watching helplessly as a trickle of blood plopped down into the gravy on the floor. Sadie felt a tightening in her chest as she remembered cowering in the corner of the kitchen, convinced that her mother was about to bleed to death in front of her very eyes.

'I'm sor—' she began. But then a bolt of anger brought her rushing back to her senses. What the hell was she sorry for? She looked up from her lap and met GL's stare head on.

'Bitch?' she asked, trying desperately to iron out the quiver in her voice. 'I thought you liked to call me babes?'

GL marched into the shop leaving the door wide open behind him.

Sadie resisted the urge to shiver as an icy breeze raced past the new releases and hit her straight in the face. 'But then, I thought a lot of things, didn't I?' she continued.

'What do you mean?' GL asked, coming to a standstill in front of the counter and slinging his sports bag on to the floor.

'Well, I thought I was the only one you called babes, I thought we were in a serious relationship. I thought I could trust you.'

'Oh, don't give me any paranoid bullshit. Is this all because I stayed the night at Wilko's? You're a nutter, you are.' GL moved right up to the counter and leant towards her, so close she could feel his breath on her face and smell the traces of day-old aftershave. Java For Men, unless she was very much mistaken. 'Have you any idea how much shit you caused me today? Have you any idea how much humiliation and ridicule I've had to endure because of your e-mail? And don't try and deny it was you who sent it, you're the only other person who knows my AOL password. Can you imagine what it was like for me to walk into that presentation and be greeted by a load of sniggers and whispers and not have a clue what was going on – until I saw the posters on the wall.'

'The posters?'

'Yeah, the posters. The posters they'd made of my passport, blown up to A4 size. The thing I don't understand, though, is what made you think you could get away with it?'

Sadie watched as GL began pacing up and down in front of the counter, rubbing the knuckles of one hand in the palm of his other.

'What did you think I'd do, just laugh it off and let you come crawling back, begging for forgiveness? I tell you what, babes, you can get down on your hands and knees right now, but you ain't ever going to get away with this one.'

Sadie looked at GL, all puffed up like Mighty Mouse in his extra-padded ski jacket and elevated heels and suddenly she had the most overwhelming desire to laugh. Why had she ever been so afraid of this pathetic idiot who stood before her? And what exactly had she been frightened of? That he might leave her? That he might run off with somebody else and leave her free to actually enjoy her life? Why had she never had any faith in herself? In one split second of almost blinding clarity she saw exactly where she had been going wrong all these years. And where her mother had gone so wrong before her. It seemed that in life you had two choices; to be led by faith or led by fear and, ironic as it seemed, it was all too easy to choose the latter. Sadie had been governed by fear for so long now, she no longer even knew what it was she was afraid of. It was only now, when the manifestation of her fears stood before her, all phoney swagger and surgically scrubbed penis, that she realised the ludicrousness of her situation.

Sadie got to her feet and walked over to the hatch in the counter. 'Do you seriously think that *I* am going to beg *your* forgiveness, Gaylord?' she asked.

GL stopped pacing and his mouth fell open. 'What do you mean?'

Sadie opened the hatch and walked around the counter to face him. GL was one of the few men she could actually look straight in the eye without craning her neck. Why had she never noticed that before? 'Well, shouldn't it be the other way round?'

'You what?'

'Shouldn't *you* be begging *my* forgiveness?'

'Ha, ha, very funny.' There was a strange sort of wobble in GL's voice now; if Sadie hadn't known better she could have sworn it was a nervous tremor.

'I don't think it *is* funny actually. To turn up at your boyfriend's work do and find him being pleasured by some tart in the ladies toilets. How many rum and blacks did you have to buy her by the way? I'm dying to know what the going rate is.'

The blood in GL's cheeks visibly drained. 'I don't know what you're talking about,' he stammered.

'Oh, I think you do, *babes*. And then of course there was the coke snorting. Honestly, GL, I thought an arrogant arsehole like you would be far too vain to risk rotting your septum.'

'You're mad, you are,' GL replied, taking a couple of steps back. 'You want to watch what you say – I could do you for defamation of character.'

'Character! What character?' Sadie gave a hollow laugh, 'Do me a favour. You've got about as much character as one of the heroes in those dire action adventure films you love to watch.' Sadie could hardly believe the words coming from her mouth now, and her voice – it was so strong, steely almost. 'Now, why don't you do me a favour and get out of my shop before *I* do *you* for harassment.'

'You what?'

'You heard me – get out.'

'You'll be sorry.' GL spat back at her. 'You're nothing without me. Nothing,' he continued, stabbing her on the shoulder with his stubby forefinger.

Again Sadie laughed. 'Wrong again,' she cried. 'I was nothing when I was *with* you, nothing but a pathetic little doormat who'd do anything to keep you happy.'

'Oh yeah? So what exactly have you got without me?' GL demanded. 'You've got no mates, nowhere to live and a shitty little job in a shitty little video store. You haven't even got any family to go running to. God, no wonder your mum topped herself with you for a daughter.'

Sadie stumbled backwards against the counter as the air drained from her lungs. Squinting, she reached out to steady herself, but it felt as if somebody was shining a searchlight right in her eyes and she could barely see a thing. It took a few seconds for Sadie to realise that she was not about to faint. A further few seconds to realise that the dazzling light before her eyes had not been caused by a sudden rush of blood to the head, but by a headlight. The headlight of a moped to be precise. The head light of a moped that just so happened to have driven right into the shop and was revving away next to the new releases.

'What the fuck?'

For the first time that night Sadie found herself in agreement with GL. They both watched, open-mouthed, as the moped rider, clad entirely in black from his biker boots to the visor on his helmet, dismounted.

'Is this little toe-rag giving you grief, Treacle?' a voice boomed out from inside the helmet.

'Terry?' Sadie asked, incredulous.

'Who the hell's Terry?' GL whispered.

Sadie began to grin. 'He's a friend of mine,' she replied. 'A very good friend.'

'With a very short temper,' Terry added.

'With a very short temper,' Sadie repeated.

'And a very large baseball bat,' Terry continued, producing a baseball bat from the back of his bike.

GL stepped away from Sadie, raising his hands slightly.

'Oh, of course, you didn't know I had any friends, did you, GL?' Sadie asked, regaining her composure and squaring up to him once again. 'You've always been far too busy obsessing about yourself. Well, for your information, I have some very good friends. People I can trust, people who care about me.

And here's something else you didn't know. I moved out of your crappy little house yesterday and I wouldn't go back there if you paid me.'

GL's eyes flitted anxiously between Sadie and Terry. 'Right, well – I'll be off then,' he muttered picking his sports bag off the floor.

'Yes, you do that,' Sadie responded, marching back behind the counter. 'Oh – and GL, before you go.'

GL stopped and turned. 'Yes?'

'You'd better take this.' Sadie fetched GL's passport from her bag and flung it at him. The passport ricocheted into the comedy section where it aptly crashed into *Dumb and Dumber* before dropping to the floor.

GL stooped to retrieve it and headed straight for the door.

'And don't you come back here neither, or I'll be having your guts for garters,' Terry snarled.

As soon as the door shut behind GL Sadie sunk down on to her chair and held her head in her hands. After being as rigid as a girder her whole body now felt as if it were about to dissolve into a pile of mush upon the floor.

'Are you all right, Treacle?' Terry asked, removing his helmet. 'I saw him hassling you as I was driving up the Parade. I thought I'd better check things out.'

Sadie looked up and didn't know whether to laugh or cry at the sight that greeted her, so she did both. 'Terry – is that a Domino's Pizza bike?' she gasped between spluttered giggles, tears coursing down her face.

Terry sighed as he came behind the counter and pulled Sadie close to his leather-clad chest. 'Afraid so, Treacle. Here, you don't fancy a stick of garlic bread, do you? I can't be arsed making any more deliveries tonight, I'll tell 'em I got mugged again or something.'

Sadie leant her head against Terry and inhaled deeply. Never had the smell of old leather, stale cigarettes and garlic smelt more comforting. 'I'd love a stick of garlic bread,' she replied. 'I'll go and put the kettle on.'

Chapter Thirty

'Do the bit where you call him Gaylord again, please,' Lana implored, grimacing slightly as she hauled herself into a seated position on the chaise longue.

Sadie's attempt at a sigh was thwarted by an inane grin. In the past week she must have recounted her tale of revenge at least fifty times to Lana, and although it was beginning to get a little tedious she knew she could never tire of her reverential audience. It felt fantastic to be the object of another's awe for once. It was as if every proud gasp that emitted from Lana was being pumped directly into Sadie, causing her to swell with pride. 'Okay,' she said, placing her cup on the floor beside her armchair and clearing her throat.

'No, no,' Lana exclaimed. 'Don't do it sitting down. I want a proper reenactment.'

Sadie got to her feet, trying hard to look disgruntled. 'Okay, but this really *is* the last time.' Making her way behind the coffee table, which was now laden with bottles of medication, assorted literature on liver disease and a framed picture of Clark Gable (a vital booster of patient morale), she stood in front of the fireplace and took a deep breath. 'Right, the coffee table is the shop counter and you're GL,' she instructed, quite pointlessly, for in the twenty-four hours Lana had been home this had become a well-rehearsed routine.

Lana nodded and pulled her woollen blanket up over her satin pyjamas. 'And – action,' she said, before launching into her Dick Van Dyke style cockney. 'What did you fink I'd do, babes, just larf it awf and let you come crawling back, begging for my forgiveness? I tell you what, babes, you can get down on your hands and knees, babes, but you ain't never gonna get away with this one – babes!' Lana sank back into her cushions, grinning from one jewelled ear to the other.

Stifling a giggle, Sadie marched around the coffee table to face Lana. 'Do you seriously think that *I* am going to beg *your* forgiveness, *Gaylord?*'

At this point both women dissolved into peals of laughter.

'Oh, stop,' Lana pleaded, clutching her side. 'What is it with that name? It makes me want to wet myself every time I hear it – I feel as if I've relapsed back to kindergarten.'

Sadie collapsed on to the floor next to the chaise longue. 'I know. I couldn't believe it when I saw the passport – I didn't think such a name existed, apart from as an insult.'

Lana nodded. 'I'm afraid so. It was pretty big in the States back in the Seventies – there's even a district in Michigan called Gaylord.'

'Maybe that's where he was conceived,' Sadie cried. 'And his parents wanted to make some kind of lasting acknowledgement – a bit like Brooklyn Beckham.'

Lana nodded. 'Let that be a lesson to all couples planning a trip to Michigan – ignore birth control at your peril,' she mused. 'Anyway, nurse, isn't it time for some more medication?'

Sadie sprang to her feet and consulted the computer printout next to the bottles of pills. 'Yes, I do believe it's time for your laxative. Would madam like it with a water or fresh juice chaser?'

Lana grimaced. 'I suppose a vodka's out of the question?' she enquired hopefully.

Sadie met Lana's imploring gaze with a frown. 'A vodka

is completely out of the question,' she retorted, topping up Lana's glass from a bottle of mineral water and passing her a pill. She was beginning to get quite concerned about Lana's repeated requests for alcohol. The day before she had returned from hospital, Sadie had completely emptied the house of booze. The previous week had given her ample time to go to the library and research the subject of cirrhosis. There was now very little she didn't know about liver function tests, jaundice and portal hypertension – not to mention liver transplants. 'You know what the doctors said – to even be considered for a transplant you have to go at least six months without a drink.'

'Yes, mother,' Lana responded sulkily, grabbing the pill from Sadie and flinging it into her mouth.

Sadie returned to her armchair, looking somewhat crestfallen. 'Sorry, I don't mean to be a nag, but isn't it worth the sacrifice? You don't want to die – do you?'

Lana looked at Sadie, whose eyes had grown as wide as a pair of satellite dishes, so shocked was she at the prospect of somebody actually choosing death over life. But it was all right for her wasn't it? At the tender age of twenty-two with everything to live for, especially now she'd finally got shot of that asshole of a boyfriend. Sadie didn't know what it was like to experience real pain, real fear. She didn't know what it was like to have woken up every morning for over twenty years and have to consume a quart of vodka before she could even bring herself to look in the mirror. And when she did look in the mirror she didn't know what it was like to truly loathe the poor excuse for a human being staring back. But more than anything, she didn't know what it was like to feel so consumed by a craving that you would literally kill to get your hands on your next drink. Lana suddenly felt a surge of fury at Sadie and her naïve concern. How dare she clear out her drinks cabinet and impose a state of prohibition upon

her home. And to think she had shown the girl hospitality
at a time when she had nowhere else to go. Like a pair
of tom-tom drums, Lana's temples began beating a tattoo.
Huh, Sadie had thought she was so smart, even disposing
of the cooking sherry in the kitchen – but she hadn't sniffed
out the bottle of tequila at the back of the airing cupboard,
had she? Lana had managed to resist it so far, but not any
longer. She'd show Sadie, sitting there so smugly, like one of
those darn doctors. They couldn't dictate whether she had a
drink or not, it was none of their business what she did to her
own body. But as she hauled herself upright and prepared
to go upstairs, the expression on Sadie's face rendered her
motionless. It wasn't one of smugness or even shock – it was
one of pure, unadulterated terror.

'Sadie, honey, are you okay?' Lana asked. Sadie's face had
drained as white as a snowman's, her eyes as dark as two
lumps of coal in contrast.

'Yes, yes, I'm fine, it's just that . . .' Unable to continue,
Sadie crumpled like a tissue into her chair, her shoulders
shuddering with each silent sob.

'Oh Jeez,' Lana sighed, throwing back her blanket and
gingerly hoisting her legs on to the floor. 'Please don't cry,
sweetie, I was only kidding. Of course I don't want to die,
it's just hard adapting to a life without drink, is all.'

Sadie nodded without looking up. 'I know,' she stammered.
'I just don't think I could bear it if anything happened to you,
but you don't even seem to care. How can a person not care
whether they live or die? I don't understand.'

Lana stared at Sadie for a few seconds before getting to
her feet and shuffling over to her armchair. 'Of course I
care, hon, but you mustn't let yourself get so upset over
things. You've got everything to look forward to now you're
shot of the Gaylord, you'll see. I'll get myself back in shape
and on to that transplant list and then there'll be no stopping

us. It'll be you and me against the world, kiddo.' Lana eased herself down on to the arm of Sadie's chair and reached out to stroke her hair. 'I know it must have been traumatic for you, finding me the way you did, but I'm going to be okay now. You heard what the doctors said – the damage to my stomach isn't that severe, and if it happens again I can have surgery.'

Sadie wiped her face with the back of her hand and looked up at Lana. 'I know,' she whispered. 'But it isn't just that. All of this – well, it's brought back a lot of memories about losing my mum – not that I see you as a mother figure or anything,' she added hastily.

'I should hope not,' Lana retorted with a sniff.

'It was just that when I found you lying there, and saw all the blood – I honestly thought you were dead. I was so relieved when you came round in the hospital. I don't understand how you can even think about having a drink when it might end up killing you. I can't handle the thought of someone actually wanting to die. My mum killed herself,' Sadie explained, returning her gaze to her lap, 'in her car, in the garage at home. My dad found her – I was at school at the time, having a history lesson. We were learning about the Holocaust, which I've always thought was quite ironic – learning about the Jews being gassed to death and all the while—' Sadie fumbled in her bag for a tissue. 'Anyway, now you know.'

'Now I know,' Lana echoed, allowing her hand to slide down Sadie's hair to the hollow between her shoulder blades, where she began rubbing in a gentle circular motion. 'And now I want you to know something,' Lana took a deep breath. 'I've made a lot of mistakes in my life, Sadie, a hell of a lot, and I have to confess I don't have an awful lot to feel proud of.'

'But surely you can't blame yourself for the way your life

turned out?' Sadie interrupted. 'It wasn't your fault your husband treated you so badly.'

Lana winced. 'I don't want to talk about that anymore – after all there's no point in constantly looking back – for either of us.'

Sadie nodded before blowing her nose.

'From now on we are going to look forward, my girl, do you understand?' Lana sighed. 'The sad fact is that before I got to know you I didn't really have anything to look forward to – or leastways I didn't think I had; but you've reminded me that life can be fun. That meal at the Caprice was the best laugh I'd had in years.'

Sadie nodded. 'Me too.'

'So, for the first time in my life I'm going to make some dreaded New Year's resolutions,' Lana continued. 'To quit drinking and start having fun. Lordy, I never thought I'd hear those words coming from my mouth – especially not in the same sentence. Now, if you'll excuse me for a moment, I need to make a quick visit to the ladies room – those laxatives appear to be mighty fast-working.'

Sadie looked up at Lana and smiled gratefully. 'Do you need a hand going up the stairs?' she asked, beginning to get to her feet.

'No, no, you stay there – see if there's any good movies on the tube. I won't be long.'

Lana shuffled her way from the living room and across the hall. With every step she took, a searing pain shot across her diaphragm, leaving her breathless before she even got to the stairs. Somehow she managed to clamber to the top, where she paused for a moment on the landing. Reassured by the sound of Sadie flicking through the channels below, Lana quickly opened the airing cupboard door and fumbled through the mountain of towels and bed linen inside. After what seemed like an eternity, the clink of her rings upon glass finally signalled the location of the tequila. Wrapping her fingers around the neck of the bottle she pulled it out and gazed longingly at the golden liquor inside. Oh, what she wouldn't give to do a line of slammers right there on the banister behind her. Clutching the bottle to her chest, Lana shuffled across the landing and locked herself in the bathroom. Her fingers trembled as they struggled with the lid, causing her to almost drop the damned thing twice. Finally, with the help of a towel for added grip, she managed to unscrew the top and inhaled deeply. God, just the smell of it was enough to send her into raptures – that sweet, summery aroma, instantly conjuring the chinking of glass and the bitter taste of lime. Lana leant against the bathroom sink to steady herself. But the smell wasn't enough – how could it possibly be? Slowly, ceremoniously, Lana raised the tequila until it was level with her face. Closing her eyes, she began tilting the bottle forwards. She knew only too well that there would never be enough tequila or vodka or Jack Daniels in which to drown her sorrows. Even if she were to fill the entire bath with booze it would not wash away the guilt and shame that clung to her skin like oil. And things had changed. She had Sadie to consider now. Watching the poor kid spill her guts about her mother had had a profound effect upon Lana. It had been heartbreaking to witness such pain and fear and even worse to think that she had in some way contributed. Well, not this time. Lana winced as she listened to the sound of tequila cascading through the plughole, but she continued to pour it away. As she had sat in the living room, rubbing Sadie's quivering back and stroking her hair, Lana had made a third, silent resolution. For once in her selfish life she was going to do the right thing – she was going to be there for Sadie and give the girl all the encouragement and support she so obviously needed.

Finally the rushing sound tapered to a trickle. Lana opened

her eyes and stared straight ahead into the mirror hanging over the sink. For the first time in years her reflection broke into a smile.

Chapter Thirty-One

'Excuse me – 'ave you got any copies of *Titanic* in stock?'

Sadie looked up from her copy of *A New Year – A New You* and sighed. The trouble with being the only film rental outlet in the area that didn't stock DVDs was that you were left with the slightly less salubrious clientele. People like the Nolan sisters for example. Of course, the young girl standing before her, fag dangling from lip, baby balanced on hip was not one of *the* Nolan Sisters of wholesome Irish girl band fame. No, the Nolan sisters who frequented Pirate Videos sprung from the bowels of the local council estate; their tattooed and pierced bodies perfectly matching their desecrated place of abode. Sadie had it on good authority that all three of them and their assorted offspring still lived with their mother, Old Ma Nolan, in a terraced house at the entrance to the estate. Hence the first sight visitors were greeted with upon arrival at Falklands Close was a burnt out Nissan Sunny and a spray painted banner on the wall telling asylum seekers to 'piss off home'.

'Yeah sure, I'll just get it for you.' Sadie's heart sunk faster than the doomed ocean liner as she got off her chair and traipsed into the shop. There was bound to be a balance owing on the Nolan account, which would mean at least twenty minutes spent listening to her delightful customer's whinging excuses of how she was sure she'd paid it off when she got last week's income support and the injustice of a single mother struggling to get by on just fifty pounds a week when the local immigrant population were all whooping it up in mansions courtesy of the Government. Just as Sadie reached the Drama section she heard a clatter behind her, followed swiftly by a slap.

'Tiara – I've told you not to bleeding touch things in shops – now pick 'em up.'

Sadie turned to see an entire shelf of Kids' videos relocated to the floor, and a snotty faced toddler sitting amid the debris, chewing on the corner of the *Assorted Adventures of Postman Pat*.

'Don't worry, I'll sort them out,' Sadie called, cringing as the Nolan sister yanked the child up by her wispy hair.

'I dunno, kids eh?' The Nolan sister remarked, placing her baby back in its tatty buggy and shoving the toddler in front of the counter. 'Now you stay there while I pay the lady.' The pitifully shabby Tiara stood rooted to the spot, staring mournfully at her mud-splattered trainers.

Returning behind the counter, Sadie keyed in the Nolan membership number and on cue a warning sign lit up the screen – *BALANCE OWING £12.00*.

'Oh, it looks as if there's an outstanding bill on your account,' she said, drawing her breath in preparation for the onslaught.

'Nah, there can't be. I ain't had a film out for a fortnight.'

Sadie checked the account history. 'Yes that's right, you got *Hellraiser* out two weeks ago, but it was four days late being returned.'

'You're having a laugh, ain't yer?' The Nolan sister snarled, her teeth an unsettling combination of nicotine yellow and amalgam grey. 'My fella returned that film the very next day on his way to community service. I know he did.'

Sadie smiled weakly and shrugged her shoulders. 'I'm sorry, but the film was booked back in five days after it was taken out. It's right here in front of me on the computer.'

'Oh – so you're going to take the word of a machine over a human being now, are you?' The Nolan sister adjusted the collars of her shell suit as if she were squaring up for a fight. 'I don't suppose it's ever occurred to you that the bleeding computer could have made a mistake?'

'I'm sorry, but—' Sadie paused. What the hell was she doing, yet again apologising when she had done absolutely nothing wrong? She put the *Titanic* cover on the shelf beneath the counter and folded her arms. 'Do you know what,' she said, forcing herself to stare straight into the Nolan sister's piggy little eyes. 'I'm getting sick and tired of having this conversation with you. Your family are always returning films late and there's always a balance owing on your account, so from now on you can either pay up or shut up.' Bloody hell! If it hadn't been for her smarting cheeks continuing to let her down, Sadie could have sworn she had morphed into Lana.

The Nolan sister seemed equally shocked, momentarily at least. 'Well, that's bloody charming that is,' she finally managed to spit. 'Do you talk to all of your customers like that – or is it just the white ones?'

'What?'

'Well – I bet if I was from Kosovo with a bit of card tied round me neck and a begging bowl in me hand I wouldn't get treated like this. Nah, the Government would give me *vouchers* for videos, wouldn't they, and it wouldn't matter if they were a couple of days late. It's bloody disgusting.'

Sadie stared at the Nolan sister in disbelief; the hatred and bitterness seemed to be oozing like bile from her pockmarked skin.

'Come on Tiara, come on Beckham, we ain't shopping where we ain't welcome.' Yanking the buggy round until it faced the door, she looked back over her shoulder at Sadie through narrowed eyes. 'From now on I'll be getting all me videos down the Paki shop.'

Sadie smiled and shook her head. The Nolans had about as much chance of getting credit from Taj as they did from Coutts. 'Good luck!' she called out before going into the kitchen to put the kettle on. What a fantastic start to the evening.

'I wouldn't bother coming in here, mate,' she heard the Nolan sister shout from the door. 'Not unless you're an asylum seeker.'

Sadie sighed. This was all she needed, her non-paying customers turning away what little remaining business she had. Peering around the corner she didn't know whether to feel relieved or alarmed when she saw a rather perplexed-looking Liam standing in the doorway. It had been almost two weeks since Sadie had seen Liam, that fateful night of the hospital visit. Since then he had obviously been avoiding the shop, or avoiding her shifts at least.

'What the hell was that about?' Liam asked, scratching his head. He had had a haircut, Sadie noticed. His curls were now skimming the top of his neck, giving even more emphasis to his chiselled jaw line.

'Don't ask,' Sadie replied. 'Would you like a cup of tea? I've just put the kettle on.'

Liam cleared his throat and scuffed the toe of his boot on the floor. 'Go on then. I don't suppose you've got the new Martin Scorsese film in?'

Sadie raised her eyebrows and sighed. 'What do you think?'

'Oh well – it was worth a try.'

When Sadie returned with the tea she saw that Liam had placed a cover on the counter. '*Mystic Pizza?*' she couldn't help enquiring – Liam hadn't exactly struck her as a chick-flick kind of guy.

'Yeah, I thought I'd get it for Tel, I was hoping it might make him change his mind about recreating a scene from *Bonnie and Clyde*.'

'Oh God, is he still going on about that?'

'He certainly is – and a word of warning,' Liam leant over the counter, his eyes twinkling as they fixed upon Sadie, 'he's got you short-listed for the role of Bonnie.'

Sadie gasped. 'Oh, no way. He can't, I won't, there's no way I'm doing it.'

'Aye, aye. What's he been asking you to do this time, Treacle? I dunno, son, you want to watch you don't get done for sexual harassment.'

Liam and Sadie looked up to see Terry entering the shop, followed closely by a rather breathless Lana.

Blushing furiously, Liam stalked over to the New Releases stand where he picked up a copy of *S Club – the Movie* and began scrutinising the blurb. 'For your information, we were actually talking about you,' he muttered.

'Oh yeah, tell me more,' Terry replied with a chuckle. 'Get the brews on, Treacle, I've got the invalid in tow.'

'I can see that,' Sadie replied. 'Are you okay, Lana? I can't believe you walked all this way – it's freezing out there.'

'Oh, quit fussing,' Lana retorted. 'I was crawling the walls back at home. And anyway – I didn't walk, Terry very kindly gave me a lift.'

'A lift? On what?' Sadie enquired disbelievingly.

'Why, on his bike, of course – and very enjoyable it was too.'

Sadie and Liam exchanged bemused glances.

'You came here on the back of a Domino's Pizza bike?' Sadie asked, even more incredulous. What the hell was happening to Lana these days? She seemed so laid back all of a sudden. Sadie was becoming rapidly convinced that one of her multitude of prescriptions had to be for valium.

'I sure did and it was fantastic – I felt like Jack Nicholson in *Easy Rider*.'

'Hmm – more like Olive from *On the Buses*,' Terry remarked to Liam with a smirk.

'Cut that out, you, and go get the food.'

'Yes, your highness,' Terry gave a meek little bow before heading back out to his moped.

'You've brought food?' Sadie asked eagerly.

'Certainly have,' Lana replied, placing her diamante clutch bag and rather battered-looking motorcycle helmet upon the counter. 'Sadie, honey, I simply could not face yet another salad for supper so I ordered a pizza instead – when Terry arrived with it and suggested we dine down here I jumped at the chance.'

Still grinning inanely at the thought of Lana on the back of a pizza delivery bike, Sadie brought a chair out from behind the counter. 'Here, sit on this,' she instructed. 'And I'll get you a cup of tea.'

'Yes, nurse. So Liam, how's it going? I understand you were at the hospital with Sadie the night of my brush with death.'

In the kitchen Sadie winced as she rinsed out the mugs. Although she had told Lana about her call to Liam and his coming to the hospital she had not told her about the subsequent disaster back at his flat – she was far too embarrassed. So, it would appear, was Liam, judging by the lengthy silence followed by extensive throat clearing going on in the shop.

'Er, yes. Well, she rang me from Casualty – I couldn't just leave her there on her own,' he added pointedly, causing Sadie to flinch as she popped a teabag into each of the mugs.

'Quite right too,' Lana replied. 'I'm only sorry to have caused such a hoo-hah in the first place. Damned liver – I should have known it would end up letting me down.

Weak livers run in my family, you know – my mother, my mother's mother, even my great-grandmother all had the same problem. I'm afraid I appear to be the victim of some hideous genetic curse.'

Sadie couldn't help smiling – only Lana would have the gall to lie so blatantly.

'Oh yeah, what hideous genetic curse would that be then?' Terry asked, the shop door slamming behind him. 'Dyke-ism or just very bad taste in men?'

'I can assure you I have impeccable taste when it comes to men,' Lana retorted, 'I just don't happen to find middle-aged pizza delivery boys remotely attractive.'

'Well, you know what – I ain't all that keen on you septic tanks neither,' Terry replied, quick as a flash.

Sadie began stirring the tea frantically – a showdown with Terry was the last thing Lana needed. Despite all of her protestations to the contrary she was still looking frighteningly frail. Luckily, Liam seemed to have come to the same conclusion and threw himself into the fray.

'All right you pair, calm down. Here, Terry, I was going to get you this film – what do you reckon?'

Sadie smiled as she heard Terry snort.

'Mystic bleeding pizza? Let me tell you, there's nothing bleeding mystic about a bit of pizza – apart from the way it always tastes so shite the minute it cools down. I found a slice of Meat Feast in me sock drawer this morning so I thought I'd have it for breakfast. Bleeding rank it was.'

'Yeah, what's with that,' Lana offered, for once in agreement with Terry. 'How does the cheese change from luscious to latex so damned quickly?'

'Sod the cheese – what about the ham? It was like eating bits of sun-dried foreskin.'

'Oh God, Terry,' Sadie groaned as she returned to the shop. 'Why do you always have to be so gross?'

Liam chuckled and passed her an open pizza box. 'Fancy a piece of Hawaiian?' he enquired, grinning warmly.

Sadie took hold of the box and smiled back. 'Perhaps it should be renamed the Circumcision,' she replied, trying hard not to look at the slivers of pink dotted amongst the pineapple.

'I thought you'd enjoy the film, Tel,' Liam continued. 'It's got Julia Roberts in and it might help you with your scene, seeing as you're working in a pizza parlour.'

'I don't need any help with me scene, do I?' Terry replied, grabbing a slice of garlic bread. 'I told you, I'm recreating a stick-up from *Bonnie and Clyde*. All I need is a Bonnie and it'll be lights, cameras, action.' He stared hopefully over the counter at Sadie.

'No way,' Sadie responded. 'I am not taking part in an armed robbery, Terry. It's wrong – we'd be committing a crime.'

'Have you seen his prices?' Terry spluttered, choking on his bread. 'One pound nineteen for a tin of meatballs; now that's what I call a crime.'

'Well even so. I couldn't rob Taj, he'd recognise me immediately.'

'You wouldn't have to, Treacle, you could just be my getaway driver.'

'You have got to be kidding. I don't even have a driving licence.'

'You wouldn't need one. Any fool can drive a moped – you should see some of the gimps Domino's employ.'

'You what?' Sadie's jaw fell open in disbelief as Liam roared with laughter.

'You're not seriously planning to get away on that scooter are you?' he asked.

'Yeah – why not?'

'Why not?' Liam shook his head. 'For a start it doesn't

go over twenty miles an hour and secondly, don't you think it stands out just a little bit? You're hardly going to give the old Bill a run for their money poodling off down the Manor on a sky blue moped. Christ, even a milk float would catch you.'

Terry shook his head and stared mournfully at the floor. 'I dunno, you lot are a right bunch of killjoys. Where's your sense of adventure?'

'You can't say I haven't got a sense of adventure,' Liam replied. 'I'm off to some island in the back of beyond in a couple of weeks aren't I? But what you're suggesting is madness. You'll end up back in jail.'

'I think it sounds kinda fun,' Lana mused, toying with a piece of stuffed crust.

'Oh no,' Sadie groaned. 'I don't know why you're all still so obsessed with recreating these scenes anyway. Take it from me – the only one of us who has actually attempted to do it – they are guaranteed to end in disaster.'

Liam glanced at Sadie curiously, but her head remained lowered, staring intently at the pizza on her lap as she studiously removed all traces of ham from the topping.

'Well, I'm sorry you feel like that, honey, because it just so happens that I need your help in recreating my scene and I absolutely refuse to take no for an answer.'

They all turned to stare at Lana who was sitting upright in her chair, brandishing her stuffed crust at Sadie like a baton.

'What? You've finally chosen one? Which one is it?' Sadie asked, her curiosity just about overcoming her sense of trepidation.

'Yeah, come on Duchess, spill the beans,' Terry mumbled, a string of mozzarella dangling from the corner of his mouth. Could all his wildest fantasies be about to come true? Could Lana have chosen a scene from a soft porn flick? One of his favourites with plenty of bird on bird action? Terry nearly had an aneurysm as he watched Lana slowly make her way towards the adult films, but to his huge disappointment she reached for something in the drama section below.

'What is it?' Sadie cried, almost as desperate as Terry to learn her fate.

'*Pretty Woman*,' Lana replied, making her way back to her chair.

'What – you want to put our Treacle on the game?' Terry enquired, licking his lips with glee. 'I tell you what, if you need anyone for the Richard Gere role, I'm your man. Birds used to call me the Gigolo when I was younger, you know – on account of my toned physique.'

'Give it a rest, Tel.' Liam put his slice of pizza down and turned to face Lana. 'So, what exactly have you got in mind?' he asked, in what he hoped was a suitably casual tone.

'Yes – what do you want me to do?' Sadie added, not even bothering to mask her concern.

'You can put your tongue back in your head, Terence, for I have absolutely no intention of putting anyone on the game,' Lana retorted. 'And I won't be requiring your services for the Richard Gere role either, as I have already cast myself in that part.'

'But you can't do it, you're a bird.' Terry's eyes suddenly lit up. 'Of course if you're in need of a strap-on, I know just the place.'

Lana shot Terry a withering glance. 'The only plastic props I'll be using in my scene are my credit cards, so drag your perverted mind back out of the sewer, you dreadful little man.'

Terry sighed and returned to his pizza.

'And you, young lady, can wipe that worried expression

from your face – the only street you're going to be walking is Bond Street.'

'Bond Street?' Sadie echoed.

'Yes – it's time to spring clean that wardrobe, because you and I are going shopping.'

Chapter Thirty-Two

If Lana was totally honest, she couldn't think of a film she'd least like to cast herself in than *Pretty Woman*. The first, and only, time she watched it, it had made her want to puke, with its corny characters and fairytale ending. There was nothing Cinderella-like about being a call girl, not even in the heady world of the 'high-class' escort. Oh sure, in her time Lana had been taken to more than her fair share of 'balls', but it had always been on the arm of a toad, never a handsome prince. And when the clock struck twelve and they went hopping back home to their wife and kids, Lana had been left feeling as undesirable as one of the ugly sisters. There had been no glass slippers in her story, only token baubles and empty embraces. Until now. With Sadie's arrival everything had changed. She might never have made Cinderella, but for the first time in her life Lana had the chance to play the role of fairy godmother. And by God she was going to grab it with both hands.

The idea of recreating the Rodeo Drive shopping scene had first dawned on Lana shortly after her arrival home from hospital. Sadie was at work, and in order to stave off the crippling urge for a drink Lana had decided to re-read her Joan Crawford biography – anything to make her feel slightly better about herself. Having rifled through the bookshelves downstairs to no avail Lana had concluded it had to be amongst the clutter on top of the spare room wardrobe. She hadn't intended to snoop through Sadie's belongings, but the minute she opened the bedroom door and saw the unfamiliar framed photograph perched on the windowsill beside the bed her curiosity got the better of her. Still breathless from climbing the stairs, she had sat down on the edge of the single bed to study the picture. The young girl on the tricycle was definitely Sadie; she could have only been two or three but there was no mistaking the soulful brown eyes and dimpled cheeks. A pale wisp of a woman stood behind her, clad in a simple floral shift, the handle of her umbrella hooked protectively onto the back of the trike. Lana raised the photo up to the silvers of pale sunlight filtering through the net curtains for closer examination. Although the woman's mouth was curved into a perfect upturned arc, the smile failed to reach her blank, staring eyes. In marked contrast, Sadie's eyes sparked with life as they gazed up adoringly at her mother. Completely without warning, Lana's own eyes filled with tears. What the hell could have happened to make this woman want to end it all? To make her want to leave Sadie? Mothers didn't *choose* to leave their children. Surely that was a fate only others could bring about. Grimacing at the thought, Lana studied the photo in search of a clue, but apart from the listless eyes there was nothing. She knew she really ought to locate her book and return back downstairs, but her curiosity was now overcoming even her craving for a drink. If only she could have transported herself back into the picture, she could have shaken that wisp of a woman by the shoulders and asked her what she had been thinking, or seen who stood behind the lens at the receiving end of such a deadened stare. Lana pulled herself to her feet and glanced about the room. She knew Sadie had travelled light when she insisted the small chest of drawers was ample space for her belongings, but she was completely unprepared for exactly how little she possessed. How could a twenty-two year old have so little to show for her time on the planet?

Lana could scarcely believe the ease with which the drawers slid open to reveal a mere handful of items of clothing neatly folded in the bottom. She almost felt ashamed when she thought of her own closets, bursting at the seams, not to mention the oak chest at the foot of her bed housing her jewellery collection. Sadie seemed to have very little in the way of documentation either. Lana couldn't find a single angst-ridden journal or gushing love letter tucked beneath her pillow or hidden amongst her underwear. It was only when she was checking the inside pocket of Sadie's suitcase that she found the unmarked manila envelope and even that seemed to be a red herring at first. Lana had rifled through the examination certificates and old payslips with a growing sense of disbelief. What was up with this kid – why did she have no intriguing mementoes from her past? But then she spotted the letter, lurking at the bottom, Sadie's name neatly printed upon the envelope. Lana had fingered it for a few seconds, her heart pounding. She knew what she was doing was wrong, but if she put the letter back now and returned downstairs the suspense would probably kill her. Carefully she eased the paper from the envelope, unfolded it and began to read.

Dear Sadie,

I am writing this letter in part explanation, in part begging your forgiveness. For many years now I have lived an inescapable nightmare and you are the only thing that has kept me going. I have tried so hard to protect you from the fear and the hurt, but I know I have let you down. The truth is, Sadie, I am a weak and pitiful person – in many ways your father is right. When you were a baby I dreamed of running away, of giving you a better life, but I knew he would always find me and bring me back. I had no money, no qualifications and, most importantly, no self-esteem. Fear is like cancer, Sadie, it eats away at you, destroying everything in its path until it gets to the very heart of your being. You are eighteen now and about to set off to university. The only thing that gives me any joy is the knowledge that you will escape from all of this. I hope that one day you will find it in your heart to forgive me for what I am about to do, but I am just so very, very tired.

With all my love, now and forever,
Mum.

Lana's hands had trembled with rage as she stuffed the letter back into its envelope. So it was fear glazing those eyes, not apathy – how dare she have passed that legacy of fear on to her own daughter! No wonder Sadie seemed so timid and tearful half the time. Lana looked at the child in the photograph, gazing so adoringly at her mother. God, some women would have given their right arm to be on the receiving end of such unconditional love, and done anything in their power to protect that child from fear and pain. Well, Sadie need never feel afraid again – not if Lana had anything to do with it. From now on Sadie would want for nothing. Beginning with her wardrobe.

Chapter Thirty-Three

'Do I really have to wear the thigh-high boots?' Sadie grimaced as she yanked the skin-tight PVC up her leg. 'I can't believe you actually possess a pair of boots like this. What on earth did you get them for?'

Lana merely smirked and raised her eyebrows before reaching over to the dressing table for her cigarettes.

'It's all right, you don't have to tell me – I get the picture.' Sadie collapsed back on to the bed, a pained expression upon her face. 'I can't believe I've let you talk me into this.'

'Relax, honey – it'll be fun,' Lana replied, tossing her a cigarette. 'Just think of all the fabulous clothes you're going to get out of it.'

'I know, but couldn't we just skip straight to that part? Do I really have to walk down Bond Street looking like this?' Sadie raised her chin slightly to glance down at her white bra top, stone-washed denim pelmet (there was no way on earth it could be described as a skirt) and the tops of the dreaded boots.

'Why, of course you do,' Lana scolded. 'We're meant to be recreating a scene here. We have to do it in its entirety – it simply wouldn't be ethical to edit out the bits we don't like.'

Sadie gave an exasperated sigh and lit up her cigarette. 'What do you mean it wouldn't be ethical? Wouldn't be ethical to who?'

'Well, to the group of course.' Lana gingerly knelt down on the floor and opened the huge oak chest at the foot of her bed. 'Now – you'll be needing some jewellery. I'm pretty sure I've still got some Eighties stuff in here. I kept hold of it in case I ever got invited to a bad taste party.'

Sadie hoisted herself up onto her elbow. 'What do you mean *the group*? We aren't some Hollywood directors' circle with our own set of rules and code of ethics, you know. This all started with a simple throwaway remark made in a video store.'

'Yes, but look at what's come out of it,' Lana replied, frowning at Sadie over the lid of the chest. 'You've got shot of that arsehole, Gaylord—' at which point they both stopped for the obligatory titter – 'I've ended up with the most delightful, if a little over-cautious, house mate. With any luck that dreadful little man, Terence, will end up in jail, and Liam is about to travel to the other side of the world.' Lana couldn't help smiling as she disappeared back behind the lid. The way Sadie's face had fallen the instant she mentioned Liam confirmed her long-held suspicions – the girl had the hots for him as sure as night followed day. And if Terry's judgement could be trusted (admittedly a big 'if') it would appear that Liam felt the same way too. Lana began to positively glow as she fished down into the chest amongst the neatly labelled boxes and pouches. As soon as her first task as fairy godmother was complete she would embark upon her second and help Cinders ensare her very own Prince Charming.

'Okay, okay,' Sadie begrudgingly replied. 'But why is it that in every scene I take part in I end up dressed like a – dressed like this?' Sadie wobbled to her feet. 'Must the costumes always involve six inch heels?'

Lana laughed as she produced a shoebox labelled *Tacky Shit* 'Honey, once you've got my credit card at your disposal I don't care if you buy the flattest things since Gwyneth Paltrow's chest, but until then the heels stay.'

Sadie staggered over to inspect herself in Lana's dressing table mirror. No matter how hard she pulled she simply could not get her skirt down to a more respectable level – like below the crotch. 'That's another thing I wanted to ask you,' she said. 'Are you sure about this? I mean, having to spend all of this money on me. It doesn't seem right.'

'Why the hell not?' Lana retorted, producing a pair of obscenely huge hoop earrings from her box. 'Hey, check these out, they're big enough to hula in.'

'Great.'

'Of course it's okay,' Lana replied, shuffling her way over to Sadie. Although she had been feeling far better over the past week, her insides still twinged with every cautious step she took. 'I adore clothes shopping, but take a look around you,' she waved a bejewelled hand at the huge oak wardrobe, chests of drawers and countless shoe racks. 'I'm all shopped out.' Lana paused to gently insert one of the silver hoops into Sadie's ear. 'And besides,' she continued, 'I wanted the chance to say thank you.'

Sadie turned to look up at Lana. 'What for?'

'What do you mean, what for?' Lana returned her gaze and for once her eyes didn't bear a trace of cynicism. 'You saved my life, Sweetie, and words can't express how grateful I am.'

Grateful was certainly not one of the words Sadie would have used to describe her own feelings, some two hours later, when she found herself tottering along Bond Street, Lana following a discreet ten paces behind. Foolish, yes. Humiliated, yes. Pissed off, extremely, but not under any circumstances did she feel grateful. The only consolation was that, unlike in the film, her bizarre appearance did not seem to be attracting the slightest scrap of attention. It would take more than a pair of thigh-high PVC boots to faze the world-weary Londoners bustling past her. Still, it was bound to be a different story once she set foot inside one of the gleaming boutiques lining the street. Sadie shivered. Although Lana had lent her a red velvet jacket to wear over her bra top, it did nothing to stop the chill February gusts from freezing her to the core. Sadie glanced over her shoulder. Behind her, Lana, clad in her black cape and fur hat was gesturing furiously towards the shops. 'GO IN!' she appeared to be mouthing.

Sadie closed her eyes, took a deep breath and headed for the first door she came to. The golden door handles were in the shape of two upright semi-circles, like a pair of Cs placed back-to-back. Oh God, it was Chanel – the favoured designer of the late Jacqueline Kennedy Onassis, global fashion icon. The mere thought of her name conjured images of immaculately tailored twin-sets teamed with dainty bags and strings of pearls. Whereas Sadie's look these days seemed to oscillate between Captain Hook and clapped-out hooker.

Okay, okay. Sadie attempted to compose herself by recalling the scene from *Pretty Woman*. All she had to do was pretend to have a browse before being unceremoniously ejected. If she could just get through that initial humiliation she would have Lana's credit card at her disposal for the rest of the afternoon. Any feelings of reluctance at spending Lana's money soon disappeared as Sadie teetered and tottered her way into the shop. God, she was going to make her pay for putting her through this exercise in abject humiliation. Out of the corner of her eye she could see a flurry of activity over by the counter. Unable to bring herself to meet the assistant's surely horrified gaze, Sadie turned to examine some clothes. But where the hell were they? She was used to the heaving rails and groaning shelves of *Top Shop* and *New Look;* a veritable riot of colour and assortment of fabrics. But not here. The boutique was like a fashion desert with just the odd display stand dotted like tumbleweed across the sand-coloured flooring. Sadie clattered her way over to the nearest podium and gingerly fingered the tartan lambswool sweater placed on top. It was hideous. A shadow loomed ominously over the stand.

'Can I help you?' a voice as polished as the flooring enquired.

Bingo! Sadie breathed a sigh of relief. Now all she had to do was get thrown out of the shop and the whole torturous experience would be over. She looked up to see a young man stood before her, one hand placed upon his slender hip, the other drooping limply from his wrist. He looked as if he were about to embark on a chorus of 'I'm a Little Teapot'.

Sadie cleared her throat as she tried to remember her lines. 'Er, I'm just checking out – checking things out,' she stammered.

'Ah, I see,' said the Teapot, tilting slightly to the left, as if he were about to pour himself out. 'And is there anything in particular you had in mind.'

Sadie began to relax. This was all going swimmingly. 'Yes, there is actually,' she replied. 'I'm looking for something conservative.'

The Teapot stared at her for a moment, taking in the PVC boots, ultra mini skirt, even skimpier top and curly auburn wig.

Sadie smiled as she waited for him to order her to leave.

'Well, of course,' he replied. 'If you'd like to follow me.'

Sadie's jaw fell open in disbelief. To her absolute horror the Teapot was smiling warmly and beckoning to her with his spout. Sadie glanced outside to where a bemused Lana had her face pressed to the glass, pretending to window shop. Sadie shrugged at her helplessly before following the Teapot to the far end of the store, where two huge leather armchairs squatted in front of an oval-shaped mirror.

'Okay, madam, if you'd like to take a seat. My name's Duane and I'd like to welcome you to Chanel. Have you shopped with us before? No? Super. Can I get you a drink before we get started? Cappuccino? Herbal tea? Mineral water? No? Right then, when you say conservative, what exactly did you have in mind? Your idea of conservative might be considerably different to somebody else's.' And with that he actually gave her a knowing wink.

Sadie groaned inwardly – this was all starting to go dreadfully wrong. The assistant was meant to be frowning at her disdainfully, not grinning broadly. Just at that moment the door opened and Lana entered the shop. 'On second thoughts, do you think I could have a herbal tea?' Sadie asked timidly – anything to get shot of him for a second so she could have a word with Lana.

'Yes, of course. I'll be right with you, madam,' Duane called over his shoulder to Lana.

'Take your time,' she replied. 'I'm just browsing. What the hell's going on?' she hissed, as soon as Duane had disappeared into the back of the shop.

'I don't know,' Sadie hissed back. 'He's being really nice to me.'

Lana frowned. 'Okay, you're going to have to be more common.'

'How?' Sadie asked, staring down helplessly at her skirt and boots.

'I don't know. Think of some of the trash you have to deal with in your own store. Imagine you're one of them.'

Sadie immediately thought of the Nolan sisters. How would they conduct themselves if magically transported from Wembley market to Bond Street? The faintest trace of a smirk began to flicker around the corners of her mouth. If she could just switch off from being Sadie Jones for a while, and become a Nolan sister instead – it might even be quite fun. A chance to experience life on the other side of the counter for a change.

Duane returned to the shop bearing a dainty porcelain cup with a gold C for a handle. 'Here you go, madam.'

'About bleeding time,' Sadie replied, grabbing it from his hands. 'Blimey, what the hell is this stuff?'

Duane paused to clear his throat. 'It's camomile tea, madam.'

'Camomile tea? Smells more like bleeding cat's piss!' Sadie heard a strange spluttering sound coming from Lana's direction. *Don't laugh, don't laugh,* she silently implored. But rather than her or Lana losing control, it was Duane himself who began to giggle.

'Ooh, don't,' he said, clutching his side, before leaning forward conspiratorially. 'It's bloody vile, isn't it? I keep telling my manageress she should invest in a box of Typhoo, but will she listen? Will she buggery!'

Sadie stared up at Duane, completely dumbfounded. Did nothing faze this bizarre little teapot of a man? 'All right then, show us the clobber,' she demanded, slamming the cup down onto the floor.

Once again Duane began to giggle. 'Ooh, you are a card,' he said. 'May I ask what kind of function madam will be attending?'

'What kind of function?'

'Yes.' Duane positioned himself in front of her as if he were a airline attendant about to run through the pre-flight safety procedures. 'Will you be requiring evening wear?' He cast both his hands to the right. 'Or will you be requiring day wear?' He cast both his hands to the left. 'Or will you be requiring both?' And he swung his hands into the centre, pointing his fingertips directly at Sadie.

Sadie shifted uncomfortably in her seat. 'Well, both I suppose,' she murmured, praying desperately for inspiration.

She thought of the Nolan sisters in all their zitty, shell-suited glory. What kind of 'functions' were they likely to be attending this week? 'Yeah, both,' she repeated, more confidently this time and crossing her PVC clad legs with a flourish. 'I've got a meeting down the DSS in the day and then I'm going to the bingo in the evening.'

'The bingo?' Duane echoed weakly.

'Yeah, and then we'll probably go for a fish and chip supper after. Oh, and by the way – the outfit's got to be motorbike friendly, my geezer's a Hells Angel.'

There, that ought to do it. Sadie sat back in her chair, a defiant smirk upon her lips, and waited for Duane to utter the immortal line, *you're obviously in the wrong place, please leave.*

'Oh my God! This is just so, like, hilarious!' Duane clapped his hands with glee. 'Okay, where are they?' he asked, looking around the shop.

'Where are what?' Sadie enquired, completely forgetting her newfound cockney accent.

'The cameras, the TV crew, Jeremy Beadle – or whoever's behind this little wheeze of yours.' Duane began pacing about the place, peering frantically behind the counter and between the stands. 'I thought it was a bit odd when Cynthia called in sick and my boss disappeared off to that meeting at *Vogue*,' he continued, 'I've never been left on my own like this before. I've been set up, haven't I? Who was it put you up to this? I bet it was Rasputin, the little rascal!'

At that moment the door opened and two middle-aged women entered the shop. They were as buffed and polished as a pair of porcelain dolls.

Completely oblivious, Duane continued marching up and down the floor. 'Come out, come out wherever you are,' he began shrieking at the top of his voice.

Sadie stared helplessly at Lana as Duane made a beeline to a mannequin at the far side of the shop.

'I bet you've got one of those micro cameras in there, haven't you?' he demanded, staring straight into the mannequin's glassy eyes. 'Hello, mum, hello nanna! It's me Duane, I'm on the telly.'

'Good lord,' one of the women muttered to her friend as they simultaneously shifted their gaze from Duane to Sadie and back again.

'It just hasn't been the same since Karl Lagerfeld took over,' her friend hissed in response.

'Ooh, more awkward customers,' Duane shouted over to the women. 'Don't tell me, you're going to ask for a new frock to wear to a swingers party – or was it going to be the old shop-lifting ruse? It's okay, ladies, save yourself the bother. You've been rumbled. Now, how about I get us all a nice cup of cat's piss, eh?'

Lana emerged from behind a pillar and beckoned furiously to Sadie, her face an absolute picture. Sadie couldn't tell if she was about laugh or cry. Either way she looked fit to burst.

'Right, well, I'd better be off,' Sadie muttered, staggering to her feet. 'Thanks for the er, tea.'

'But aren't you going to reveal your true identity?' Duane asked, his face beginning to fall. 'How am I supposed to know when I'm going to be on telly?'

'My name's Vivian,' Sadie called over her shoulder as she followed Lana through the door. 'Vivian Ward.'

'It's absolutely scandalous. This country has gone to the dogs,' remarked one of the middle-aged women, following closely on Sadie's heels.

'Quite right,' her friend agreed. 'You wouldn't get this kind of service on Rodeo Drive.'

Chapter Thirty-Four

'Quit giggling and hold still for a second,' Lana ordered, removing a hairpin from the corner of her mouth and inserting it into Sadie's hair just above her nape. 'Now for the final touches.' Lana gently teased a few tendrils from the mass of curls piled upon Sadie's head until they formed a frame of ringlets about her face.

'I'm sorry,' Sadie spluttered, trying desperately to remain still. 'I just keep thinking about him yelling "come out, come out wherever you are". What must those women have thought?'

A smirk snaked its way across Lana's face as she fetched a globe-shaped bottle of perfume from her dressing table. 'Honey, that was nothing – how about when he offered them a nice cup of cat's piss? I assume that wherever those ladies lunch, cat's piss is strictly off the menu.' Lana gently squeezed the gold-tassled vaporiser and a mist of scent settled upon Sadie's hair. 'Okay, that's the hair and make-up taken care of; now for the clothes.' Lana sighed theatrically as she stared at the mountain of Top Shop and Miss Selfridge bags covering her bed. 'I still can't believe you passed up on the chance of a proper designer wardrobe.'

Sadie smiled. 'Honestly, Lana, designer clothes really aren't me. And besides, think of all the money you saved.'

'I told you before, money isn't a problem. Believe me, honey, I may be a sucker when it comes to affairs of the heart, but when it comes to pecuniary matters I put Bill

Gates to shame. Now, aren't you going to check out my masterpiece?'

Sadie turned to look at herself in the dressing table mirror and couldn't help gasping in surprise. 'God, I look so – glamorous.' She couldn't believe what a difference it made simply wearing her hair up. For once it seemed sleek and sophisticated rather than wild and unkempt. And given how much time Lana had spent on her make-up it looked surprisingly natural. It was as if she had taken an airbrush and magically erased all shadows and blemishes, leaving a luminous glow in their place. 'Thank you. Thank you so much,' Sadie leapt to her feet and planted a gloss-coated kiss upon Lana's cheek.

'Don't mention it.' Lana hurriedly turned away to hide her smarting eyes. 'Of course all my hard work will be totally wasted once you've put on your outfit. What's it going to be then, hon? The army fatigues or the tracksuit?'

Sadie giggled as she began emptying the bags upon the bed. 'Combat gear and leisurewear are all the rage these days, Lana. Don't you read *Heat* magazine? Honestly, you sound just like my—'

An awkward silence fell upon the room.

'Well, I guess I'll leave you to it. After all, I do have a dinner party to prepare for.' Lana picked up her cigarettes and made her way to the door, her eyes brimming over and a smile wider than the Mississippi illuminating her face.

The dinner party had been Lana's idea, formulated on the journey home from the West End. As their train trundled into Baker Street a soppy-looking teenager clutching a grotesque pink teddy bear had clambered on board. The teddy bear was so large it had to have a seat all to itself, right opposite Lana. Upon its heart shaped chest the immortal words *True Love Always* had been embroidered in scarlet. Lana had wanted to vomit right there on the spot. Then, as any fairy godmother worth her salt would, she spotted an opportunity to weave more magic.

'Lord above, do you realise what day this is?' she asked Sadie.

'Friday?' came a muffled response from behind the mountain of carrier bags beside her.

'No – I don't mean what day of the week. I mean what day of the year.'

Sadie peered out at her from a gap in the plastic. 'No.'

'Why, it's Valentine's Day of course.'

'You're joking.' For the first time since she had been aware of its existence, Sadie had actually forgotten about Valentine's Day. She had completely forgotten to feel unhappy, unloved and unwanted, whilst the rest of the world indulged in a collective love-in sponsored by *Hallmark*. She sat back in her chair and smiled contentedly.

'So you know what this means?' Lana continued.

'No, what?'

'Well, it's the perfect excuse to celebrate of course.'

Sadie took a while to ponder this statement. Celebrating her new-found single status on Valentine's Day was not something that would ever have occurred to her. 'What do you mean?'

'Well, let's throw a party and invite our other single chums.'

Sadie's heart began to sink. 'What other single chums?'

'Why, Terry and Liam of course. It's days like these us single folk ought to stick together – unite against the tidal wave of mush sweeping the nation.' Lana cast a menacing glare at the teddy bear.

At the mention of Liam's name Sadie couldn't help warming to Lana's idea. 'Well – if you're sure you're up to it.'

'Of course I'm up to it. What's a little dinner party after the day we've had?'

Lana leant against the kitchen sink and filled herself a glass of water. The truth was, after her trek around the West End she felt far from up to hosting a dinner party. Her head felt woozy and her legs like lead. Previously she would have taken herself straight to bed with a flask of hot toddy and a copy of *Gone With the Wind*. Lana sighed wistfully at the recollection before forcing down a mouthful of water. But not now, in her new incarnation as fairy godmother. Now she must weave her magic and create a feast fit for four. Lana pulled open the drawer next to the sink in search of her book of culinary spells – or rather Mr Ming's take-out menu.

One hour later both the guests and the food had arrived. Unfortunately in that order, so Lana's cover as hostess with the mostest was immediately blown. Not that anyone seemed to care.

'I tell you what, I'm so Hank Marvin I could eat a scabby horse sandwiched between a pair of old mattresses,' Terry exclaimed, tearing open a carton and grabbing himself a spring roll. 'Mind you, I don't know what I'd have done if she'd ordered pizza, eh Liam?'

'Mmm.' Liam nodded distractedly. He wouldn't have cared if Lana had ordered a Wimpy quite frankly, he was far too busy feasting his eyes upon Sadie.

'You look nice,' he said, passing her the special fried rice. 'I like your hair.'

Sadie blushed as she took the rice and spooned some on to her plate. 'Thanks, but it was all Lana's work – it was compensation for the way she made me look earlier on.'

'I don't know why you couldn't have kept the hooker clobber on for us,' Terry remarked. 'We was looking forward to that, wasn't we Liam? Especially them thigh-length boots.'

Liam grimaced as he hacked away at the crispy aromatic duck.

Lana scooped up some chicken noodles with her chopsticks, the light from the fire catching on her charm bracelet, causing sparks of gold to dance about her wrist. 'Never mind Sadie, what's with your outfit, Terence? You look like a delegate at a peeping Tom convention.'

All eyes fell upon Terry and his poorly fitting, powder blue suit.

'I wanted to make a bit of an effort, didn't I.' Terry replied, fiddling uncomfortably with the huge kipper tie around his neck. 'This is the only suit I've got. I don't have much call for executive clobber. To tell the truth I've never been invited to a dinner party before. Normally I wear this for court appearances.'

'Jeez! It's a wonder they didn't throw away the key,' Lana retorted. 'Anyone for some noodles?'

As the four of them munched their way through Mr Ming's set meal D, pausing briefly for Terry's uproarious impression of Marlon Brando on stilts (involving four sweet and sour pork balls and a pair of chopsticks) Lana and Sadie recounted their day's events.

'So it's two scenes down and two to go,' Terry said, attempting to lick a splattering of black bean sauce from the bottom of his tie.

'Yes, and so far both have been a complete disaster,' Sadie replied.

'Oh, I wouldn't say that,' Lana responded, passing Terry a tissue. 'Okay, so neither have gone exactly to plan. But the first scene made you realise what an arsehole you were living with and the second – well, we certainly had a laugh, *and* you acquired a new wardrobe full of clothes.'

Liam glanced across the coffee table to where Sadie sat cross-legged by the fire, smiling contentedly. So she had given her bloke the elbow then. Terry kept telling him that she'd moved in with Lana, but he had learnt long ago to take anything Terry told him with about a kilo of salt.

Sadie looked up and caught Liam's gaze. 'So, it's your turn next, Liam. When do you leave?' As if she didn't know. As if the date on the airline ticket hadn't become etched upon her mind the very second she spotted it in his bedroom.

Liam shifted awkwardly at the end of Lana's chaise longue. 'Next Tuesday,' he mumbled.

'Great.' Sadie forced her mouth into a grin and began gathering up the empty cartons.

'You leave all that, honey – just relax and enjoy. Terence and I will take care of the clearing up.' Lana said staring pointedly at Terry.

'But I was just going to tell you all this blinding joke about a bulimic biscuit taster,' Terry began, before wilting under Lana's gaze. 'Oh, right you are, Duchess. Yes, you young uns make yourself comfortable while we take care of the dishes – and other more pressing matters.'

'Like what?' Liam enquired, running a hand through his hair and stretching his legs out in front of him.

Terry tapped the side of his nose with his finger. 'Never you mind, son, never you mind.' And with that he followed Lana into the kitchen. 'Chocolate *digesteds* they were,' he called back across the hall.

Liam looked at Sadie and grinned. 'What do you think that's all about then?'

Sadie shrugged her shoulders. 'I dread to think. You don't suppose there's anything going on between them, do you?'

Liam shook his head vehemently. 'What, as in jiggy-jiggy? No way. It would be like Liz Taylor getting it together with Benny Hill.' Liam moved along the chaise and patted the space beside him. 'Come up here if you want, it's fractionally more comfortable than the floor.'

Sadie pulled herself to her feet and brushed a few stray grains of rice from the front of her new hooded top and combats. 'He's been round to see her quite a few times in the past couple of weeks, you know,' she confided as she plonked herself down next to Liam. 'She hasn't told me herself, but sometimes when I've got home from work I've found pizza boxes in the bin and the living room reeking of his aftershave.'

Liam chuckled. 'Terry must be the only bloke alive who still wears Brut. Smoke?'

Sadie nodded and took a cigarette from Liam's slightly battered pack. For some infuriating reason her fingers had begun to tremble.

'Have you got a light? I can't seem to find mine.' Liam asked, fumbling in his jeans pockets.

Sadie reached down to the coffee table for Lana's huge marble lighter and struggled to ignite it.

'Steady,' Liam whispered, cupping one of his huge hands around hers and lowering his head towards the flame.

As she watched his tousled hair tumble forwards Sadie's stomach flipped. There was something simultaneously terrifying and tantalising about being in such close proximity to Liam; a sweet and sour assault upon her senses, as her throat tightened and her skin tingled.

'Are you okay?' he asked, raising his head, but keeping his hand exactly where it was, wrapped around hers like a glove.

Sadie nodded. The flame from the lighter continued to flicker, illuminating his face with a sheen of gold.

'You seem to be shaking a bit, that's all.'

Sadie looked down at her hands nestled inside Liam's. 'So do you,' she replied, her voice barely audible.

Liam's eyes twinkled as his mouth broke into a grin. 'It's bloody freezing in here, isn't it?'

They both turned to look at the flames leaping hungrily about the hearth and began to laugh.

Liam placed his cigarette in the ashtray on the table and brought his hand back up to join his other one until they formed a complete circle around Sadie's.

'I wanted to ask you something,' he said, bringing his face in closer to hers.

Sadie loosened her grip upon the lighter and the flame spluttered out, causing shadows to fall in the hollows beneath his cheekbones.

'Go ahead,' she managed to utter.

'That night, after the hospital, when you came back to mine.'

'Yes.' It felt as if the whole room had been wired to the National Grid. Sadie's scalp tingled and her skin crackled into goose bumps. If her hair hadn't been pinned down so tightly she felt certain it would have been standing on end. In that one moment she wanted Liam more than anything she'd ever wanted in her life. And then, faster than you could say, irritating cockney in powder blue stay-pressed, it was gone.

'All right, pop-pickers, I'm just going down the mini-mart to do a quick reccy for my scene and I'm going to pick up some afters while I'm there. Anyone for a nice bit of Arctic Roll?'

Chapter Thirty-Five

Lana had read somewhere that more people commit suicide on Sunday than any other day of the week. As she stalked across the landing, wiping her fevered brow on the sleeve of her dressing gown, she wondered what the favoured day for committing murder was. One look at her wild-eyed reflection in the bathroom mirror and she concluded that it had to be Monday. After all, it had been a Monday that she herself had taken somebody's life and now here she was, all those Mondays later, once again fuelled with murderous intent. Admittedly, it was a drink that she could quite happily murder this time, but all the same.

Lana took hold of both sides of the sink and inhaled deeply. Great waves of tension were rolling into her head, like leaden banks of cloud warning of an imminent storm. Ever since the 'dinner party' the tension had been mounting, and with Sadie working two twelve-hour shifts over the weekend she had had precious little to distract her – apart from a couple of visits from Terry to discuss his scene and watch *Bonnie and Clyde* for the umpteenth time. But if anything Terry had only made her feel more uptight, sabotaging her match-making plans for Sadie and Liam and then boring her senseless with his Warren Beatty impersonations. By the time she had gone to bed on Sunday night, feeling quite aptly suicidal, her craving for a drink had reached critical point. And then she'd had the dream.

It had been quite some time since Lana had last had the

dream – in fact, since she had been home from hospital her permanent state of exhaustion had left her blissfully dream free. But last night it had come back to haunt her, like the technicolour remake of a vintage horror flick, even more garish and gruesome than before.

Lana soaked a flannel in cold water and pressed it over her burning face. She could almost hear the hiss of steam as her inflamed cheeks greedily sucked the icy moisture from the cloth. Letting the flannel drop into the sink, Lana slumped down on to the edge of the bath. Flashes from her dream flickered through her mind like some twisted action replay of all the very worst moments. Her hand upon the bedroom door; a young, unblemished hand, way before the veins had begun to protrude through the back like some three-dimensional map of the Underground. The glint from her rock of an engagement ring as she pushed the door open. And then, in double slow-mo, the real gut-wrencher; the bizarre naked monster flailing about on her bed, thrashing its limbs and throwing back its two heads. And that god-awful sound it was making – a groaning, gasping sound as if it were in its death throes – a sound that was amplified in her dreams to the point where Lana's eardrums felt as if they might burst. And then, as always, the series of quick close-ups – a woman's leg, Guy's back. A woman's leg wrapped around Guy's back. A woman's chin coming to rest upon Guy's shoulder. A woman's face staring blankly at Lana and then beginning to smile. Her dream would always linger upon that smile, before cutting straight to Lana behind the wheel of the car. The rain would be lashing against the windscreen, completely obscuring her view of the freeway. Not that it mattered. Her vision was already filled with the super-imposed images of before – her husband of just four weeks and that awful, smiling woman with the tanned leg and the gold ankle chain. In her dream Lana would begin stepping down harder and harder on the gas, completely consumed by rage. Sometimes she would wake to find her quilt kicked into a pile at the foot of the bed. Oftentimes she would become aware at this point that she was actually having a dream but she was unable to wrench herself from it. It was as if she had to see the damned thing through to the bitter end. Like this morning when the screech of brakes and smash of glass had seemed to reverberate throughout the house and the sound of the young girl crying had been so chillingly real that she'd had to stumble across to the spare room to make sure it hadn't been Sadie.

Lana pulled herself back to her feet and stared blankly at the mirror. Who the hell was the haggard old crone staring back at her? Two decades had passed since that fateful Monday and yet somehow she had managed to shield herself from the passage of time beneath a haze of alcohol and a layer of slap. But not any more. 'The chickens are coming home to roost, honey,' Lana told her reflection with a wry smile – or perhaps it was the crows coming home to roost, judging by the lines unfolding like fans at the sides of her eyes. Who was she trying to kid? She was no fairy godmother, she was a fraud. How could she ever expect to be a true friend to Sadie without being completely honest about her past? The dream was obviously a message from her subconscious telling her it was time to clean out her closet, both literally and metaphorically. But not just yet. She would wait until this evening, when Sadie got home from work. That way she would be able to partake in a little Dutch courage in between times.

It was more than Dutch courage that Sadie required when she arrived at the video store later that morning. Not only had the phantom crapper paid a visit, but it appeared he was suffering from the most dreadful stomach disorder imaginable.

Diarrhoea would have been a woefully inadequate diagnosis.
Sadie clutched her own stomach as she gazed in horror at the
pebble-dashed porcelain and beige mass clogging the pan. It
had to be dysentery at the very least. It took three flushes
for the water to clear and even then, what appeared to be
three kernels of sweetcorn absolutely refused to go down,
taunting Sadie as they bobbed merrily upon the surface.

'For God's sake!' Sadie cried, before flinging down the
toilet brush in despair. 'No job is worth this crap.' A statement
which would come back to haunt her two hours later, when
Vince arrived in the shop, a wilting bouquet of forecourt
flowers in one hand, a huge padlock in the other.

'I'm afraid it's sayonara, sweetheart,' he announced, dropping the padlock on to the counter with a clatter and thrusting
the flowers into Sadie's face. 'This place just ain't cutting the
mustard, d'you know what I mean?'

Sadie examined the bedraggled bunch of *Floral Favourites
(guaranteed for fourteen days, fifteen days ago)*. She knew only
too well what Vince meant, she just wasn't prepared to accept
it yet. 'No. What's going on?'

'I'm shutting up shop, darling, calling time, selling up. This
place just ain't bringing in the spondulicks, you know what
I'm saying?' Vince waved a hairy hand towards the flowers.
'I may be kind-hearted, but I ain't no charity.'

'But this place would be fine if we got some new releases
– and DVDs. When I first came here it was a goldmine, you
said so yourself.' Sadie grimaced as Vince positioned himself
in front of her, legs akimbo, his furry eyebrows furrowed in
fake concern.

'I know what you're saying, darling, and don't think for
one minute I don't appreciate all the graft you've put into
this place.' Once again he gestured to the flowers. 'But at
the end of the day, I ain't got the cash flow to support
no sinking ship. Not even a pirate ship, geddit!' And with

that he leant forward and gave Sadie's eye-patch a play-ful ping.

Sadie leapt to her feet, ripped her eye-patch from her head and flung it on to the floor. 'Have you any idea how much work I've put into this shop?' she fumed. 'Have you any idea how much time I've spent thinking up promotions to try and get customers back in through that door?'

Vince began backing off towards the wall, his eyebrows now knitted together in real concern, forming a miniature mohair scarf across his face.

'Every single day I have to humiliate myself in this ridicu-lous get-up.' Sadie yanked her plastic cutlass from its scabbard and began stabbing it in Vince's direction. 'And every single day I have to clear up after the phantom crapper and put up with the stick I get for being the only video shop in existence not to stock new releases – not to mention DVDs.'

'Easy,' Vince whimpered.

Sadie flung her cutlass at the counter where it ricocheted off the computer and landed with a plunk in the plant pot. 'And do you know why I do it? Why I keep coming back day after day for my pittance of a wage?'

Vince shrugged helplessly.

'Because I love my job. Because I love films and I love talking to other people about films. I love the atmosphere in this shop. The way customers drop in for a chat and a cup of tea as well as a video. This shop isn't like *Blockbusters* or some other impersonal chain store. Friendships have been formed in this shop. Confidences have been exchanged, relationships have been ended. But to you it's all a big joke.' Sadie slumped back down on to her chair. 'This place means nothing to you, does it? That's why you think you can march right in and make your stupid jokes about closing it down and I'll skip off merrily into the sunset.'

'Well, you're wrong there, as it happens,' Vince retorted,

flexing his stubbly chin in an attempt at outrage. 'For your information, young lady, I was hoping you'd be skipping off merrily to my new store in Hackney. So what have you got to say to that, eh?' Vince's face broke into a chuffed grin.

'I say – no thanks.' Sadie got to her feet and fished her bag from beneath the counter. 'If it's all the same to you I think I'll take the redundancy option. Speaking of which, I expect a generous settlement, in light of the all work I've put in here. After all, it would be a terrible shame if the Inland Revenue were to find out about the dubious manner in which you conduct your business. I've heard you on the phone to your accountant. *You know what I mean?*'

Vince nodded meekly and pulled his wallet from his back pocket. 'Phew, you are one feisty little lady,' he muttered, peeling off a wad of notes. 'You sure you don't want the Hackney job – you'd see them Yardies off in no time.' Vince handed Sadie the money and placed a stocky arm around her shoulders. 'I tell you what – you come down here tomorrow lunchtime and help me box up the stock and you can take your pick of videos. Can't say fairer than that now, can I?'

As Sadie trudged her way back to Lana's, she felt completely dejected. So what if she had finally stood up to Vince and won herself a generous redundancy package – it was nothing more than she deserved. The truth was she would return it in an instant if it meant getting her job back. It was only when Vince had provoked her into a fury that she'd realised quite how much the shop had come to mean to her. And as with everything that came to mean something to her, it was now being snatched away. As Sadie turned into Lana's road she thought of Liam, no doubt packing his rucksack in preparation for his adventures down under. Oh yes, he was promising to be back for the summer now, but Sadie had seen *Mutiny on the Bounty*. She knew how Fletcher Christian ended up, and knowing her luck Liam would also fall in love with a beautiful Tahitian, never to return. Although she'd been livid at the time, she was now hugely relieved that Terry had barged in on them when he did. If she and Liam had kissed at the Valentine's 'dinner party' it would have made his departure even harder to bear. The thought of a life without the shop and without Liam seemed about as miserable and uninviting as an Ingmar Bergman season on Channel Four. Still, at least she had Lana.

Sadie fumbled in her pocket for her door key as she made her way up the garden path. Perhaps if Lana was feeling up to it she would let Sadie have a go on the sex line, God knows she could do with a laugh – and a new source of income. Sadie cautiously opened the door and tiptoed across the hall. She didn't want to wake Lana if she was napping; she had been looking rather fragile since their shopping expedition and could probably do with all the sleep she could get.

Sadie eased open the living room door and crept into the room.

'Oh my God!' she yelled out in shock, letting her bag clatter to the floor. 'What are you doing?'

Lana was reclined on the chaise longue, a horrified expression upon her face and a bottle of vodka in her hand. An open bottle of vodka, poised above a large glass tumbler.

'What is wrong with you?' Sadie shouted, launching herself at the bottle and sending it flying towards the fireplace. 'You promised me you wouldn't have another drink. You told me you wanted to live.' Sadie dropped to her knees and set the bottle upright. She searched the coffee table for a box of tissues to mop up the pool of vodka, but all she could see were old newspaper cuttings. 'What are all these?' she asked, grabbing one from the top of the pile. *NEW YORK MODEL IN DEATH SMASH!* The headline screamed.

Lana fumbled in her cigarette case for a smoke but her

fingers were shaking so much and the cigarettes were jammed in so tightly she couldn't get one of the bastards to budge. 'It's not what you think,' she stammered. 'I was only going to have one.'

'One what?' Sadie retorted. 'One bottle? What's wrong with you, Lana, didn't you hear what the doctors said? You have to be clean for at least six months before they'll consider you for a transplant. How can you even think about having a drink?'

Lana flung her cigarettes to the floor and turned to face the wall. 'You don't understand. It's not as simple as that.'

'Not simple? What could be more simple than wanting to live?'

'For you, maybe, Miss Everything-to-Live-For, but for some of us life isn't quite so clear cut.'

'Oh, spare me the sermon – please.'

'Honey, this isn't a sermon.'

Sadie sat back on her heels and stared at Lana defiantly. 'Oh, no? What is it then?'

'I guess you might say it's a confession.' Lana reached down for her cigarettes and somehow managed to wrench one from the case.

'What do you mean?'

Lana lit her cigarette and stared forlornly into her lap. 'I haven't exactly been straight with you, Sadie. I'm so sorry.'

Sadie sighed and shuffled along the floor until she was kneeling alongside her. 'It's okay – I think I know what you're going to say.'

'You do?'

'Yes, but it's okay – I don't think any the worse of you. Lots of people have drink problems – it's an illness, not a weakness. The important thing is to face up to it and admit that you need help. I'd never judge you, Lana, especially after everything you went through with your abusive husband – I'm not surprised you turned to drink.'

'Oh sweetie.' Tears began coursing down Lana's face. 'If only it were that simple.'

'I don't understand.' Sadie looked up at Lana, bewildered.

'That's exactly my point – you can't possibly understand because I haven't told you the truth.'

'The truth about what?'

'The truth about me, the truth about my marriage. Everything I've told you has been a pack of lies. I'm not from the Deep South, I'm from plain old Missouri. I didn't come here to escape from an abusive husband, I came here to escape from myself and the awful things I'd done.' Lana grabbed a newspaper cutting from the table. 'You want to know the truth about me – it's all here in black and white.'

Sadie took the cutting from Lana and blinked away the tears that were massing at the corners of her own eyes. 'The picture,' she muttered, staring down at a grainy photograph of a young Lana. 'It's you.'

Lana nodded.

'But it says it's somebody called Mary Latimer.'

Lana drew heavily on her cigarette and looked away. 'As I said, everything I've told you about myself has been a pack of lies.'

As Sadie hoisted herself up on to an armchair she felt a welter of dread and curiosity envelop her. Much as part of her wanted to know the real truth about Lana, or Mary, or whoever the hell she was, another part of her felt terrified. She could tell from the fear etched upon Lana's face that the secrets contained in the faded newsprint before her were going to alter the course of their friendship for good. From this moment, things would never be the same again.

Chapter Thirty-Six

LAST MINUTE REPRIEVE FOR
DEATH SMASH MODEL

The case against model Mary Latimer was sensationally thrown out of court yesterday. In a shock turn of events, the victim's family have decided to drop all charges. A grim-faced Joseph Ellroy, father of the deceased, had no comment to make as he left the courthouse accompanied by his attorney. It is thought that a financial settlement has been reached out of court, with the husband of the accused, investment banker Guy Latimer, expected to foot the bill.

It is now almost eleven months since that fateful Monday morning when, for no apparent reason, Mary Latimer's car veered into oncoming traffic on the Long Island Expressway, resulting in the tragic death of Harlem mother Kimberley Ellroy, aged just nineteen. Thankfully Ellroy's four-year old daughter Cissy (pictured right) escaped with only superficial injuries. Eyewitnesses reported Latimer's car being driven erratically for at least half a mile before it ploughed headlong into Ellroy's Buick. Although the defense counsel has repeatedly claimed mechanical error was responsible for the accident, police investigators found no evidence of faulty engineering and tests have conclusively shown the brakes on the six-month old Porsche to be in full working order. Latimer's refusal to take a roadside breathalyser test also raised huge question marks about the real cause of the incident.

It is no secret that Mary and Guy Latimer are lead players

on the New York Society scene. Their wedding last year was
celebrated in lavish style at the newly opened Trump Tower,
with most of Wall Street's finest and NYC's fashion glitterati
in attendance. The champagne bill alone was rumoured to have
been in the region of seven thousand dollars. In marked contrast,
victim Kimberley Ellroy was raised in the Harlem Projects and
left school at just fourteen when she became pregnant. The identity
of Cissy's father is unknown and it is believed that her maternal
grandparents have now become her official custodians.

For the inside view on the Latimers' marriage please see our
exclusive interview with their former housekeeper in today's
Society Section.

After re-reading the article three times, Sadie took a moment
to examine the accompanying photographs. A bewildered-
looking child gazed out from beneath a mass of curls on
one side of the piece and the posed shot of a young woman
stared sullenly from the other, her glossed lips betraying the
faintest hint of a smirk. There was no mistaking it was Lana,
even if the caption read '*Mary Latimer models Mary Quant.*'
Sadie put the cutting back on the table and sat on her hands
in a vain attempt to stop them shaking.

'You were a model?' she finally managed to whisper, staring
blankly into her lap. She just couldn't bring herself to look at
Lana or utter the question she really wanted answering – *you*
killed someone?

Lana nodded.

'And your husband was an investment banker?'

'Oh, he was that all right.'

Sadie looked up with a start. How could Lana be so
flippant? How could she even attempt to make a joke?

'Did he – did he used to beat you? Was he possessive,
paranoid? Were you trying to get away from him when you
crashed the car? Was any of that stuff you told me true?'

Lana shook her head.

'So you were drunk – was that it?'

'Not exactly.'

'What do you mean not exactly? Either you had been drinking or you hadn't.' Sadie gestured to the newspaper cutting. 'It says here that you refused to take a breathalyser test. Why would you do that if you hadn't been drinking?'

Lana ground out her cigarette and stared at the wall. 'I was scared, confused. I didn't know what I was doing. I was terrified I was going to lose everything.'

'You were terrified *you* were going to lose everything? What about that little girl? What about her mother? What about what they lost?' Sadie stared beseechingly at Lana, but still Lana refused to meet her gaze.

Finally she spoke, her voice as brittle as an old gramophone recording. 'Okay, I'd had a drink – I wasn't drunk, but I knew I was over the limit.'

'But it was Monday morning.'

Lana gave a derisory snort. 'So it was Monday morning?'

'Don't you dare patronise me.' Sadie leapt to her feet, her eyes blazing. 'Most people do not have a drink first thing on a Monday morning.'

'And most people do not find their husband screwing another woman first thing on a Monday morning either.' Lana replied, staring up at Sadie hopefully, but one look at Sadie's expression caused her breath to catch in the back of her throat. There was something all too familiar about that look of loathing and disgust. It was exactly the same look Joseph Ellroy had shot her as he marched from the courtroom the day the case was thrown out. Oh yes, he had taken the cash, but it was no settlement, not after Guy's defense team had revealed the dirt they had on his daughter. The payment had been a bribe, plain and simple. After all, what decent man would want the entire world knowing that his daughter had been turning tricks since the age of fourteen?

'Every man has his price,' Guy had crowed later that day over a bottle of champagne. *What about me?* Lana had wanted to cry. *What about the price I ought to be paying for killing his daughter?* But there would have been little point, for she had realised by then that Guy didn't view mistakes as something you rectified; they were just something you flung money at until they magically went away. And wasn't that exactly how he had treated her? Paying for her to see that shrink in the aftermath of the accident, and when that hadn't worked, when he grew sick of returning home night after night to find her in a drunken stupor upon the carpet, discarded bottles littering the apartment like glass corpses, he had made her disappear too. All it had cost him was an airline ticket to London and her very own 'out of court settlement'. When he had left her in that grotty Earls Court hotel there hadn't been an ounce of compassion in his parting stare. No, the expression on his face had been almost identical to Sadie's. Lana screwed her eyes shut and shuddered.

'I think I need a breath of fresh air,' Sadie muttered, picking her bag off the floor.

'Yes, that's right, you go,' Lana replied, hoisting herself upright. 'Go on, you're far better off out of here.' She swivelled her legs on to the floor and gingerly got to her feet. 'You do yourself a favour honey, and get as far away from me as possible.'

Sadie watched as Lana shuffled her way over to the empty vodka bottle.

'I'm bad news,' Lana continued, almost defiantly, as she picked up the bottle and raised it to her lips. 'I'm nothing but a low-down, lying killer. A nice girl like you shouldn't want anything to do with me.'

Sadie shook her head as she watched Lana drain the

remaining drops from the bottle. 'No, I'll tell you what you are,' she replied, her voice trembling with a curious mixture of rage and fear. 'You're a pathetic, self-pitying, coward.'

Lana threw her head back and emitted a shrill laugh. 'A coward? Me? I may be a lot of things, honey, but a coward sure isn't one of them!'

'Of course you are. Oh, don't worry, you hide it well behind your brash exterior and sarcastic one-liners, but underneath all the make-up and the wisecracks you're nothing but a pathetic wimp.'

'Now hold on just a minute,' Lana slammed the bottle on to the coffee table and adjusted the belt on her robe.

'No, you hold on,' Sadie demanded, actually squaring up to Lana across the table. 'What's so brave about running halfway across the world to escape from your mistakes? What's so brave about turning to drink? Drinking is the coward's way out – and so is killing yourself. Look at you. Look at what you did.' Sadie gestured at the pile of cuttings.

'I know very well what I did – I killed someone, and do you think a day doesn't go by when I don't think about that young woman and her kid? When I don't torture myself with what I took from that child? I stole her mother from her, for Christ's sake. How do you think that makes me feel?'

'See, there you go again.'

'What do you mean?'

'There you go again – feeling sorry for yourself.'

'I don't feel sorry for myself – I hate myself.'

Sadie sighed. 'But it was an accident.'

'Yeah, right.' Lana snorted and made her way back to the chaise longue.

'But don't you understand. Sometimes things happen and you have absolutely no control over them. It's only afterwards you wish you could hit a rewind button and do things differently, but you can't. Sometimes you have to accept that your life is stuck on Play and just go with the flow.' Sadie put her hand to her throat to try and quell the lump that had suddenly risen out of nowhere. 'When my mum killed herself, I spent weeks walking round in a daze. And then, when it did finally start to sink in, all I could think was, if only. If only I'd seen it coming. If only I'd been a better daughter. If only I'd been there for her. If only she'd loved me more, then she wouldn't have gone and left me.'

Lana looked up, her eyes filling with concern. 'Oh Sadie, honey, you can't blame yourself for what your mom did. It wasn't your fault at all. She was sick, she was living in fear of your father, she wasn't thinking straight.'

Sadie felt the onset of nausea expanding like a fur ball in the back of her throat. 'How do you know she was living in fear?'

Lana gulped. 'You told me, the day we had the fight about the booze.'

'No I didn't. All I told you was that she had killed herself. I didn't tell you she was afraid of my father.' Horrible tremors of rage began coursing through Sadie's body, emanating from the pit of her stomach and reverberating to the very tips of her fingers.

Lana sighed and coiled her legs up in front of her on the chaise longue. 'I guess I must have read it someplace.'

'Read it?'

Lana nodded.

'Read it where? I don't have a collection of cuttings about it.' Sadie gestured wildly at the coffee table. 'You've read her letter, haven't you? You've been through my things and read her letter. How could you?'

Lana shivered and hugged her legs tightly. 'I'm sorry. I guess I just wanted to get to know you a little better, is all. I'm not the only one who's been playing her cards close to her chest, you know.'

'But it was private. It's the only thing I've got left of her.'

'I know, I'm sorry, I just wanted to know what happened – Sadie, honey, please don't go.' Lana stumbled to her feet, but it was too late. By the time she got to the hallway Sadie had gone – the slam of the front door ringing around the house like the sound of a slap.

Chapter Thirty-Seven

As Sadie marched along the endless Drives, Lanes and Avenues of Ruislip Manor it was as if she had an invisible walkman attached to her head, with the volume and mega bass all cranked up to the max. But instead of playing one of her favourite homemade compilation tapes, designed to motivate and uplift, it was pumping out the kind of vicious diatribe that would have made Eminem proud.

The lying, deceitful bitch, Sadie fumed, very nearly marching straight under the wheels of a Renault Espace people carrier. 'Fuck you!' she yelled in response to the prolonged toot of the horn, before giving the driver the finger. (Having previously ascertained that the driver was a harassed young mother, rather than a shaven-headed bruiser, of course.) *How dare Lana snoop through my things like that? How dare she lie to me?* Sadie continued with her internal rant, careering into an old lady who happened to be hobbling out of the library. A large-print copy of Danielle Steele's latest clattered to the floor causing the old lady to cluck in dismay. Ordinarily Sadie would have scurried to pick it up, proffering profuse apologies along the way – but not any more. Why the hell should she bother being polite and civilised, when all she got in return were lies, hurt and deceit? As Sadie strode across the roundabout – after all, why the hell should she bother traipsing all the way up to the zebra crossing? – she weighed up the evidence in the case against everyone else in her life. Firstly, her parents. Sadie laughed a horrible, tight, sarcastic laugh as she somehow made it to the head of the Parade in one piece. *Hadn't she drawn the long straw there? With a bully for a father and a coward for a mother – a coward who preferred to take her own life rather than face up to her responsibilities to her daughter. Then of course there was her one and only boyfriend, the great 'love of her life' – Gay-fucking-Lord, a self-obsessed liar and cheat, who had done nothing but belittle her since the day they met.* Sadie glowered as she strode past the butchers. *Oh, what she wouldn't have given to see GL's miserable little carcass suspended from a meat hook before being shoved into the mincer and ground into sausages – the arrogant pig! And speaking of which – what about her wonderful boss, old hairy mammoth features, Vince?* As she stalked past Babs' Beauty Parlour, Sadie fantasised about treating Vince to an all over body wax – the fluorescent yellow sign in the window informed her that if she booked it before the end of the month she would even get thirty percent off. Sadie's rage began to ebb slightly as she approached Flaming Fires and thought of Liam hunched over his workbench, a pair of eye protectors resting on top of his tousled mane of curls. But one glance inside the shop and all her bitterness came flooding back. Liam's partner, Jim, was sat at the bench, his bald pate shinier than one of the finished surrounds and a spotty teenager was wrestling with a wrought iron furnace heater in the window. Liam was nowhere to be seen. *But why on earth had she expected to see him there? He was leaving for New Zealand tomorrow morning. He would be at home packing, of course. Work would be the last thing on his mind.* Sadie wanted to kick herself for being so stupid. *How could she have allowed herself to develop such a stupid crush on him, when she'd known all along she would end up getting hurt? As with Lana, she'd lowered her defences to Liam only to be kicked in the teeth – never again. They were both a pair of* – Sadie came to a halt outside Pirate Videos and searched for the right adjective to describe her two so-called friends –

motherfuckers – that would do. Sadie gazed forlornly into the darkened shop and vowed to buy herself an Eminem CD at the earliest possible opportunity.

Although it had only been a few hours since Vince had arrived to close it down, the store already had an abandoned air about it. Without the reflected glow from the fairy lights the poster display in the window looked faded and worn and although the shelves inside were still fully stocked the shop seemed eerily empty. Sadie placed a hand upon the cold glass as if she were reaching out to console a friend. With a sinking feeling she realised that she could see her reflection peering back both in the glass and beyond it; she had become nothing more than an abandoned shell too.

'Penny for them.'

Sadie jumped as another reflection loomed up behind her own. A tall, smiling reflection, clad in a lumberjack shirt and jeans. 'Liam!' The pounding bass line from her invisible walkman was miraculously replaced by the swooping melodies of a string quartet.

'What's happened to the shop?' Liam asked as she spun around to face him. 'I couldn't believe it when I saw it all locked up. Terry's been having kittens.'

Sadie forced a smile. 'Vince has finally shut it down. He turned up this morning and asked me to leave.'

'You're kidding – just like that?' Liam stared at Sadie in disbelief. 'What a shit. I hope he's given you a decent pay-off after all the work you've put in.'

Sadie nodded. 'Yeah. And he said if I helped him box up the stock tomorrow I could help myself to videos. Oh, and he did offer me a job in his new store in Hackney.'

Liam raised his eyebrows. 'What did you say?'

'What do you think?' Sadie cast her eyes forlornly along the Parade. 'So as of now I am officially unemployed.'

Liam shook his head and sighed. 'That's bad news. Well

– if you're not doing anything, why don't you come up to mine for a cup of coffee?'

Sadie pretended to contemplate his offer for all of five seconds. 'Well . . . if you're sure you don't mind. I won't get in the way of your packing or anything?'

'No – it's all done – apart from this,' Liam produced a bottle of sun cream from the paper bag in his hand. 'Jealous?' he asked, giving Sadie a playful dig in the ribs.

Sadie made a feeble attempt at a smile as she followed Liam up the stairwell. 'Of course not; I've got weeks of hanging out with Terry to look forward to.'

Liam laughed. 'Just think, you can even go and sign on together.'

'So where is the lodger from hell?' Sadie asked as she took a seat at the kitchen table.

'God knows,' Liam replied, filling the kettle. 'He disappeared about two hours ago saying something about buying me a leaving present.'

'Oh God, what do you think he's going to get you?'

'I dread to think.'

'I bet it's a copy of *Playboy* to read on the plane.'

'Yeah, and an inflatable doll for a travel companion.'

They both looked at each other and sniggered, but before their laughter had even finished echoing around the kitchen Sadie felt the rather inconvenient onset of tears welling behind her eyes. It was so unfair. She liked Liam so much, he was the only person she felt she could trust, the only person who could still make her laugh. Why oh why did he have to be going?

'Do you fancy a biscuit?' Liam asked, removing a bucket of cleaning products from beneath the sink and fishing out a slightly battered packet of custard creams. 'It's my latest hiding place,' he explained. 'The one place Tel is guaranteed not to look.'

Sadie opened her mouth to giggle, but to her dire embarrassment a sob escaped, followed by another and another until torrents of tears were spilling down her face.

'Hey, it's not that bad,' Liam soothed. 'They might taste more like Shake'n'Vac than custard, but at least he doesn't get his paws on them.' Liam placed the biscuits on the table and crouched down in front of her. 'Sadie, what's up?'

But Sadie couldn't bring herself to speak. After all, what on earth would she say? *Please don't go off and abandon me to my sad, lonely existence?*

'Bloody hell, I've done it again, haven't I?' Liam asked, standing up and looking around the kitchen in despair. 'Okay – what am I doing wrong? Would you prefer tea, but are too polite to ask? Or do you have some deep-rooted phobia of caffeine but you're too ashamed to admit it? Or perhaps you find the way I fill the kettle offensive?'

'What do you mean?' Sadie stopped mid-sob to stare at Liam blankly.

'Every time I try to make you a cup of coffee you end up going into one,' Liam replied. 'Well, this time you're not going to do a runner until you've at least given me an explanation why.' He marched over to the kitchen door, where he stood with his arms folded in front of his chest. 'You could give a bloke a right complex carrying on like this, you know.'

Sadie wiped her face with the back of her hand and started to smile.

Liam threw her a tea towel. 'Here, wipe your face on this. I wouldn't mind, but you get upset before you've even tasted the bloody stuff. For all you know, I could be the Jamie Oliver of the percolating world.'

Sadie laughed. 'You can't be,' she replied, pointing at the coffee jar. 'It's instant.'

Liam looked momentarily perplexed before grabbing the jar from the counter and studying the label. 'Okay – I could

be king of the Rich Roast then. You haven't seen me let loose
with a teaspoon – it's like watching a maestro at work. It's all in
the wrist action, you know.' As soon as he said it, Liam could
practically hear a shriek of *Carry On*-style canned laughter
echo around the kitchen.

'Hmm – I bet it is,' Sadie replied, her eyes twinkling through
the tears.

Liam put the jar back down on the counter. 'Please don't
run off again,' he said, scuffing the toe of his boot against
the floor.

Sadie dabbed at her face with the tea towel and began
opening the packet of biscuits. 'I'm sorry, it's just been
quite a day. Of course I won't run off – besides, I haven't
got anywhere to run to.'

As Liam set about making the coffee, Sadie told him all
about her afternoon at Lana's, the shock revelations and the
heated exchange. She even ended up telling him about her
mother's note – at which point one of Liam's shovel-sized
hands gently came to rest upon her own.

'I can't believe she went through my things like that. I know
it sounds stupid, but that letter was like my final connection
with my mum, my one clue to what was going on in her head
that – that morning,' Sadie shivered. 'And now I know Lana's
read it, it doesn't feel personal anymore.'

Liam pulled his chair around the kitchen table until it was
next to Sadie's. 'Don't be silly,' he said, his gruff voice
strangely soothing. 'So she's read it – so what? She wasn't
there when your mum wrote it. She'll never be able to change
the sentiment behind it. It's still a connection to your mum –
it always will be.'

Sadie sighed. 'I know what you're saying, but I feel as if
Lana's betrayed me, and the fact is she's not the only one.
I tell you what, since the start of this year it's as if people
have been lining up to let me down – the motherfuckers.'

Liam raised his eyebrows and stared at her quizzically. '*Motherfuckers*?'

Sadie blushed. 'Sorry, but they've got me so mad.'

'So who are these *motherfuckers*?' Liam asked with a wry grin. 'I hope I'm not on your list.'

'Oh no.' Sadie picked up the packet of biscuits and tried to disguise her increasing embarrassment by studying the calorific content of a custard cream. 'Well, first I find out that my boyfriend's been cheating on me, then Vince closes the shop and now all this with Lana – how am I supposed to trust anyone at all?'

Liam laughed. 'You're not.'

'Oh.'

'If you want my humble opinion, there's only one person you can rely on in life and that's yourself.' Liam took the packet from her and helped himself to a biscuit.

Sadie frowned. 'Isn't that a tad cynical?'

'No, I don't think so.' Liam paused to dunk the biscuit in his coffee. 'I think it's realistic. If you put all of your faith into another human being they're guaranteed to let you down. How can another person ever fulfil all your expectations?'

'But surely you have a right to expect certain things from your boyfriend or your friends or your parents?'

Liam nodded as he consumed his biscuit in one easy mouthful. 'Yes, of course, in an ideal world those people would and should be there for you, but life *isn't* ideal, is it? You never know what it might throw at you. Christ, look at me – I've wound up with Tel for a lodger and living in permanent fear for the safety of my biscuits.'

Sadie laughed. 'Point taken. You're quite thoughtful for a man, aren't you?'

Liam glanced at her cautiously, unsure if this was a good or bad point.

'My boyfriend – *ex*-boyfriend – he didn't really think about anything much apart from himself.'

Liam grinned and leant forward, causing a lock of hair to fall over his face. Brushing it away with the back of his hand he stared at Sadie intently. 'Believe me – when you spend hours on your own every day carving the same damned thing over and over again you get plenty of time to think. I haven't quite got the meaning of life sussed yet, but another couple of months ought to do it.'

Sadie smiled and tried to ignore the tingling sensation emanating from the tips of her toes to the tops of her legs. If Liam moved any closer, their feet would be touching. 'Go on then, oh wise one, what have you worked out so far?'

'Well, apart from the fact that washing machines enjoy snacking on socks and birds never die – where do all the bodies go?' He offered in response to Sadie's blank expression. 'I suppose the main thing I've realised is that you have to take responsibility for your own life. Actually, I realised that when I was about ten years old, but there's not been a day since that has caused me to think otherwise.'

Sadie nodded. 'But isn't that stating the obvious? Surely we're all responsible for our own lives.'

'Yeah, but how many of us actually take that responsibility?'

'What do you mean?'

'Well, look at you and your list of motherfuckers. By blaming them for everything, aren't you shirking your own responsibility?'

Sadie's smile slid into a scowl. 'What are you saying – that it was my fault GL cheated on me, that it was my fault Lana snooped through my belongings?'

'No, of course not,' Liam replied anxiously. Christ, if he wasn't careful Sadie would be hot-footing it out of the door again and she'd only drunk about an inch of her coffee. 'Of course you're not responsible for *their* actions, but you are responsible for your *reactions*.'

'What was wrong with my reactions? I think I was perfectly entitled to dump the cheating—' much to Liam's relief, Sadie began to grin, '—*motherfucker*. And I think I was quite within my rights to have a go at Lana.'

'Yes, of course you were. The cheating motherfucker deserved to be shot, let alone dumped. And Lana needed to be told a few home truths, but you don't deserve to be eaten up with anger for the rest of your life just because of them.'

Sadie stared at him thoughtfully. 'So what are you saying I should do?'

'I'm saying this is *your* life, Sadie, nobody else's. Don't let other peoples' problems or inadequacies wreck it. It's obvious Lana thinks the world of you but she's an alcoholic, she's full of guilt. She never meant to hurt you, she's just completely fucked up by the sounds of it. Oh God, speaking of which.' They both started as they heard the front door slam.

'Greetings, pop-pickers!' Terry bounded into the room and flung a nylon suit cover on to the table. 'Treacle – just the person I wanted to see. What's up with the shop? What's the padlock in aid of?'

Sadie sighed. 'I'm afraid I've got some bad news, Terry. Vince has finally closed it down.'

'Stone me! You're having a laugh, aren't you? Where am I going to get me vids from now?'

'Blockbusters?' Sadie replied with a shrug.

'I can't, angel, I'm on their most wanted list aren't I?'

Sadie groaned. 'Don't tell me you staged a stick-up in *Blockbusters*?'

'Nah, of course not,' Terry retorted, grabbing the custard creams from the table. 'I just had a bit of a dispute with the South Ruislip branch over me non-payment for *Dirty*

Dancing, didn't I.' Terry squeezed the remaining four biscuits from the packet. 'Dirty bleeding Dancing? I've seen raunchier action down the Darby and Joan. I said to them, if you expect me to pay for that load of guff I'll 'ave you under the Trades Descriptions Act.'

'Help yourself to a biscuit, Tel,' Liam said, raising his eyebrows to Sadie.

'Yeah, don't mind if I do,' Terry replied, stuffing one into his mouth. 'How about I fix us some tea? You'll be needing a bit of fuel in your belly son, with the journey you've got ahead of you. How about I heat us a couple of them canned fry-ups?'

Liam visibly recoiled with horror. 'Oh I don't know, Tel, I've been feeling a bit dodgy all day. I think my belly could do with a break – probably pre-flight nerves.'

'I'm not surprised, son. I tell you what, you wouldn't catch me going on a plane in this day and age. You see anyone with a tea towel on their head in that departure lounge you make a run for it, you hear. Are you sure you don't want to go tooled up? I can easily sort you out with a sawn-off.'

Liam and Sadie both groaned.

'I'd better get going,' Sadie said, getting to her feet.

'Are you sure?' Liam practically implored. 'You're welcome to stay for another Rich Roast.'

Sadie smiled. 'No, it's okay. I'll get out of your way. You've got a big day ahead of you and anyway I have things of my own to take care of – you know, responsibilities.'

Liam grinned. 'That's the spirit.'

Sadie stopped as she got to the kitchen door. 'Oh Terry, if you're interested in earning yourself some free videos come down to the shop tomorrow lunchtime and give me a hand boxing up the stock.'

Terry's face broke into a smile as he reached into his shirt pocket for his roll-ups. 'Nice one, Treacle. Here, will that include the top shelf jobs?'

'You can help yourself to whatever shelf you like as far as I'm concerned. Vince is going to be dumping whatever we don't take. He's finally realised that DVDs are the way forward.'

As Sadie reached the front door she could hardly bring herself to look at Liam. Her heart was pounding louder than a hip-hop bass line and an annoying lump was once again forming at the back of her throat. It took every muscle in her face to manoeuvre her mouth into a cheery grin.

'Well, good luck with the scene,' she said, her voice literally squeaking with forced jollity. 'Make sure you send us a postcard when you get to Pitcairn Island.'

'Of course I will.'

Sadie studied Liam's face. For a man about to embark upon a swash-buckling adventure he appeared remarkably grim.

'Will you be all right now?' he asked. 'With Lana – and everything.'

'Of course I will – especially now you've talked some sense into me.'

Liam smiled and held out his hand. 'Well, good luck,' he said, his voice gruffer than ever.

Sadie stared at his hand for a moment before realising that it was obviously being offered as a parting gesture. 'Yes, you too,' she stammered, awkwardly placing her hand in his and attempting to shake it. It felt heavier than a brick. 'You too.'

It wasn't until she reached the end of the Parade that Sadie began to regain her sense of composure. A whole welter of emotions were jingling about inside her, from abject embarrassment at the whole hand-shaking debacle, to utter sorrow at the prospect of not seeing Liam for the next couple of months and not even getting a farewell kiss. But thankfully, rising above all this internal pandemonium was a reassuring top-note of calm. For as Sadie negotiated her way back along the Drives, Lanes and Avenues of Ruislip Manor, paying great heed to her Green Cross Code and respecting the right of way of any oncoming pedestrians, she felt emboldened by a new sense of certainty with every step. Liam had been spot on. It was high time she took responsibility for her own life. Perhaps being made redundant was the best thing that could have happened to her. In fact, now she came to think of it, her entire list of recent woes could easily be redefined as wake-up calls.

As she turned into Lana's road Sadie smelt the familiar aroma of wood smoke suspended in the crisp early evening air. Sure enough, a thin grey coil was wisping its way out of the chimney stack, creating a charcoal smudge upon the tangerine sunset. Sadie stopped at the garden gate and inhaled deeply. It smelt of winter and warmth all rolled into one. It smelt of home.

When Sadie entered the living room Lana was kneeling before the hearth, prodding at the fire with a brass fork.

'She's dead you know, Sadie,' Lana said, without turning round. 'Mary Latimer – she's dead and she's never coming back.'

Sadie watched as a glowing fragment of newspaper leapt out of the flames and spiralled up the chimney.

'I've changed, I promise you,' Lana implored, finally turning to face Sadie, her eyes glassy with tears and wide with concern. 'Please give me another chance.'

Sadie knelt down beside her and took the fork from her hand. 'Of course I will,' she replied. 'Now, why don't you put your feet up and I'll make us a plateful of smores.'

Chapter Thirty-Eight

'*Would passengers for flight BA 457 please make their way to the departure lounge. Thank you.*'

A flurry of activity broke out across the terminal concourse, as tickets were double-checked, passports were relocated and farewell embraces were exchanged. Liam picked up his bag and looked at Terry. 'Well, this is it then.'

Terry nodded mournfully. 'Yep, I suppose it is.'

'Blimey, Tel, lighten up. I'll only be gone for a couple of months – think of all the porn you'll be able to watch while I'm away.'

'What do you think I do when you're at work?' Terry retorted, gazing sorrowfully about the terminal.

Liam frowned. 'I don't know why you've got such a chin on. You're going to have your own pad for God's sake – think of the pulling power you'll have down at the Legion.'

'Yeah, that's what I thought last year when you buggered off to Asia, but it ended up being a right anti-climax, in more ways than one. I only got lucky once and it turned out she was on blob week.' Terry pulled his leather jacket around his scrawny shoulders and shuddered. 'I tell you what, the bed looked like something out of the *Chainsaw Massacre* by the time I'd finished with her. I ended up having to burn your sheets and everything.'

'*My* sheets?' Liam yelled in horror.

Terry scuffed the toe of his cowboy boot against a conveniently placed ashtray stand. 'Yeah, well, I could hardly give her one in my cot of a bed – she was a right hefty piece – we'd have probably shagged the legs off it. Don't worry, once I turned your mattress over it was as if the stains had never been there.'

Liam groaned. 'Jesus, Tel, are you trying to put me off going or something?'

Terry's face lit up. 'Why? Is it working?'

'No, it is not.' Liam made a last check in his pocket for his travel documents. 'You know me, Tel, once I get the travel bug there's no turning back. And anyway I've got my scene to re-enact, haven't I. Shit, I was the one who came up with the idea in the first place – I can't bottle out now.'

Terry nodded unenthusiastically. 'Hmm, I suppose so.' He paused to relight the roll-up suspended like a paper bat from his bottom lip. 'You go, son. Don't worry about us. You just go and enjoy yourself. I'll do me best to look out for young Sadie, but I can't guarantee anything, mind.'

Liam turned and stared at Terry. 'What do you mean?'

'Well, you know, I can't guarantee she'll still be there for you when you get back.'

'She'll still be there for *me?*'

'Yeah. Obviously I'll keep putting in a good word for you, but there's no saying some other young pup isn't going to come sniffing around while you're off gallivanting. A little corker like her, she ain't gonna be on the market for ever now, is she?'

Liam dropped his bag to the floor and buried his face in his hands. 'Oh Tel, why can't you just leave it alone. Sadie's a free agent and so am I. I don't need you putting in a good word for me.'

Terry hollered with laughter, causing a ripple of turning heads. 'Of course you do. How long have you fancied her for now? Bleeding months – and in all that time you haven't even got a snog, let alone a bit of 'ow's your father. No, on the rare occasion you do get her back to the flat all you bleeding do is natter. What's up with you, son? You scared or something? Or has the cat got your knackers?'

'I'm not scared of anything,' Liam retorted, puffing out his chest. 'Just because I respect women and see them as more than just a shag, it doesn't make me a wimp.'

'Oh, don't give me none of that new man nonsense. Birds don't want to be respected, they want to be rogered, simple as that.'

'Can you please keep your voice down,' Liam hissed, smiling apologetically at two passing air hostesses.

Terry sighed and begrudgingly lowered his voice. 'I can't help it, son, but I've got to say my piece. I'm older than you – and, if you don't mind me saying – a great deal wiser. I suppose in a way I look upon you and Treacle as the kids I never had, and Gawd knows it can be hard for a father to stand by and watch two of his nippers bodge everything up.'

Liam didn't know what to be more dismayed about – the fact that Terry had been putting in a 'good word' for him with Sadie or the fact that he viewed them both as his adopted offspring. 'I really ought to get going,' he muttered, picking up his bag and heading towards the Departure Lounge.

'Well, if you're sure,' Terry replied, trotting after him.

'I'm sure.'

'Okay then, son. Well, you have a safe journey, and make sure you wear my present when you do your scene.'

Liam couldn't help grinning at the thought of Terry's leaving gift. 'I can't go dressed in a sailor's outfit, Tel, I'll feel like a right twat.'

'Hey,' Terry retarted indignantly. 'You're meant to be Fletcher Christian, aren't you? And besides Rancid Ron went to great lengths to get hold of that get-up for you. It's the real McCoy, you know. Regulation naval attire as issued by Her Majesty – back in the nineteen-eighties, mind. Here, you never know, that uniform could have seen some action down in the Falklands.'

'All right, all right,' Liam came to a halt before the entrance to the Departure Lounge and turned to face Terry. 'Well, take care of yourself – *Dad*.'

'Stone me, I'm coming over all emotional,' Terry spluttered, flinging his arms around Liam. 'You too, son, you too. And hey – sod the duty frees, try and smuggle one of them Tahitian birds back in your suitcase for us. Tell her I'll even marry her if she's prepared to wash me skids.'

Sadie studied the array of video cases in front of her and scratched her head. Here she was with the opportunity to take her pick of free films, and yet for some completely bizarre reason not one of them held any appeal. She could have understood it if she were in the Action Adventure Section, presented with shelf after shelf of Jackie Chan and James Bond, but this was the Drama Section, housing her staple viewing diet for the previous twelve months. Not even the cover of *Thelma and Louise* could elicit the slightest tingle of excitement. The fact was, Sadie felt all videoed out. She was sick of watching pretend characters embarking upon road-trips or high school romances or star-crossed love affairs. She wanted adventures of her very own. For the first time in her life she felt ready to assume the lead role, and not in some vain attempt at a re-enactment either. Sadie didn't want to follow a script. She didn't want to know the ending before she had even begun. For the first time ever she felt brave enough to take a plunge into the great unknown.

Sadie smiled as she reached into her pocket for Lana's list of requests. 'Has anybody seen *Casablanca*?' she called.

'Nah, but I've got two copies of *Sheryl's Shaven Haven*

here if anyone's interested,' Terry replied from the top of the stepladder.

'Dirty old perv,' Brian muttered from behind his reflector lenses, piling the entire music section into a cardboard box on the floor.

'*Jason Donovan's Greatest Hits*,' Sadie observed as she made her way past him to the Golden Oldies. 'I didn't realise you had a penchant for Aussie pop, Brian. I thought you were strictly a Floyd man.'

'I am,' Brian replied with a scowl. 'It's background research for my college thesis – How Ramsay Street has become the Axis of Evil of the Music World.'

'Stone me,' Terry sighed. 'You want to get yourself a proper job, son, get out in the sunshine once in a while – all that studying's mashing your brain.'

Brian snorted. 'Oh yeah? Lot of opportunities in the pizza delivery trade are there, old timer?'

'Now just you hold on a second, sonny,' Terry fumed, stalking down the stepladder, several soft-porn covers tucked under his arm.

Sadie threw up her hands in despair. 'All right, all right, calm down. Vince will be back from the estate agents in a minute. Who fancies a cup of Pirate Video's finest? For old time's sake.'

Finally getting Terry and Brian to agree on something, Sadie beat a hasty retreat to the kitchen. She sighed as she looked around the cupboard-sized alcove, gazing fondly at the chipped mugs, coffee splattered jars and solidified sugar. She still couldn't quite believe this would be the last time she switched on the rusty old kettle to make a brew. But things were changing, life was moving on and she had to move on with it. Sadie looked at her watch. It was half-past twelve. Liam would be boarding his plane at any moment. Sadie felt a shard of pain slice through her as she pictured Liam

all the way on the other side of the planet, so far away that
he would actually be upside down. But then she recalled his
advice to her from the day before. She had to stop letting other
people's actions dominate her life and take responsibility for
her own destiny. If she couldn't actually be with Liam then
at least she could let his attitude be an inspiration to her, and
become empowered by that same sense of fearlessness. As if to
prove this point, Sadie unlocked the back door and prepared
to confront the outside toilet for the very last time.

Liam was feeling far from fearless as he stood at the departure
gate, staring helplessly through the glass. There, looming in
front of him, was the cavernous belly of a 747. Liam sighed
and turned his back to the window. For the first time in his
life he was viewing a plane as more of a monster than some
kind of saviour. He had been seventeen when he made his
first flight, a late developer compared to most of his peers,
whose parents had been able to afford annual jaunts to the
Costas Brava and Del Sol. But he had certainly made up
for it since. Nothing had beaten the adrenaline rush of that
first take-off, *en route* to a lads' holiday in Goa. As he'd
pressed back into his chair, gripping the armrests so tightly
the colour had completely drained from his hands, he felt
like a tank of aviation fuel ready to explode from the sparks
of excitement and fear igniting throughout his body. And
then there had been the beautiful come-down after the rush,
when the seatbelt light pinged off and the stewardesses began
their first round with the drinks trolley.

But even the recollection of his maiden flight couldn't
raise the slightest trace of a buzz in Liam. As he watched
his fellow passengers handing over their boarding passes
and scuttling off down the tunnel he felt completely and
utterly flat.

A tearful woman accompanied by an air stewardess and

a slightly bewildered looking young girl came to a halt just in front of him.

'Your father will be at the airport to meet you,' the woman said, stooping down until her face was level with the girl's. 'Now, don't forget what I said about the sunblock. Make sure you put some on every time you go out – especially on your nose.'

The girl nodded and gave a tight little smile.

'You have a good time, and I'll see you next month,' the woman choked, grabbing the child to her and showering the top of her head with kisses.

Liam thought of Sadie and sighed. Why the hell hadn't he given her a hug good-bye? What had he been thinking of, offering her his hand as if she were some kind of business acquaintance when all he'd really wanted to do was wrap his arms around her and bury his face in her hair?

The woman's sobs echoed around the by now deserted departure gate as the little girl disappeared off down the tunnel with the stewardess, a battered-looking teddy bear clutched to her chest.

I can't do this, Liam thought, *I can't leave.* Much as he was loathe to admit it, Terry had been right. He was acting like a wimp, legging it off to New Zealand when all he really wanted was to be with Sadie. What had he been thinking of, making pathetic excuses about having to recreate a film scene? For fuck's sake, there were millions of other scenes he could have chosen, ones that could have included Sadie too. Liam wracked his brains as he made his way over to the departure desk, smiling apologetically at the overly made-up attendant. What was that film his mum always watched with a slab of chocolate and a box of tissues? The final scene in that would be perfect – thanks to Terry he already had the outfit. If he could just make it back to the shop in time.

*   *   *

Sadie winced as she listened to the outraged voices hollering throughout the shop.

'There's no way that horse's head scene was worse than anything in *Taxi Driver*,' Terry seethed. 'I tell you, when it comes to blood and guts, Scorcese beats that Canneloni geezer hands down.'

'Don't you go dissing *The Godfather* in my presence.' Vince replied, equally indignant. 'I'm from Sardinia mate, you know what I mean?'

Their argument over the comparative gore content of *Taxi Driver* and *The Godfather* had been raging for almost an hour now, during which time Sadie had taken refuge behind the counter, slowly clearing the back shelves and placing the videos in their correct covers. It was a thankless task at the best of times, but with Vince, Terry and Brian going at it hammer and tongs Sadie was beginning to long for the moment when it was time to leave.

'If it's real blood and guts you're after you want to see *Foetus Eaters From Hell, Part Three*. It pisses all over your Hollywood glory boys,' Brian muttered, instantly causing howls of derision from the other two.

'Who rattled the hippy's cage?' Vince yelled. 'I tell you what, if you was from my neck of the woods, with your attitude, son, you'd have said adios to your knee-caps long ago. You know what I mean?'

'I know exactly what y—' Terry began to reply, before breaking off mid-sentence with a gasp of disbelief. 'Stone me, it's the Village People.'

Hearing the collective hoots of laughter from the front of the shop Sadie looked up in surprise. 'Oh my God,' she cried, dropping the cover of *Top Gun* in shock. 'Liam, is that you?'

Liam was stood in the doorway, clad in the most outrageously naff sailor's outfit, complete with a natty embroidered anchor on the left breast pocket of the tunic. It also appeared to be about three sizes too small, with the hem of the slightly off-white trousers flapping around his calves and a square shaped hat perched jauntily on top of his curls.

Liam took a deep breath and, ignoring the collective sniggers of Brian and Vince, marched straight up to the counter.

'If you're looking for the Seaman's Institute you're about two hundred miles too far inland, sailor,' Vince spluttered, clutching his side.

'What are you doing here?' Sadie asked. 'Why aren't you on the plane? Why are you wearing that – outfit?'

Still saying nothing, Liam marched around the counter and swept Sadie up into his arms.

'What are you doing?' Sadie shrieked, spluttering with laughter. 'Why aren't you on your way to New Zealand?'

'I'm not going,' Liam replied, carrying her back round the counter to the front of the shop.

'But – what about your scene?'

'I've decided to do another one,' Liam replied, removing his sailor's hat and placing it upon Sadie's head. 'I'm doing it right now, as it happens.'

'You are?' Sadie asked.

'Yes. Please don't tell me you're the only woman alive not to have seen *An Officer and a Gentleman*?'

'Fucking stone me,' Terry cried, bursting into a round of applause. 'The boy's finally come good. I'm proud of you, son.'

Sadie flung her arms around Liam's neck and buried her face in his chest. 'I can't believe you're doing this,' she murmured.

Liam started to laugh. 'Neither can I,' he whispered. 'Now let's get out of here before I get arrested by the fashion police.'

Chapter Thirty-Nine

'So let me get this straight – every morning when you arrive at the shop somebody has taken a crap in the toilet?' Liam hoisted himself on to his elbow and stared down at Sadie, the furrow of concern upon his brow completely belied by the twinkle in his eyes.

Sadie nodded and giggled. Excrement was hardly a typical subject matter for pillow talk, but then in the twelve hours they had spent in bed very little had been typical. The way Liam had made her feel, for a start. From their very first kiss – the moment he carried her over the threshold into the flat – to the way he was stroking her arm now, causing goose-bumps to arise in the most unlikely of places. There was a contrary mixture of strength and tenderness about Liam that was driving Sadie wild. The feather-light touch of his calloused fingers; the protective aura of his intimidating physique; his gruff displays of emotion. 'I've been waiting nearly a year to do that,' he had whispered huskily in her ear, when they finally tore apart from that initial kiss.

Sadie had no idea kissing could be so enjoyable. GL had always used his tongue in much the same way as he had used his penis, like some kind of mechanical digger, thrusting away randomly and with considerable force. With Liam, however, kissing – and indeed sex – was obviously just as much about the emotional as it was the physical. The notion that sex could be used to as an expression of feeling rather than a basic biological function was an entirely alien concept to

Sadie, but one she had quite literally embraced with open arms. From the moment their lips met, an whirlwind of passion and desire had been unleashed, causing a CD stand to be sent flying, a wooden Buddha to be unceremoniously upended and the bed to be stripped bare. It was only when the dulcet tones of Joe Cocker began booming throughout the flat that they were forced to pause for breath.

'What the hell is that?' Sadie asked, glancing anxiously about Liam's bedroom, getting her bearings for the first time. What the hell were they doing on the carpet beneath the window? Completely naked on the carpet beneath the window? Sadie instinctively reached for the mound of sheets that had somehow become dislodged from the bed and pulled it over them.

Liam sat up and scratched his head. 'It sounds like Joe Cocker,' he replied and then his face broke into a grin. 'It's the bloody theme tune to *An Officer and a Gentleman* – Tel's obviously trying to give me a hand creating the right ambience.'

'I think you were doing pretty well by yourself,' Sadie whispered, rolling herself on top of Liam in a quite shameless show of sexual abandon. 'The door is locked, isn't it?' she added, before sinking back into Liam's embrace.

It was only when 'Up Where We Belong' came on for the eighth time that Liam had to leave the room to confiscate the CD. Terry was nowhere to be seen, but the stereo had been set on repeat, with a battered box of Neapolitan chocolates placed on top. *Seeing as you've finally started following my advice you might want to give her these chocs*, the attached note read. *According to the Daily Star something in the cocoa solids makes birds well up for it.*

And so it was, in another break with convention, Sadie found herself nibbling on a square of out of date, orange flavoured chocolate, whilst discussing excrement with her new lover at six o'clock in the morning.

'I can't believe the phantom crapper doesn't even flush away the evidence,' Liam continued, by now woefully unable to disguise the amusement upon his face. 'It's as if he wants to show off his crime, like one of those killers who have to leave some sort of calling card by the body.'

Sadie grimaced. 'I know, and the last couple of days it's been vile. I don't know what he's been eating, but the after-effects have been horrific.'

'Have you never thought about trying to catch him out?'

'What – like setting a crap trap?' Sadie shook her head and laughed. 'Look, it's bad enough having to confront the crap let alone the crapper. God knows what kind of an animal is responsible for it.' Sadie shuddered. 'I swear, what I found yesterday looked more like elephant dung than anything produced by a human!'

Liam glanced at his bedroom window and then at Sadie. 'But aren't you even the *least* bit curious?'

Half an hour later they were back beneath the duvet, giggling like a pair of schoolkids.

'I can't believe what we've just done,' Sadie sniggered. 'He's bound to notice it.'

'Of course he won't, it's pitch black out there and besides if he's still got the runs he's not going to be bothering with a pitch inspection, is he. What was that?' Liam sat up with a start.

'What?'

'That creaking noise.'

'It was probably just the greengrocers arriving next door.'

'No, listen.'

Sadie craned her head towards the window and sure enough she heard a faint creaking followed by the clatter of a bolt being drawn. 'It's him,' she cried, leaping from the bed. 'Come on, let's get the motherfucker.'

Liam looked at her and smiled. He couldn't believe he had ever had Sadie down as the shy and retiring type. Okay, so she wasn't exactly a mouth almighty, but there was a feistiness beneath that delicate exterior that was like the fizz inside a lemon sherbert. He watched as she pulled on her tracksuit, back to front and inside out, her hair springing from her head like a mass of telephone wire and he felt like a life-long loser at the bookies whose horse had finally come in.

As they crept their way down the wrought iron fire escape from Liam's kitchen they heard a muffled yelp from inside the outhouse.

Liam turned to Sadie and quietly began to sing to the tune of *Ghostbusters*. 'If there's something vile in your outside bog, who you gonna call? Crap-Trappers! If there's something weird and it don't smell good, who you gonna call?'

Sadie clutched hold of Liam's arm and bit on her hand to stifle her laughter. 'I'm going to wet myself,' she spluttered.

'Hang on in there,' Liam soothed. 'I've got a funny feeling the toilet's going to become available any second now.'

Sadie crossed her legs and bent over double. 'You have got to be kidding. After what we've done, I dread to think what kind of state it's going to be in.'

'Here he comes,' Liam whispered, before resuming his song. 'I ain't 'fraid of turds.'

They both stood motionless on the bottom step as the bolt slid undone and the door came crashing open. A sinewy figure stumbled out into the darkness, his trousers rucked around his ankles and his head twisted over his shoulder as if he were trying to catch a glimpse of his backside.

'Fucking stone me!' the figure gasped. 'What the hell's going on?'

'Terry!' Liam and Sadie cried in unison.

The phantom crapper froze for a second before clapping

his hands around his genitals. 'Oh shit,' he muttered, staring sorrowfully at the ground.

'Precisely,' Liam replied, leaning against the railings of the staircase and folding his arms. 'So what's going on?'

'Yes – what do you think you're doing?' Sadie demanded, trying hard to keep her eyes fixed upon Terry's face, although gravity seemed to keep dragging them back downwards.

'I was having a Tom-tit,' Terry replied sheepishly. 'Leastways I was trying to, but something really fucking weird happened. It was like an explosion or something and it all seemed to fire back up me arse.' Once again, Terry attempted to peer over his shoulder. 'Me backside's covered in it.'

Sadie and Liam looked at each other and grinned.

'But what were you doing using that bog, anyway?' Liam asked, 'What's up with our one?'

'Well it's me log-a-rhythms, ain't it,' Terry replied.

'Your what?'

'Me log-a-rhythms. Me internal digestive clock. Ever since I was a nipper I've always needed a crap in the early hours, but I don't like waking nobody up, see, with the flusher and all that. Nipping down here seemed like the perfect solution.'

'But that's my toilet,' Sadie retorted. 'Have you any idea what it's been like for me having to face your faeces every morning when I arrive for work?'

Terry hung his head in shame. 'I'm sorry, Treacle. I thought you'd think it was a homeless person and take pity on them.'

'Take pity on them?' Sadie fumed. 'You've got to be joking. The other day it took three flushes before the toilet was clean.'

Terry nodded proudly. 'I know, I've done some right monsters, ain't I?' Upon seeing Sadie's scowl, Terry hastily lowered his tone to a more morose levels. 'Don't be mad, Angel; I'm not a well man.'

'You can say that again,' Sadie retorted.

'No, I mean it. It's those breakfast-in-a-cans I've been eating. From can to pan to man it says on the label – well, they bleeding missed out the end bit, didn't they? From can to pan to man *straight back to pan*, it ought to say. I've had the squitters for three days and now it's shooting up me back an' all.'

Liam looked at Sadie and they began to snigger. 'You stupid old fool,' he said. 'It was us – we'd set a trap for you.'

'You what?'

'We'd set a trap – the old cling-film over the toilet number. Don't tell me you never pulled that one back in your child-hood days.'

'You pair of sods,' Terry muttered, stumbling towards them shaking his fist and in the process revealing a full frontal.

Sadie screamed with laughter and ran up the stairs.

'Keep away!' Liam shouted, following hot on her heels. 'Don't even think about setting foot in the flat until you've cleaned yourself up. Oh, and Tel,' Liam paused on the balcony and looked down at Terry. 'Perhaps you want to pay a bit more attention to that golden rule of organised crime you're always going on about.'

'Oh yeah, which one's that then?' Terry enquired sullenly.

'Never crap on your own doorstep!'

Chapter Forty

'What do you reckon, Lana – do I make a convincing flapper girl?'

Lana watched in wry amusement as Sadie pulled a feather boa from the closet, wrapped it around her neck and attempted to dance the Charleston across the bedroom floor.

'God, where did you get such beautiful clothes?' Sadie sighed, tripping to a halt at the foot of the bed. 'They ought to be on display in the Victoria and Albert.'

'Honey, I discovered vintage when Sarah Jessica Parker was still crawling around in diapers,' Lana retorted, taking a hefty drag on her cigarette. 'Now where the hell is that burnt orange sweater?'

Sadie returned to the gargantuan wardrobe and began rifling through the rack of lambswool sweaters. 'You must have every other shade under the sun in here,' she replied, 'Does it have to be orange?'

'Of course it does. You've seen the film cover. Bonnie's wearing a burnt orange sweater, a tweed pencil skirt and an oatmeal beret.' Lana yanked open the top drawer of her mahogany chest and began flinging handfuls of hats on to the floor. 'Aha! Here's the beret – it's a bit on the beige side, but I guess it'll do.'

Flicking her boa over her shoulder, Sadie sashayed round to join Lana. 'God, very *Arabian Nights*,' she remarked, fishing a bejewelled turban from the floor and pressing it down on top of her curls.

Lana couldn't help staring at Sadie. Not since Michael Jackson's skin bleach had she seen such a radical transformation in a person. The chrysalis of fear previously surrounding Sadie had finally been chipped away, and the most vibrant social butterfly had fluttered her way to freedom. Lana frowned and sat down on the bed. 'So I guess you'll be moving in with Leroy soon,' she muttered, stooping forward to pick the discarded hats from the floor.

'Leroy?' Sadie repeated, removing the turban and taking a seat next to Lana.

'Leroy, Liam – it's a simple enough mistake,' Lana snapped, slinging the hats into the drawer.

'Are you okay, Lana? You seem a little distracted.' Sadie unravelled the feather boa from her neck and stared at Lana anxiously.

'Of course I'm okay. I'm not pissed if that's what you're thinking. Jeez, I've been to a meeting every day for the past week, haven't I? I'm just tired is all.' Lana rather unsteadily got to her feet and raised her right hand. 'My name's Lana and I'm an insomniac.'

Sadie laughed nervously as Lana sat back down again.

'Anyway, you didn't answer my question – has he asked you to move in with him or not?'

'No, of course not.' Sadie frowned and began picking at the brocade on Lana's bedspread. 'Why, you don't want me to move out, do you?'

Lana face broke into a grin. 'Are you kidding? I love having you here. I just thought, now you're madly in love and all, you may prefer to be with him. And God knows I wouldn't want to come between a pair of star-crossed lovers.'

Sadie placed her hand over Lana's and gave it a gentle squeeze. 'Liam and I have only been together for a few weeks, Lana. There's no way I'm going to make the same mistake I made with GL.' Sadie shuddered at the mere recollection. It was bad enough admitting she once knew GL, let alone thinking she actually allowed him to put his pristine penis inside her. 'Do you know something, when we first met at college I was so desperate for a boyfriend I plunged in headlong without even stopping to consider if he was the right person for me. I just felt eternally grateful that somebody had finally shown an interest. Sad, or what?' Sadie linked her fingers through Lana's and stared straight ahead determinedly. 'But I'm a different person now – I know that life doesn't revolve around whether you have a man or not.'

'Atta-girl!' Lana cried, raising their joined hands in salute.

Sadie turned to face Lana, her cheeks aglow and eyes sparkling. 'Besides, I'm far too busy making plans for us. Guess what, Liam said he's going to teach me to drive and when I've passed my test and you've had your transplant we should go away somewhere – have a girls' adventure. We could drive down to Cornwall, or maybe we could tour around the Scottish Highlands. The air's so clean up there, it would do you the world of good. Oh, Lana, there's just so much I want to do.'

Lana looked at her and grinned.

'What?' Sadie asked. 'Why are you staring at me?'

'I'm just wondering where that timid little mouse went to,' Lana replied.

Sadie's gaze fell to her lap 'Oh, she's still in there somewhere, but every time I hear her squeak, do you know what I do?'

Lana shook her head.

'I think to myself, how would Lana handle this situation? It never fails.'

'Well, honey, I don't know what to say. I'm really touched.'

'Yes, within seconds I've turned from a timid mouse into a belligerent old battleaxe.' Sadie laughed as a purple pillbox hat caught her square on the chin.

'Well, I'm glad our friendship has been a two way thing,' Lana replied, once their laughter had subsided. 'After what happened last month I was terrified I'd blown it. You have to believe me Sadie, – I never meant to hurt you, and I wish to God I'd never lied to you. I can't help feeling I've let you down terribly.'

'How can you say that?' Sadie stared at Lana bewildered. You've helped me so much, from the moment you took me to Le Caprice and showed me that birthdays can actually be happy. I mean it Lana, you've turned my life around.'

Lana shook her head, but couldn't help smiling. 'Nonsense – you've turned it round yourself. All I ever did was get you barred from one of London's premier eateries and introduce you to smores.'

'Well, what could be more life changing than a smore?' Sadie sighed, licking her lips.

'I just want you to know that I'll never let you down again, Sadie. I promise. And I'm determined to repay you for everything you've done for me.'

Sadie looked at Lana blankly. 'What have I done for you?'

'Oh, more than you'll ever know, honey. More than you'll ever know. Now, how about you help me get ready for that dreadful little man's scene.' Lana sighed wistfully as she picked up her beret. 'Too bad I'm going to be playing opposite Warren Mitchell rather than Warren Beatty.'

Chapter Forty-One

One blonde wig, several layers of kohl, a beige beret, burnt orange sweater and tweed pencil skirt later and Lana could have sashayed right off the cover of *Bonnie and Clyde*. The only things detracting from the femme fatale effect were her trembling hands and somewhat glazed expression.

'Are you sure you're up to this?' Sadie asked, studying Lana anxiously. 'It's not too late to pull out, you know. Terry can always do this scene on his own.'

'No way,' Lana retorted. 'I told you – I'm just a little tired, that's all. Now where did I put my purse?'

Sadie pointed to the hall table, where Lana's handbag was lying on top of a still uncompleted job application for Blockbuster Video. 'I'm just worried that the stress might be too much for you. You are supposed to be recuperating, after all. When the doctors told you to take it easy I think they had meditation, poetry, and Melody FM in mind, not holding up your local mini-mart. What if Taj recognises you? What if he calls the police?'

'Oh honey, take a chill pill. Jeez, if anyone needs to meditate around here it's you. Now for the last time, will you quit worrying about me.' Lana grabbed her bag from the table and put it over her shoulder. 'I am going out of my mind cooped up in this place twenty-four seven.' To emphasise the point she threw her hands up to the ceiling and contorted her face into an expression of rabid horror. 'And do not talk to me about Old Fart FM; believe me, there is nothing "easy listening" about Julio Inglesias on repeat. Now, how do I look?'

'Great,' Sadie conceded. 'you look great.'

'I know,' Lana purred, admiring herself in the hall mirror, as she ran her bejewelled hands over her hourglass hips. 'I guess a glamour icon never truly loses her style, does she – even when her body has been utterly ravaged on the inside, externally she always maintains a sheen of sophistication. Just think of poor old Princess Margaret.'

Hearing the squeak of a horn from outside, Sadie opened the front door. 'They're here. Oh my God!' she pushed the door to and turned to face Lana, 'Oh. My. God!'

'What? What is it?' Lana demanded, pushing past Sadie to peer out of the door. 'Oh, Jeez. What the hell is he wearing?'

They both watched in stupefied silence as Terry and a rather ashen-faced Liam disembarked from the pizza delivery bike. Whereas Lana looked every inch the nineteen thirties sex siren, poor old Terry looked more like he was on his way to place a twenty-pence bet at the bookies in his ill-fitting powder blue suit and brown felt trilby.

'Well – if it isn't my leading man,' Lana remarked, through gritted teeth. 'Please tell me that isn't your best effort at Warren Beatty? I know you can't do anything about the looks – barring major reconstructive surgery – but you could at least have acquired some stylish attire. Bonnie and Clyde? We're going to look more like Ma and Pa Hillbilly. You're going to make a complete laughing stock of us.' She shook her head in disgust.

'Now, now, no need for that kind of talk,' Terry replied, opening the pizza container on the back of his bike and producing two huge Technicolor pistols.

'And what in God's name are they?' Lana hissed.

Terry looked at Liam and raised his eyebrows. 'What are

they, she asks! They, my dear, are two top of the range, pump action, semi-automatic water pistols.'

'Water pistols?' Lana shrieked, 'You mean we're going to hold up a store armed with no more than a few rounds of tap water?'

'Two pints,' Terry corrected.

'What do you mean, two pints?'

'Each pistol takes two pints. These ain't no piddly kids toys, you know. In the wrong hands these can be lethal – as young Liam found out tonight when he got home from work, didn't you son?'

Liam scowled at Terry. 'Yeah, really fucking hilarious that was, Tel.' He strode up the garden path and placed an arm around Sadie's shoulders. 'The bastard drenched me,' he explained, stooping to kiss the top of her head. 'He was lying in wait on the balcony.'

Terry swaggered up to the front door, brandishing both pistols. 'I gave it to him lock, stock and two soaking barrels. Vinnie Jones, eat your heart out. Well helloooo, Miss Bonnie,' he drawled as he drew level with Lana. 'You are looking mighty fine tonight, girl.'

'Oh my God,' Lana replied with a shudder, refusing to join in with Sadie and Liam's laughter. 'Keep away from me, you dreadful little man.'

Terry shook his head and frowned at Lana. 'Somebody ain't been doing their homework.'

'What do you mean?'

'I mean – in the film, Bonnie's all over Clyde like a bleeding rash.' Terry passed one of the water pistols to Lana. 'Don't worry, we can save the shag until after we've done the job.'

Still studiously ignoring the hilarity going on behind her, Lana pointed her pistol in Terry's face. 'It sounds as if you haven't been doing your homework either,' she retorted,

'Unless my memory is completely failing me, I do believe that Clyde was never able to get it up – such a pitiful waste of Warren Beatty's true talent, don't you think,' she added under her breath to Sadie. 'Now let's get this freak show on the road, before I return to my senses and go back indoors for tonight's scintillating episode of *Peak Practice*.'

As Sadie watched Lana gingerly clamber on the back of the bike and even more gingerly take hold of Terry's waist she leant back against Liam. 'I hope it doesn't end in complete disaster,' she muttered, forcing herself to wave enthusiastically as the bike putt-putted its way down the road.

'Of course it will,' Liam replied with a chuckle. 'For Christ's sake, look at the pair of them – they're like the Munsters do Mafia. Anyway, enough about them – how are you?' Liam took hold of Sadie's shoulders and eased her round to face him.

'I'm fine thank you – now.' As soon as their lips met, Sadie felt the tension drain from her body, almost as if Liam were draining it from her. For all of her feisty talk earlier about the world not revolving around men, part of her had come to view her time away from Liam as some kind of self-imposed exile. It was the part of her that was now pounding away excitedly in her ribcage, sending little darts of excitement rushing to the outermost reaches of her body. 'I've missed you,' she whispered, cupping her hands around his face, letting her fingers sink into the hollows beneath his cheekbones.

'Good, because I've missed you too,' he whispered back, his breath sending shockwaves of lust racing through her ears and burrowing deep into her brain.

Suddenly they were crashing on to the floor in the hall, ripping at each other's clothes, biting at each other's mouths. They didn't even bother to shut the front door properly. It wasn't until she could feel Liam inside her that the frenzy within Sadie began to abate.

'Hello,' he whispered, gathering her to him and cradling the back of her head with one of his huge hands.

As they stared into each other's eyes Sadie felt a rush of emotion the like of which she'd never experienced before. She loved the way Liam made her feel so wanted and safe, she loved the way his understated confidence and sense of calm wrapped itself round her like a blanket, the way he didn't put any pressure on her to be anything other than herself, the way she felt so incredibly relaxed in his company, as if she had nothing left to prove. She loved his shy laugh and his endearing clumsiness, she loved the way he always looked good, in a somewhat dishevelled way and even more – she loved the way he only had one stick of deodorant and one can of shaving foam to his name. She even loved his name. Liam Costello. Liam Costello. Sadie Costello.

The ensuing bolt of fear that reverberated around her body was like an intruder alarm designed to keep out unwelcome emotions. Sadie's eyes flew open and her body stiffened.

'Are you okay?' Liam asked, breathlessly.

Sadie nodded and clung on to him tightly. Of course she was okay. Wasn't she?

At the Manor Mini-Mart things were far from okay.

'I told you – there's only one job I'll be on tonight and that's getting my revenge on this money-grabbing bastard,' Lana hissed as she removed Terry's hand from her backside and gestured angrily at the shop. 'Now, do you have your lines ready?'

'I sure do,' Terry replied, in the worst attempt at a drawl Lana had ever heard.

'You're supposed to be from Texas, Terry, not Tipperary,' Lana retorted, toting her water pistol. 'Okay, let's kick some ass!'

On the count of three they burst through the shop

door, causing the bell housed in the joist above to jangle wildly.

'This here's a stick-up,' Terry muttered.

'Louder,' Lana barked.

'I said – this here's a stick-up!' Terry repeated, shouting this time. But his words echoed around an empty shop. 'Where the hell is the tight git?' he asked as they tiptoed their way up the central aisle, past the piled packs of Bombay mix and vast array of bizarre tinned vegetables.

'Don't ask me,' Lana whispered, as she peered over the loosely constructed wall of greying flapjacks on the counter.

'Don't tell me he's already been done over,' Terry groaned, 'be just my luck, that would.'

'Don't be so ridiculous,' Lana glanced over her shoulder to check the coast was clear, before letting herself behind the counter. 'He's obviously nipped upstairs for something – unless of course he's been abducted by aliens.' Studiously avoiding the shelves of outrageously over-priced liquor, Lana began filling a carrier bag with cartons of cigarettes. 'Come on then – what are you waiting for?' she hissed.

'Oh, yeah, right you are.' Terry pulled a bin-liner from his jacket pocket and headed straight for the tinned meat section.

'Jeez! What the hell was that?' Lana's hand froze over the Marlboro Lights as the sound of crockery smashing rang out from upstairs.

'Search me. Let's just get the gear and get out of here.'

'What – leave without any shooting?' Lana cried. 'You've got to be kidding. Think of the money he's embezzled from us over the years. This is our one chance to make the bastard pay.' Having completely cleared the shop of cigarettes (apart, of course, from the Lambert and Butler, which everyone knew were the chosen smoke of the clapped out, Patsy Cline loving, bingo-hall queen), Lana returned to the front of the shop to select a gift for Sadie. The only chocolates on display were a couple of boxes of dusty and woefully out of date Neapolitans. Replacing them with a disgusted sigh Lana examined the rather precariously rotating display stand housing a variety of grotesque plastic toys. It was a veritable choking hazard fest. In desperation Lana snatched a beaded pink purse and stuffed it on top of the cigs.

Suddenly a voice yelled out through the ceiling, followed swiftly by the thud of footfall on the stairs.

'Come on, let's make a break for it,' Terry cried, turning for the door, his sack of tins clanking loudly.

'You're kidding,' Lana replied, her eyes glinting as she cocked her water-pistol. 'Don't tell me you're chicken, Terry. Not a hardened criminal like you.'

'Well, that's just it,' Terry replied anxiously. 'I've got previous, haven't I. The last thing I want is to end up in the slammer again – and let me tell you it ain't no place for a lady.'

Lana laughed shrilly. 'Why the hell should I care? Jeez, by the time the case goes to court I'll probably be six feet under.'

But before Terry could counter with the argument that much as he liked prison grub he couldn't bear the thought of being banged up with another cell-mate like One-Ball McCall, with his penchant for thrash metal and Thai lady-boys, the door behind the counter burst open and Taj stumbled in. His normally slicked-back hair was sprouting from his head like strips of liquorice and his turquoise satin shirt had been ripped open to the waist. Lana studied the resultant exposed expanse of hairy paunch with a grimace.

'Ah, Terry,' Taj muttered, his eyes darting wildly about the shop. 'I'm just about to close up, boss. What is it you want?'

Meanwhile, having shared a post-coital packet of Revels on Lana's stairs, and several post-coital arguments about who had had the most toffees, Liam and Sadie decided to make their way down to the Parade.

'What's the betting they've already been arrested,' Sadie remarked as they approached the mini-mart.

'Either that or they've been sectioned,' Liam replied. 'Terry's probably being fitted for his straightjacket as we speak.'

'It would make an improvement on that awful suit I suppose.' Sadie snaked her hand inside Liam's coat pocket and entwined her fingers in his. 'How about this for a prime stakeout location?' She pointed to a bench situated about four shops up from Taj's.

Liam nodded and followed her over. 'Happy?' he asked, as he sat down beside her.

'Very,' Sadie replied with a smile.

'I've come to get what I'm owed, haven't I?' Terry snarled waving his water pistol menacingly in Taj's direction.

'What do you mean *what you're owed?*' Taj responded, seemingly oblivious to the pistol, glancing anxiously over his shoulder in the direction of the back door.

'What I'm owed,' Terry repeated.

'Ah – your magazine,' Taj shook his head in despair. 'I told you, boss, I've had to order it direct from Amsterdam. It should only be about another week. Now, if that's all I really must shut the shop.'

With the beads of sweat lining his top lip and the frenzied manner in which he was wringing his hands, Taj certainly looked the part of the terrified-shopkeeper-mid-stick-up. Unfortunately however, the cause of his obvious concern did not appear to be Terry and Lana, but some unknown force emanating from upstairs. Hardly a second went by when Taj did not glance anxiously towards the ceiling or over his shoulder to the back door.

Lana sighed. This really was not good enough. She thought

of all the bottles of over-priced vodka she had bought in this goddamn shop, all that money poured down the drain, or down her neck to be more precise. A few packets of smokes and a beaded purse were hardly suitable compensation. She wanted to see the cocksucker plead for mercy at the very least. Lana hoisted her pump action up to her shoulder and took aim.

'Listen mate, I don't think you understand,' Terry continued, thinking fondly of prison gruel and the way the lumps seemed to melt in a geezer's mouth. 'I ain't talking magazines here, I'm talking loyalty bonus, reward points, rip-off recompense. Me and Miss Bonnie have come to get what we're owed.'

'I've told you a million times, boss, I don't give credit. Surely we can talk about this some other time. Right now is really not the best.' Taj gave another ceiling-ward glance. 'Why don't you come back tomorrow?' Jangling his huge ring of keys – just like a prison screw, Terry couldn't help thinking – Taj moved around the counter and gestured towards the front door.

'Show him, Bonnie,' Terry commanded, pointing to Lana's swag bags.

'Sure.' Lana plonked the bags on the counter in front of Taj.

Taj glanced from the bags to the shelves behind the counter, completely barren apart from the Lambert and Butler. 'Have you just stolen those cigarettes?' he gasped. Finally they had his undivided attention.

'Yeah, and that's not all,' Terry said with a swagger, holding his bin-liner open in front of him.

'Meatballs?'

'That's right,' Terry nodded brazenly. 'And I tell you what, while we're at it how about you sling in a couple of Pot Noodles, sausage madras flavour, please.'

'What are you telling me?' Taj's voice scaled two octaves in panic. 'You're not going to pay for these goods? You expect me to just hand them over to you without a word or expression of protest?'

'Damn right, sucker,' Lana seethed.

'Yeah, this here is our expression of protest, not yours,' Terry added, 'Now get them Pot Noodles or I open fire.'

Terry and Lana both took aim but before they could unleash their liquid ammo somebody upstairs began unleashing a verbal assault of her own. Although they couldn't discern a single word she was saying, the voice was clearly female, clearly incandescent and clearly getting louder – which thereby implied that she was clearly getting closer.

'Oh shit!' Taj cried, moving back behind his counter. 'You really must go. I beg of you. Take the goods, take them all, just go. Please.'

'Who the hell is that?' Lana enquired, as all three of them stared ceiling-ward with a mixture of fear and awe upon their faces, as if observing an incoming plane from the runway. An incoming plane with engines screaming and smoke billowing from its under carriage.

'It's my wife,' Taj whispered.

'Jeez, what have you been doing to her – getting her to try out the merchandise?' Lana quipped.

'I told you – take the god-damned things – just get out of my shop.' Taj clutched his head in his hands, practically in tears.

Lana slammed her fist down on the counter. 'This isn't good enough. You're not supposed to let us go without a fight. You're meant to threaten to call the cops. How the hell are we supposed to shoot you if you act so damned reasonably?'

'What say we just cut our losses and get out of here,' Terry said, remembering the day One-Ball McCall had followed him into the prison showers and threatened to make a wife of him. 'The geezer's obviously having a few problems with her indoors. Best we leave them to it, eh?'

'Thank you, boss,' Taj whispered and he grabbed a handful of pouches of Golden Virginia from the shelf behind him and dropped them into Terry's bin-liner. 'There you go, have a smoke on me.'

'Holy shit!' Lana exclaimed, staring over Taj's shoulder in horror. There in the doorway, bursting through the beaded partition, stood an incandescent Asian woman. Although she was only about four feet tall, the machete she was wielding above her head added at least another two feet to her height. 'Open fire!' Lana called to Terry, pumping furiously on her water pistol in the direction of the woman.

Faced with the combined water-power of both Lana and Terry's pistols the woman was forced to shield her face with her hands and in doing so, dropped the machete to the floor.

'What in Allah's name are you doing?' Taj cried, diving for the machete and backing away from his wife.

'What am *I* doing?' she retorted, wiping the water from her face and stalking towards him. 'How about you tell me what *you* have been doing with that badchalan, that strumpet from the Cash and Carry. And who the hell are these?' she asked gesturing at Lana and Terry. 'Friends of yours, are they?'

'Good God, no,' Lana replied hastily. 'We're just customers. Very *dissatisfied* customers.'

'Join the bleeding club,' Taj's wife sighed, returning her furious stare to her husband. Grabbing the tray of sunset-yellow samosas from the counter she began flinging them one by one at Taj in time with every word she spat from her mouth. 'So tell me, dhokebaaz, what the hell has she got that I haven't?'

'I told you, it was just a one-off. She offered me a cut-price deal on gram flour, she turned my head. I was flattered. It didn't mean anything,' Taj implored, darting behind Terry.

'Fucking stone me,' Terry spluttered, hastily opening his bin-liner to catch any airborne Indian appetisers going begging.

Lana clutched on to the rotating display stand and began to laugh and laugh. She was suddenly experiencing the warm, woozy feeling normally associated with half a litre of Smirnoff and a plateful of smores. A kaleidoscope of colours was bombarding her eyes and the sweet smell of incense was flooding her nose – never had the world seemed so vibrant, so fresh, so fun. 'You guys are a scream,' she gasped, holding her hand out to Terry. 'Come on Clyde, let's split.'

'You got it, Miss Bonnie,' Terry replied, slinging his bag over his shoulder. 'Miss Bonnie?'

Lana felt the ground rush out from beneath her feet and begin swirling around her body. Could she really be drunk? Had somebody spiked her drink? But she hadn't had a drink since leaving home. Clinging on to the display stand to stop herself being sucked into the vortex, she felt herself begin to teeter sideways. Suddenly the warm wooziness was replaced by an icy chill of panic. What the hell was happening to her? As the colours racing before her became increasingly discordant Lana screwed her eyes tightly shut and was immediately plunged into a well of darkness. 'Help me,' she gasped as she was sucked deeper and deeper into the black. 'Help me someone, please.'

Chapter Forty-Two

Outside, the Sunday evening traffic coasted by, transporting lemonade-bloated kids home from visits with grandparents, and chilled-out couples on a last gasp search for fun before the weekend drew to a close. Sadie squinted until the trail of headlights formed a golden stream gliding past her eyes. So what if she didn't have a new job, so what if she missed Pirate Videos more than she could have imagined possible; right here, right now, at this very moment, on this very bench outside Big Tone's Tattoo Parlour she was happier than she had ever been at any other time in her life. She snuggled up against Liam and sighed.

Liam wrapped his arms around her and rested his chin on top of her head. It was that time every bloke dreaded, the time you staked everything you had, your pride, self-respect, entire reputation, on three little words. Three harmless little words, with no fewer than eight letters combined, and yet said in the wrong way, at the wrong time, to the wrong person, and their effect could be deadly. They were the verbal equivalent of anthrax – unless of course you were Nigel fucking Havers, in which case you could look like a weasel, produce more oil than the Saudis and still women were somehow 'charmed' into submission. Liam frowned. This really was not the time or place to start obsessing about his plummy-voiced nemesis. He took a deep breath and attempted to empty his mind of all negative thoughts. He had almost revealed his feelings for Sadie back at Lana's house, on the stairs, after their mind-blowing session. It would have been the perfect time, but then Sadie had started going on about bloody Revels and how much she loved the toffees and wasn't it a sickener when you unexpectedly got a peanut, and the moment had been lost. But now as Sadie nestled her head against his chest and entwined her tiny fingers in his the moment was back with bells on – and he, Liam, part-time Zen Buddhist that he was, had to seize it with both hands. Liam opened his mouth in preparation to speak.

But how should he say it? Should he just blurt it out, completely unexpected, or should he build up to it with some kind of cheesy preamble? He wracked his brains for a suitable intro for his declaration of love. *Since meeting you. From the very second I laid eyes upon you. Do you come here often? You know you love toffees – well guess what, I love you.* Liam groaned. This was torturous. Part of him was even starting to hate Sadie for putting him through all this. It wasn't as if he hadn't told a woman he loved her before, but before he had always been stoned and he had never really meant it. Everybody loved everybody when they were travelling. It was one big, drugged up, beach party love-fest after another. But this was different. This was a freezing cold bench in Ruislip Manor, this was the real world, this was the real thing and there had never been so much at stake. Liam opened his mouth.

'I love you,' the words popped out in an awful, girly squeak.

'What?' Sadie asked. The cruel, heartless bitch.

Liam cleared his throat. 'I love you,' he growled, in a gravelly rasp to make Barry White proud.

So her ears hadn't been deceiving her. Every nerve ending in Sadie's body leapt to attention. The way Liam had just barked the words out could leave her in no doubt – he loved her. Liam loved her. The question was, how did she feel? Sadie paused for a moment to monitor her reaction. Physically, the signs were very promising indeed. Her mouth seemed to be grinning inanely. Her skin had begun to tingle and it definitely wasn't from the cold; the March air was positively springlike. There was no sickening lurch in her stomach, just the faintest fluttering of butterfly wings. From the effortless way in which she was turning to face Liam she had obviously not been paralysed by fear and there were no alarm bells going off in her head. Or were there? Suddenly, out of nowhere, a bloody great siren began to wail. Sadie glanced around in confusion.

'Oh, for fuck's sake,' Liam groaned, 'Taj must have called the old Bill.'

Sadie leapt to her feet, blinking in the face of the swirling blue lights. 'It's not the police – it's an ambulance,' she cried.

Something about the way in which the doctor was standing, framed by the door, with his hands behind his back, reminded Sadie of her father standing by her headmaster's window all those years previously. But this time she didn't feel numb, this time she felt huge bolts of panic ricocheting against the back of her throat.

'What do you mean, liver-induced?' She somehow managed to splutter the words out. 'How can liver disease lead to a coma?'

Liam attempted to take her hand but Sadie shook it off. If she accepted any support now she would surrender what little reserves of strength she had left.

The doctor brought his hands back around to the front of his body and fiddled with the ID badge hanging from his neck. 'Because Ms Loveday's liver is so badly scarred, the blood from her intestines can no longer flow through it.'

'Portal hypertension,' Sadie interrupted. 'That's what she

had the last time she was brought here, but I thought that was under control now. She was on medication, she'd stopped drinking.'

'Yes I know, but she was still at a very high risk of complications.' The doctor glanced nervously around the private waiting room before continuing. 'Because the blood displaced in portal hypertension circumvents or goes around the liver, it tends to contain high levels of ammonia and other toxins. When these toxins reach the brain they can cause varying degrees of mental impairment.'

'So what are you trying to say, doc, has it sent her doo-lally, or what?' Terry enquired, from his perched position on the corner of the coffee table. Taking his trilby from his head he removed a roll-up from inside the band and placed it in his mouth.

'I'm sorry sir, but this ward is No Smoking. If you'd like a cigarette you'll have to go outside.'

'I wasn't going to light it, Doc – it's just a comfort thing. You know, like sucking me thumb. I'm in a state of shock, aren't I? Me bleeding nerves have been torn to shreds.'

Sadie frowned at Terry before turning back to the doctor. 'What exactly do you mean by mental impairment? Is it permanent? Is she going to be all right?'

The doctor moved out of the doorway and edged closer to Sadie. His forehead glistened with a veneer of perspiration under the fluorescent strip light. 'I'm afraid the prognosis isn't good. In many cases the changes are quite subtle – loss of memory, slight confusion or absent-mindedness, but in Ms Loveday's case I'm afraid the effects have been quite profound.'

Quite profound. Sadie allowed his words to echo round and round her head. It was quite ironic really that he should have chosen a word like profound, which was normally used in a positive context, to describe such a catastrophic event.

How could there be anything *profound* about being rendered comatose? It was like calling the Tiananmen Square massacre awesome.

'Can I see her?' Sadie asked, feebly, sure that his answer would be no.

'Yes, I really think you ought to. We don't know how much time she has left.'

'Oh God!' Sadie lunged at the water cooler to steady herself.

'Are you all right, Treacle?'

She could feel Liam and Terry positioning themselves around her, hands shelving her elbows, arms propped against her back. How could she possibly be all right – everything about this was wrong, wrong, wrong. Nothing made sense any more. One moment she had been sat on a bench, happier than she'd ever been in her entire life, with the man of her dreams bellowing that he loved her – the next she was clinging on to her seat in the back of an ambulance, watching helplessly as the paramedics worked on Lana. Lana, who only an hour or so earlier had been setting off to hold-up a mini-mart, all sultry swagger and witty wisecrack. And now – now this doctor was standing here, telling her they didn't know how much time Lana had left, and wasn't it *profound*! Sadie felt as if she had been wrenched from the closing scene of a romantic chick flick straight into the climax of a stomach-churning horror. If only she could hit stop and rewind back to the bit where everyone was happy, where everyone was well.

But life wasn't like that, was it? What was it she had told Lana only a few weeks previously? Sometimes you have to accept that your life is stuck on Play and go with the flow. Sadie took a deep breath.

'I'm okay,' she whispered. 'Take me to her.'

By focusing on the heels of the doctor – who bizarrely

appeared to be wearing Nike trainers beneath his greens – Sadie somehow managed to negotiate her way through the labyrinthine corridors leading to Lana's room. Along the way she tried in vain to get her head around the enormity of the night's events. Could this really be it? Was Lana really going to die? By the time they arrived at the room she half expected to see the grim reaper sat in the chair beside the bed, his scythe propped against the life support machine as he helped himself to a beaker of water.

As Sadie made her way over to the bed she experienced an overwhelming sense of déjà vu. It was just like before. Lana lying there, motionless, with only the beeps of a monitor to break the silence.

'I'll leave you alone for a while,' the doctor whispered, backing out of the room, his mind already elsewhere as he consulted the pager attached to his belt.

'Oh, Lana,' Sadie whispered, pulling a chair right up to the bed and taking hold of her hand. 'Wake up, wake up, please.'

But Lana just lay there – her breathing so shallow, Sadie had to lean right over her mouth to feel the faintest whisper upon her cheeks.

For a long time Sadie remained in this position, like a mother observing her newborn baby, drawing comfort from its every breath. But then a wave of panic began to well inside her. What if Lana really was about to die? What if she never had the chance to speak to her again? There were so many things she wanted to say to her, so many things she had to thank her for. If she died now they would all gone unsaid and unheard and Sadie couldn't bear the burden of another mound of unfinished business upon her shoulders.

'Oh Lana, please wake up,' she implored. But again, nothing. Sadie studied Lana's false eyelashes for the slightest flicker of life, but to no avail. Her fingers trembling, Sadie began tracing the contour of Lana's angular cheekbones, gently stroking her powdery skin, painfully aware of the sanctity of each passing moment. Finally she let her hands drop on top of Lana's and shut her eyes. 'I just want to thank you for everything you've done for me,' she whispered, a wall of tears forming behind her eyelids. 'Since that day in the shop, when you invited me out for lunch my whole life has changed. I know you'd say you hadn't done anything and it was all down to me, but you're the one who gave me the courage to do it. You're the one who gave me the strength to stand up for myself. God knows what kind of mess I'd be in now if you hadn't been there for me.'

'Bitches!'

At the sound of Lana's gasp, Sadie's eyes sprang open, unleashing a sheet of tears upon her face. 'Lana? Did you say something? Lana, please, say it again. Who are bitches?'

Sadie stared expectantly at Lana and although her eyes remained closed her lips began to quiver into life. 'I said Beaches,' Lana hissed.

Sadie leant forward to hear her properly. 'Beaches?'

'Yes.' Lana took a laboured breath and squeezed Sadie's hand. 'I do not want my final scene to be turned into something out of godamned *Beaches*. Understand?'

Sadie nodded, her whole body convulsing with awful spasms of involuntary laughter. 'I understand,' she whispered.

Lana's eyes flickered open a crack. 'Good,' she whispered. Then she turned her gaze to the ceiling. 'Oh,' she gasped as if suddenly recognising an old friend. She slowly turned her head to Sadie and smiled. 'Well, I'll be darned. It's not the least bit scary after all.'

Chapter Forty-Three

All the way back from the hospital, Sadie felt an unidentifiable emotion building inside her. With every crackle of static on the cabbie's radio, every rasping cough from Terry in the front passenger seat and every stroke of Liam's hand upon her head, the pressure inside Sadie built, like trapped air in an over-inflated balloon. It wasn't until they got back to Liam's flat that the choking feeling was able to burst free in an explosion of incandescent rage.

'How about I fix us all a bite to eat?' Terry suggested, tipping the contents of a black binliner on to the kitchen table. 'Anyone fancy a samosa – or a Pot Noodle?'

'How can you even think about eating?' Sadie cried, swiping wildly at a tin of meatballs and sending it clattering to the floor. 'Our friend has just died and all you can think about is your bloody stomach. That is so typical of you.'

'I was only trying to do the right thing, Treacle. I thought maybe a bit of grub would make us feel a bit better, that's all.' Terry stared mournfully at the meatballs as they careered to a halt by the foot of the stove.

'Huh – the day you do the right thing is the day I start believing pigs fly,' Sadie spat.

'Easy,' Liam soothed, sitting down next to her and taking her hand. 'Tel's only trying to help.'

'It's all right, son. Truth be told, I ain't got much of an appetite neither.' A tear formed in the corner of Terry's eye before spilling down one of the crags in his face. 'If only I hadn't picked that bleeding scene. If only I'd gone for *The Bridges of Madison County* instead.' He wiped his face with the back of his hand. 'I think I better turn in. Good night, Treacle, you take care.'

Sadie refused to look up as Terry shuffled out of the door.

'That was a bit harsh,' Liam whispered. 'I know Terry's not the most tactful of blokes, but his heart's in the right place.'

Sadie shrugged Liam's hand from hers. 'Whatever.'

'Come on, Sadie, I know you must be going through hell right now, but don't forget you've still got us.'

Sadie gave a bitter laugh. 'Yeah, right – and for how long?'

Liam stared at her blankly. 'What do you mean, for how long? For as long as you want.'

Sadie shook her head. 'It's a nice idea, Liam, but it never quite works like that, does it?'

'I don't understand – what's the matter with you?'

'Oh, there's nothing the matter with *me*, it's everybody else – it's life.' Sadie got to her feet and began pacing up and down the kitchen. 'Every time – every single time I get close to a person – they end up leaving me. Every time I open up my heart to someone, every time I place my trust in someone they end up betraying that trust and deserting me. First my mum, then GL, now Lana and next it'll be you. Only there isn't going to be a next time.' Sadie marched up to Liam and stared at him defiantly through tear-filled eyes. 'From now on *I'm* going to be the one doing the leaving, do you hear me?' And with that she turned on her heel and fled to the front door. But just as she got to the door, just as her trembling fingers managed to negotiate the lock and open it a crack, a huge hand came flying past her shoulder, slamming it shut.

'Oh no you don't!' Liam shouted, grabbing her arms and spinning her round. 'I am *not* having you running out on me again, no way.'

Shocked into submission, Sadie watched as Liam pushed his hair back from his face. It was the first time she had ever seen him angry. The twinkle in his eyes had been replaced by a fiery spark, and his jaw was set as rigid as stone.

'I know you're upset and I can't imagine how painful it must have been to watch Lana die, but I am not going to let you turn it into an excuse to walk out on me.' Although Liam was no longer shouting, his voice was steely with determination. 'And I am certainly not going to stand here and let you compare me to that useless little toe-rag you used to go out with.'

Sadie gulped and lowered her gaze to the floor. Suddenly her anger was being replaced by shame, a far more difficult emotion to handle.

'I might not have a flashy sales job and I might not spend my life poncing around all suited and booted like some man from Burtons, but at least what you see is what you get. I've never lied to you, Sadie and I've never claimed to be something I'm not. Jesus Christ, earlier tonight I actually told you I loved you. Have you any idea how hard it is for a bloke to say that when he really means it and he's not just trying to get a shag?'

Sadie shook her head ashamedly.

'Well, it's bloody hard. Especially when you haven't got a clue how the other person feels about you because she always keeps everything under wraps.' Liam sighed and leant against the hall wall. 'I know I can't force you to stay, but I won't have you leaving here because you think *I'm* about to walk out on *you*. For fuck's sake, I'm the one who came *back* for you. I could have been sunning myself on Pitcairn Island right now if it wasn't for you.'

Sadie covered her face with her hands and began to sob. 'Oh Liam, I'm so sorry. I'm just really scared.'

Liam put his arms around her and held her tight. 'Don't worry, I understand.'

'Do you? Do you understand?' Sadie wiped her face with the back of her hand and gazed up at him. 'It's because I feel the same way about you that I feel so scared. I love you, Liam.'

'Well, thank Christ for that!'

Sadie and Liam disentangled from their embrace to see Terry standing in the shadowy recesses of the hall, clad only in a pair of tartan boxers and holding out an envelope. 'I thought I was going to have to turn me water-pistols on the pair of you, blast a bit of sense into those idiot heads of yours.' Rather cautiously, Terry handed Sadie the envelope. 'Here you go, Treacle. Lana gave me this a couple of weeks ago. She said I was to give it to you if anything should happen to her. Completely slipped me mind until a moment ago.'

Sadie took the envelope with trembling hands. 'Thanks, Terry, and sorry about before. I didn't know what I was saying, I was lashing out.'

'Don't you worry about it, my dear. I've had to deal with far more slanderous remarks in my time, believe me. I'll just put it down to a hysteria-induced lack of judgement. Now if you don't mind, I think I'll turn in. I take it there'll be no more shenanigans from you pair tonight.'

'No, it's all right, Tel, we're fine now. You try and get some kip.' Liam gave Terry a hug before ushering Sadie into his bedroom and helping her on to the bed. 'Now I'm going to make us a cup of coffee and give you a chance to read your letter,' he said. 'I take it you'll still be here when I get back.'

Sadie nodded. 'Oh yes,' she replied with a weak smile. 'I intend to be here for quite some time.'

Sadie couldn't help laughing as she removed the letter from

the envelope. There was no mistaking who it was from – only Lana could seal her correspondence with a generous squirt of her signature scent. Sadie held the thick creamy paper to her face and inhaled the heady fumes of *Obsession*. 'Oh, Lana,' she whispered, leaning back against the pillows and bringing her knees up under her chin. As she unfolded the letter her eyes raced over the elegant script.

My dearest Sadie,

If that dreadful little man has given you this letter then I guess the worst has happened and I have departed this mortal coil. (Please God I had a glamorous exit and didn't meet my fate under the wheels of a milk float or something equally hideous.) I hated having to entrust Terence with this letter, but he was the only person I could talk to about my concerns for the future. You see, I've known all along that my outlook wasn't good – doctors have such a wonderful knack for putting the fear of God into a person. But you had your heart so set upon the transplant and I didn't want to be the one to rain on your parade. (You might want to check this letter for gravy stains, honey, as I have my doubts Terence will be able to keep his weasely little nose out of our business.)

Half laughing, half crying, Sadie took a moment to examine the pristine paper for any evidence of snooping. Amazingly, it appeared stain-free.

And so down to business. Ever since childhood I have been blessed with the uncanny ability for fucking things up. Calamity Jane, my mother used to call me – and believe me that was one of her fonder pet names. It was as if I had some in-built self-destruct button and no matter what successes I achieved they were never enough, I was never satisfied. But at least up until the automobile accident I only ever hurt myself. And I swear to God, Sadie, that day was exactly the same. When I saw Guy with that floozy I wanted to die. I was so cut up that all I wanted to do was drive and drive until I just dropped off the edge of the planet, I didn't care what or who I had to mow down along the way. But that's the rub. You see I knew her car was there, I knew and yet in that one split second I truly didn't care. I just put my foot on the gas and ploughed straight ahead. There was nothing wrong with the brakes on that car, and unfortunately there was bugger all wrong with the accelerator either. Oh Sadie, you have to believe me – from the moment I heard the smash and that poor child's screams I knew I had done something completely unforgivable and yet it was too late. The moment was over, there was no going back and ever since I have lived my life filled with self-hatred and remorse. As that god-awful walrus of a doctor on the Oprah Winfrey show would say – I have an extremely low 'self-image'. That's why I allowed my asshole of an ex-husband to dump me over here like a discarded plaything and why I found it so easy to sell my body for sex – what more did I deserve? I was alive and she was dead, what claim could I possibly have on happiness or self-worth?

And then I met you. I remember when I heard you crying in the shop, the day Gaylord (I hope you're having an immature giggle right now) did the dirty on you, and I was so close to walking out. To be honest it was only the pissing down rain and thought of a cup of tea that made me stay, but I am so glad I did. Oh Sadie, honey, you have given me something I never dreamed possible. You have taught me how to care, not only about you – and God knows I love you as if you were my own daughter – but also for myself. The way you have made me feel and act has taught me that I can't be all bad. I have watched as you go from strength to strength, *kicking that little shit into touch, rebuilding your self-esteem and captivating the heart of that colossus, Liam, and my own heart has filled with pride to think that in some small way I may have helped in this process.*

I guess if you're reading this now then I'm no longer there to provide you with fashion tips and killer putdowns, but don't you dare go feeling sorry for yourself and thinking that I've deserted you. Shit, I gave up vodka for you, girl, there is no way I would leave you high and dry. And that is why I dragged my sorry ass down to the solicitors today and had my will rewritten. I never had the chance to make my peace with the Ellroy child – I was always far too ashamed to track her down. I know that Guy took care of her financially with his 'out of court settlement', but I always intended leaving everything to her as a way of saying sorry. Typical of me, don't you think? Taking the coward's way out even in death. It's not a cheque that poor girl wants or needs from me, it's some form of explanation. So I have left a letter and details of how to track her down with my solicitor with the instruction to forward it on in the event of my death. I know it won't bring her mother back but at least my regret and remorse might provide her with some form of closure. As for my worldly goods, with the exception of my drink and couture habits, I have been fairly shrewd over the years. My house is paid for and there's money in the bank. I want you to have it all, Sadie, on the proviso that a) you occasionally wear my jewellery, but NEVER with those god-awful army fatigues you're so fond of, and b) you use the cash to follow your dreams.

Quit fearing life, Sadie, and grab it with both hands. And if at times you hear that nagging doubt in the back of your mind, just think to yourself how would my old pal, Lana deal with this and I will somehow communicate some kick-ass advice via the spirit world (I am not talking a bottle of Smirnoff here, although the thought is kind of appealing!)

So what the hell are you waiting for – go get 'em girl.

All my love,

Lana xxx

Chapter Forty-Four

Upon arriving at Lana's Movie Lounge, Sadie's opening-up routine went something like this: Unlock door. Leg it to back of shop to reset alarm. Leave door open to allow the late summer breeze to circulate and chase out previous night's stale cigarette fumes. Boot-up computer system. Put *Casablanca* or other Hollywood classic on DVD player. Turn on screens housed in elegantly carved alcoves between shelves. Plump up cushions on the re-upholstered chaise longue for the next batch of weary customers. Polish the huge Oscar statuettes positioned either side of the All Time Classics stand. Refill and switch on coffee percolator on counter. Check there are plenty of paper cups. Empty ashtrays and flick a duster over the framed stills from *When Harry Met Sally, Taxi Driver, Bonnie and Clyde, Pretty Woman, Mutiny on the Bounty, An Officer and a Gentleman*, and, of course, *Grease*. Take petty cash from pleasantly crammed safe and place in till. Check appearance in new, indoor toilet.

Sadie passed a hand over her elegantly sculpted chignon and smiled. Although she was still getting used to the figure-hugging aspect, Hollywood glamour was a far more preferable working look than Long John Silver any day of the week. As she checked her eyeliner for smudges and applied a quick squirt of Obsession she could hardly believe that just a few months previously she had shuffled into this very same shop clad in a bandanna and eye-patch. Just as the shop had undergone a total over-haul (thanks mainly to Liam's handiwork) Sadie herself felt completely transformed. 'I hope you're proud of me,' she whispered, fingering the string of pearls around her neck and inhaling the reassuringly familiar scent upon her wrists.

Lana's death had precipitated some kind of psychological detox within Sadie, purging her body of all manner of painful emotions, from anger and horror to anguish and despair. Most unbearable and unexpected of all, however, had been the tidal wave of mourning she'd felt for her mother. Although she'd been through the initial stages of grief at her mother's death – the shock, the questioning, the anger – during the previous four years, it was only once Lana died that Sadie was able to move on to the final stage and experience the overwhelming sorrow and sense of loss. For days she had been unable to get out of bed as her grief spilled out in sheets of tears and her mind was flooded with childhood memories of her mother. The velvety lilt of her voice, the cushiony softness of her chest, so perfect for resting a weary head upon whilst listening to yet another story. And the way in which her mother's sorrowful eyes would sparkle as she brought these stories to life; not dully reciting from books but conjuring up from some enchanted kingdom inside her head. A land crammed full of flaxen-haired maidens, goblins, witches and frogs turned princes. A land where good always triumphed over evil. A blissful escape from reality. How could Sadie have forgotten those stories? How had it been possible to erase whole chunks of her past? She had had no control over her mother's suicide, but she didn't have to kill her off in her own mind as well.

Finally rid of the toxins of anger and pain, Sadie began to feel cleansed. It was as if the gallons of tears had washed her hurt away and left her with a new sense of acceptance.

Finally she realised that what had happened to both Lana and her mother had not been her fault – how could it possibly have been? Lana was an alcoholic and her mother had been systematically bullied into submission, but they had both loved her and they both lived on inside her. And besides, not everyone was screwed up. Some people could be relied upon. Liam was a testament to that. Liam, who had got her through Lana's funeral, the sale of her house and the purchase of the shop. Liam, who had guided her through the darkest days of her grief, supplying her with a constant source of tissues, coffee and cigarettes. Liam, who had accompanied her to Norwich and hung around outside the cemetery in the cold for two hours while she paid her first visit to her mother's grave. It wasn't just the shop Liam had helped transform. His unswerving love and unyielding strength had helped bring about the most amazing change in Sadie too.

'Anyone for breakfast?'

Sadie smiled as she heard Liam call out from the front of the shop. 'Definitely. Did you get bacon or sausage?' Sadie let herself out from behind the counter to join Liam on the chaise.

'Both,' he replied, handing her a brown paper bag, shiny with grease.

Sadie hurriedly unwrapped the sandwiches and sighed contentedly as her teeth sunk through the fluffy white doorsteps to crunch into the salty bacon below.

'Well, this is the life, eh?' Liam mumbled through a mouthful.

'You're telling me.' Sadie turned to him and smiled. 'Do you know what? At the start of this year I was so fed-up, I seriously wished my life was a film.'

'Yeah, I know – *Grease*, wasn't it?' Liam smirked.

'No – well, yes, admittedly I did used to fantasise about

being Sandy,' Sadie's cheeks began to blush the colour of the ketchup oozing from her sandwich. 'But what I meant was, I used to wish I could just fast forward through all the bad bits and keep replaying the occasional good scene. But now I'm happy to let life take its course. Look at this place,' she gestured at the polished wooden shelving housing ranks of DVDs, the shiny glass cases containing Lana's collection of Hollywood memorabilia and the plush red carpet forming a path from the counter to the door. 'Look at me. Look at us. Who would have believed things could turn out this way? That's what I love about life,' Sadie concluded. 'You never know what's going to happen next.'

'Greetings, pop-pickers!'

'Jesus Christ, Tel,' Liam spluttered, winking at Sadie. 'What's with the vampire clobber? You look as if you're on your way to a Grateful Dead convention.'

Terry stood frowning in the doorway. Silhouetted against the brilliant morning sun and clad in black morning dress, complete with slightly battered top hat, he did indeed possess something of the night about him. 'Bleeding hell, son, show a little respect,' he replied, removing his hat and placing it under his arm, 'It's me new uniform, ain't it? Here, any of them sarnies going spare? I'm so hungry I could eat a scabby horse between—'

'I know, I know,' Sadie interrupted, hastily passing him a sausage sandwich. 'What new uniform? I didn't know you were changing jobs.'

'Don't tell me – you've been offered the lead role in the remake of *The Munsters*,' Liam teased. 'I suppose you'll be wanting us to call you Herman from now on.'

'Yeah, yeah, hil-fucking-arious!' Terry retorted, refusing to even look in Liam's direction. 'I thought it was time for a change, Treacle. I've watched what you and old smart-arse over here have done with this place and it set me thinking.

I was never cut out to be a pizza boy. Not a man of my advanced years – and experience.'

'So what is it you're going to be doing?' Sadie asked, trying desperately to control the falsetto of panic in her voice.

'Well, I thought I'd try me hand at a bit of the old undertaking. Seems more fitting somehow.' Terry's expression was fixed on Sombre as he adjusted the black cravat around his neck.

'You're going to be an undertaker?' Sadie didn't know whether to laugh or cry as her head filled with the potential disasters Terry could be about to unleash upon the unsuspecting mourners of Ruislip Manor.

'Yeah, old Maurice Grimstead said he'd give me a three month trial. It was being a pall-bearer at Lana's funeral what first gave me the idea,' Terry paused to give a cursory salute to the framed photograph of Lana smirking at them from behind the counter. 'Gawd rest her soul. I said to Maurice then, Maurice, you done the lady proud. When they played the theme from *Bonnie and Clyde* as we came marching in – still brings a tear to me eye it does.' Terry fumbled in his pocket for a black satin handkerchief and began dabbing his eyes.

'It was when you opened fire with your water pistol over her grave that brought a tear to my eye,' Liam muttered. He took Sadie's hand and gave it a squeeze. 'What was that you were saying about life's unexpected twists and turns?' he asked with a chortle.

'Tell me about it,' Terry butted in. 'I've only been in this job a couple of hours and it's already been a right eye-opener. Here, did you know that a person continues to pass wind up to twenty-four hours after they snuff it? I nearly bleeding shat meself this morning when one of them stiffs let rip.'

Sadie leant back against the chaise longue and for the first time in months she began to laugh and laugh. 'Oh Terence,' she gasped, in her best attempt at a drawl. 'You really are the most dreadful little man!'